PPL
14.95

The Last Good Night

The Last Good Night

EMILY LISTFIELD

BEELER LARGE PRINT

Hampton Falls, New Hampshire, 1997

Library of Congress Cataloging-in-Publication Data

Listfield, Emily
    The last good night / Emily Listfield.
        p.   cm.
    ISBN 1-57490-128-1 (alk. paper)
    1. Television new anchors—New York (State)—New
York—Fiction. 2. Mothers—New York (State)—New
York—Fiction. 3. New York (N.Y.)—Fiction.   I. Title.
    [PS3562.I7822L3 1997b]
    813'.54—dc21   97-32935
                                                                      CIP

Published in Large Print by arrangement with
Little, Brown and Company.

BEELER LARGE PRINT
is published by
Thomas T. Beeler, *Publisher*
Post Office Box 659
Hampton Falls, New Hampshire 03844

Typeset in 16 point Times New Roman type.
Printed on acid-free paper and bound by
BookCrafters in Chelsea, Michigan

In Memory of Ingrid Schwartz Dudding
and for
Sasha

Life is but a dream whose shapes return
Some frequently, some seldom, some by night,
And some by day.

—James Thomson, *The City of the Dreadful Night*

AUTHOR'S NOTE

I would like to thank the television news anchorwoman and the studio who so graciously let me in to pry, Detective Brian Dennigan of the New York City Police Department for his continued help and good humor, Suzanne Gluck for her patient readings, invaluable insights and advice, Frederica Friedman for her early faith and unfailing guidance, the Writer's Room for time and space, Helen and Leonard Listfield and Andrew Listfield for the gift of child care, and, of course, George for all the intangibles.

The Last Good Night

Part One

One

IT WAS THE LAST GOOD NIGHT, REALLY.

The light from the all-night deli across the street filtered through the lace curtains and fell in shadows across my legs. Outside, the West Village street was deserted except for a delivery truck unloading bundles of the next day's newspapers by the closed metal shutters of the corner store. The wind blew dried leaves across the pavement and the season's first blast of steam heat gasped and sputtered as it made its way through the radiator.

Sophie whimpered softly in my arms. I looked down at her puffy slit eyes neither awake nor asleep, focused up at me. Her irises are black, bottomless. Sometimes I think she can read my mind, literally read my every thought. She pursed her full red lips. It was one of the first things David noticed about her as we rested in the recovery room those first hazy drug-soaked moments five months ago, the baby across my chest, David by my side. "Someone stole your lips," he said. I traced their outline now, wiping a tiny bubble of spittle from her chin and then licking it from my finger.

Sophie's face suddenly turned purple, deep as an eggplant, as she began to sob. Her arms, her legs are pillows of flesh, boneless, pliant. Her wrists are fat, smooth, and hairless, like the wrists of a plump old lady. The only thing missing is a narrow gold watch and lilac

2

perfume. I offered her the bottle of formula sitting on the floor and held her close to my face while I continued rocking back and forth in the mission chair. The smell of talc and formula and a musty amber scent all her own, like dank cherry wood and cobwebs, engulfed me. I shut my eyes and inhaled deeply, swallowing it, drowning in it. Her fine dark hairs tickled my nose. Sophie's hair is straight, like David's, on the top and sides of her head, but erupts into a patch of wild curls, like mine once did, in the back. I've tried to wet down the renegade ringlets, tame them, this unexpected fragment of my past self, recognizable as if from a foggy distance, but they always bounce stubbornly back.

I wonder what else will spring out suddenly, unbidden.

I sat her up, burped her, wiped the white liquid that spilled from her mouth. Her cheeks, red and chubby, had patches of parched skin from drool and dry heat. Sometimes, in profile, there is a fleeting expression on her face that is exactly like my mother, Astrid—a puzzled consternation nestled in fat. This is what David says "Nature versus nurture is a joke. Babies come out with their own little agendas. It's all genetics after all, don't you think?" He never met my mother, and wouldn't know, even if I told him of the resemblance, if I'm right or not. Certainly, he wouldn't be troubled by it.

I heard David snoring in our bedroom down the hall. It amazes me that he is able to sleep through the crying, that he truly does not hear, the way I do, every whimper, every breath in the night, hear it in his sleep, in his very bones.

It was another hour before Sophie finally fell to sleep.

3

Before I left her, I stood in the doorway looking back into the dark room, and hurriedly made the sign of the cross on my forehead three times. It is one of my secrets, this ritual, always three times, always furtive If anyone ever catches me at it, I pretend to be rubbing something off my skin, an eyelash, a piece of dust.

I'm not Catholic, I have no religion at all.

I only crave protection.

I shut the door to Sophie's room and climbed quietly back into my own bed, with its soft mattress, Porthault sheets, and extra pillows. David was sprawled on his back, the eyelet quilt across his stomach, his caramel-colored hair standing up on end. I closed my eyes and tried to sink into all the plushiness, but my body only skimmed the surface, rigid and resistant.

I lay still a moment more and then got out of bed.

I closed the bedroom door behind me and padded barefoot into the living room. Kneeling by the television, I felt behind a stack of magazines for a videotape, pulled it out, opened the black plastic box, and slid the tape into the VCR. After five seconds of static, music piped up, a graphic of Manhattan's skyline filled the screen, and the title appeared: The *New York Nightly News with Laura Barrett and Ron Kheeler*. I turned the sound down, embarrassed at the thought of David coming out and finding me.

I looked at the two faces on the screen, smiling and then still, as the titles and music dissolved and the camera moved in closer.

My own face, so smooth and confident as I began, "Good evening," my eyes opening expressively, my hands resting on the desk. When I first started in television, my eyes roamed the screen nervously, looking to connect with the unseen viewer—are you

4

there? or there? My arms rose from the desk, explicating, distracting. Early errors in out-of-town debuts. The way I clutched the microphone in two hands, as if praying, because I had once seen Barbara Walters do it. The makeup I applied myself, too vivid, with glossy lips that surrounded my words in pools of obscene red light. Small markets, small starts.

I slid my hands into the pockets of my silk bathrobe and sat back on the sage velvet couch.

Years ago, I took all of my savings and hired a coach to view my tapes. Maggie Tildon sat in silence through the entire first half hour, her scrawny legs crossed at the ankles, her lips pursed, as she took copious notes. When the tape ended, she pulled her thick glasses lower on her tiny nose and started reading her comments in a gentle voice, couching her criticisms, dulling them, until, frustrated, I insisted: Tell me the truth; don't spare me. That's how badly I wanted it.

After that, we spent weeks watching and rewatching the tapes. She had me slow down my speech, still my eyes and hands, lower my voice. She told me to smooth my hair closer to my head so it didn't look so cheap, dull my lips, square my shoulders to look more authoritative. She changed the way I dressed to more conservative suits, and told me to favor stronger colors. Even when they hurt, I welcomed every suggestion as she cut deeper and deeper, deconstructing me, remaking me. I was just so desperate to leave the past behind.

I watched the tape until the end. It was recorded a week ago, a memento of my last broadcast as co-anchor of the local evening news.

Often during the last week at home, I put the tape in and stared at my own face on the screen, a comfort, a reminder, a lie. This is who you used to be, this is who you are.

And all the while I watched it, I was wondering this: What did they see in it, in me, the network honchos in their leather and art-filled offices high above Manhattan, to make them offer me the national slot?

Others were wondering exactly the same thing—the media critics who thought co-anchors were by their very nature a bad idea, the network reporters who had been dutifully trudging through the ranks from small domestic bureaus to Washington and then overseas, all aimed at getting them to the anchor desk, only to find the network had chosen someone who'd only done the local news. Not everyone wished me well.

When the tape ended, I got off the couch, ejected the video, hid it once more behind the television, and went to make a pot of coffee. While I waited for it to brew, I picked up the copy of *People* magazine that was resting on top of the refrigerator. I turned to page seventy-three. My own face smiled back at me from the right-hand side, greasy with fingerprints from secretive studying, blurring the words that trumpeted my soon-to-be debut as co-anchor of the *National Evening News* with Quinn Hartley. This was what the network had figured on, all the hoopla that came with their unexpected choice, the frenzy that a new face can bring.

I poured myself a cup of coffee and sat down at the butcher-block counter. Outside, dawn was just beginning to break, pearly gray and wintry. I sipped the hot black coffee and stared once more at the print.

All last week, I wheeled Sophie back and forth past the newsstands, eyeing the magazine displayed in multiples, my face inside each and every one. And each time, a wave of nausea and fear washed through me. It hadn't seemed real before.

I've had press before, of course, but it was always strictly local, circulated only within the borders of whatever city I found myself working in. Who recognizes the news anchor of Burlington outside of its city limits, or Pittsburgh? The fame was contained, held in check. Restaurants seated me in front to impress the other customers, and people looked twice at me on the street. But I could leave the city, and twenty miles away, no one knew me, no one looked.

I was safe.

There are things you don't let yourself think about, things that you cram into a molten ball and stash deep within the caverns of your gut. Even as I moved to bigger and bigger markets and finally New York, I put out of my mind where it might be headed.

Sometimes now I look back and try to find the exact point where I should have put a halt to it all, when I should have thought about the consequences.

But I didn't.

I went along with the tests to see how I worked with Quinn Hartley, how we sounded together, how we looked, to see if there was that incalculable something between us: chemistry, alchemy, ratings magic. Part of it was simple curiosity—would I make the grade? Part of it was ambition. It is difficult, after all, to say, *This is enough. I'll stop here,* when you are being offered so much more.

Anyway, I never thought I'd get it.

I rested my mug on the countertop and carefully ripped the article out of the magazine. Folding it in half, I took my coffee in the other hand and returned to the living room with its double-height swagged windows, Aubusson rug, and custom-made Italian chairs, all the

7

carefully accumulated accouterments of permanence. When we moved in, I was seven months pregnant. It was our first real place as a family, and I wanted it to be perfect. The scent of all the anonymous apartments I'd had in all the anonymous cities still clung to me, gray impersonal rooms that could be vacated at a moment's notice when I got the call to move on. And all the while, longing for a home.

On the bookshelf, there is a large burgundy leather loose-leaf, and I pulled it down gently. Inside, I had pasted the articles that trailed after my professional career, from Burlington, Providence, Pittsburgh, a scrapbook of the past fourteen years until I made it to New York, complete with grainy photographs of my face behind a series of studio desks. I flipped past the page that held tabloid photos of my wedding to David three years ago, inky shots of us standing outside Tavern on the Green. Our faces, perhaps because of the long-distance lens, seem strangely expressionless, handsome cutouts of a bride and groom. We had only known each other six months, love was still most of all a hunch.

David has clippings of his own. A professor of urban planning, he wrote what everyone thought would be a well-received if sleepy book three years ago tracing the history of a single Manhattan block from colonial times to the present. Somehow it became a surprise bestseller and was even optioned for a miniseries. Magazines were suddenly clamoring to do profiles of him, intrigued by his ideas as well as his shaggy handsomeness and charm, hostesses wanted him for dinner. Women, enamored of his book jacket photo, so studious and so sensitive, sent him love letters disguised as philosophical analyses of his work. I had just come to

New York to anchor the local news and one of my first assignments was to interview him.

My arrival, heralded in the press and in repeated promos on television, fully occupied me at first, but after the initial onslaught, I found myself left much to my own devices to fill the twenty-three hours when I was not on-air. The city left me breathless and unsteady. David, who had grown up on the Upper West Side of Manhattan, had seen a lifetime of people come here to conquer it anew. "Just like you," he teased on our first date. "It's a city of phoenixes, all that small-town ambition burning up whoever comes near it. Everyone here is the one who got out of wherever it is they can't wait to forget. It's a whole goddamned city of amnesiacs."

"What about you?" I asked.

"Me?" He laughed. "When I went to college, they asked me the name of my hometown paper in case I did anything particularly notable. The only thing I could think to answer was the *New York Times*." He smiled. "Actually, I'm jealous. No one who was born here has nearly as much energy as you infiltrators."

I wonder if he looks at the articles about himself behind the closed door of his study, or if he rereads the love letters on discouraging afternoons. I suspect that he does, though I've never caught him at it.

I came to an empty page and pasted the *People* article onto it.

I was on my third cup of coffee when David came up behind me and kissed the back of my neck, his lips still dry and caked with sleep. "Good morning."

"Morning."

"So today's the big day."

9

"Yup."

"Nervous?" he asked.

"Why should I be nervous? Just because every television critic in the nation will be watching and every women's group has written to tell me I'm their next great hope?"

"I'll take that as a yes." David poured himself a half-cup of coffee and filled the rest of the mug with milk. He took a sip and leaned back against the counter, the white T-shirt he had slept in falling in ripples against his solid frame. I knew if I touched it how soft it would be, how warm. "You'll be fine. They wouldn't have chosen you if they didn't think you could do the job." He smiled. "Of course, that's what they said about Connie Chung, too."

"It's your optimism I find so irresistible."

"Not my piercing intellect?"

"Don't flatter yourself."

"So, how did our little peanut do last night?" he asked.

It was what we always came back to, Sophie. It was where we found each other.

"All right," I answered. "Only one bout of projectile vomiting."

"Don't you think we should talk to someone about this?" David asked nervously. He was a first-time father at forty-one, the baby melted all his usual wryness, it just dripped away.

"I put in a call to the secretary of health, but she hasn't gotten back to me yet."

"And I thought you finally had some clout."

"Seriously, David, she's fine. We can't call the doctor at every sputter."

"Actually, we could."

"Does the story of crying wolf ring any bells with you?"

"No. I don't believe I've heard of that one." He smiled, but he still looked worried.

I smiled and ran my hand down his bare arm. When we first met, his parents had both recently died and, beneath his sheen of sophistication, there was a stunned, raw quality about him, as if nothing had quite scratched him before. The first night we slept together, he clutched me even in his sleep with such tenderness that I felt something deep within soften, shift. The largeness of his six-foot-three-inch body, the way it wrapped so thoroughly about mine, seemed to offer a refuge when I thought I had long ago given up the possibility of such a thing. It was so alien to me at first, and so welcome, this first real taste of security. It still is.

"Come on," I said now, prodding him gently. "Let's go look at her."

We tiptoed into the baby's room and stood together over the wicker bassinet. Sophie was snoring lightly, the fluffy white blanket up about her ears. "Our perfect little girl, our perfect little peanut," David whispered.

She opened her eyes and stared up at us.

"Come here, precious," David said as he reached his large hands into the bassinet and picked her up. "Mmmm." He nuzzled her neck and then looked over her drowsy marshmallow body and smiled at me. "We did a good thing," he said softly.

"We did."

"Family hug," he said, and he reached his free arm around me, the three of us clinging to each other in the center of the room.

These are things I never thought I'd have: a husband, a

child. Family.

Sometimes it feels like luck, pure luck. Someone else's luck, a mistake to be corrected.

Our new nanny, Dora, arrived twenty minutes later, bundled in layers of wool, two scarves, and a baseball cap, her wire-framed glasses misted with condensation. She washed her hands and went in to look at Sophie, who was swaying contentedly in an electric swing and batting with athletic determination at the hanging plastic rings. "Hello, little girlie, hello, little baby," Dora cooed in her nearly impenetrable St. Lucian accent. I often found myself nodding in polite agreement when I hadn't the vaguest idea of what she had actually said.

I went to the bathroom and splashed cold water on my face. Then I lay on the bedroom floor, did seventy sit-ups, twenty lifts with each leg, and fifteen push-ups before showering. I've always been terrified there's a fat woman lurking within, just waiting to escape. Staring in the mirror, I began to apply makeup to my long, narrow face with extra care. I paused for a moment and appraised myself. My thick shoulder-length hair is cut into a bob by the most expensive stylist in New York. Its once unruly curls are chemically straightened so that they fall in a smooth, perfectly natural-looking sheet by someone else, who uses a secret formula from Italy that frizzy-haired women fly across the country for. A third person painstakingly paints it with four different shades of blond, completely erasing any evidence of its black beginnings. My brows are professionally shaped and lightened to match. I even have a new nose, thinner, straighter, shorter than the original, acquired twelve years ago because I was told it would look better on camera. Is it any wonder that celebrities sometimes slip and refer to themselves in the third person? I leaned closer and patted cream underneath my eyes to cover the circles. Other on-air women I know go to the studio bare-faced, letting the makeup artist start fresh, but I never do.

"You look good," David said as I came out of the bathroom.

"Really?"

"You always look good."

"Oh."

"That was meant to be a compliment."

"Thanks."

"Did they messenger over an outfit? Did they give you rules about jewelry?" he asked. "Did they remind you that an open neck means an open person?"

I frowned.

"Come on. You need me to keep you honest," he teased.

David maintains a certain ruefulness when it comes to the background of my work, as if the politics and image-making are somehow unseemly, or worse, amusing. His own brush with notoriety left him glazed, intrigued no doubt, but winded and suspicious. Within six months his book was off the bestseller list, the magazines were hungry for the next new face, and David was back where he said he preferred it, in the quieter and more manageable world of ideas, teaching his classes, working late in his study, giving occasional quotes to the more academic journals. Still, there was a passion and a pleasure in his eyes during that singular period of glare that I sometimes miss, even if he doesn't. Or says he doesn't.

"And you need me to keep you from being too sanctimonious," I replied.

13

He laughed. "I'll be rooting for you," he said as he touched the small of my back, and I knew that he would be. It is one of the things we understand about each other, the love we both have for what we do, the room it takes. He leaned over to kiss me. "Good luck."

After he left, I stood in the foyer fingering the gold clasp of my pocketbook that rested on the otherwise empty marble table. I've always been wary of tabletops, fearful of what the artifacts that accumulate on their surfaces might betray. The choice of books, the odd necklace, the lipstick. The papers, the tissues, the detritus. When I was young, I thought: If a Martian landed here and saw this tabletop, what would he presume about my life? And I carefully chose and arranged the fragments accordingly. Though I no longer think of Martians, I am still careful.

I told David about it once. Before I even finished speaking, he came up with a theory that had something to do with my being an expatriate (I came from Germany when I was nine, settling first in Florida). "You didn't know anyone, you didn't speak the language, so surfaces took on a particular importance," he suggested, pulling thoughtfully at a stray lock of hair behind his ear. David has theories about so many things—the layout of a perfect city, how a married couple should divide their finances, the proper way to peel a cucumber—each embraced with equal hope and fervor.

"Maybe," I said doubtfully, and let it go.

I finished collecting my papers and then, slipping out of my heels, I tiptoed once more to Sophie's room, hiding behind the door. Dora was on the floor rattling toy keys at Sophie, who lay on her back with her feet and arms in the air, wriggling with delight.

I watched them a minute longer, and then, reluctantly, I left.

The cab careened down a block of crumbling tenements, soiled liquor stores, hunched-over men, puddles of garbage, turned the corner, and pulled up to a row of brick buildings on the far west side of Manhattan. I paid the driver, gave him an autograph for his wife, and got out in front of the only clean façade. Looking down the broad street, with its Toyota and Chrysler showrooms like glass-plated slabs of suburbia somehow misplaced on the edges of the city, I saw a wedge of the Hudson River, gray and forlorn in the late autumn sun. Across the street, where one of the more rabid of the daytime talk shows is filmed, a few tourists walked by, pulling cameras out of thick down jackets and taking pictures of the marquee. The buildings are lower here, squat outposts with vast satellite dishes on their roofs aimed diagonally up at the sky, while on the ground, limousines and town cars wait to whisk guests away from this otherwise forsaken part of the island.

I turned to the scrubbed creamy building with its famous matte gold logo sitting proudly above the entrance. My heart lurched a fraction of an inch. I wondered if it always would, if it does for all of them.

I walked into the main lobby. The receptionist, Donna, a light-skinned Puerto Rican woman in a white appliqued sweater, glanced up from behind the large round desk and smiled. I smiled back and we looked awkwardly at each other, uncertain of whether to go further, inquire about health, ask for baby pictures. I often see other people pause and rest their attaches on Donna's while they ask after her two-year-old daughter with cystic fibrosis, but she never mentions the child to me, just smiles shyly across the divide of those who go on-air and those who don't.

I stepped to the left where the entrance is watched over by two uniformed security guards standing beside the steel arch of a metal detector. I nodded to them both and walked slowly by the hip-height security scanner, which read the ID card inside my jacket and emitted four high-pitched beeps of acceptance.

Instead of turning left to the local studio as I had for the past three years, I went right and walked down a long corridor of thinly painted white brick to the elevator that would take me to the studios of the *National Evening News*. My pulse raced and a film of sweat began to trickle down my back. I kept waiting for someone to tell me I had made a mistake, tell me to go back, who did I think I was kidding?

Finally, I reached the studio and pushed open the heavy glass door. I walked past the reception desk and paused at the edges of the main newsroom. The far wall was dominated by a large map of the world, the countries marked off in pastel colors, at once vast and manageable. Beneath clocks set to every time zone, forty people sat huddled over desks cluttered with video monitors, computers, and straggly copies of the day's newspapers, calling out to each other, glancing up at the four television sets overhead each tuned to one of the networks, rushing thin white and pink sheets of copy back and forth, eating candy bars, yelling into telephones. Up front at the assignment desk, three women sat monitoring the wire reports and the constant hum of their voices mixed with the churning of the computer printers and the newsroom banter. The sound wrapped around me, seeped into my skin, wriggled into my arteries, the insistent hum that obliterated everything around it, outside it, with its steady pulsing rhythm of *now, now, now.* It is what I love best.

Susan Mahoney, the assistant producer of the news, glanced up from her computer and smiled. "Well, well. Look who we have here."

Others in the room turned. A slow ripple of applause waved through the air and then trickled out as people called out greetings, wishes of good luck, congratulations.

Susan stood up and began to wend through the narrow aisle between the desks, her legs, encased in black leggings and intricately stitched cowboy boots, moving with a sure athletic stride. Her long blond hair was tied back in a ponytail, and she wore no makeup on her pretty dry-skinned face. With her Chapstick and her readiness with a curse and her delicate gold pinkie ring with its aquamarine flower, she is a unique blend of the girlish and the macho that thrives in the hothouse of newsrooms, fueled by alcohol and sarcasm and working hours inhospitable to outside romance. "Welcome to hell," she said as she came up to me. "Are you ready?"

"I hope so."

Susan stepped back and looked me up and down. "So do I." She smiled. "You'll be great. Just don't let Quinn big-foot you. He's sure to try to step on every line." Susan knows on-air talent well, how to treat us, coddle us, soothe us, and she knows too how to set us up against each other just enough to get the best results. We are children to her, talented and precocious children.

Just then, an assistant hurried over and announced to Susan, "The tape on the Metro bombing just came in."

Susan nodded. "We'll talk later," she said to me, and rushed away to one of the fourteen editing rooms that line the newsroom behind walls of tinted brown glass.

17

I walked around to a few of the other producers' and writers' desks, said hello, and then went into my new office to the left of the main room, shutting the door behind me. I flipped on the lights. With its pale pink walls, gray couch and carpet, it had the sterile cleanliness of a hotel suite. There were no loose papers yet, no photographs. The large Sony TV was dusted and blank, an imposing matte black. I slid out of my coat, put it on the mahogany stand, and walked over to my desk, where three bouquets of flowers were waiting. I quickly read the cards to see who they were from—the executive producer, Frank Berkman, the network news vice president, Ken Draper, and my agent, Jerry Gold. I slipped the white cards into my desk drawer and sat down.

The buzz outside was distant now, the voices neither male nor female, just a carpet of words. Occasionally, when something is happening, something big, involving wars, flames, hostages, guns, ambulances, death counts, the intonations change and the heightened syllables spread through the room like a virus. But today it was just a steady even pulse. I glanced at the corner of my desk, where there was a basket stuffed with unopened fan mail forwarded from the local show. I had asked the station to stop messengring it to me at home after reading too many letters filled with unwarranted advice on child care, diatribes about my hair style, descriptions of problems in the writers' own lives, sad and intimate scrawls from people who thought they knew me. The worst were filled with rambling sexual fantasies, with dangerous offers, with a fierce if incomprehensible anger.

There was one man who wrote me every week for a year. He broke into my house and ate dinner in my

18

kitchen, leaving dirty plates and a love letter behind. When the police finally caught him trying to sneak into the studio, he didn't understand what all the fuss was about. He was certain we belonged together. Couldn't they see that? Sean McGuirre, his name was. He only got six months.

I shifted my eyes, turned on my computer and brought up the station's NewsMaker program where the stories that were slated for the day were listed. Next to each story there was an initial to specify who would read it, "L" for me, "Q" for Quinn. I carefully counted the "L's" and then the "Q's," making sure that they were balanced. Airtime equals power, and I learned early on that you won no points for sweetness or self-sacrifice. Quinn would always do the lead-ins, though. It was one of the many things he made sure of when he got the bad news of my arrival.

I leaned forward and began to scan the stories themselves. The second item was about a terrorist bomb on the Paris Metro that had killed two young girls. I stopped, shuddered. Since having Sophie, any story about children being hurt makes my stomach collapse and a well form in my throat. More than once during my maternity leave, I found myself tearing up while watching the local news, which specializes in such catastrophes. I told myself it was hormones, that it would stop, lessen, but it hasn't. I'm terrified that it will show on-air, that I'll drip, leak. I know that a single blunder, a drop of sweat, a blank stare, an emotional gaffe, will be instantly more memorable to viewers, and to the network, than an entire career of professionalism. On television, where two seconds can come to define a life, the only truly unpardonable sin is losing control.

I moved on to the item on negotiations in the Middle

East. Though I miss reporting now that my job is behind a desk, the recitation of the action fascinates me in itself, the irrefutable fact of other lives, other calamities, other triumphs, other worlds.

And then there is the camera. The camera that grants life with its glass eye.

The very first time I sat before it and let it train its eye on me, I felt like an amorphous shadow finding its contours, its colors, its fit at last.

Though it's more fashionable now to deny that. To talk only of the responsibility, the importance of the news. And surely that is part of it.

Still, everything pales next to the time I spend before the camera, when every gesture, every breath, every nanosecond matters as I speak live to thousands and thousands of people—and they listen. Tonight, it would be millions.

I pulled my chair closer to the desk, my forefinger moving down the computer screen, my lips moving soundlessly.

But somewhere during the read-through—was it the third story, the fourth?—I realized that I'd been running through the print without seeing it, without connecting to it at all. What I was watching instead, as if through the wrong end of a telescope, far away, miniaturized, adrift in space, was Sophie, curled up soft and fleshy, wriggling exactly as she had when I left.

I wondered if she was sleeping, one dimpled hand pressed to her perfect mouth, her tiny fingers bent, or whether she was beginning to stir, to cry.

No one told me how physical this love would be, like a craving. I was startled out of my reverie by the ringing of the white phone on my desk. I picked up the receiver. "Hello?"

No one answered.

There was breathing, only breathing, a man's, a woman's, I couldn't tell.

"Hello?" I said again.

After a few more breaths, the other person hung up.

I put the receiver down. It was probably just someone who had forgotten that I had moved into this office.

I moved the cursor three pages back, and started again.

At five o'clock, I left my office and headed for the makeup room down the hall. I settled into the thickly padded mustard vinyl chair and stared into the mirror. The makeup artist, Perry, looked up from her brushes and her pots. "Well, hey there."

I smiled, and watched the smile form across my face in the mirror. "Hi. How are you?"

"Fine. Well not really fine, but you know. Okay. I finally broke up with my boyfriend, Billy. I forgot, you're new, you don't know about Billy, the alcoholic, can't commit, sometime Broadway stagehand. Anyway, it took me two years, but I finally ditched him. I'll tell you all about it later. More important, how are you?"

"All right. A little nervous, I guess."

Perry stepped closer and tipped my face up to the fluorescent lights as she began to wipe off my old makeup. "Not bad. Not bad at all. Motherhood agrees with you. You wouldn't believe the under-eye cream I usually have to use. I'm impressed."

"You're easy."

"I may be easy, but I'm honest." Perry laughed. Twenty years ago, she was a cheerleader in Nebraska, and though her waist has thickened an inch or two, she still has the pert-nosed clear-skinned good humor of one of the truly popular girls, just bad enough around the edges to make her interesting. I'm fascinated by her, by all of them, the girls things came so easily to, the girls who, even when they stumble, do it with an innate confidence that I can only imitate. "Pictures," Perry demanded. "Let's see some pictures."

I slipped a single photo out of my suit pocket. Sophie, just after a bath, swathed in a hooded towel, her skin dewy, translucent, her grinning face as fat and ruddy as a Brueghel.

"God, you're lucky," Perry exclaimed.

"I know."

I smiled and put the photo back in my pocket while Perry pushed aside the black quilted imitation Chanel bag on the Formica counter and reached for her instruments. She began to apply foundation to my face with a wedge-shaped white sponge. I closed my eyes, soothed by the strokes, by the thick creamy layers themselves, and listened to Perry's love problems.

She stopped talking when Quinn Hartley strode in. "Nice suit," she said to him.

"Armani." He glanced at himself in the mirror, straightened the lapels of his jacket, smoothed the temples of his black gray-streaked hair, and turned to me. "Just stick to script tonight, all right? Let's not try any of this ad-lib stuff right off the bat."

I nodded. I'd watched Quinn Hartley, and respected him, for years, first as a White House correspondent then as an anchor, impressed with his deep resonant voice and his debonair clothes, his disheveled hair and his ruthless questions. Known for his fiery attacks on the status quo in his younger days, he now projected a calm and erudition that fledgling anchors around the country imitated. Still, I'd heard rumors that he once punched a colleague in the face in an effort to get to the President first as he rushed to board the helicopter on the White House lawn, that he had purposefully left the blood streak from a bullet graze on his forehead when he reported from Angola. In a business where a large ego is considered a necessity, his is legendary. We both knew he didn't want me here, sharing the show that had been his alone for the last six years. Everyone knew that.

Quinn sat down and waited for Perry to finish with me. "So," he said, "today's the anniversary of the California earthquake. Last time I checked, they were still arguing about whether to show the famous 'dead woman on the freeway' footage."

"The one with the mutilated arm sticking out the window?" I asked. "I was in Providence when that happened. We didn't show it, but the rival station did. And let me tell you, they whupped us in the ratings."

"That was local. You're in national now. Decisions have more far-reaching implications," Quinn said. He turned to Perry. "What do you think of this tie? The colors looked brighter in the store. Is it too dull?"

Perry picked it up and fingered the cool heavy silk. "It's perfect."

"Armani."

With my hair and face in place, I went to say hello to the people in the control room. I walked up the back stairs by the side of the studio and entered the long narrow room, where two levels of desks and computers sat facing a wall of forty monitors. The engineers and assistant directors were just settling in for the newscast. Tony DeFranco, whose job was to slug in the by-lines beneath the faces on the news, was the first to look up.

"Well, L.B., good to see you." He wiped a sprinkling of fine white powder from his jelly donut off his hand and offered it to me. It was a good sign that I already had a tag, L.B.

"How's it going?" I learned from the very start, a number of cities ago, that these men and women who others never saw could make me look good, or not. I needed all the help I could get.

"Just fine, ma'am."

"Ma'am? When did I become a ma'am?"

"When you went from local to national."

I smiled, shook a few more hands, and left.

When I got back to my office, about sixty percent of the newscast had been completed. I began to read the stories that were tagged for me out loud, playing with intonations, "The thirteen-year-old boy doesn't *consider* himself a hero. The thirteen-year-old boy doesn't consider himself a *hero*."

Over the loudspeaker that reached every corner of the newsroom, I heard the announcement, "Five minutes."

My foot began to jiggle rapidly up and down beneath my desk. I turned off the computer, went to the locked file cabinet, got out a pair of gold button earrings, put them on, took them off, put them back on, and left my office.

No one in the newsroom looked up, no one talked to me as I made my way to the studio. Everyone has their pre-show ritual, ridiculed but respected, and this is mine. I pumped my fists again and again until my knuckles ached.

All I could think of was this: Don't fuck up, don't fuck up, don't fuck up.

The studio was dark save for the brilliant white lights trained on the small set itself, the desk with its built-in video monitors and two chairs anchored in the harsh white light, a separate constellation. The air surrounding it was black and icy, the air-conditioning cranked as high as it would go to counteract the heat under the lights. The cameramen wore sweaters and leather jackets. I stepped carefully over the thick black cables on the floor and said hello to the studio director, Al.

"Welcome to the nuthouse," Al said.

"Thanks."

I walked up to the set and settled into my chair, into the warmth of the lights. I glanced down at the three video screens inset in the desk, and then up at the TelePrompTers, at the cameras aimed at me, and at the clock, ticking away the seconds in red.

I touched the edges of the desk, the papers.

I plugged my tiny headphone into the desk and heard Susan Mahoney up in the control room say hello into the earpiece.

Fifty-four seconds before we were to go on-air for the six-thirty broadcast, Quinn hurried in and sat down beside me. It's a game to him, how close he can cut it, how fine, how dangerous. "Do us all a favor and don't screw up," he said.

I looked over at him and decided to take it as a joke. "I'll try."

Quinn nodded as he leaned back in his chair and began to whistle "Hard Day's Night." His ritual.

I checked myself one last time in the small compact I stashed behind the desk while Al rushed up and put the last of the fresh pages of copy in front of us.

I heard Susan whisper in our ears, "I have a good feeling about this." And then, "Twenty seconds . . . fifteen seconds . . . ten seconds . . . and go."

I could feel the blood rush to my face and suddenly

everything was gone, everything but this. I looked directly into the camera and smiled as I heard Quinn say, "Good evening. Tonight I'd like to welcome Laura Barrett to the *National Evening News*...."

Three minutes into the broadcast, while film of the Paris Metro played across the screens, Susan spoke into my ear from the control room. "You're doing great."

I smiled. Despite all the odds, I am one of those who flourish before a live camera. I can feel its magnetic particles shimmering in my pulse, my heart, my brain. I've known better reporters, better *news* people, who are not so lucky, who become dull and flat and thickened in the camera's presence. There are many honest people who appear shady and untrustworthy, while credibility, the ultimate coin of a news broadcast, emanates from others with little effort. Luck, again.

When the tape ended, I leaned forward and read the story of a San Diego high school hero who rescued his teacher from drowning on a class trip with more authority than I ever could have alone in my office, without so many eyes on me, without the thrilling risk.

"How come the heroes are always honor students?" Quinn asked no one in particular while a commercial played. "Even the psychopaths always turn out to be honor students. 'He was such a nice guy, until he opened fire in the mall that day.' " He stood up to stretch, cracked his knuckles, and turned to me, his eyes piercing. "You have a drop of sweat on your upper lip. It's been there for the last four minutes. I tried to motion to you."

I didn't have time to check in my compact before Al stepped up and said, "Fifteen seconds to us, two shot,

26

then Laura to camera four."

Distracted, I read the next story too quickly, skipping a line and tripping over the name of the secretary of defense. In the end, we had twenty long seconds to fill because of my mistake. There was no choice but to banter.

"And we're off," Al finally announced.

Quinn leaned back and smiled out into the dark studio. It was an odd smile, rising only on the left, baring no teeth.

After the broadcast, Frank Berkman, the executive producer, came out of his office for a brief postmortem. Berkman, who came armed with a string of Emmys and a reputation for journalistic innovation, was brought in ten months ago from a rival network to help the show rise out of third place. I was his idea. Everyone quieted at his approach. He is an achingly thin man with thin dry lips and thin hair and thin gray skin, as if the incessant rhythm of the newsroom had eaten through his flesh. Even his sentences are parsed, thin, minimal. Unlike many in the business, he keeps his personal life out of the office and out of the press, which only adds to the rumors and the mystery about him. He is loyal, untrustworthy, brilliant, or merely lucky, depending on whom you believe. The only hard facts that had become known in the newsroom so far were that he always walked to work no matter how bad the weather, he ate lunch at his desk as often as possible, he never returned phone calls, and he had a predilection for Savile Row suits.

He leaned against an empty desk and crossed his arms before his concave chest. "Not bad," he said, looking at me.

"Thanks."

"But what happened at the end?"

I said nothing, just shrugged apologetically.

"I realize that you were used to happy-talk on the local news," Berkman continued, "but we do not engage in banter on national broadcasts."

Quinn stood with his rolled-up *Wall Street Journal* in his hands' banging it against his thigh.

I looked nervously back to Berkman, who had nothing more to say. He slowly uncrossed his arms and turned back in the direction of his office.

"Thanks for the flowers," I called after him as he began to walk away.

Berkman swiveled, looked at me, nodded, and left.

"Flowers?" Quinn asked. "What's next? Heart-shaped boxes of chocolates?"

I went back to my office and shut the door.

I sat at my desk, resting my head in my hands, my eyes shut, feeling my skin peel off my body layer by layer, leaving a pulpy space behind. Only during the live broadcast did it seem to fit airtight.

I glanced at my watch.

David would be waiting for me at home, Sophie snuggled tightly in his arms. Sometimes he dances about the living room to Patsy Cline with her, Sophie smiling at the first notes of Patsy's smooth and mournful voice, turning to the speakers, anxious for more.

There had been offers of celebratory dinners from my agent, Jerry, from the network news director, from people who suddenly wanted to know me better, but I only wanted to go home.

The air was dense and moist as I left the building. I

28

pulled up the collar of my coat. The streets were dark save for the pools of yellow light from the street lamps. I had gotten into the habit long ago of walking at least part of the way home alone, though David tried to talk me out of it, reminding me of the muggings and rapes I reported every night on the local news, about the dangers of the neighborhood, and the possibility of deranged fans. He even bought me an illegal Mace spray to carry in my pocket. Still, I continue, finding in the night streets the promise of anonymity that first brought me here. Even now, I told myself, I can change neighborhoods, change names, dye my hair, who would find me?

I turned the corner onto Eleventh Avenue, where a trio of men stood before the liquor store pooling money, and headed south, walking quickly, my arms wrapped about me while I played it over and over in my mind— Quinn's lopsided toothless smile, Berkman's voice, "We do not engage in banter on a national broadcast"— dissecting it, putting the fragments back together one way, and then another.

And I thought of Sophie, of going home to Sophie, with her scent of cherry wood and cobwebs, and the way she fit into my chest like a long-lost puzzle piece.

Half a block away, I turned around suddenly, thinking I heard someone behind me. I fingered the tiny canister of Mace in my pocket. But there was only emptiness, silence. I continued walking.

I heard the voice again, just a mumble at first, the words indistinguishable.

And then I heard it clearly. "Marta."

I kept on, my head down, my arms tight about my torso.

"Marta," the man said louder.

I froze, the blood suddenly still in my veins as I turned around and saw him.

Two

HIS DARK BLOND HAIR WAS PUSHED STRAIGHT BACK and his face was whittled as if someone had taken a chisel and removed everything extraneous until all that was left was its purest geometry. A nearby street lamp cast conical shadows across it, striping it with light.

"Jack," I said at last.

He reached to touch me, his fingertips grazing my cheeks, then pressing into my flesh as if to verify—*you are here*. "Marta." His voice was anxious and defiant, scratched with longing and disbelief.

"My name is Laura," I said quickly.

He looked blankly at me.

"Laura," I repeated.

He nodded and continued to stand in silence, taking me in, as if looking for scraps whose shape and texture he could recognize, seize, and stand on as dry land.

I took a deep breath and was just about to speak when a young couple in matching down coats walked by and turned to do a double-take, seeking my face, embracing it.

He watched me take in the recognition, meet it, absorb it, let it go.

"Jack?" I said when they were out of earshot.

"Yes?"

I shook my head, looked down at the street and then slowly back to him as an iciness spread across my scalp, the back of my neck, my throat. "What are you doing here?" My own voice was dim and tinny in my ears.

30

"I saw your picture in the magazine."

Our eyes met and held before slipping off to a more comfortable distance. Our breath curled white between us.

"It's been so long," I said.

"Twenty-one years," he answered. "Twenty-one and a half years, actually. Since that night." There was a bitterness in his tone that made me wince.

Two men in suits and woolen overcoats were walking in our direction, their footsteps audible down the street.

Jack did not see them, did not care. "Marta?"

"Not here," I whispered urgently.

"What?"

"I can't do this here," I said, stealing another look at the approaching men, both from the publicity department at the network.

"But I came all this way to see you. You owe me that much, at least," he insisted. "Don't you think?"

My body was completely still except for my fingertips, tapping nervously against my thigh again and again. "Yes," I admitted.

He took a step closer. "Marta."

"Please, Jack. Not here," I repeated nervously.

"I can't believe I finally found you."

The two network executives were just a few feet away now, regarding me curiously. I stared at Jack another moment, unable to speak, and then I ran out into the street, waving my arm wildly at a passing cab. It screeched to a halt and I jumped in, slamming the door.

The taxi raced down the avenue until, when I looked back through the rear window, Jack was lost in the traffic, in the night itself.

I slipped my keys quietly into the top lock.

"Congratulations," David called out. "You were great."

I went into the living room, still wearing my coat, and found him on the couch with a spiral sketchpad balanced on his knees, a rapidograph in hand. It's a nervous habit of his, this continual drawing of lines, of buildings, of rough city overviews. I find them on napkins, envelopes, sometimes even on toilet paper. Tonight, there was an unopened bottle of champagne on the coffee table in front of him and he was smiling broadly. "Look," he said, holding up a stack of yellow telegrams. He began to read the names of the senders, all people we knew well enough to give our closely guarded home address.

I nodded and tried to appear pleased.

"You look wiped out," David said. "Are you all right?"

"I'm fine."

"Just fine? That's it? You're jaded already? How was the dapper Mr. Hartley? Does he spit when he talks? Did you play footsie under the news desk? Should I be jealous? What did everyone say afterwards?"

"I bantered."

"What?"

"I bantered. You know, unscripted talk that has the distinct ring of mindless chatter."

"You mean like our dinner conversations?" He smiled, leaning forward. "Laura, don't you think you're being a little hard on yourself?"

I shrugged. "David, did I have a bead of sweat on my lip?"

Before he could answer, Sophie began to whimper. "You relax, I'll do it," he said, pushing his papers aside.

"No, it's all right. I'll go," I interrupted hastily, glad

for the excuse to get away.

When I reached down into the wicker bassinet, Sophie stopped whimpering and grinned up, her toothless mouth a single gummy squiggle, her fists banging into the mattress as if her body could not hold all of her delight at seeing me. Her back, as I lifted her, was damp with sweat.

I held her against my chest tighter than usual, bending down to sniff her scalp, and in the rolls behind her neck, in the three creases of her thighs, trying to memorize the woodsy odor, imprint it on my lungs. Finally I rested her back in my arms and watched as she clasped the bottle greedily.

Perhaps I had always known Jack would find me.

Years ago, when I first left, I was waiting for him, waiting with every corner I turned, every bus I boarded. And then when he didn't find me (was it possible that he never even looked, that none of them had?), I began slowly to relax, unknotting one muscle at a time, stretching out—but warily, always warily. It is not always so simple to tell when something is over, after all—love, for instance, or grievance, is sometimes only hiding no matter how hard you try to convince yourself that it is gone.

My skin burned where his fingertips had pressed into me under the street lamp.

Sophie closed her mouth tightly, stubbornly refusing the last ounce of liquid. I looked down at her face, her eyes closed now, myriad expressions playing across it, flickering contortions of worry and of pleasure. Sometimes when I return to bed, I feel my own face unconsciously mimicking hers. I watched a few moments longer and then put her back in her bassinet, angling her around the black-and-white geometric mobile and tucking the white blanket firmly about her.

And then I went out and drank champagne with David.

Later, I lay beside him, trying to fit my body to his, my breath to his breath, so steady and so regular and so oblivious.

But each inhalation caught in my throat as my heart beat out its wild staccato adrenaline-laced rhythms.

I moved my hand gradually down my stomach and wriggled it between my legs, working slowly, and then faster.

In the last months of pregnancy, there was a frantic immediacy to my desire for sex that riled me, gnarled me. I would bring myself to orgasm three, four times a day. It only took a minute, sometimes less. Once or twice, I sat behind the desk in my office, the lights and the conversations of the newsroom moving busily just outside my door, as I worked my hand recklessly between my legs, biting my lip into a relieved silence. I told myself it was the pressure of the baby, so low and so heavy, and maybe it was that.

David murmured something deep inside his dreams. I stopped, lay completely still. He was grinding his teeth in his sleep, gnawing at tensions he rarely admits to in waking hours.

And then I started again.

I shut my eyes and felt my body seize up and then ease.

I dreamt that night of the tropics, of being trapped in the thick wet Florida heat, always the same heat, the same dream, the gnats that filled my eyes, my mouth, my nostrils, my lungs, the noose of arms tightening and tightening about my throat as I tried desperately to breathe, to scream, to escape . . .

A large hand spread across my back.

Terrified, I slapped and clawed at it, my arms flailing.

"Laura. Laura, wake up."

Gradually, I became aware of David kneeling beside me on the floor. "It's okay," he said gently. "It was just a nightmare."

I ran my hands over my neck as I struggled out of the darkest recesses.

"Sshhh. It's okay. Come back to bed now."

I nodded, my heart still thrashing in my chest.

David helped me up and led me back to bed. He smoothed the damp hair from my forehead and picked up the sheets from where I had wrangled them to the ground.

"You're still shaking," he said. "Come here." He wrapped his arms about me. "What was it? The same one?"

"I don't remember," I mumbled.

I don't know whether he believed me or not.

As soon as I got to work the next day, I told my secretary, Carla, that if a man by the name of Jack Pierce called not to put him through. Guilt coiled through me as I spoke, as I pictured his face, as I remembered. But I was too scared to change my mind. Carla looked up curiously, waiting for an explanation, but I offered none. She is a consummately efficient woman who believes above all in playing by the rules. In her late forties, she favors well-made knee-length tweed skirts that are never quite in style and never quite out of style, sheer stockings and pumps. Her fair skin and cerulean eyes only sometimes exhibit surprise and betrayal that, in this business at least, it is the people who don't play by the rules who get ahead. "It's important," I reiterated, and walked away.

I closed the door of my office and breathed in the thick sickroom odor of too many flowers, too much heat. On my desk, there was a stack of messages congratulating me on my debut, including one from the network news head, Thomas Greenville, as well as various other memos that needed my attention. I read a few and then I walked to the window, looking down at the street below, looking for Jack.

He was not there.

I returned to my desk, sat down, and punched up the NewsMaker program, waiting impatiently for its primary colors to fill the computer screen, waiting for the stories, the hum of the news wires, the ticking of the second hands on all the newsroom's many clocks to do their work, draw me in, wall me in with the immediacy of their demands.

The lead story so far was the President's upcoming budget proposal, a dry report made only slightly more interesting by the scare tactics of threatened cuts in Medicare.

I tried to make sense of the figures, but the digits remained abstract, meaningless. The story was not yet tagged "L" or "Q" and I knew that I'd better have a good working comprehension of the sums, the implications. Quinn was sure to throw me unexpected questions to make me nervous as well as expand his own airtime. I was beginning to realize I couldn't trust him. I ran my forefinger along the screen, reciting the numbers out loud.

I got through the entire story once before looking over the monitor at the window again.

All that was visible was a tiny sliver of the empty street below and the beveled steel cutout of the city's skyline.

I crossed my legs and returned to the computer, still filled with details of the budget proposal.

As the hours passed and I did not see Jack on the street, did not hear from him, I began to think that I dreamt the incident last night, his face beneath the street lamp, his touch.

Or perhaps he had changed his mind, gone away, back to wherever he had come from, back to the past.

Susan Mahoney barged into my office without knocking. "I guess you've heard by now that the overnight ratings were the highest they've been in months. Seven point nine. That's only a quarter-point behind second place," she said excitedly. She didn't mention that the reviews in the morning papers were only mixed. One critic quoted "an anonymous network source" who doubted I'd still be here in six months.

I looked up from my computer. "People just tuned in to see if I'd screw up," I replied.

"I don't care why they tuned in. The trick is to make sure they keep tuning in. Look, half the magazines in the country have been calling, but I think we have to be careful about overexposure right now. The only one I agreed to was *Vanity Fair*. We can reevaluate later and maybe hit the women's magazines."

"You agreed without asking me?"

She looked taken aback. "I'm sorry. I just assumed you'd say yes. Do you know how many television personalities would kill to have a feature in *Vanity Fair*?"

"I'm not a 'personality,' I'm a news anchor."

"Of course. Look, if you're worried about your image, they've assured me they have every intention of treating you seriously. We're not talking glamour girl shots here."

"I need to think about it."

Susan frowned. "You're not going to give me this 'I don't owe the public anything' crap, are you?" she asked. "They're the ones that keep you in business. The fastest way to get in trouble is to forget that."

"I'm not forgetting it."

"So?" She leaned forward.

It was too late, I was beginning to see that now. Too late to stop it, control it. Any of it.

I looked away, said nothing.

She took my silence as a yes. "Talk about your baby a lot, okay?" Susan suggested brightly. "They love stuff like that. It'll humanize you. And babies always help ratings. Look at Katie Couric. Look at fucking Kathie Lee Gifford."

"I can think of people I'd rather look at," I groaned. And then, more seriously, "I'd like to leave my daughter out of this."

"Just think about it."

"All right. Listen," I said as she began to turn the door knob to leave, "would you mind arranging for a studio car for me tonight?"

"Of course not. Why?"

"No reason. I just had trouble getting a cab last night."

"No problem. We can have one every night if you'd like.

"Maybe that would be a good idea."

She smiled and I saw in her face a flicker of both condescension and relief. I would be like all of them, then. Grabbing all the perks, suddenly convinced that we deserved them.

On the newscast that evening, Quinn leaned forward with a veneer of interest across his famously taut face and asked me a complicated question about the exact percentage of proposed cuts in Medicare under the President's proposal, but I was ready for him. Everyone agreed that there was a level of energy, of concentration, almost a feverish competence to my work. If I sweat, it didn't show. And I certainly didn't banter. Jerry called right after the broadcast to say I was beginning to look more relaxed, beginning to look like I belonged.

I left the building at 7:46.

I saw the studio's black town car waiting for me by the curb. Relieved, I pushed open the glass doors and walked across the three yards of sidewalk to the car. At my approach, the uniformed driver got out of the front seat and stood holding the back door open for me. I was just bending my head to get in when I felt a tug at my arm.

I looked up, startled.

Jack returned my gaze and tightened his hold, squeezing my arm beneath my heavy coat.

The driver stepped up to protect me. "Hey," he said loudly. "What do you think you're doing?"

I swung around, fearful of loud voices, of commotion, attention. Out of the corner of my eye, I saw the matte gold network logo looking down on us. "It's okay. I know him," I said, smiling wanly to reassure the driver. "We just need to talk for a minute."

The driver stood still for a moment and then walked reluctantly around to the front of the car and got in.

I straightened up and looked at Jack. His lips were

tucked into his teeth and the lightly tanned skin of his cheeks fell into deep creases.

"Where are you going?" he asked.

"Home."

"What about us?" He held my arm with one hand, the open door with the other. "We need to talk."

Through the building's glass doors and windows, I saw the receptionist watching me intently.

"Not here."

"That's what you said yesterday."

"Tomorrow."

"Where?"

"Café del Petore," I answered without thinking. I wanted only to be in the car, the door closed, moving away from him. "It's downtown. Look it up."

"When?"

"Twelve-thirty."

"All right," he said, and held the door open, watched me get in, and then closed the door behind me.

I leaned forward and told the driver to go.

This is what I thought later: How quick, how ready he was to believe me, to believe that I would meet him, after everything, after all.

The next morning, I was working at my desk when Carla buzzed to remind me of the production meeting for the new magazine show Quinn and I were going to start doing the first Wednesday of every month. It was in my contract, in his. Actually, ever since the networks discovered how cheap and profitable magazine shows are, it's in just about everyone's contract.

Everyone was already sitting in the conference room when I got there—Berkman, the director, Barry Fried,

Quinn, Quinn's agent, my agent, Jerry Gold. A platter of donuts and bagels sat untouched in the center of the table.

"Are you ready?" Berkman asked as I sat down.

I nodded and they ran the videotape of the new graphics, set, and music.

Though the show, to be called *In Step*, had been in the planning stages for months, long before they settled on me as the co-anchor, there was still some uncertainty about its precise tone and pace, whether it would be mostly taped or live, and what the balance between hard and soft news would be. Often, it can take months on-air for a magazine show to find its rhythm. None was successful right off the bat, not even the hallowed *60 Minutes*, if anyone cared to go back that far, and a network had to be patient for it to pay off. Berkman had hoped for at least a year's commitment from the brass for our show, but he hadn't gotten it. Still, ads had begun to appear in magazines and on the sides of buses: "Get *In Step* with Quinn Hartley and Laura Barrett."

Berkman got down to his list at hand. Though we'd leave a slot for late-breaking stories, the first show was slated to include an investigative report into welfare reform, an interview with Tom Hanks, and a talk with the secretary of state about the progress of peace talks in the Middle East. While Quinn and I would share the anchoring duties, other network reporters would contribute pieces. Everyone hoped a good scandal or a particularly sexy news event would happen our first week, but we had to be prepared if not.

Berkman looked down at his yellow legal pad. "We've decided to go with Olivia Redding for the secretary," he said. Redding was the network's veteran Washington correspondent who was rumored to be

41

furious I'd been granted the nightly anchor spot instead of her.

Jerry leaned forward. "I think Laura should do the secretary." He spoke in a gruff Bronx-ridden voice that clashed with his cashmere turtleneck, tweed jacket, and well-pressed jeans. His accent, purposefully unrefined, perhaps even exaggerated, was one of his trademarks, along with a year-round tan that he swore was natural.

"I thought she was doing Hanks," Quinn protested.

"She can do the star part next time. This time she'll do the secretary."

"Reading has the contacts," Berkman countered in an uninflected tone.

"And she's obviously been lobbying hard," Jerry retorted. "The competition among reporters at your own network is worse than with their rivals. If that works for you, fine. Far be it from me to tell you how to run your news division."

"Thank you, Mr. Gold," Berkman replied.

"But," Jerry continued, "the best way to showcase Laura as an anchor is to prove her news mettle. She should do the secretary."

Berkman leaned back. "I'll think about it. Quinn, tell us what you've lined up. Do you think you'll be able to get a quote from the President on welfare?"

"I have a tentative commitment from the White House," Quinn answered. "Especially if we get the timing right and this airs the week the Senate votes on it." I sat back and doodled in my pad while Quinn outlined his piece, riddled with numerous illustrious sources. "I'd like to do most of it live," he said. "We can get a satellite hook-up between the senators, the White House, and at least one welfare recipient grilling them. That way, fireworks will be inevitable," he finished up, and everyone nodded approvingly. It is a measure of success of any magazine show not just to report the news but to make it, to be quoted in the next day's newspapers and broadcasts.

After the meeting, Jerry followed me to my office and sat down.

"Why didn't you speak up?" he asked. "You don't win any points for niceness. Look, they want to give you all the celeb shit, there's nothing wrong with that. But not just yet. We've got to show you can do the hard stuff first. And you can, you know. You're not some fucking Twinkie. I didn't groom you through twelve years of street reporting so they can put you on the woman's page."

"Why did you?"

He frowned slightly. "Because you have talent. Real talent. Do you know how many people send me their demo tapes every week? Every two-bit reporter from Podunk, Ohio, to Bumfuck, Egypt. Every goddamned weather girl dreaming of the big time. Every horse's ass with a journalism degree. Do you know how many have real talent? I can count them on one hand."

I looked at him steadily. "There is no woman's page anymore," I said.

He leaned back, smiling. "Don't kid yourself."

"I know."

"So?"

"I thought you told me not to make waves."

"Some waves, honey, you've got to make some waves or they won't respect you. The trick is to look confident even if you're not. Fake it. No one's gonna believe the news from someone with a quivering voice. On-air or off." He sighed and ran his hands over his stubbled chin. He began talking, talking again, talking about something, but I did not hear the words. Finally, he leaned forward. "Am I boring you, Laura?"

I smiled apologetically. "No. I'm sorry. But I'm late for a lunch appointment. I've got to run."

My eyes adjusted gradually to the dark lighting, absorbed by the wood-paneled walls and low ceiling of the Café del Petore. The only brightness came from the spotless white linen tablecloths.

I was twenty minutes late but only two tables were occupied. The restaurant, on a scruffy side street, did not do a big lunch business, which was why I had chosen it. Jack was sitting at a table in the back room, drinking a scotch. He was wearing a blue and white seersucker suit and a crisp white shirt, a southern gentleman's outfit, mildly absurd but somehow touching in the somber northern air. He drank slowly, shifting his gaze between the front door and his watch.

I saw the relief in his eyes as he followed my progress in his direction.

"I wasn't sure you'd come," he said softly when I reached his table.

I smiled despite myself. "Neither was I." I felt a part of myself, caked on, encrusted, fall away in one large sheet. We had been youngest together.

"But you did."

"Yes."

"You look good," he said, studying me. "Different, but good. I never thought of you as a blond."

I felt my face flush, embarrassed suddenly by the artifice that I had grown so used to. When the waiter came, I ordered a glass of wine, something I rarely do at lunch.

"How did you find me?" I asked.

44

"I saw your picture in *People* magazine. It was a fluke, really. I only bought it because there was an article about a cartoonist I admire. I wasn't even sure it was you at first, but there was something in the eyes. I woke up in the middle of the night seeing them in front of me. I got up and went back to the kitchen where I left the magazine." He paused to take a sip of his drink as he remembered. "I was terrified of turning on the lights and looking at the picture again. I was terrified I was wrong." He looked up. "But I got a Magic Marker and darkened your hair, then I changed the shape of your face with a pencil. I pulled out an old photo of you and there was no question. Marta, you had to know I'd find you once you had your face in the magazines and on TV. Did you really think I wouldn't recognize you just because you have a different name and a new nose?"

"I don't know. So much time has gone by. Sometimes I don't even recognize myself."

He looked directly at me. "Maybe you wanted me to find you."

I didn't answer.

"Have you been here in New York this whole time?" Jack asked.

"No. I think I've lived in half the cities on the East Coast, and some in the middle. At least it felt that way. I didn't make it back to New York until three years ago."

"And now you're a big success."

"I guess."

"You don't sound sure."

"I don't know. Sometimes it feels like it doesn't have anything to do with me." I stopped abruptly. "Where do you live?"

He laughed, and it was not entirely pleasant, not entirely benign. "Flagerty."

45

I looked at him curiously. "You never left? Even afterwards, later?"

"No."

"I'm surprised."

"Are you?"

I didn't reply.

"Maybe I thought you'd come back," he said. "Maybe I was waiting for that all this time. Waiting for you."

I flinched. "I'm so sorry, Jack."

He swirled the ice about his drink. "Are you?"

"Yes," I answered quietly.

Our eyes locked. There was a faint relief map of lines about his, and I nearly reached to trace it with my fingertips.

"I guess waiting became something of a habit," he said. "I almost stopped noticing it. And then suddenly, when I saw your picture and I realized you were actually within reach, the waiting stopped."

The waiter returned with my wine and took our lunch order, stealing lingering glances at me as he wrote in his little white pad.

"Tell me about your life," I said when he had gone. "What is it like?"

He leaned back. "How can anyone ever really say what their life is like?"

"Are you married?"

"I was. I'm separated now."

I was surprised at the pang I felt. "Who did you marry?"

"Carol Hendricks. Maybe you remember her? She was two years behind us in high school."

I shook my head no.

"She certainly remembers you."

46

"Do you have children?"

"I feel like I'm being interviewed."

I smiled. "Sorry. Professional hazard."

"No, there were no children. Carol wanted one desperately, but it never happened. We spent three years and almost all of our savings seeing every fertility expert in the state. Even after they told Carol she couldn't conceive, she kept on trying every shady cure she could find. Everything from Chinese herbs to lighting candles. She was obsessed with it." He took a sip of his drink and carefully put the glass down. "She thought I left because she couldn't have a baby, but that was never really it."

"What was it?"

His leg skimmed mine under the table. "The truth was, I was in love with someone else," he said. He stared at me unabashedly, with none of the feints and sidesteps of politesse. It was one of the things I had once loved about him, though it unnerved me now. I looked away.

"You have a baby, though," he said. "I read it in the magazine article. A girl, was it?" he asked.

"Yes."

"That must be nice for you."

I nodded. I'd been drinking quickly, nervously, and I felt the wine begin to form a hazy scrim across my mind. I played with the edges of my large linen napkin, staring at Jack's hands resting on the table, his long thin fingers knobbier, more callused now.

"Tell me about Flagerty," I said. "Has it changed much?"

He laughed. I had forgotten his laugh. "Sure. One step forward, two steps back. We lost the store, you know."

47

"I didn't know. I'm sorry."

He shrugged. "Back taxes."

"What do you do for a living?"

"Well, I obviously couldn't practice law," he said dryly.

I winced. It had been his dream once. When we first met, just after the Vietnam war and Watergate, Jack had a great burning optimism, an overriding belief in using the law to correct all the injustices that he took so personally. All that righteousness had given him a certain nobility that seemed so wounded now, by age, by events, by me.

"There was a small inheritance," he said. "And I draw."

"You draw?"

"For the paper. You know, editorial cartoons, caricatures of local events, stuff like that."

"I didn't know you could draw."

"Neither did I." He paused, inclining his face to me. "Do you want to know how I discovered it, this wonderful talent of mine?"

" Sure."

"Drawing you."

I looked at him curiously.

"That first year away, when I began to realize you wouldn't come back, I started to draw you over and over again. So I wouldn't forget what you looked like." He stopped and, looking down, he pulled out his scuffed leather wallet and opened it up. Slowly, carefully, he extricated a small pencil drawing, the paper thin and cracking, its creases worn almost into oblivion. He looked at it once and then handed it to me.

It was me, exactly me at sixteen, my long dark wild hair, my scared and insolent eyes. My throat caught.

They were strangers both, the man across from me, the girl in the picture, strangers and yet not, and for a moment I was lost in the dark vertiginous tunnel between the past and present.

I looked slowly back to him. "Oh, Jack."

With a single motion, he took the drawing back from me, tenderly folded it, and replaced it in his wallet.

"Do you remember the boat we had, how we used to get splinters every time we sat in it?" he asked.

I took another sip of wine. "We were kids," I said. "Just kids."

"No one ever truly changes. Not really."

I said nothing.

Our food came and we began to eat. I looked up at Jack, at once so familiar and so new, twirling his angel hair pasta, taking the fork into his mouth, swallowing. "That's what you eat for lunch?" he asked.

I looked down at my plate of steamed baby vegetables, my standard fare, and wanted to disown them, their glazed primary colors, their preciousness.

Jack leaned across the table suddenly. "I couldn't believe you would just vanish like that," he said in a pained voice. "We could have explained what happened. If you'd stayed."

"I'm sorry."

"So you said."

"I mean it."

He looked at me closely to gauge my expression.

"Jack, I know I can't make up for what I did. But if there's anything I can do for you, anything I can do to help you . . ."

"Help me?" he asked. "I don't need your help. Is that why you think I came here?"

"No," I admitted.

For a few minutes we ate in silence and then we both stopped, stopped the pretense of it.

"Have you ever been to New York before?" I asked.

"No. I don't travel much. Funny, the way things turn out, isn't it?"

I pushed my plate away. "How long are you staying?"

"I don't know."

"Well, as long as you're here, you might as well see some of the city."

I began to list sights that Jack should visit, the Metropolitan Museum, the Staten Island ferry, the World Trade Center, the Forty-second Street Library with its majestic lions, whatever came most immediately to mind, grabbing at them quickly, hopefully, cruise ship chatter among strangers.

He was hardly listening. "I didn't come here to see the goddamned Staten Island ferry," he interrupted.

"Why did you come?"

"To see you," he answered simply.

"Jack?"

"What?" His eyes were watery with sadness and defiance.

"What do you want?"

"I don't know."

I looked away. I wanted to tell him that people didn't say that here, I wanted to tell him to play by the rules, rules that I had studied, assimilated, clung to. But I didn't.

I glanced at my watch. "I've got to get back to work."

"Busy lady. Aren't you going to invite me to dinner, meet your husband, talk about old times?"

I stopped and looked at him. "Jack, I meant what I said. I'm sorry, more sorry than I could ever say for what happened. But it was all so long ago."

"Not to me."

When the waiter brought our check, I reached for it, but Jack quickly put his hand on mine, his fingers dry and warm. I withdrew first.

"I'll pay," he said. "Don't worry I may not be as rich as you, but I can afford it."

I nodded and followed him out.

The sky had darkened while we were having lunch, and a coming storm had turned the only remaining light to mercury. We stood just outside the restaurant's doors, our hands thrust deep into our pockets. "Goodbye, Jack."

"Just like that?"

"I don't know what else there can be."

"I'm staying at the Hotel Angelica, on Twenty-seventh Street," he said.

I nodded and, at the last moment, I leaned over quickly to kiss him on his hollow cheek.

He pulled me closer and I felt his moist breath as he whispered in my ear, "Don't forget, I know you better than anyone. I always will."

The lover's lure, the lover's threat.

Three

I LAY IN BED TRYING TO SHUT OUT THE EARLY morning sounds, to shut out the day itself, postpone its arrival as long as possible. I closed my eyes, trying to go back to sleep, but Jack's face, his words, his hurt, swam before me. I jumped when the telephone rang. It was just seven o'clock. David, already showered, picked up the cordless phone on the other side of the bedroom, mumbled a few words, and then handed it to me. "It's

51

for you. It's Jerry."

"Why would he be calling so early?"

"Joan Lunden called in sick and they want you to sub?" David suggested, and left to finish dressing.

"What's up?" I asked as I took the receiver.

"I might ask you the same."

"Jerry, it's too early for riddles. Shouldn't you be out jogging, or having a ten-dollar bagel in a midtown hotel?"

"Have you seen the *Post*?"

"Not yet. Why?"

"There's an item in it about you having lunch yesterday with a mystery man at some hole in the wall."

"What?" I sat up.

"It doesn't actually come out and say anything, just goes into the wife-and-new-mother thing. Implications, you know."

"That's ridiculous."

"I hope so."

"I can't believe you're taking this so seriously, Jerry."

"Yeah, well let me tell you something, a lot of people who would never admit it take it seriously, too. If the supermarket tabloids pick up on this, they'll have a field day."

"Jesus Christ, can't I even have lunch without explaining it?"

"No. Not anymore. Let's be honest, at least with each other, okay, kiddo? The network could have gone with a diva like Sawyer or maybe even Walters, for chrissakes, but they figure they've got their hands full with Hartley. Part of the charm of taking someone from local and making them a star is they're easier to control, at least at first. But people have to trust you, that's the whole point of a news anchor. You've got to project sobriety,

52

responsibility, not secret rendezvous. Laura, this is the best chance you're likely to get. Don't blow it."

"But it was nothing like that," I protested.

"Listen, in your business illusion is reality. You should know that by now."

"Don't worry."

"You're paying me big bucks to worry. And right now, you're getting your money's worth. You've got to know the tabloids are all going to be scrounging around for dirt on you. It's how they make their money. Just stay clean, okay? Don't give those fuckers anything to work with."

"All right," I said and hung up the phone.

"What was that about?" David asked, dressed now in a charcoal suit.

"Nothing. Just some bullshit on Page Six."

He went to the kitchen and picked up the top of the three newspapers we had delivered every morning. He opened the Post to the gossip page and read the item about me out loud while he walked back to the bedroom. He dropped the paper on the bed.

"Not bad. Upper-right-hand corner. Boldface."

"Very funny."

"All right, I'll bite. Who was your hot lunch date?"

"It was nothing, David. I had lunch with an interior decorator, and all they saw was me with an unidentified man."

"Are we decorating something?"

"We've been talking about fixing up the bedroom since we moved in. It was going to be a surprise," I said indignantly, convinced for a moment of my own righteous anger.

"Oh." He went into the bathroom and shut the door. I heard him turn the water on and begin to brush his teeth.

53

I lay in bed picking at my fingernails for a couple of minutes and then I got up and opened the bathroom door without knocking.

"I'm sorry about the paper," I said as I came up behind him.

"It's okay. I know it's not your fault What's that expression, 'No press is bad as long as they spell your name right'?" He reached for a towel and dried his face. "It's not your fault. It's just going to take some getting used to, that's all."

David once told me that he didn't particularly like watching me on television, that there was something disturbing to him about the smoothed and sanded version of me, a small portion of the woman he knew sprayed and buffed and shrunken onto screens throughout the city, his and yet not his.

"It doesn't have anything to do with us," I tried to reassure him now.

"Doesn't it?"

"Not if we don't let it."

I wrapped my arms around him and kissed the back of his neck beneath the soft fringe of his hair, and then his ear, his throat.

"What's this?" he asked.

"Sshhh." I moved my hand over his chest and into his pants, down through the thicket of hair until I felt his cock, already thickening.

He turned to face me. "I'll be late."

"So?"

We collapsed back onto the bed and he moved into me, the sheets and the quilt sliding about beneath us.

I wanted to want only this, this man, my husband, his hips grinding against mine, going in and in.

I dug my fingers into his back and shut my eyes.

54

But what I found waiting in the darkness was Jack.

I wondered what it would be like to make love to him now, this new and whittled Jack, wondered if I sniffed him closely I would once more smell the salt, the sea, the heat itself on his skin.

David gave a single final lurch, reared, and then collapsed against me.

After he left, I dressed quickly in jeans and a merino wool turtleneck and, as soon as Dora arrived, I tucked my hair under a baseball cap, put on sunglasses, and took a cab downtown to the Red Hat diner on the corner of Essex and Delancey on the Lower East Side where I met Shana Joseph every second Wednesday. She had been my little sister, as the jargon goes, for the past year and a half. In fact, she was seventeen, three inches taller than me, and weighed at least forty pounds more.

Shana wasn't there yet.

I sat down at one of the peeling linoleum tables in the back under a string of neon red hats and ordered a cup of coffee. The breakfast rush was over, and after the waiter brought me my coffee, he began mopping the stained gray floor. The smell of ammonia made my eyes water.

When I first volunteered years ago in Burlington for a similar program, I thought they'd give me a sweet motherless nine-yearold whom I could make popcorn with on rainy afternoons and gossip with about boys. But most of the girls turned out to be teenagers, and their mothers weren't dead, just disinterested, or worse. Which was something I understood. Perhaps that's why I do it.

Or is it to prove something to myself, that anyone can change if given the right chance, that the possibility of redemption exists for all of us?

Anyway, it is part of my personal deal with God, my endless attempt to rebalance the scales I had tipped so long ago. If I try to be good now, really try to be good . . .

Shana came in fifteen minutes later. She walked slowly, as if to show how little she cared to be here, her wide thighs dimpled beneath kelly green leggings. As soon as she sat down, she called out her order of a bagel with extra jelly and two cups of hot chocolate. We both watched the waiter reluctantly put down his mop and go to the counter, where he opened twin foil packets of cocoa into mottled white mugs and poured hot water in.

Shana downed the first one in a single gulp and wiped the corners of her mouth before she looked across the table at me. Her long blond hair was frazzled and lifeless except for the oily black roots. Her pasty face was heavily rouged. Still, even with the sullen expression, there was a certain prettiness that another girl, an uptown girl, would have been able to do something with. I noticed she was wearing gold button earrings just like the ones I'd worn on the broadcast two nights ago. It was odd, really. She often managed to find a scarf like one she'd seen me wear, the fabric a little shinier, the colors too brightly acidic, but close. Or use a complicated word I'd used, an expression. An intonation, even. She had lately begun to hold her hands as I did, interlaced and still.

We always start this way, her surly, withdrawn, every look designed to remind me that this is just a condition of her probation—going to school, meeting with me. But there are times when I break through and it feels like such a victory I keep coming back. Once, when I took her on a tour of the local studio, she was so shy and silent, so cowed, and her smile was so broad afterwards, that it made my heart ache. After that, she slowly began to release pellets of information about her life. Her mother had moved in with her boyfriend and his four kids a few blocks away, leaving Shana alone with her older brother, Cort. Cort was on crack again after four months in Rikers. There was no mention of a father. Shana never exhibited any surprise, any pain or anger, when she spoke of her family. She only shrugged as if to say, Everyone has a story, after all.

She took a bite of her bagel and then looked under the table to see what I was wearing. She was disappointed it was jeans. Shana felt I didn't dress suitably for what she called my "station in life." I didn't tell her it was because I was uncomfortable wearing expensive clothes to meet her.

She straightened up. "I watched you on TV," she said.

"What'd you think?"

Shana can be a surprisingly accurate critic. She once told me I talked too quickly whenever I had a hard name to pronounce and when I rewatched the tapes, I realized she was right. She was good on clothes, too, though she wouldn't give up trying to get me to wear false eyelashes. "Jay thought you had to chill out a little, but I thought you were all right," she said.

I frowned. Jay was Shana's new boyfriend. She and I had a deal that she wouldn't tell anyone who her "big sister" was, but she told him right away. She even brought him to our apartment on a Saturday afternoon without calling first. Jay stood in the center of the living room, scanning the decor like an auctioneer at a wake. "This real?" he asked, picking up a Cartier travel clock we had gotten as a wedding present. "What about this?" Since then, Jay has been something of a sore spot between us. Sometimes when we meet for coffee, I spot him cruising by the window of the diner in his baggy jeans and massive hooded leather coat, back and forth, back and forth.

"You get a raise when you went on that new show?" Shana asked.

"Yes."

She nodded. "That's good. How much they pay you for doing that shit?"

"More than they should and less than the other guy. So how's school going?" I asked. "Have you been getting to English class?" She had a special dispensation to meet me during gym on Wednesday mornings, but she didn't always make it to the English class afterwards. When I had time I walked her back to the large tan brick building filmed with soot and made sure she at least entered the front door.

She shrugged.

"You're making me look bad," I said. "You want the principal to call me and make me sit in his crummy office?"

"That ever happen to you when you were a kid?"

"Sure."

"No, I bet you were one of those fucking cheerleader types, straight A's, hall monitor, all that shit."

I laughed. "Not quite."

"Right," she said sarcastically. "You were stealing hubcaps and getting tattoos."

"Well, we can't all have your sterling résumé," I countered, "but I had my fair share of trouble."

She looked at me condescendingly. "Sure."

I took a sip of my acrid coffee.

"Jay says you're just one of those do-gooders," Shana continued. "He says all of you feel guilty about something. He says you think you can buy yourself a good night's sleep for the two dollars you spend on my goddamned hot chocolate."

"Jay says, Jay says. Don't you have a mind of your own?" I teased.

Shana stared blankly at me, puzzled as always by my nudges toward feminism. "How's your little girl?" she asked finally.

The only time I had really gone up in her estimation was when I had a baby. I knew that she wanted one herself. It was one of the things I was trying to talk her out of.

"She's fine."

"How much does she weigh?"

"Nineteen pounds."

"Is she sitting up on her own?"

"She just started to."

"I'm gonna come see her again soon."

"I'd like that. Shana, you're not thinking about having a baby with Jay, are you?"

She shrugged.

"How are you going to go to college with a baby?" I asked.

"Girls like me don't go to college."

"There's no such thing as 'girls like me.' You can be whatever 'kind of girl' you choose to be." I realized that I sounded like some irritating self-help book, but I believed it nonetheless. I had to. Shana sighed theatrically.

Nevertheless, I pulled out a catalog from the State University in Syracuse from my bag. I brought her a different one every time we met, thick glossy catalogs of verdant quadrangles and fresh-faced kids, hoping that the pictures would prove to her that there were other worlds out there, other climates. "I can help with the applications," I offered. "And I'd be happy to write you a recommendation."

"They have a communications department?" she asked. "You know, like, TV?"

"Yes. Why? Is that what you're interested in?"

She shrugged noncommittally, and slid the catalog into her knapsack. "Jay wants me to ask you if he can meet Quinn Hartley," she said as I motioned for the check.

"I'll think about it."

"Is your husband jealous of him?"

I laughed. "Not that I know of."

Shana didn't smile, she only nodded, taking in the information, collating it. She has a disconcerting habit of asking me the most personal of questions with no warning. Once, she asked me how many times a week David and I had sex. Another time she wanted to know precisely what I ate at every meal. Whatever I answered, she always took it in impassively and added it to whatever map she was trying to chart.

"Come on," I said. "English starts in five minutes."

We left the diner and found Jay leaning up against a stoop three feet away, his enormous foot in complicated sneakers propped up on the railing, waiting for us.

When I got to my office, I turned on the computer, looked at it briefly, and then began to go through the stack of mail on my desk, mostly a barrage of speaking requests for various civic groups and charities that had already passed initial network standards. I flipped through them quickly, separating them into two piles, those to be discarded and the few I would consider. As soon as I put one in the "discard" pile, though, I had

60

second thoughts and moved it to the "to be considered" pile. They were all worthy, after all, the Women in Media Network, the Girl Scouts, the Central Park Conservancy, the Breast Cancer Awareness Foundation. How do you say no? Of course, if I said yes to each, I'd have no time to do the news and then they wouldn't want me anyway. I turned the television on to CNN, muted the sound, and continued shifting envelopes back and forth between the two piles.

I only saw its edges at first, colorful, crenelated. I wasn't even thinking as I pulled it out.

I froze.

It was a small old-fashioned postcard, with a picture of a yellow U-shaped motel, the courtyard filled with royal palms, the water in the distance. The sky was a lurid blue. I turned it over to read the legend but I already knew the motel's name. The Breezeway Inn. Flagerty, Florida.

There was no handwriting on it, no note.

But in the space where an address should have been, there was a meticulous black ink line drawing of a coffin.

I shut my eyes and sat very still, my heart pounding.

And then, shaking, I rose and went out to the reception area. "How did this get in with my mail?" I asked Carla.

"What?"

"This postcard."

"I suppose the way mail usually gets here. With a stamp and a prayer." Carla's simple gold jewelry, her flowery perfume, and her soft-spoken voice make her sometimes edgy remarks all the more surprising.

"Well, there's no stamp on this. And there's no address."

Carla shrugged. "I don't know anything about it."

"Did you see anyone go into my office?"

"No." She bent down to answer a ringing phone.

I clutched the card as I stared out at the newsroom. Everything was as it should be, everyone was busy with their wires and their computers and their sheets of copy.

I went back to my office and locked the door.

I looked at the postcard one more time, staring at the motel, and at the coffin on the back, before I crammed it deep inside my purse. Then I phoned the studio's head of security, Hank Baldwin. It's his job to protect us from the numerous fans, besotted, beleaguered, lonely, mad, who occasionally seek us out. "Congratulations on the overnight ratings," he said.

"Thanks." I was only somewhat surprised that even he studied the overnights. I asked about his wife and then I got down to business. "Hank, no one can get into the studio without proper ID, can they?"

"Of course not. Why?"

"No reason. Just checking."

"You worried about that guy McGuirre again?"

"I don't know. Not really."

"He's got two more months before he comes up for parole. Getting some headshrinking, I hear," Baldwin said. "They'll let us know when he gets out."

"Okay."

I heard the rustling of papers, a deep breath. "Look, has anything happened?" he asked. "Is there anything I should know about, anything you want to tell me? Confidentially, of course."

I paused, stumbled. "No, nothing like that."

Hank sighed with disappointment. "Well, no one who's not authorized can get into the building, Laura, but if you're nervous I'll put the guards on extra alert."

"Thanks."

What both of us knew but did not mention was that people did slip through, the zealots, the lovelorn, the possessed. They had disrupted live broadcasts with political demands, they had cornered another anchorwoman in her office, holding her hostage for two hours, they had followed a talk-show host to his home in Connecticut and broken all his windows, slashed his tires, jammed his locks. There are a whole litany of deaths that fame has caused. Those of us within its domain only mention them in whispers, if at all.

Baldwin reassured me that under no circumstances would anyone give out my home phone number or address, and then he added, "I'll check on McGuirre."

I thanked him again and hung up.

There was no way that Sean McGuirre could have known about the Breezeway Inn.

Or what happened there.

I went back to the computer, back to the news, went back to doing my job.

What else could I do?

Still, I felt it, the card in my bag, like a scab.

Berkman had a new idea of spending the last five minutes each evening on a single topic under the headline "Nightly Notes." The pieces would be filed by bureau reporters as well as Quinn and me. Jerry told me to make a list of ten possible topics. "Exposés are always good," he said. "Think government waste. Or anything to do with radiation. Money, that too. Always money. Especially when it's being squeezed from little old ladies." Though I'd always prided myself on my ability to generate story ideas, I'd only come up with three viable possibilities so far. I wondered how many Quinn had. Whatever it was, he wasn't talking. I stared at my list for a few minutes, adding nothing, and then, distracted, I called Dora to check on Sophie.

"She's fine, our little girlie is fine, thank the Lord," Dora said. "Sleeping like the innocent she is."

Dora thanked the Lord so repeatedly and for such prosaic events, a good bowel movement, a well-attended bottle, that everyday occurrences took on a miraculous and ominous air. She was, as David said, a woman after my own heart.

I hung up, checked the progress of the evening's broadcast on the computer, and then, at four-thirty, I went to makeup.

Perry was perched on the counter alongside her brushes, her small rounded figure tightly encased in a black knit dress, as she talked on the telephone. She put down the receiver as soon as I walked in.

"That sounded bad," I said, settling into one of the clammy vinyl chairs. "Billy?"

"Worse. The *National Enquirer*."

"What did they want, makeup tips from the stars?"

"They're not *Vogue*. They don't pay big bucks for my ideas on mascara," Perry said. "Half the hair and makeup people at the studios are on the tabloid payrolls. They're great sources. You wouldn't believe the stuff we hear."

"You're kidding me."

Perry laughed. "I didn't figure you to be the naïve type." She glanced over me at her own reflection in the mirror, fingered a red strand of hair from her forehead, and then went back to applying my foundation.

"What were they asking?"

"We didn't get that far. They know I don't dish."

I nodded.

"So how is Billy, anyway?"

Perry laughed and rolled her eyes. "Italian men, they're the best. Impossible, but the best. All that Mediterranean blood makes them wild in bed and all that Catholic guilt has them crawling for forgiveness."

I laughed. "You sound like you've given this a lot of thought." Quinn, walking by, peered in, frowned at the sound of our laughter, and walked away.

Perry stuck her head outside the door to make sure he was gone, then turned back to me and held up her forefinger and thumb an inch apart. "This big," she said.

I laughed. "How do you know that? Don't tell me you . . .?"

"I told you, we hear everything," she said. "Maybe that's why his wife's leaving him," she added as she put the finishing touches on my face. "Poor Quinn. He's losing the woman he wants, and getting the woman he doesn't."

"Who's that?"

She looked at me and smiled. "You, of course."

An hour later, I sat in my studio chair beneath the hot lights while the clocks clicked by the final three minutes, now two, now one.

Quinn came in with forty-three seconds to spare. He clipped on his mike, pulled down his jacket, whistled one refrain of the Beatles, and stared out into the camera.

It was a slow news night. The lead story was about the upcoming anniversary of the U.N. After that, there were pieces on a train derailment in New Mexico and the last hurricane of the season threatening the coast of Texas.

Quinn and I alternated stories, passing the ball back and forth, the perfect team, the perfect husband and wife, which was what we were subconsciously supposed to mimic.

The lights pierced the skin of my face, heating it, sharpening it.

There was no external time, there was no postcard, no coffin, there was only this.

During the first commercial break, Quinn stood up, cracked all his knuckles, rolled his neck, and then sat back in his chair. He leaned over to write a note on my pad. We were both miked and it was the only way for us to communicate without everyone in the control room and the studio hearing what we said. I waited until he was done scribbling before I leaned down to read it.

"Don't trust Perry," he had written.

I took his pad, annoyed. "The politics here are worse than the Kremlin," I wrote back.

He shrugged. "Nice item in the *Post*," he said out loud.

I heard snickering in the dark studio.

Susan whispered in our ears, "Nine seconds to camera four."

We both smiled serenely as the red light signaled that we were back on the air.

When I got back to my office, I unlocked the safe where I had crammed my pocketbook, and pulled the postcard out.

I looked at the Breezeway Inn one last time.

I looked at the carefully rendered coffin.

And then I ripped it in half, and ripped it again.

I ripped and ripped it until the pieces were no longer recognizable as anything but shreds of color, tatters of

66

confetti, and then I ripped it more.

But nothing could rip it from my brain.

Four

ALEXANDRA HARRISON, THE JOURNALIST FROM *VANITY Fair*, arrived at nine-thirty the next morning with a photographer in tow.

She wore a short fitted black suit and flat scuffed penny loafers. There was a milky stain on her left lapel that didn't look entirely new. Her deep red hair was expensively streaked but it needed to be washed. It was hard to reconcile her disheveled appearance with her prose, known for the sharpness of her observations, the way she captured a telling nervous tic, a verbal gaffe. I always used to wonder why people agreed to be interviewed by her, if it was because their egos were so big they thought they could outsmart her, or if it was an unquenchable desire for fame at any cost. Whatever it was, the same quotients had helped me as a reporter for years—people's need to talk, the universal desire to be understood—so it was hypocritical of me to criticize her now, even if I didn't like the whole idea.

"Do you want some tea or coffee?" I asked as she made herself at home on the couch. Her tape recorder fell out of her large Prada bag and crashed to the ground at her feet. She flushed, embarrassed, as she reached down to pick it up. "No, I'm fine thanks."

"Are you sure that thing will work now?" I asked, suddenly worried for her even as I was aware that it could all be premeditated, the milky stain, the clumsiness, anything to get her subjects to relax. She tested the tape recorder once and then got out her

67

notebook. A few feet away, Mark, the photographer, was busy setting up lights and umbrellas. He had a vague foreign accent and a chestnut ponytail. I wondered if they were sleeping together. When Mark tripped over a plastic lady bug pull-toy on the floor, Alexandra jumped almost imperceptibly.

I sat down on the chair facing her.

"Nice house," she said. "How long have you lived here?"

"Just a year. You won't print our address?"

"Of course not."

I noticed the tape was going, though I hadn't seen her turn it on.

"Your publicist warned me that I only have forty minutes for this initial meeting so we might as well get started." She didn't glance once at the notebook on her lap as she began. "How does it feel to be the only woman co-anchor on the network evening news?"

"Well, I hope we get to the point where women at the anchor desk are not such an uncommon sight," I responded. "The only relevant issue should be talent not gender."

She nodded politely at the predictability of my answer. "How do you respond to criticism that you were not the most qualified contender?"

"There are an incredible number of talented reporters at all of the networks now. I think I was very lucky. But I'd also like to set the record straight about the impression that I don't have the journalistic background. I've been a reporter for over twelve years. I didn't get here by winning a beauty contest."

"Though you have to admit your looks haven't exactly hurt your career."

I smiled without answering and the questions

continued: How do you get along with Quinn Hartley? How do you balance motherhood and career? Each time I spoke, Alexandra leaned forward, smiling, nodding, hoping for more. It was her job to throw me off, mine not to be thrown off.

"Let's talk about your past," she said. "You grew up in Florida? Your parents must be very proud of you."

"Actually, they're both dead."

"Oh, I'm so sorry." She feigned surprise, but if she'd read any of the previous articles about me, she must have known that.

"Before you came to New York to do the local news you were in Providence?"

"And Burlington, and Pittsburgh. And St. Louis. It's easier to get your credentials in smaller markets first." I remembered suddenly what it was like when I arrived at each new city, each new station, holding back, watching, learning the politics and the style, changing myself accordingly, adjusting my hair, clothing, vocal intonations, delivery, until it seemed as if I had been born there. I remembered the loneliness. But it wasn't something I was going to describe to a stranger with a microphone.

I saw her glance down surreptitiously to make sure her tape recorder was still going before she looked back to me. "Were you always interested in the news?" she asked. "What role do you think celebrity plays in television journalism? What are the plans for *In Step*?" She continued on, her eyes never wavering from my face. I tried to stay as still as possible, not to betray any discomfort or nervousness, not to betray anything at all.

I only eased when I heard the front door open and Dora come in with Sophie from a trip to the supermarket. "Excuse me," I said, and went to greet them. Sophie was so bundled up she looked like the Michelin tire guy. Dora is a firm believer in the benefits of fresh air and takes Sophie out on the most inclement of days, but she hedges her bets by insisting on overdressing her. When I picked Sophie up and rubbed her upturned nose with mine, her arms and legs remained immobile, sticking straight out.

"I guess we're done for now," Alexandra said when I returned to the living room. I noticed that she had been writing in her pad while I was gone. "I'll turn you over to Mark."

She sat in the corner, watching intently while I posed on the couch, holding my chin slightly up and to the left, my eyes wide, as I'd learned worked best over the years. I had refused the magazine's offer of a hair and makeup team, as well as their suggestions about clothing. Though a glamorous and provocative layout may sell copies for them, it would do nothing to help me be taken seriously as a journalist.

"How about one with Sophie?" Alexandra asked. It made me nervous how easily she used my daughter's name, as if she knew her.

"No," I answered quickly. David and I had agreed that there should be no pictures of Sophie in newspapers or magazines. It was unfair at best, dangerous at worst.

"Why don't I just take a few for you," Mark asked in his mellifluous accent, "and send you the best ones as a gift?"

And I have to admit I agreed. Who doesn't want a record of her child's beauty?

I balanced Sophie on my lap, bending my head to hers, smiling genuinely for the first time as I fingered the downy soft tip of her ear. Her weight and her heat were an anchor to me as Mark continued to snap away.

When they were done, I walked them to the door and we shook hands.

Alexandra smiled. "We're off to a good start. Of course, I'd like to ask you follow-up questions after I gather some background information. You know how it is."

Unfortunately, I did.

"Oh, by the way," Alexandra said as she turned to leave. "I hear you're interviewing the secretary of state."

"Yes."

I tried not to register my surprise. No one had told me that.

"Be careful. Don't let his stiff upper-class act fool you. He may know his way around a treaty, and frankly even that's a matter of opinion, but he's nothing but an old lecher at heart. He still thinks grabbing anything in a skirt is his droit du seigneur. I'd sit as far away as possible."

I thanked her for her advice and closed the door behind her.

As soon as I got to the office, Carla raised one eyebrow to note my lateness.

"I had an interview to do. Susan set it up," I said.

Carla smiled slightly. "You don't have to explain yourself to me. "

I nodded, embarrassed. "Old habit," I said.

She looked at me impassively. "Berkman's waiting for you in his office."

"What's it about?"

"The day he tells me what anything is about is the day I get stock options in the company. Quinn is already in there."

"All right. Thanks."

Berkman's office was at the far end of the studio. It was an austere affair, with a stiff leather couch against one wall, a mahogany desk, three chairs, and some highly polished chrome accessories. The single surprising note was a large Brice Marden painting that looked like a chalkboard hanging on the wall behind the desk. I'd heard rumors that Berkman had a substantial contemporary art collection in his townhouse on the Upper East Side but I'd never been invited to see it. It was hard to imagine him, so serious and so gray, haunting the galleries and the artists' studios, but it was said that he did, preferring that to letting an agent do all the legwork for him. Whether it was vanity or passion, I didn't know.

Quinn was slouched in his chair, looking glum, when I walked in.

"Hello, Laura," Berkman said. "Have a seat. I've just been talking to Quinn."

I sat down beside him and waited.

Berkman leaned forward and the monogrammed cuffs of his shirt peeked out of his suit jacket. There were no how-are-you's or chat about the weather. There never was with him. "Your on-air chemistry is not exactly rivaling Tracy and Hepburn's," he said bluntly.

Quinn was staring down at his glossy black wing tips. I was beginning to see why.

"The viewers aren't fools, you know," Berkman continued. "It's a mistake to think they don't sense what's going on between' you two. I'm not saying you have to be kissy-kissy, but the cold war you two have engaged in is going to affect ratings. It certainly has to improve by the time we launch *In Step*."

"Didn't Malcolm X say you can't legislate love?" Quinn asked.

72

I frowned. I'd buy a lot of things, but not Quinn Hartley as an expert on Black Power.

"I'm not talking about love," Berkman said. "But last time I checked, we'd negotiated détente in three-quarters of the world. I'd like the same in this office."

"Speaking of *In Step*," I said. "Alexandra Harrison came to interview me today."

Berkman raised one eyebrow. "Yes. Susan told me she set that up. How did it go?"

"Fine. But before she left, she gave me advice on interviewing the secretary. I wasn't aware that you'd made a decision about that."

"Weren't you?"

"No. How did she know before I did?"

"Good reporting on her part, I'd say." Berkman looked down and muttered to himself. "I'd love to get her on television. Anyway, as I was saying, I've made dinner reservations for the two of you tonight after the show."

We both groaned.

"At Orbilé. Eight o'clock. Back room. I've been bribing the headwaiter for years so don't even think about not showing up."

Orbilé was housed in an elegant white brick building on Fifty-seventh Street known for its celebrity occupants and its double-height windows. The restaurant itself had gone through a vogue in the eighties when it was the setting for a number of Warhol-attended parties of aging socialites, English brewing heiresses, and disturbingly good-looking artists, which was doubtlessly when it had become a favorite of Berkman's. Most of the others had moved on by now to whatever was in fashion this year, mostly dark living room-inspired dining rooms that gave even the most democratic of partiers the satisfyingly patrician feeling of being in a private club. Orbilé remained what it had been before the peacocks had come and gone, a bland gray-carpeted affair frequented by people on expense accounts.

We were shown to a table in the rear.

Quinn ordered a scotch on the rocks and I ordered a glass of white wine. We both looked around the room, avoiding each other's eyes.

A few feet away, I recognized a curly-headed minor rock star from a duo that had been popular in the seventies. He was attached from the waist up to a young girl with infinite lengths of blond hair that made no attempt to appear natural. Her thin arms, wrapped in a low-cut flesh-toned leotard, were draped about his neck and engaged in tiny flicks of constant motion. Their lips were grazing, locking, withdrawing, grazing again. Their half-closed eyes were focused only on each other.

Quinn watched them for a minute too. "You know what the real joke is?" he asked.

"What?"

"They're married." He shook his head in wonderment. "When was the last time you kissed your husband like that?"

We both turned to look at them once more.

"Actually, the real joke is that he doesn't have any money. Only she doesn't know it yet," Quinn said.

"How do you know that?"

"My wife, my soon to be ex-wife, was hired to do their apartment. His checks bounced, and his credit cards have all been canceled." He sighed. "Who knows, maybe she does know. Maybe she loves him anyway. What do you think, Laura? Would you venture money on that one?"

74

"I'd like to think love is at least a possibility," I said.

"Wouldn't we all."

"Are you as cynical as you appear or is it just an act?"

"I'm not sure myself anymore," he said, almost laughing but not quite. "I'm not even sure it matters."

The tabloids had been tracking the ups and downs of Quinn's divorce for months. His wife, an interior decorator renowned for her daring combinations of sisal and swag, had walked out on him, taking their three children with her. I'd read that he'd just bought a second apartment in the same building as hers, as well as a second home in the Hamptons a few blocks from the old one to remain close to the children.

"You have three kids, right?" I asked.

"Is this the 'getting to know you' part of the evening?"

I frowned.

"Yes," Quinn said. "I have three kids. All girls. Funny, huh?"

"Why is that funny?"

He shrugged, unable to explain the joke to me.

"Let me ask you something," he said, resting both elbows firmly on the table and leaning forward.

"All right."

"Why do you want this job?"

"I wasn't aware I was still auditioning. I thought I already had it."

"Answer the question."

"Okay." I smiled. "Because it's there?"

He laughed. "That's why everyone wants it. Even me. It's such a fucking joke. This job is supposed to be the pinnacle of television journalism and it has nothing to do with journalism at all. It's all about the illusion of power. Hell, it's all about the illusion of journalism. In

75

England, they call us news readers, did you know that? So much for the fourth estate. So much for the fucking sacred trust."

His unhappiness leached out across the table as he took a sip of his scotch and motioned for another.

"I used to be a real reporter," he said.

"So was I."

"Yeah, well."

"Maybe with me at the desk beside you, you'll be freed up to go out into the field more," I suggested.

"That's the party line, isn't it? That's what they say when they want you to step to the side."

"No one's asking you to step aside."

He raised one eyebrow. "I didn't say aside. I said to the side. There's a difference."

We were heading onto dangerous ground and I tried to change the tone. "You'll be able to do real reporting on *In Step*."

"Yes." Then he added, "The ninety percent that isn't shaped by producers will be all ours."

Our meal came, monkfish for me and liver for Quinn, and we began to eat.

"How's the piece on welfare reform going?" I asked.

For a moment his face lit up. "It looks like the Senate will be voting the week following our broadcast. So not only does everyone suddenly want to be on it, everyone wants to know what the other guy is going to say. Even the President realizes it's a great platform. I've got a welfare mother in Detroit who wants to go back to school so she'll be more qualified to find a job. One of the proposed changes in the system will make her lose her welfare check if she does. I'm going to have her question each party on their plan for her. With any luck, even the President will agree to talk to Miss Gina

Marks."

"Careful," I said. "You're sounding suspiciously like someone who cares."

"Am I?"

"Yes. You still think what we do matters."

For an instant his eyes turned steely and sure. "Of course I think it matters." Then he leaned back and smiled that lopsided no-teeth smile. "And so does my accountant."

When the waiter brought our coffee, Quinn turned to him before he walked away. "See that couple over there?" He pointed to the rock star and his wife, still tangled up in each other's arms, their food untouched. "Send them a bottle of Dom Perignon. On second thought, make it two. And put it on Frank Berkman's tab."

We watched as the bottles were brought to their table. "He was always the less talented of the duo, anyway," I said.

Quinn smiled. "All the more reason for alcohol."

The cold air assaulted us as we stood out on the street a few feet from the restaurant's entrance, figuring out how to extricate ourselves from each other, from the evening. "This has been very nice, Laura," Quinn said as he held his hand up for a cab, "and I for one will be sure to thank Berkman first thing tomorrow morning for the brilliant idea. But I've got to tell you something. I'm not looking for a new best friend. There's no goddamned job opening for that particular post." He paused as a taxi pulled up by the curb. "Then again, I don't suppose that's the job you're after."

He reached for the door and climbed in. "Goodnight," he said as he shut it with a persuasive slam.

Berkman did not ask us how the dinner went.

If there was any of the desired result evident on-screen, he did not mention it.

He only tracked the ratings and took notes.

For the rest of the week, I went in early and spent every moment when I was not preparing for the broadcast working on my segment of the magazine show.

There were nights when I dreamt in print, the simple block letters of the TelePrompTer playing across my mind, though I could never quite figure out the words.

There were nights where I dreamt of the coffin.

There were nights, too, when I dreamt of the minor rock star and his wife, dreamt of their lips coming close, touching, melding.

Though it wasn't them at all, of course.

Fame is an odd thing.

It sits just outside your front door, waiting for you, and the moment you step from the confines of your home, it wraps itself about you, a cloak, a shield, a magnet, and sticks to you like glue, just like fucking glue, so that others can only see you through its gauze. Try as you may, you can never quite see it yourself, your fame, only feel the effect.

On Thursday night, I had to go to a black-tie dinner honoring Lloyd Parker, who was retiring after twenty-eight years with the network. The sportscaster was everything I despised about television journalism, a showman with a cigar caught permanently between his teeth who had, in the last ten years, been elevated to doing interviews with heads of state, as if his celebrity alone granted him the expertise. Nevertheless, network orders had come down for me to make an appearance. I was, after all, their latest inductee.

I raced home after the broadcast to change clothes. David was standing before the full-length mirror on his closet door, straightening the jacket of his rented tuxedo. At six-foot-three, it wasn't easy to find the right fit.

"Why don't you just buy one?" I asked as I slipped out of my suit and into a Calvin Klein dress that cost more than anything without an engine and wheels that I had ever bought.

"Because it'll be like that baseball field in, what was that movie? You know, build it and they will come. Buy it and I'll have to use it. It will just attract more invitations like this one."

"To say nothing of attracting the ladies."

"I can hardly handle the one I have."

I smiled. "Seriously, you look great."

"Isn't that supposed to be my line?"

"I'm waiting," I replied.

"You don't look half-bad for Mom."

I poked him in the ribs. "Thanks a lot."

"You look simply gorgeous," he said theatrically. "Better?"

"Better. And so heartfelt."

"I try. Now that we've agreed on our mutual attraction, I don't suppose you'd want to stay home and put it to good use?" he asked.

"I'd love to, but you know I can't." I leaned up to kiss him. "Thanks for doing this tonight."

"I haven't done anything yet."

"You will. Wait till later."

"Promises, promises."

The studio had offered to send someone over to do my hair but I refused and, frustrated, I pulled the bobby

79

pins out of my latest attempt at a chignon and decided to wear it down.

"Ready?" David asked.

"Ready. "

We stepped out into the cold night.

And there it was, that cloak, sliding on so silkily that I didn't even feel it at first.

When we got to the midtown hotel where the reception was being held, a horde of paparazzi were waiting at the entranceway beneath the international flags flapping in the wind. As each limousine pulled up, they turned to see who emerged, their immense cameras raised hopefully, their down-coated arms waving for attention, a single dark mass punctuated only by their yells and the blinding flash of their cameras—was that Paul Newman? Peter Jennings? Don King? Jane Pauley? Cindy Crawford?

We got out and headed up the velvet-roped path to the ornate gold-leafed doors while the lights, the clatter swirled about us. David took my arm, muttering as he hurried our pace. The commotion thickened and I thought there must be someone behind me, a model, a star, whose glare we had somehow gotten caught in. But I heard my name and realized it was me they wanted.

I turned around, turned to that name, my name.

I saw him just before my eyes were blinded by the white light of the cameras.

Jack, deep inside the crowd, standing completely still in his seersucker suit, staring at me.

The flashbulbs exploded.

When I refocused my eyes, Jack was gone.

"Come on," David said, urging me inside.

By then, the cameras had moved on to someone else.

We were seated at a table with an aging Hollywood actress starring in a Broadway revival, a network producer, a Wall Street junk bond king and his fourth wife, and a model from the seventies who now had her own talk show. David was at the opposite end of the table and the insistent pattering of small talk came between us, the brittle chatter of strangers united only by a sense of privilege. I let it swell about me for a minute and then I gave myself up to it, desperately, rebelliously, as if it could erase Jack's face in the light. I heard my own voice mingling with and rising above the others, high and shrill, only vaguely recognizable.

I glanced over at David and saw him picking at the first course of carpaccio, while he smiled and bantered obliviously with his neighbors. I turned back to the Wall Street raider's fourth wife. I'd seen her picture in the society pages before. She was famous for the blackness of her hair, the extreme slightness of her waist, and the vastness of her apartment. I've always been fascinated by women like her, women who'd grown up plumbers' daughters in Iowa or Indiana, who'd worked as stewardesses or panty hose models, but through sheer will, sheer determination, reinvented themselves as arbiters of society and devoured the city whole. She pushed the food about on her plate without actually putting any of it in her mouth. "We must get together for lunch," she said. "I'd love to talk to you about co-chairing the benefit for the Cancer Institute." She was leaning forward to me, the me ensconced in the cloak of fame.

David was deeply enmeshed in conversation with the woman seated beside him, his hazel eyes unwavering, the hair behind his ear curling over his stiff white shirt. I watched closely and then returned reluctantly to the fourth wife and her gossip about the love lives of clothing designers I had barely heard of.

It was during the lull between the last course and the start of the speeches that I saw Olivia Redding walking in my direction. She stopped in front of me.

"I see they hijacked you, too," I said—we are in this together, we can be in this together if we choose.

"We all love Lloyd." She smiled. Her hair, of that particular cool shade of blond that can be found only on television, was sprayed into a perfect helmet. Her chiseled cheeks and hooded eyes somehow managed to project both sex appeal and authority, an unlikely combination that undoubtedly added many thousands to her network contract. Of course, she also had phenomenal contacts in the Pentagon, Congress, and the White House. "I just came to congratulate you personally for winning," she said.

"You make it sound like a contest."

"Well, it was a contest, wasn't it? There aren't enough good slots for women for it not to be."

I nodded. "You were probably just too good at what you do in Washington. They knew they couldn't replace you."

"We'll see. New York never really pays attention to what goes on in Washington anyway. So," she said, "I see the overnight ratings fell a half-point. Well, I wouldn't worry about it. They were inflated to start with. That always happens at the beginning. People tuning in out of curiosity, boredom."

"I'm not worried," I said.

"Good. I was just telling Quinn the same thing. I only wish he was as relaxed about it as you. I don't know how you do it. In your place I'd be much more nervous. After all, you'll get all the blame if the ratings fall." She straightened her long black sheath dress. "By the way," she said, "I hear *Vanity Fair* is doing a profile."

"How did you know that?"

"Oh, they've been calling everyone. Alex always does her homework."

"Alex?"

"Alexandra Harrison."

"Of course."

"Well, I should get back to Wyatt," she said. "We see little enough of each other as it is. Of course, I've always believed that's the secret to a successful marriage, don't you?"

I watched her walk back across the floor, an army general in Chanel pumps, waving to people as she went, until she came to her own table. She sat down next to her husband, Wyatt Hargrove, the columnist for the *Washington Post*. Together they were one of those brainy and ambitious couples whose dinner parties are comprised of the most important names in politics and media. One or both of them always seemed to turn up on the Sunday morning news shows, and there were rumors of standing tennis dates with the Vice President. It was hard to imagine them fighting over the dishes, it was hard to imagine them making love.

They both bent their heads to talk and it was then that I noticed the third head in the huddle, Quinn. All three had their hands over their mouths to cover their laughter. Of course, there was no reason to think that it had anything to do with me.

As soon as the speeches were over, I motioned to David that I wanted to leave. I was suddenly exhausted by it all, the noise, the smiling, the effort it took to be one of them. David, too, was ready. The woman he was talking to had left to find her husband.

The paparazzi were gone when we stepped back out into the night.

There were no faces in the light.

There was no one there at all, just a lineup of bored drivers standing before the strand of shining black limousines.

We found a taxi and rode the first few blocks in silence.

"Who was that woman you were talking to?" I asked.

"She's on the City Planning Commission. She's overseeing the renovation of the Hudson River piers."

I nodded.

"She knows my work," he said. "Remember my work?"

"Of course I remember your work. I'm sorry, David. I had to do this tonight."

"I know."

The cab pulled up to our building and David paid the driver.

I shrugged it off outside the door, the fame, and stepped back inside—as who?

While David paid Dora and saw her to a taxi, I ran a hot bath, poured in half a bottle of French herbal bubble bath, and then felt instantly guilty. I still cannot help adding up how much everything cost, a remnant of being poor. Outside the door, I heard David returning to the bedroom, listening to the late news while he undressed, clicking it off when he got into bed. I lay back and let the steam fill my nostrils, my mouth. The only sound came from the cars outside. There had been so much solitude once, too much, all those frantic empty years when I thought I'd never be held, really held again. Now it was something I could find only behind locked doors. I lay still until I grew lightheaded from the heat.

I climbed out of the bath, put on one of David's worn-out T-shirts, and got into bed, quickly falling into a heavy sleep.

But I woke at three in the morning in a cold sweat, breathless.

I sat up, pushed the damp hair from my face.

I lay back against the pillows, terrified to shut my eyes, terrified to sleep, to see them again, the gnats, the noose of hands, the eyes, the blood.

I got out of bed, made myself a cup of coffee, and watched the sun rise.

Five

THERE ARE LULLS THAT ARE SO SWEET, SO SIMPLE, SO calm, that for a little while you can almost convince yourself that this is how your life really is, this is how it will always be. Later, of course, you realize it was just a brief respite, a pocket.

After the broadcast on Friday night, David and I bundled up Sophie and then made three trips downstairs to the car. The amount of paraphernalia we suddenly needed for a weekend away was overwhelming: a stroller, a folding crib, a baby monitor, blankets, diapers, diaper wipes, formula, bottles, a bottle warmer, a first aid kit, toys, clothes. "So much for the days of traveling light," David said grimly as the turquoise diaper bag slid from his shoulder. He wasn't really displeased, though, neither of us were. We had come to parenthood late enough to doubt that we would ever find ourselves there and now that we had, it was so new

85

and wondrous, all this encumbrance, that even complaining about it gave us a sense of pride.

I strapped Sophie into her new car seat and settled in the back beside her, too uncertain of how she would react to sit up front with David. David never likes talking until he has maneuvered out of the city, and we rode in silence through the Village streets crammed with taxis and people anxiously hurrying into those first promising hours of the weekend. I tucked a blanket about Sophie and stroked her fuzzy scalp. By the time we made it out of the Holland tunnel and were on the highway headed south through New Jersey, she had fallen into such a deep sleep that I shook her firmly to make sure she was okay. When do you get over the fear that your baby will somehow die, simply cease, the moment you turn your back, as if it is your attention alone keeping her alive? Sophie opened her eyes once, stared at me mutely, and then fell back into her motion-drugged slumber.

The dusky smell of the artificial heat filled the car. Outside, the night suddenly blackened and broadened, pierced only by the headlights of other cars. I looked up at David, his tall tousled head, his broad shoulders. He turned halfway and smiled back, and suddenly the world was only here, in this car, together, driving through the night, away. When we pulled into a rest stop forty minutes later, I climbed into the front seat beside him. I opened the package of gummy bears I had bought in the neon-lit gas station and put one in David's mouth as we got back on the highway. "Guess which flavor," I said and watched him roll it about his tongue. It was something we always did in cars, eat gummy bears until our teeth grew matte with sugar. Last summer, I had left an open pack on the dashboard by mistake and they had melted into a glazed plastic river of yellows and greens and reds. I leaned forward now and peeled up remnants of it. "Red," David said. "Was it red?"

I leaned across and kissed him.

Three hours later we followed the signs into Cape May and found the Victorian guest house we had reservations at on a street of other wedding cake houses a block from the Atlantic Ocean. I carried Sophie wrapped in blankets into the reception area crammed with floral rugs, wing chairs, and mahogany tables with yellowing doilies. The woman who ran the hotel stood behind the desk in a period floor-length dress, white cap, and apron. "Breakfast is at eight," she told us as David signed the register "Mr. and Mrs. David Novak." "And there's sherry every afternoon at three." Her husband, standing next to her in nylon jogging shorts, his ginger hair combed and sprayed to cover a bald spot, added, "There are bikes out back, and beach chairs if the weather holds." We thanked them and walked carefully up a narrow staircase to our room, scented with cinnamon sachets, the four-poster bed covered in a floral duvet, lace and needlepoint pillows, the walls lined with silhouettes and cameos, a cluttered Victorian theme park. David opened the portable crib, and we both stared at its brilliant primary colors, suddenly so garish and synthetic. Sophie whimpered softly when we put her in it.

I bent over the crib to pick her back up.

"Don't," David said. "Let her be. She'll put herself to sleep."

I knew that he was right, but every cell in my body was pushing me to reach for her, hold her, comfort her.

"Come here," he suggested, patting the bed.

I lay still beside him, staring up at the ceiling, my

stomach in knots, while we waited for the crying to subside. When it finally did, we both exhaled. Slowly, David's fingers reached for mine, stopping, intermingling, squeezing, before moving up my arm, along the sides of my chest, my stomach. I rolled over to him and we pressed into each other, our outlines new and unfamiliar, the gift that travel brings, while Sophie slept a few feet away, the restriction of silence adding to our excitement. I traced the muscles of his arms, his butt, his long thighs as he kneeled between my legs.

I remember the exact instant I fell in love with David. One late blustery Saturday afternoon, three months after we started seeing each other, we were sitting at a wood-paneled bar in Soho, drinking port after having made the rounds of galleries. I had left my pocketbook, a Bottega Veneta woven pouch, on the stool next to mine, and when we stood to leave, I noticed for the first time that it was gone. The owner, immediately disavowing any responsibility, told us there had been a rash of such thefts in all the bars and restaurants in the area.

David slapped some money on the bar and stormed out into the darkening streets.

"They probably just took your wallet and ditched the bag," he told me. He hurried to the first garbage can he saw, a block away, and rifled through the papers and half-eaten food looking for it, and then the next, and the next, circling the block, moving on, a determined gleam in his eyes.

Long after I had given up hope and begged him to forget it, David kept on, his circle ever widening.

Finally, he took me home. As we sat on the front steps of my brownstone in the wet cold night, waiting for the locksmith, I looked over at him, his hands ragged and stained with dirt, his hair disheveled, and I realized that this, too, was love.

David opened his eyes now and watched his cock moving in and out of me and for a moment I watched him watching himself. He always likes to see himself come, where I want only forgetfulness, the flash of obliteration.

The next morning, we walked with the stroller down streets lined with ornately layered Victorian houses to the ocean. The seaside scent of taffy and popcorn and hot chocolate poured from the open stands next to the video arcade, mixing with the coconut suntan lotion of the diehards soaking up the season's last rays. We settled Sophie onto the sand and watched her roll into it, nervously at first, and then avidly. She had learned just a week ago to feed herself a cracker and before we could stop her, she grabbed a handful of sand and began to practice her new technique. We dug our bare toes into the cool and clammy mounds. David let the sand drip slowly onto Sophie's belly and she laughed, her nose crinkling with delight.

"It's odd to think that she won't remember any of this," I said.

"But it's in there somewhere," David answered. "It will always be in there somewhere."

Later that afternoon while Sophie napped upstairs we drank sherry out of tiny engraved glasses on the empty porch, sitting in wicker rocking chairs and playing backgammon, the red light of the baby monitor between us. The pastel bed-and-breakfast next door had a large gold cross on its roof, and a trio of nuns in heavy black habits emerged out of the screened door and settled into rocking chairs on the porch, their faces round and pink, their eyes hidden by sunglasses while they slept in the waning sun.

In the evening, the woman who owned the hotel baby-sat and David and I went to dinner at a restaurant on the docks famous for the freshness of its seafood. We sat outside eating clam chowder, lobster salad, fried clams, and onion rings, and drinking cold beers while we watched the fishermen unload their wares from the belly of a large boat before us.

"New York is one of the few cities I know of with such a dreadful waste of its waterways," David said in between spoonfuls of the spicy chowder. "In my perfect city, there would be promenades along every river's edge, there would be . . ." I listened to him talking while I watched the gulls clustered on the boat's deck waiting for handouts. There's a dreaminess, a glow when David speaks about his work (the very term *urban planning* bespeaks a certain optimism, after all, as if cities can actually be managed, the future itself plotted out in grids), and it was this dreaminess that first intrigued me. A pragmatist by nature, grounded in facts, in the limitations of history, I've never been able to afford such dreaminess. For isn't it a luxury, as much as a character trait?

He looked up suddenly. "I'm boring you."

"No," I said, smiling, and we kissed, tasting the seafood in each other's mouths.

"Go on," I urged, and he did, we did, continued playing the game of city planning together. It was something we used to do all the time, back when we were new. Walking through the snow in Washington Square Park, eating Chinese food on the floor, taking turns planning the streets and the avenues, the buildings and the parks, a perfect world of ours.

"In my perfect city," I said, "we'd always have

dinners alone like this."

"Don't turn into some sappy romantic on me, okay?" David warned.

"It must be all those cinnamon sachets rotting my brain."

"Maybe that's what happened to the Victorians."

The waiter cleared the table and brought our dessert.

We took turns dipping our forks into the pecan pie. "Why don't you write another book?" I suggested as I put down my coffee.

"About what? How too many sweet odors lead to a plethora of wedding cake houses?"

"I'm serious."

"Why? Because you'd feel better if I published again?"

"I didn't mean that."

He stabbed a piece of crust and ate it. "Never mind."

"I'm sorry."

He chewed, swallowed, relented.

It was just a flash, though, the kind all couples have.

He put his arm around me as we walked back to the car and we were together again.

"I love you," I said.

"I love you, too. You can go sappy on me anytime."

"I've had worse offers."

When we left the following afternoon, the weather turned suddenly cold, and a hard freezing rain pounded against the windows and roof of the car. David drove slowly, carefully. It was as if nature had given us this weekend, and only this weekend, but it was over now.

It was dark when we saw the Manhattan skyline loom before us. I remember the first time I saw New York. I was nine years old, coming with Astrid from Germany by boat because she was too nervous to fly. After six days, we arrived in the harbor early on a shrouded morning, the city's outline a majestic gleaming paste-up in the distance.

New York spread before me then, a vortex of strange tempting smells and rapid indistinguishable words, but I was whisked away to Florida before I was allowed to enter it. Even then, it felt like banishment. The city loomed before me, a destination, a promise, a last resort, through all the difficult years that followed.

I didn't see it again until I was seventeen, riding in on a bus with everything I owned hurriedly crammed into one small floral canvas suitcase. The Manhattan skyline had risen up, a picture postcard of skyscrapers, steppes of glittering glass against the sky, but I was too frightened to admire it. I had come to lose myself there.

I dreaded entering it tonight, dreaded finding myself once more within its confines, with the studio, with Jack, with all the unlit corners, waiting for me.

David looked over at me and smiled. "Almost home," he said, and gently squeezed my hand.

When we got upstairs, the red light of the answering machine was blinking. I didn't check it until David went to take a shower.

But there were no messages from Jack, no unexplained breaths, no hang-ups, nothing.

Sometimes even forty-eight hours away can give you enough distance to glance back at the workings of your days and believe that they are manageable, changeable, if only you put your mind to it. It is all a matter of control, of discipline.

When I headed back to work on Monday morning, I was determined not to let myself grow flustered, on-air or off.

I was half an hour earlier than usual, my head buried in briefing papers the studio had messengered over, when I walked through the glass door and was surprised by Shana and Jay waiting for me on the white couch in the reception area. Their hands were entwined and their faces were as grim as if they were in the waiting room of an oncologist. Shana looked down at Jay's hand in hers, tracing the crude homemade tattoo of a cross near his thumb while Jay stared blankly at Carla, answering the incessant phones on her desk while she unconsciously straightened the gold-framed picture of her nine-year-old son in his crisp navy parochial school uniform.

Carla looked up at me with relief. "They say they know you."

I nodded. "Yes."

They both stood up as I turned to them. Shana was wearing a short purple suede skirt and a black single-breasted blazer not unlike the one I had worn two nights before. Jay's light brown skin was freshly shaved and speckled with tiny red pricks rising across his prominent cheekbones. His long leather jacket was zipped up to the neck, and his short curly hair glistened with pomade. "What are you two doing here?" I asked.

"Jay wanted a tour," Shana said.

"How did you get past security downstairs? No one is supposed to get up here without an appointment."

"We told them you was expecting us."

"And they didn't check?" I glanced back to Carla, who shook her head.

"Goddammit," I muttered. "What's wrong with them? This is the second time something like this has happened."

"The second time?" Carla asked.

I looked up, alarmed. "Never mind."

Jay turned to Shana angrily. "I told you she didn't want us here. It's one thing to meet downtown in some lousy diner, but come up here and she don't know you. See?" He grabbed Shana's hand and took a step to the door.

"Wait."

Shana turned her blue-lined eyes anxiously to me. I knew that look, had felt it wash across my own face, protective and fearful of the boy, the man, her man.

"I'm just surprised, that's all." I looked at Jay. "Maybe if you had called first. That's what people do," I said pointedly.

He shrugged.

"Well, come on, you're here now, so let's start off in my office."

We walked in single file down the corridor of the newsroom. Shana kept her hands deep in her pockets as she went, taking in every detail of the computers, the writers bent over keyboards, the editors rushing by clutching videotape, the maps overhead, the clocks, the wires. Jay's step had an even more pronounced roll than usual, lifted by rebelliousness or boredom, I wasn't sure.

I shut the door to my office behind us. "Sit." I motioned to the leather couch on the far wall and they perched on its edges while I hung up my coat and pushed the mail aside.

"What is it you'd like to see?" I asked.

Shana looked to Jay. I wanted to take her face in my hands, tell her to look at me, to speak for herself, but I didn't.

"Everything," Shana said.

Jay shrugged. "Whatever."

94

They came around to my side of the desk while I showed them the NewsMaker program on my computer. The treacly smell of Shana's perfume and Jay's hair cream made me dizzy and I shut the program off. "Come, I'll take you to the studio."

I ushered them back through the newsroom and down the barren corridor to the studio. At this hour, it was empty, dark, and cold.

"It looks so small," Shana said as she stared at the news desk that filled the entire screen when she watched it at home. I glanced back at it. She was right, it did look small.

Jay didn't say a word, but he looked about intently, noting every cable, every camera. Even in the dark, I could see his chocolate eyes shining.

On our way back, I showed them the makeup room. Perry wasn't there yet and Shana sat on the Formica counter, dipping her fingertips into the pots of liquid and powder.

"How long does it take you to get all this stuff on?" she asked.

"About twenty minutes."

"So you come right before the broadcast?"

"If I can. It depends if there's a late-breaking story."

"Men wear this shit too?"

"They have to. The lights would bounce off your skin otherwise."

Shana nodded.

"Actually, some of the men are far more vain than the women on TV. And you should see the politicians. Half of them come with their own hairdressers."

"I believe that shit."

"Well, I really do have to get to work," I said at last. I walked them to the reception area. As I opened the glass

95

door for them, Jay suddenly held out his hand solemnly and I shook it. "Thank you," he said.

"You're welcome."

"Yeah, thanks," Shana said.

I watched as they stood side by side waiting for the elevator, their backs to me. Shana reached for Jay's hand, and I saw him shake it off, reject it. I hurt for her, for that hand hovering alone in midair, slowly returning to her side. But I understood, too, the rebuff, the need to be alone, to absorb without hindrance .To plan.

They stepped into the elevator without looking back.

I returned to my office and flipped the computer back on. A good deal more of the night's broadcast had been written and I rushed to study the copy and rewrite what I felt needed improvement. I was an hour behind schedule.

When I heard a knock on my door, I looked up, annoyed. "Yes?"

Quinn walked in. "Do you have a minute?"

Surprised, I nodded. He had never been in my office before—it had been up to me to go to his if we needed to talk for any reason—and he looked around curiously before sitting down opposite me.

"Who were those two people you were showing around?" he asked.

"Just some kids I know."

"Did you get clearance? You've got to get clearance. I thought you knew that."

"Security sent them up without asking me."

He frowned. "I find that hard to imagine. That's never happened before."

"Well, it happened this time. Take it up with them, not me."

He leaned back and ran his hands through his hair, breathing once deeply. "Maybe I didn't make this clear at dinner, but I'm not the enemy, you know," he said.

"I didn't know there was an enemy."

"Look, Laura, we both know I wasn't the most enthusiastic supporter of your arrival. Why would I be? I was doing just fine by myself. Would you have wanted a co-anchor?"

I didn't answer, I didn't need to.

"But you're here now. The way I figure, if you look bad, I look bad."

I put down my pen, listening.

"How old are you, Laura?" he asked.

"Thirty-eight."

He nodded. "This business can devour you," he said. "And if it doesn't get you, it gets everyone around you. Your kids, your marriage." He wasn't looking at me anymore, he wasn't looking anywhere at all. "It's a hungry fucking beast, is what it is. You spend all this time getting here, and you think once you do you'll be able to make up for all the times you fucked up in the past, all the dinners you missed, all the school plays your kids were in and you didn't get to see, but you know what, Laura? You can't. By the time you get back to them, they're already someplace else. In the case of my beloved wife, in the arms of a two-bit diplomat from the British foreign office. But it's okay, because you want to hear another secret? It takes just as much time to stay on top. Ambition is just another bad habit that's impossible to break."

"Without ambition there's no accomplishment. You make it sound like a crime to want to better yourself."

"A crime? Hell, no." He laughed. "It's the great American dream." He picked a piece of lint off of his pin-striped pants and dropped it on my floor. "Well." He sighed and rose slowly. "I'll see you in the studio."

I watched as Quinn closed the door quietly behind him, and then I returned to my computer.

The broadcast went smoothly for the next few nights.

There was only one slipup on Wednesday when we started to speak at the same time, but we quickly recovered.

No one said anything afterwards, not Quinn, not Berkman.

The initial onslaught of media criticism died down and I tried to concentrate on the business of settling in to the job, to the increased numbers of looks on the street when I walked to lunch, to the extra berth people gave me in the hallway.

But all the while, I knew that I was waiting. I didn't know the shape the blow would take, I didn't know the form. I only knew that it would come.

I thought I had given it up years ago, the waiting that once burned through all of my energy, my very being, so that it was my only true activity—waiting. It had faded gradually, but I realized that it had never really dissipated at all, only burrowed deeper in, so that now, when it reappeared, it was as recognizable as an old wound that throbbed in bad weather.

I crossed myself three times when I shut Sophie's door at night, and kissed her three times on the forehead every morning.

I tried not to wake David when I woke breathless and shaken by nightmares.

I dug my nails remorselessly into my skin until it bled whenever I thought of the past, of what I had done.

Psychologists say the fear that something you love

will be taken away from you stems from guilt.

And there is that. Oh God, there is that.

But who's to say it isn't also simply a matter of being realistic?

Two nights later, in the middle of the broadcast, I saw the red light of the telephone beneath my desk blinking. I waited until the next commercial break, my pulse racing, my imagination working behind the words I was uttering. The phone was used only for pressing communiqués from the studio chiefs and true emergencies.

I thought of Sophie, Sophie bruised, Sophie mangled, while I raced through my copy.

As soon as the lights over the camera signaled that we were off the air for ninety seconds, I picked up the receiver. "Yes?"

"Hello, Marta," Jack said.

"How did you get my number here?"

"You'd be surprised at some of the things I learned how to do." He paused. "There's something I forgot to ask you at lunch."

My back stiffened. I could feel everyone in the studio watching me. "What?"

"Do you ever think about what happened?" he asked.

"Of course I do," I whispered.

"I think about it all the time," he said.

I gently hung up the telephone.

When Quinn threw me the lead-in for the kicker, that last amusing story of the evening designed to leave a pleasant taste in the viewer's mouth, I stepped on the tail end of his sentence by mistake.

We both stopped, recovered, started again.

And then, smiling, we said goodnight to each other,

to America.

After the broadcast, I called David and told him there was a post-production meeting I had to go to.

"I won't be long," I said, "but you might have to put Sophie to bed without me."

"Are you sure?"

"I just can't get out of it. I'm sorry. Give her a kiss for me, okay? Give her three. Tell her I love her."

"All right."

I hung up the phone, stayed in my office another ten minutes, my head in my hands, and then I left.

The black town car was waiting for me outside the studio door.

I went up to the driver, Mike, and said hello.

"I think I'll walk tonight," I told him.

He looked at me skeptically. "I have orders to take you home."

"I'm not an invalid."

"Sorry. You know what I mean. I can follow you if you want to get a little exercise. I do that for some of them."

"That's okay, Mike. Really. You have a good night now."

He stood a moment longer by the door and then finally got in and, with one last glance to be sure, drove away.

As soon as he was gone, I hurried around the corner, looked both ways to be sure that there was no one I knew in sight, and hailed a cab. As we headed downtown, I wrapped my hair in a large navy wool scarf and, despite the darkness, put on a pair of black sunglasses.

100

The desk clerk at the Hotel Angelica stared at me as I strode quickly through the lobby. "Can I help you?" he asked loudly when I reached the desk. He wanted to make me squirm. Maybe it would help relieve his boredom.

"What room is Jack Pierce staying in?" I asked in a low voice.

"Pierce? Let me look." He took an inordinately long time with the guest book before he glanced back at me. "Six fifty-eight."

The deep walnut elevator, a vestige of the hotel's grander days, creaked ominously as it jerked its way up to the sixth floor. I clutched the mottled railing tighter with each lurch.

I walked hurriedly down the thinly carpeted corridor until I found 658 and knocked cautiously on the door.

Jack opened it after the third knock, dressed in a clean white shirt and chinos, but with cloudy tired eyes. "Come in." While I entered, he went to turn off the television that had been playing. We both watched the image fade slowly, shrinking to a luminous white circle in the encroaching blackness, smaller and smaller, until that too was gone. He looked back at me and smiled.

"You don't seem surprised to see me," I said.

"I'm not. I knew you'd come."

I nodded. I was standing between the neatly made-up bed and a table by the window. Looking out, I saw a mountain of garbage bags in the alleyway below. "Jack?"

"Yes?"

"I know that I owe you more than I could ever repay."

He stood completely still, watching me.

"Is there anything? Anything I can do?" I asked.

He remained silent.

101

"I have a life, Jack," I pleaded.

"I lost everything because of you," he said bitterly.

My lungs folded up, I could hardly breathe. "I know."

"Was it so easy for you?" he asked.

"What do you mean?"

"Did you ever once think about going back?"

"Of course I thought about it. I thought about it all the time."

"But you didn't."

"No," I agreed painfully. The nylon of my stockings squeaked as I shifted my weight.

We were staring into each other's eyes now, listening to each other's inhalations, exhalations, to the mysterious rhythms of each other's bodies.

"Did you even think of me? Did you ever wonder what it was like for me?" he pressed on.

"Yes."

"Don't," he said. He pressed his curled forefinger to the side of my chin and turned me around to face him. "Don't look away."

I looked at him, straight at him, I had no choice. "I'm sorry. I'm so sorry for everything."

"Tell me one thing," he said. "Did you ever love me?"

"Oh, Jack."

"Answer me."

"Yes. You know I did." Tears began to cluster in my eyes. "I loved you."

He reached over and pulled me to him with one swift motion. Suddenly he was kissing the side of my cheek, my neck, his lips chapped and rapid and raw.

I shut my eyes and felt my neck bending to him, giving in to him, to the blackness that was encroaching.

"Marta," he moaned.

I broke away. "No." I looked down, pushing my hair from my face. "I can't do this."

The radiator made a loud creaking sound and we both turned to look at it as if at an intruder before returning to each other.

"There can't be any more phone calls, Jack. And no more calling cards."

"What are you talking about?"

"The postcard."

"What postcard?"

"You didn't leave a postcard of the Breezeway in my office?"

"No. Of course not. Where would I have gotten that?"

"Are you lying to me?"

"I'm not the one who lies."

Confused, I looked away.

He took a step closer and touched my arm.

If there had been only sadness in his eyes, I would have been relieved.

But there was sadness and other things too.

"I thought you'd like to know," he said, his voice suddenly hard and brittle, "that I followed your suggestion and went to see some of the sights. The Empire State Building, Times Square, the Staten Island ferry. I even went to the Forty-second Street Library. Pretty impressive, all those ancient reading rooms and banks of computers." He took a breath, held it, and finally exhaled while we both waited. "I thought I'd punch your name into one of those computers, see what came up. You know, see what you've been up to, catch up on lost time. I even looked you up in that big black book they have, what is it, the *Celebrity Register*? Funny thing, your official bio. Interesting. But not quite accurate, is it, Marta? Not exactly what you'd call complete." He shook his head. "Did you really think you could get away with murder?"

Part Two

Six

WHERE DID IT BEGIN?

Did it begin with Astrid, with Garner, did it begin with the men, with the moment I met Jack? Did it begin with bad luck? Or did it begin with something within, a stain, a scar?

Of course, there are those who say it doesn't really matter where it begins, where any of it begins.

All that matters is the act itself.

I can still hear them, still feel them, each of them.

I can still feel the heat.

I hear my mother and stepfather in the living room of our apartment behind the office of the Breezeway Inn, eating their breakfast, the television turned up loud to cover their voices. Still, the words passed through the thin yellow walls like ghosts, forming, disintegrating, re-forming.

"Just tell me why you won't do it," Astrid said.

"Because she's not my daughter."

"But if you adopt her, she will be."

"I never said I would. Did I?" Garner demanded. "Did I ever say I was going to adopt her? Answer me,

104

Astrid, did I?"

I'd heard the words before, sometimes strident, sometimes plaintive, since my mother had married Garner Clark. I knew that Astrid would quickly drop the subject, ask about dinner, make a joke. Astrid, figuring the odds, moving on, forgetting.

"Just tell them your last name is Clark anyway," Astrid said to me, "instead of Deuss. Who'll know the difference? Who asks for papers here?" Astrid, who believed you were whoever, whatever you said you were, why not?

I got up and walked soundlessly past them, slipping through the screen door in the kitchen. I hurried down the path that ran along the back of the motel where we piled trash between pickup days, and onto the empty two-lane road. The nascent sun was sharp and clear, its edges not yet blurred with humidity. Out here, you could see a storm forming miles away, tell when it was raining by the striations of light in the large and open sky, watch the storm moving toward you, over you, away from you.

It was only eight-thirty in the morning when I got to the public beach a quarter-mile from the motel. Except for a few elderly couples taking their constitutionals, it was deserted. The waitress at the Driftwood Café was setting up its outdoor tables, putting napkins beneath the salt and pepper shakers so they wouldn't blow away, filling ketchup bottles. Her face was a weathered brown with soft pouches beneath her eyes, her hair was cropped short in a tight wiry gray perm. "You're awfully early today, hon," she said. "We don't open for another half an hour."

"I know."

"You want a cup of coffee?"

"Sure."

The waitress, Thelma, went inside and brought me a cup of black coffee in a paper cup. "Don't let no one see you." She winked.

I nodded. Thelma often got me coffee in the morning and free refills of ice tea on days when I managed to come after school, sitting at an empty table after the lunch rush, doing my homework, killing time, avoiding Garner.

I took the coffee and perched on the wooden banister, staring out at the ocean as I drank it. It was calm today, and there were no early morning surfers. It hardly seemed the same ocean I had crossed all those years ago, coming with Astrid from Germany. Then it had been a livid monster.

A few of the hardier passengers spent the afternoons playing cards and drinking whiskey in the lounge, and on the second day, they asked Astrid to join them. "Go play with the other children, sweetie," Astrid instructed. "You must be bored with me." I moved a few yards away and watched Astrid settle down at the small table with the men, take their proffered liquor, and put her money on the table. Every now and then one of them nodded in my direction and they all laughed. Embarrassed, I left to walk alone around the perimeters of the boat, climbing over ropes, running my hands around the cold steel railings and ladders. But within an hour, I returned and, standing a little farther away, once more kept watch over my mother.

At night, after tucking me in, Astrid went back to the lounge for more whiskey, more cards. It was three, four in the morning before she returned to our tiny cabin, her makeup smudged, her dress crooked. Sometimes it was later, dawn.

I knew that time, for Astrid, had a tendency to melt, to slip away.

"So German," Astrid remarked scornfully of the others in our crowded tenement in Dortmarr who watched her progress disdainfully, who could not forget, would never forget that Astrid had me when she was just seventeen, and unmarried. And worse, unapologetic. "So staid," she complained. "So set in their ways."

For as long as I could remember, Astrid dreamt of escape from the dingy Ruhr Valley town, where the only beauty came from the sunsets made brilliant by the coal dust rising from the mines. Astrid and her plans, her endless talk of *opportunities*, always looking for a way out, out of Dortmarr, out of Germany, out of poverty.

And so regularly disappointed.

Still, she almost always lost her sadness in the night and rose cheerfully to search for the next big chance. If not, there was always a man, men, a parade of nameless, faceless men who came and went in the dark, staying for just an hour or two and leaving behind small gifts, a gold-plated bracelet, a scarf. Money.

On those nights, I slept on the couch in the living room, and though I rarely saw the men, I heard them sneaking past me to the bathroom, the sound of the hard steady stream of their urine a fearful portent of masculinity.

But always, before and after, Astrid came back to me, just to me.

Sometimes, on bad nights, empty blue nights, Astrid slipped into bed beside me, her soft squishy breasts pressed against my back, her folded hands between my legs, warmth cupping warmth.

Until Garner Clark.

One day, I came home from school to find Astrid writing and rewriting drafts of a letter, an English dictionary by her side to help her fill in the blanks of her schoolgirl vocabulary. The man in the butcher shop, whom she had grown up with and who secretly pitied her, had a brother in America who played poker with a man who was looking for a wife. The American still remembered the German girls he had seen during his stint there after the war and was amenable to meeting one.

"Why does he have to get a wife in the mail?" I asked.

"People meet all kinds of ways," Astrid answered peremptorily. "Anyway, we have friends in common, don't we?" She never believed in examining any details, drawbacks, or unpleasantness that might hinder her plans. Why be negative?

Astrid repeated the word reverently, *America*. America, with all its land and its inventions and its belief only in the future, surely that was the place for us.

She had her picture taken, enclosed it in the letter, and waited.

It was two months before Garner Clark wrote. He told her that he'd never done anything like this before, but that she looked nice. He told her that he owned a motel on the gold coast of Florida, thirty miles above Palm Beach. "I have the ocean and the palm trees and the sun," he said, as if they were his personal possessions. He enclosed a photo of himself in skimpy bathing trunks perched on the edge of a motorboat. He had a lean torso and slicked-back wavy hair. There were no visible defects, no obvious scars or withered limbs.

She had me take another picture of her in a lacy black

negligee, her short dark hair tousled suggestively about her pretty face, and enclosed it in her reply.

Six months later, we came here.

I finished the bitter coffee and wandered to the scalloped edge of the ocean. The wet sand rose between my toes as I headed down the shoreline, bending now and then to pick up interesting shells, examining them closely and then discarding even the most beautiful of them. I did not like the idea of possessions, of being weighed down, did not like most of all the possibility that I might wake one day and find that what I had once thought exquisite was really nothing at all.

By noon, I had walked three miles down the coast to where the white hotels were clustered, identical rectangles with balconies overlooking the sea. Hot, I dove into the water, hearing it rush past my ears as I closed my eyes. For a moment everything was gone, just gone.

When it was finally late afternoon, I walked back to the motel.

Back in my room, I stripped off my wet clothes and brushed my long tangled hair before the mirror, watching as it fell in black dripping ringlets across my bare shoulders.

Suddenly, I saw Garner's reflection in the mirror, his eyes stuck to my skin.

By the time I turned around to face him, he was gone.

I picked up the brush and began again, my fingernails scraping my scalp as I stroked.

Moments, looks. That is what you remember, That is what you try to forget.

And touch. That too. That most of all.

They seem, later, like a ladder, leading up and up to

the single inevitable landing.

Do they seem like that at the time? Perhaps.

The motel was crumbling about us. The yellow paint on the two-story U-shaped structure was peeling. The docks of the fourteen boat slips were splintered. Only when you sat at the end looking across the intracoastal to the state park, a dense wall of pines, did it look anything like the postcard. Maybe that's why Garner brought us here years ago, to help save it. There didn't seem to be anyone else. By the time we arrived, the German friend he played poker with had disappeared, along with the game. He had no friends in Flagerty, and his efforts at the simplest public transactions were painful to watch, his fear and distrust of strangers coming out in short angry exchanges. He came quickly and completely to depend on Astrid for most of his communication with the outside world.

Our apartment was separated from the front office by a narrow door. The office itself had royal blue walls, a ceramic vase of plastic flowers, a rack of local maps, and a large wooden fish painted in iridescent blues and pinks. There was a bell to call us, the motel's only phone, the large reservation book, and a machine that took credit cards. It was always very neat and tidy, organized and dusted. Behind the door, though, our apartment had long since grown into chaos. There were the tools that Garner was always using to fix the constant stream of broken appliances—faucets, mowers, sprinklers, even beds. There were the stacks of towels and sheets, the chlorine for the pool, the slatted plastic chairs that needed mending, the suntan lotion and dog-eared paperback books that guests left behind. The smell of cooking oil, suntan oil, machine oil, hovered thick in the air.

Often guests tried to peer behind the door, but even Astrid, whose weight had been ballooning since the day we arrived and now, six years later, was well over two hundred pounds, was adept at slipping through and closing it tightly behind her.

But if the guests themselves never quite saw the chaos, its scent and its havoc seeped through the vents.

Maids quit every other week, tired of Garner following them around and barking at their flaws. None of the local boys would even cut the grass. Most of the time, there was only the three of us to clean the twenty rooms, tend the lawn and pool, organize the boat slips.

When I didn't retreat to the beach, I went to Rosie Jenson's house, where we sat behind the closed door of her bedroom, painting our toenails, smoking, analyzing and reanalyzing our faces, our chests, our chances. All the other girls at school, the ones who ruled in perfectly coordinated outfits, their long slender arms and legs tanned a uniform gold, their straight hair swinging loose down their backs, ignored us.

When I first arrived in Florida, I had watched them silently, unable to understand what they said, but I began to learn English quickly from long lonely hours watching television and listening to the guests in the motel. "English now," Astrid used to insist whenever I tried to talk to her in German. "Only English now. We are in America."

Within the year, I could speak a clearer English than Astrid, and unlike Astrid, who, not having my child's malleability, never lost her accent, it was not long before strangers no longer asked where I had come from, and when, and why.

Soon, I no longer even dreamt in German, dreams that I had treasured and been comforted by, the familiar sounds and sights of home only attainable alone in the night—now gone even from reverie. I tried to will them back, but I couldn't. I began to forget my old language.

I tried then to make friends with the popular girls. I tried to look like them, dress like them, laugh at their jokes that I never quite got. I even tried to tame my curly hair to be like theirs. At night, I ironed it on the table and slept with it wrapped tightly around my head. Each day, it was smooth and straight when I left the motel, but by the time I got to school the relentless humidity had already frizzed it. The air itself became my enemy.

They had long since tired of Rosie, with her gray plastic glasses and her perfect grades and her fat. That is how we found each other, sitting in the back of the classroom, ignored. And that is what we now spent most of our time plotting to escape—the back row, the girls, Flagerty itself.

"I think San Francisco is best," Rosie said. "California. That's where I'm going." She had seen a picture in an old *Life* magazine of a long-haired boy with high cheekbones and a haunted look in his eye standing in front of a record shop in Haight-Ashbury. She was much taken with the idea of free love. Surely some of it would have to rub off on her.

I listened once again. I wanted to tell her that there was no more summer of love, that there probably wasn't even a Haight-Ashbury anymore, not the way Rosie meant, we had missed all that, the war was over and Patty Hearst had just been caught and looks mattered, they always had, but I didn't want to hurt her feelings.

"I'm going to New York," I said instead, the glimpse

I had seen from the harbor already working through my dreams.

I stared at the rain falling outside her bedroom window and dropped the butt of my Winston into an empty can of Tab, listening to the fizzle as it fell into the liquid. "Do you ever hear your parents doing it?" I asked.

"No," Rosie answered, embarrassed. "I don't think they do."

"Of course they do it. Everyone does it."

"Why do you always ask me that?" she demanded.

"I don't always ask you that."

"Yes you do."

"Well, what do you want to talk about?" I asked.

"I don't know."

I lit another cigarette and looked down at the pages of *Sixteen* magazine, filled with boys and their guitars, their satin pants tight about their bulging crotches, their long hair loose about their necks.

I had seen Astrid once in the bedroom of our tiny apartment in Dortmarr. One night, I crept to the door and opened it a crack. I saw my mother and the man just as they were prying away from each other. Saw him give Astrid's loose breasts a final squeeze. Saw, as he turned his back to pull on his pants, Astrid reach for the money he had left on the night table, count it twice, and put it beneath the mattress.

I looked up at Rosie standing before the full-length mirror on her closet door, sucking in her chubby cheeks. Behind her, I saw my own reflection, outlined with new swells and indentations, the early etchings of breasts, hips.

"Come on, the rain's stopped," I said. "Let's go out."

The storm had brought no relief. The sun was once

more severe and unrepentant as we wandered downtown to buy ice-cream cones. The streets were filling with other kids anxious for release after the rain, and we walked along watching the first tenuous couplings of our classmates, boys and girls pressing into each other as they leaned against parked cars, holding hands, touching lips, pushing each other away, pulling each other back, their arms and legs bare, their shirts rolled up on their tanned stomachs, skin brushing against skin.

I walked faster than Rosie, my eyes darting to the couples and then quickly away, not wanting to be caught, my curiosity and longing sputtering messily about. But Rosie, plodding a foot behind, was not disturbed by them. It was as if they had nothing to do with her.

We rounded the corner and sat down on a wooden bench in the shade across from the movie theater where *Jaws* was playing, our thighs sticking to the splintery wooden bench. I looked over at Rosie, her moon face placid, a drop of chocolate chip ice cream on her lower lip as she watched people line up for the afternoon showing. We had already seen the movie twice, sitting in the back, listening to the other girls' screams that signaled to their dates to hold them tighter.

"What about Mark Birch?" I asked.

"What about him?"

"He'd be a good boyfriend for you."

Rosie rolled her eyes. "He'd never go out with me."

"Why not?"

Rosie looked at me seriously. "Boys won't go out with me now," she said. "My mother says I'm a late bloomer. All the women in my family are. It's okay."

"You can bloom whenever you goddamned want," I said, my irritation with Rosie's resignation mixing with the afternoon's heat, the anxious couplings, my own restlessness.

Rosie smiled patiently. "Actually, you can't. I've thought about this, and you can't. Bloom is completely beyond your control."

I regarded her closely and then looked away, thinking of the boys and girls against the parked cars, the way their fingertips met so slowly in the heat.

In a little while we rose and started to walk back on the endless flat road that led out of town.

"They will later," Rosie said quietly after a long bout of silence.

"What?"

"The boys. They'll go out with me later. That's the type I am. I think they'll appreciate me when I'm older."

I looked over curiously at her, jealous of her patience and her certainty, jealous that she had complete theories about herself, about the future, when I had only loose fragments, random and troubling, swirling about within.

We said goodbye where the road forked.

As I continued the final half-mile alone, my head grew dizzy from the heat and my peripheral vision began to blacken. I rested on the sidewalk beneath a live oak on the edge of someone's front yard but rose again as quickly as I could. Garner had no patience for those who complained of the heat. "Your blood's too thick," he told me. "That's the problem. Another few years here, it will thin out."

There were things I wanted to tell Rosie.

About my real father, whom I had only seen once.

About Astrid and her men.

About Garner. Garner and his gimlet eyes watching me, always watching me.

115

But I didn't.

How could I? Rosie, with her pharmacist father who always smelled of antiseptic, and her mother with her shirtwaists and her garden club.

All I could do was try to keep her away from the motel.

Some moments are like spotlights that will not disappear even when you shut your eyes, while everything else falls away, into the blackness of the past.

Midweek the motel was often empty, desolate. Astrid and Garner slept late, stayed indoors, left the mail unopened.

So I was surprised to open my eyes to see Astrid standing over me, dressed in a loose turquoise shift, her naked white forearms pendulous and dimpled with fat, her bright red lipstick already beginning to melt. I pulled the sheet over my face.

"Wake up," Astrid insisted. "Dad's going to take us on an outing."

"Don't call him that. He's not my father."

"What would you like me to call him?"

"I don't know, just don't call him that."

I looked up and saw Garner pass by wearing faded plaid shorts and soiled sneakers, his belly pushing against a gray cotton sweatshirt.

"Why do I have to go? You go," I said to Astrid.

"He wants you to come, too. It'll be fun."

"I have school."

"This is a special occasion. School can wait. Be nice, sweetie. Promise me? Just meet him halfway."

I got reluctantly out of bed.

We drove along deserted roads until we came to a

116

wooden shack on the Indian River with a sign that promised Budweiser, fishing tackle, worms, and pontoon boat rentals. Inside, it was dark and musty, the walls lined with rods and buckets, maps of the tides, ancient postcards, and a refrigerator full of sodas, beers, and worms. Astrid and I stood a few feet away while Garner argued with the owner about money. "Four dollars an hour means four dollars an hour," the man said. He was missing one front tooth, and when he spoke, certain syllables seemed to get lost in the hole. He showed no inclination to bargain, but Garner, who always suspected that someone was trying to pull something over on him, could not resist trying. In the end, he paid the asking price and then led us onto the boat. Astrid smiled at me as we began to move slowly through the water, the breeze running into our faces, the sun pushing at our backs. "This is an adventure, isn't it?" she said. "Admit it."

Garner commandeered the wide flat vessel downriver, muttering to Astrid about the conservationists who had just managed to get Florida to outlaw the cutting down of mangroves, while I lay on the deck, feeling the sun bake my skin, and then seep in and bake me inside too, layer by layer until it reached my very marrow. I loved the way the heat became a universe unto itself, scalding all in its wake, so that everything—my mother's and Garner's voices rising and ebbing a few feet away, the occasional airplane overhead, the buzzing of mosquitoes—everything but the sound of my own blood thrumming in my temples seemed a million miles away. I loosened the neck ties of my lilac bikini top and lowered them so that only tiny patches of my breasts were covered, and then I rolled down the sides of the bathing suit bottom beneath the sharp rise of my hip bones.

At noon, we ate bologna sandwiches and then I watched Astrid and Garner climb down the rope ladder on the side of the boat and swim in the river. Their heads bobbing in the green water as they wrapped their arms around each other's necks, laughing and splashing. Kissing. When they climbed back onto the boat, I could see my mother's large nipples and dark bunchy pubic hair outlined beneath her white suit.

I shut my eyes as Astrid went to the other end of the boat to see if there were any potato chips left in the picnic basket. In a moment, I felt a shadow pass across the sun. When I opened my eyes a slit, I saw Garner standing over me, smoothing his wet hair off his forehead, staring down at me, his mouth parted.

He took a step closer.

His big toe skimmed my skin just under my rib cage and began to work its way slowly down.

I shut my eyes again, immobilized, unable even to breathe.

His toe moved over my hip to my bikini bottom and wiggled underneath.

But as soon as Astrid came sashaying back, smiling and licking her greasy fingers, Garner stepped away.

That night, I ran away from home. I crammed my schoolbooks and a change of clothes into my green canvas knapsack and then sat on the edge of my bed waiting for the light in Astrid and Garner's bedroom to go out. As soon as it did, I slung my bag over my shoulder and left.

The unlit streets hummed with the night sounds of the tropics, a constant background of wings and antennae. I passed a rare lit window among the sparse houses, the sparser trees, but other than that the world seemed suddenly deserted, vast and dark and empty. There was only my heart beating against my chest, and my footsteps.

When I came to the end of Loyola where it petered out into an unpaved dirt lane, I walked onto the field before me, the tall grass tickling my shins. Exhausted, I curled up on the ground, using my knapsack as a pillow and an extra shirt as a blanket.

I lay awake, staring up at the sky. My body was alien in its aloneness, cut off, unmoored. I touched myself tentatively, my forearm, my belly. My breasts. There was no one, nothing within sight. I looked up at the brilliant pinpoints of white stars amid so much blackness. The motel seemed as far away as the constellations themselves, and I saw it rising into the night, leaving only the smoky tail of a comet in its wake, until that too disintegrated.

When I woke, it was dawn. The sky was lighting up in gradual increments, as if the night was being erased before my eyes, revealing a fragile gray and pink sheet behind it, pearly as the inside of a shell. My skin was clammy with dew. I hadn't eaten dinner and my stomach grumbled, but there was no one there to hear it. Astrid was always so brazen about bodily functions, grumbling, farting, snoring, but I was ashamed.

That afternoon, I told Rosie I'd had a fight with "the asshole" and went home with her, setting up camp in a corner of the Jensons' garage behind a lawn mower. In the evening, she brought me food she had sneaked from the dinner table.

We sat in the dark garage amid bags of old clothes, and Rosie watched as I ate. When I was done, we both curled up on the quilt she had brought in, our bodies close enough to feel the rise and fall of each other's breath, our faces invisible in the blackness.

"If I tell you something, do you promise never to tell anyone?" I whispered.

"Yes."

"You know how I told you my real father was dead?"

"Uh huh."

"He's not."

"Where is he?" Rosie asked.

"In Germany."

"Do you write to him?"

I shook my head. "I only saw him once, on my fifth birthday. He brought me a gingerbread house. It was two stories high, with icing on the roof and three front steps."

We lay in silence for a long time.

"My mother wouldn't let me touch the cake," I said quietly. "It sat on the kitchen table for days, but she kept saying it was too beautiful to eat." I paused. "Sometimes, when she wasn't looking, I broke off tiny pieces of the steps and ate them."

"How come you never saw him again?"

"He was married to someone else," I answered matter-of-factly. "He broke my mother's heart."

Rosie nodded.

I rolled onto my back, pulling the quilt up to my neck. I parted my lips and began to speak again, but the words clumped like glue in the center of my throat.

In a little while, I heard the soft steady murmur of Rosie's sleep.

I slept in Rosie's garage for three nights before Astrid showed up to claim me. In fact, Rosie's mother had found out about me the first evening and called Astrid to

120

tell her not to worry. When it appeared that Astrid was too busy to come for the first couple of nights, Mrs. Jenson made sure that the leftovers Rosie brought me in the garage were particularly plentiful and savory. Finally, on the fourth night, Astrid drove up just as the Jensons were locking the front door.

She stood inside the dark garage and reached over to touch the side of my head, her hand lingering in my unwashed hair, and despite myself, I leaned into the warm soft palm as familiar as my own soul. "Let's go, sweetie," Astrid said. I gathered my things while Rosie and Mrs. Jenson watched wordlessly.

I sat close to my mother as we drove, the car filled with her breath and her particular smell, her Astridness, sweet and acrid at once. I wished that we would never reach home, but could drive on like this in the dark together forever. "Why do you stay with Garner?" I asked.

Astrid breathed deeply. "It's not so easy to explain. You'll understand when you're older."

"Adults always say that when they don't understand something themselves."

"I made a choice," Astrid said.

"So? You can change your mind."

"He made us a family," she said. "That was the choice I made. That was what I wanted. To be a family."

We drove in silence for a few minutes.

"When you were first born," Astrid began softly, "people wanted me to give you away. You have to understand, it was very hard for me, with no husband. So I agreed."

"You gave me away?"

"There was this couple in the country who couldn't have any children. They wanted you. A nurse from the hospital took you to them."

"I can't believe you gave me away."

"I couldn't stand it. A week later, I brought you back."

We stopped at a light.

"He's loyal to me," Astrid added thoughtfully, looking for the briefest moment at the continental spread of her thighs, her belly in heaps upon her lap. "He's a loyal man." She turned to me. "I love you," Astrid said quietly.

She rounded the last corner onto our street. "We've always had each other. Don't ever forget that." She pulled into the driveway and cut off the ignition. "Come on, sweetie, I bought some cheesecake on the way. I'll bet you're hungry."

The rest, the time between then and the night he came to me, was nothing, just waiting, blank.

I'm getting there, getting there despite myself.

It was a Friday night. I sat at the front desk, checking in the sport fishermen with their big bellies and gold chains with medallions nestled in the coarse gray hair of their chests. Garner was outside fishing leaves, gum wrappers, and dead chameleons out of the pool, scrubbing down the barbecue grills, and emptying the stinking garbage bins of fish refuse and Budweiser cans. Astrid sat beside me, smiling pleasantly at the never-ending requests for more towels, suntan lotion, a phone, restaurant recommendations, for refunds and reservations and postage stamps.

Finally, at nine o'clock, all of the expected guests had checked in and I went back to my room, put on the record player, and began to change my clothes.

I reached into the top drawer and wrapped my bare

122

torso in a royal blue paisley silk scarf I had stolen from the accessories department at Dearfields, wrapping it across my chest like the strapless gown I had seen in *Vogue*. I stared, entranced, at the cleavage this gave me, and then I rimmed my eyes with black Maybelline liner.

Outside of the bedroom, I could hear Garner and Astrid fighting about how we never had any money and whose fault that was.

Their voices faded to a low angry murmur and then the front door slammed.

I painted my lips a deep crimson and sat down on the floor, my head between the speakers of my tiny plastic stereo, blasting the Rolling Stones' *Exile on Main Street*. I didn't hear Garner come in.

"You could have knocked," I said when I looked up from his bare hairy feet and yellow toenails to his face.

"It's my house. I don't have to knock."

"What do you want?"

"I want you to turn that racket down."

"It's my room."

"I don't want an argument, just do it." Garner turned and left.

I reached over and turned up the volume knob on the console as far as it would go.

When Garner came back, I glared up at him, my face flushed. He glared back. Both of us were, for an instant, speechless, caught in the moment, finally caught in it.

He bent over and began to sweep the albums that 1 had lined up in meticulous alphabetical order into a large trash bag he had brought in. The corners of the LPs poked against the black plastic, ripping it in spots.

"What are you doing?" I demanded.

"You don't listen to me, you pay the price."

I rose quickly and grabbed Garner's arm. "Give those

123

back, they're mine." I pried his fingers until he dropped the records and they scattered about the floor. We both stared down at them, and then back at each other.

Garner suddenly yanked the silk scarf from my chest. "You look like a goddamned whore," he said. "Well, I shouldn't be surprised. Like mother, like daughter."

I froze.

I felt my breasts standing out in the open air, laid open, exposed, Garner's eyes all over them.

And then in a second, his hand was on me too, his callused hand.

Open-palmed, spread-fingered, it fell slowly down from my collar bone, rubbing across my skin, lingering over the small swell of my breast, cupping my nipple, which grew instantly hard and sore as he pinched it.

I did not move.

Garner's hand rested in the shallows just below my rib cage, and then it fell farther, his fingers landing on the top of my panties, grasping them.

He pulled the lace edge down a half-inch below my tan line, where my skin was pale and untouched. The jagged border of my pubic hair curled up into view, black and kinky. His forefinger wriggled into it as a drop of spittle fell from his lower lip.

With his other hand he unzipped his soiled khaki pants and pulled out his penis, purple and swollen. He began to jerk his fist up and down it, slowly and then faster.

I stood completely still, mesmerized, horrified, while the head touched my skin, pulled away, touched again.

He swallowed once, loudly, deeply.

A groan escaped from his throat and a sticky liquid shot out over his hand and onto my belly.

The whites of his eyes shone as he gave my panties

one final victorious snap, zipped himself up, and left without saying a word, slamming the door behind him.

I stood for a long time naked in the center of the room, my stomach dripping.

Seven

WHAT DID WE DO? WE WENT ON. WHAT CHOICE WAS there, really?

I sat at the front desk, checking people in and out, I began to cut school, individual classes at first, and then whole days, I kept to myself. I told no one what had happened. My sixteenth birthday came and went with no event. The only person who remembered was Rosie, who called before she left for school that morning.

"Sweet sixteen," Rosie said and laughed, because that is what we did and because girls like us were never sweet sixteen, not really, maybe no one was anymore.

You go on. But not the same, never the same.

Or maybe that's just an excuse for what happened later.

This is what I wanted: for Garner to look me in the eye.

He still hadn't, not since that night.

Sometimes, I could feel him watching me, feel his eyes burning across the contours of my body as I passed him, but whenever I turned around to catch him at it, his eyes were already somewhere else.

At night, I lay awake long past the time I heard Astrid and Garner close their door.

He would come to my room after Astrid had fallen asleep. This time, I would yell, claw, fight. I would push him away from me.

My skin tingled in anticipation.

But he did not come.

Somewhere, so deep beneath the weariness and the hatred and the shame that it could not be found even in my dreams, there was a certain deflation, even disappointment.

There were times when I wondered if it had ever happened at all, his hands on my breasts, my belly, his penis, wondered if it hadn't been some awful dream, a splinter in my imagination, and it was in those moments of doubt that I hated him the most.

There are poisons that flood the system, infecting every movement, every view, poisons that cluster and build like a boil, with no place to go, no release. I rarely left the Breezeway's grounds. I did not go to the beach, or to the ice-cream store a mile up the road, I did not go past the motel's carefully demarcated acreage, but like a cat, traced and retraced its perimeters. I rarely went to school. If Astrid or Garner noticed, they said nothing.

I sat at the end of the dock, drinking a Tab in the strong morning sun. The day spread before me, shapeless and silent. I thought of school, of the bell ringing at the end of each class, of gathering up books, fastening the rubber strap about them, hurrying down the hallway to the next class. But I did not move. I wore a man's large Timex watch a guest had left behind and sometimes as a game I timed how long I went without speaking to anyone, two hours, three.

I got up and fished the previous day's paper from the large garbage can near the barbecue, and sat back down.

The only real news was a report of the first shark attack of the season. A pregnant woman in Stuart had gotten a chunk of her left thigh bitten off. It had required seventy-two stitches. The baby was said to be doing fine, thanks to the woman's quick thinking. She had curled her arms and legs over her bulging belly to protect the baby. "It was just instinct," she told the reporter.

I folded the newspaper, flung it back into the waste can and headed back to the office to get my cleaning supplies. We were once more without a maid and I was left to tidy the rooms, scour the toilets, collect the stained sheets, vacuum.

Maybe it didn't begin with Garner. Maybe it began here.

I wheeled the heavy canister vacuum cleaner into room 202 and picked up the bedspread, peering underneath. I was always surprised by what guests left behind. Money, stray shoes, rolls of film, used condoms, checkbooks, rusty razors. Pieces of themselves—lost, forgotten, deemed unnecessary. I vacuumed, dusted, bleached the bathroom sink and tub, made the bed, and then carried my supplies to the next room.

Room 203 was occupied by a single middle-aged man, Lewis Harmon, with a great carbuncular nose and ferret eyes who had been at the Breezeway for two weeks. Every afternoon, he sat by the pool in a long-sleeved linen shirt, bathing trunks, white knee-socks and sandals, reading detective novels while he drank tap water out of a paper cup. I was startled to find him in his room now, perched on his bed, reading.

"I can come back later," I offered.

"That's all right. I don't mind. Just pretend I'm not here."

I hesitated, but he nodded his encouragement and went back to his paperback. I bent over to turn on the

127

vacuum. I could feel him watching me as I arched my back and began to move slowly about the room. I glanced over at him and he smiled slightly and turned a page. His eyes were puffy, bloodshot. I turned off the vacuum cleaner, flexing my calves, my butt out, and stretched as I rose, testing it, this new power, trying to gauge its weight and its effect while Harmon watched from beneath his heavy drooping eyelids.

When I reached over to wipe a ring of water stains from the night table, I suddenly felt his hands on my back. Steadily, firmly, they traced my shoulder blades and then inched down the incline of my waist and out again over my hips. The hands stopped, grasped me, turned me around. Lewis Harmon, sitting up with his feet on the ground, pulled me between his legs and buried his face in my chest. I looked down at the top of his head, his coarse hair flecked with dandruff. I felt his lips on my skin, not kissing, but pulling mouthfuls of my flesh in. My hands were on his shoulders, steadying myself. There were no questions asked, no answers given.

He pulled me down onto the bed. I did not speak, did not protest. I looked up into his face, his red-webbed eyes, his slab of a nose, and then I shut my eyes. He untied the straps of my halter top and threw it on the floor.

I helped him slide down my shorts and parted my legs for him.

It would be easier to say that I didn't, but I did.

He smelled faintly of mothballs.

He held me tightly and entered me as I reared up, swallowing my own cry, this is it, so this is it. I felt him go an inch, and then further, all the way up to where it was black and marshy and uncharted. He was riding me now, absorbed in his own tides.

He bucked suddenly, grunted, and collapsed.

He lay on top of me for a moment and then rolled off. My chest was sticky with his sweat.

In a minute, I heard him snoring.

I sat up slowly and looked at the sheets. I expected to see a lucent crimson pool of blood, but there was none. I bent over and pulled on my clothes.

As I began to tie my shirt, I noticed that Harmon had left a pile of money and his keys on the night table.

My eyes still on him, I reached over, pulled two ten-dollar bills from beneath the keys, and stuck them in my pocket before I quietly left the room.

It was still sunny out, still the same day. That was what I remembered later, that it was somehow still the same day. That, and the burning sore ache between my legs, and the money like a rock in my back pocket.

Back in my room, I sat down on the floor and spread my legs. The lips of my vagina were puffy and swollen. I touched them gingerly, testing, examining.

I stood up and smoothed the bills across my dresser, and then placed them in my top drawer.

I did not feel regret or remorse or sadness or shame. I did not feel free. I felt, more than anything, let loose, as if a wall I had not seen before had been shattered and I was spinning from its shards, my own atoms tumbling out and out and out, unstoppable.

I changed my clothes and went back out. I was still washing the weekend's sheets and towels long into the night. In between cycles, I stepped outside and stared at the fireflies, brilliant orange pricks of light darting about in concentric circles and then disappearing into the air stained with the odor of cheap detergent and lint from the dryer and the musky smell of sex.

The next day, Lewis Harmon was again by the pool, reading his detective novel, drinking his tap water. When I walked by, he peered over the top of his book at me. He closed his book, laid it across his belly, put on his sunglasses, and studied me from behind their forest green shield.

That afternoon, I went back to his room.

It was four o'clock. He lay on his bed, fully clothed, waiting for me. The lights were off and the air was faded brown from being trapped inside on such a sunny day.

I closed the door behind me.

"I would have given you the money," he said.

I shrugged. "You were sleeping."

He grunted. "Don't steal. Just don't steal. I don't like that."

This time, because he knew he was going to pay for it, Harmon did exactly what he wanted. He squeezed and pushed me and when he entered me he stuck his fingers up my ass. "Bite my nipples," he whispered hoarsely, and I did.

I was watching myself, watching him, wondering where he would go next, where I would go.

And then I wasn't watching myself at all. I was inside it.

He rammed into me so hard it hurt, and the pain and the pleasure mixed up in my brain, my spine, my gut. For there was that, too—a darkly hued pleasure. And release, not a release that flew gleefully up into the air, but a release that spiraled down and further down, into some murky swirling bottomless pool where I found myself waiting.

When I left, he slipped a twenty-dollar bill into my back pocket. I felt his hand, fingers spread, slithering into my tight jeans, slipping around my ass, cupping it, leaving the money behind, slithering out.

When Lewis Harmon checked out five days later, I had eighty dollars in my top drawer. I liked looking at the bills, smoothing them out, folding them, counting and recounting them. I did not think of spending them, of new clothes or nights out. It had nothing to do with that at all.

A week later, I sat on the gate by the parking lot, swinging my legs back and forth, watching the Jensons' car drive up. It was a Sunday afternoon and because the next day was a school holiday, it seemed the perfect time for Rosie to spend the night. It was her idea. I had tried to avoid it, but here she was.

Rosie jumped out of the car, clutching her overnight bag as she said goodbye to her mother. Mrs. Jenson chatted briefly with me and then drove off, leaving us alone by the side of the road. I hadn't seen Rosie since the last time I was in school two weeks ago, and we were both suddenly uncomfortable with each other.

"So," Rosie said.

"So."

I glanced more closely at her. She looked exactly the same. I wondered if I, too, looked the same to her. I couldn't believe that Rosie, so earnest and so vigilant, would not see a change, would not smell it, sense it, suspect it. But if she did, she gave no sign. I was relieved and disappointed. "Let's drop off your bag," I said.

We turned and headed through the courtyard. "Not

bad," Rosie remarked. I followed her eyes to the palms, the pool, the boats bobbing by the docks in the tranquil water. It looked impressive enough.

We went inside where Astrid and Garner were sprawled at the living room table surrounded by piles of loose papers trying to figure out how much tax to pay, or not to pay, on the room rentals. They both looked up briefly to say hello and then returned to their work.

"What do you want to do?" I asked Rosie.

"I don't know. What do you want to do?"

"How about the beach?"

We changed into our suits and headed down the road lined with motels and citrus stands to the public beach. I had never been a hostess before, and I felt responsible for the lawns, for the cars on the road, for the day itself.

We continued along the shore until we came to a deserted patch of dunes, where we spread our towels across the slight incline and lay down. Rosie, whose skin never tanned, scrupulously covered herself with a gooey white suntan lotion.

"I have news for you," she said as she settled back and closed her eyes. "It's about Lydia Warner."

"What about her?"

"You ready? Her mother came home and found her in bed with Barry Johnson. They had all their clothes on and everything, but isn't that the grossest thing you've ever heard? I mean, with his skin, yuck."

I nodded up into the sun. "Which would you rather do," I asked, "lick Barry Johnson's face or have to eat that entire bottle of suntan lotion standing naked in front of homeroom?" It was a game we used to play, offering up options of disgust.

Rosie stuck out her tongue and pretended to lick the lotion's cap and we both broke up, meeting inside the

132

sound of our own laughter once more, grateful to find each other there. Eventually, the laughter drifted off and melded with the soft steady crash of the waves and then we listened to that.

"Don't your parents care about you missing school?" Rosie asked.

"Not really." The truant officer had called a few times, but Astrid just told him I was sick and never mentioned it again.

"Aren't you worried about catching up?"

"I haven't really thought about it," I answered. School, classes, bells, were another thing that had faded, a story from the past.

"What do you do all day?"

"I don't know. Stuff. There's always things that need doing."

"But you're going to go back, aren't you?"

"Eventually."

"I sent away for college catalogs," Rosie said. "I am going to try California after all. U.C.L.A. looks good. Or maybe Berkeley."

I said nothing.

In a little while, I turned on the transistor radio we had brought and we listened to the new Led Zeppelin song and then the news. President Ford, who was gearing up for the coming election, had taken a tumble on a ski slope in Utah. I followed the report closely. Lately, I had gotten into the habit of listening to the radio late at night, skipping around the dial looking not for a better song, but for the news. I looked forward to the time each day when I could close my door and listen to the announcer's voice in my dark shadow-infested room, gleaning the facts, storing them up, welcomed evidence of a world beyond my own.

"So, have any cute boys checked in?" Rosie asked.

That night, we made cottage cheese-and-jelly sandwiches and ate them sitting on the edge of the Breezeway's docks. A huge ship was visible off-shore, outlined in a string of white lights, and we both stared out at it as we spoke.

"Supposedly there's a pirate ship buried a mile from the shore," I said. "This guy checked in last weekend with all this incredible diving equipment and he was telling us about it. He said the treasure was finders keepers. It could be millions of dollars in old gold coins and shit."

"Do you believe him?"

"No." I threw a crust of bread to a pelican and watched its prehistoric profile as it dove into the water. "But my mother does. Not that that's a recommendation."

Rosie sighed. "God, it's so romantic here."

We both lit cigarettes and smoked them with our hands cupped about the tips, shielding the red embers from view, an old habit when parents were in the vicinity, though really there was no need. Astrid and Garner were buried in the apartment and anyway, they wouldn't have cared.

Later, Rosie and I carried our things to room 214 and settled onto the double beds, two feet away from each other, in oversized T-shirts and underwear.

We watched television for a little while and then, tired from the beach, from the reunion itself, we turned off the lights and lay on our backs in the dark, talking quietly as if someone might hear. The room had the minty odor of the Noxzema we had both used to wash our faces.

There was a long pause and I felt myself swimming in

it, fighting through it, trying to come out armed with the words, the sentences, I could give to Rosie to make her understand, make her know.

But I couldn't.

I retreated back into the bed, the silence.

Though Rosie was lying an arm's span away, I missed her, missed most the person I used to be when I was with her.

For a long while we both lay listening to each other's breaths, murmuring now and then, and then not at all.

Long after Rosie had fallen asleep, I crept from the room and sat on the docks alone, shivering in the cool night air, the tiny white lights of the far-off boat blurred by my own tears.

We kissed goodbye the next afternoon, and promised to see each other in school the following day, but I didn't go.

Two weeks later, on a Saturday afternoon, a man named Frank Xavier rang the office bell and asked for a room. Though he was short with a slight build, there was something grandiose about his ears, eyes, lips, even his limbs, as if the features of a much larger man had somehow gotten attached to the wrong body. His voice was low and gravelly, and Astrid, standing beside me, had to lean forward to hear it. "We don't usually get people checking in on Saturday," she told him. "Most of our guests try to make a weekend of it." She glanced down at his four matching vinyl suitcases.

"I'm a pharmaceutical salesman," he explained. "I cover most of the hospitals from here to the Keys."

Astrid smiled, buoyed by the prospect of regular routes and recommendations to fellow salesmen.

"I'd like to stay till Wednesday, if you can find

something for me," Xavier said. The tips of his teeth, white and even, were also oversized.

Astrid smiled once more. Midweek guests meant unexpected money.

She told him that there was only one room available for the first night, room 110, with an entrance to the rear of the courtyard, facing the road, but that she would change him to a better location after everyone checked out on Sunday.

Xavier took the key and followed her directions along the path to a door partially hidden by palmettos.

We did not see him again all evening.

Sunday morning was always busy, with people trying to cram as much vacation into their last hours at the Breezeway as possible. The children's yelps by the pool were shriller, the sport fishermen, who did not have time to go out on their boats, loitered about the dock drinking beer for breakfast and dreading going home to their wives and jobs, the married couples stayed behind the drawn curtains of their rooms, making love one final time and then beginning to squabble while they packed.

Frank Xavier lay on a lounge chair by the pool. His bare belly was flat and muscular, with a triangle of coarse dark hairs. He was reading a newspaper when I walked by on my way to empty the trash. He watched me pull the large black plastic bag from the wooden container, knot it, and replace it with a fresh one before he spoke. "You're Marta?"

I stopped and looked down at him. "Yes."

Xavier nodded. "I'm a friend of Lewis Harmon's," he said. He stared directly up into my eyes without squinting from the sun.

Just then, Astrid stuck her head out of the office door and called to me. "Can you come help me, sweetie? The

Weinsteins and the Littles both want to check out."

I glanced back at Frank Xavier and then I hurried away.

The next morning, Astrid offered to move Xavier to a better room with a door and window directly on the courtyard.

"There's no need to go to all that trouble," he told her. "I'm fine where I am."

"What a nice man," Astrid remarked as we watched Xavier leave the office. "So easy to please."

It was an overcast day, the sky a patchy gray quilt, and the courtyard was empty. Xavier settled at one of the round tables with a carton of orange juice and *Time* magazine's year-end issue.

I glanced curiously at the "Women of the Year" cover as I passed. I had already stripped the beds in half the rooms, and was on my way to the laundry room with a basketful of sheets when I heard his voice.

"Come talk to me."

I turned around.

"I've got work to do," I said.

"I'll help you."

He stood up and took the full plastic basket from my hands, following me to the narrow unlit laundry room, with its two washing machines and single dryer.

"We're going to be friends," he said, as he rested the basket on top of one of the machines.

I began to pull sheets from it and load them into the washer. "What makes you think that?" I asked.

"Call it a hunch."

I had to maneuver around him to reach the detergent, and our forearms brushed against each other. "Good friends," Xavier added.

Why do you go to what you are most afraid of? Later, when I had to think of something, I thought of that. Why I went, knowing even then, from the very first, that there was something, a glint, a warning.

Sometimes, I tried to go back and make myself run in the opposite direction.

But I couldn't.

I walked along the walls of the courtyard path and turned the corner to the barely visible door of room 110. I knocked once and he let me in.

He looked me straight in the eyes. "Come in."

The only light was from the reading lamp on the night table.

"Sit," he instructed.

He got two Budweisers out of the small refrigerator and handed me one. I had never had beer before and was surprised by its bitterness. We drank in silence for a minute.

"So what did Lewis Harmon tell you?" I asked.

Xavier smiled. "He told me you like it."

I didn't answer.

"You've got a good body, Marta," Xavier said. "Slim, with tits. That's rare. Usually you get one or the other."

Instinctively, I wrapped my arms in front of me.

Xavier took another sip of his beer and wiped his mouth with the back of his hand without taking his eyes from me. Then he reached into his pocket, pulled a crisp twenty-dollar bill from his wallet, and put it on the table.

"It's thirty," I said

"That's not what Harmon said."

"The price has just gone up."

Xavier looked at me stonily and then erupted into

laughter. "You're awfully smart for a girl your age." He got another bill out and added it to the twenty. "I think we're going to like each other. I think we're going to like each other just fine."

He began to unbutton my shirt. We were standing six inches apart now. His eyes traveled across my body unabashedly, taking me in, my breasts, my nipples. I felt more naked than I had ever been and I moved over to him, pressing my chest against his. At least he couldn't see me that way.

He laughed. "You're an eager one, aren't you?" And with that, he yanked me roughly onto the bed. He held both of my arms above my head, clasping my wrists so that I couldn't move. With his free hand, he pulled down my shorts.

He stripped off his own clothes and then he flipped me over, slapping my ass once before entering me from behind, pushing me down into the bed, my face pressing deeper and deeper into the mattress, where all I could see was blackness.

And when I thought of it all those years later in my frequent wakeful moments between night and dawn, this is also what I thought: That what I was most terrified of was not him, but myself, the part of myself that responded to him, and that is what I should have run from.

But I dove right into it, right fucking into it.

It didn't feel like I had a choice.

We did it the next day in broad daylight, lying on the cement path behind his room beneath the spray of palmettos, the ground scraping my naked butt and ankles, the cars driving past just a few yards away.

It took ten minutes.

Then he slipped into his room and got the money while I scurried into my clothes, pieces of dirt sticking to my skin.

These are not things I am proud of.

In fact, it feels like someone else did them. In a way, it was someone else.

I realize that's no excuse, of course.

Maybe the past always feels that way. Maybe everyone has a separate self lost back there, connected by only the thinnest thread to the person they are now.

Who, after all, would repeat the past in exactly the same way, given a choice?

The last time I went to Xavier, he was sitting at the table cutting a cord into four pieces. The money was already laid out. I sat down at the table and watched him work.

"Where are you from anyway?" I asked.

"Georgia."

"You don't have an accent."

"I've only been there two years. Before that Ohio. Then there was Maine."

"Why do you move around so much?"

"Just making a living."

"Are you married?" I asked.

"I was."

"Do you have any kids?"

"One. A girl. I haven't seen her in a long time. Four, five years."

I leaned forward, alert. I was endlessly curious about absentee fathers. "Why not?"

Xavier stopped playing with the cord for a moment and stared down at the scissors. "I guess it's inconvenient," he answered at last. He frowned. "Christ, you ask a lot of goddamned questions. You see me asking you questions? Nosirree. Not one. I figure your business is your business and mine is mine." He measured and snipped the last piece of cord. "You ever done this?" he asked.

"What?"

"I'll show you."

He tied a knot around my wrist and fastened my left arm to the bed. Then my right arm.

My left leg.

And finally my right leg.

I was splayed open.

He stared at me, his mouth parted, his eyes gleaming. "You got any questions now?" he asked.

I turned my head away.

My ankles and wrists strained against the rope, toward him or away from him, I wouldn't have been able to tell, and I knew then that people were wrong, that it was possible to leave your body behind after all.

Afterwards, he sat up, wiped himself, and walked naked to the refrigerator to get a fresh beer while I was still tied up. I thought at first that he had forgotten me, but he turned once, glanced down at me, and then went into the bathroom to pee, leaving the door open.

"Hey," I demanded when he returned.

"Yes?"

"Are you going to untie me?"

"I don't know. Should I?"

"That's not funny."

"Isn't it?"

"No."

He stood completely still for over a minute, and then he picked up the scissors and cut the bonds on both of my hands. He handed me the scissors as I sat up, rubbing my wrists. I cut the ropes on my legs myself.

"Don't lose your sense of humor, Marta," he said. "Nobody likes a girl who loses her sense of humor."

When I got back to my room, I ripped up the money he had given me into tiny shreds and buried them in the trash can behind the motel.

The next morning, Astrid and I sat at the kitchen table together, balancing our coffee cups on top of the papers and leaflets and phone books that never seemed to move. On the second Wednesday of every month, we totaled up the previous month's credit card receipts. Astrid had the stack of inky slips before her and she read out numbers while I punched them into the adding machine.

I sat with one hand on my lap, a woven string bracelet about the wrist of my other hand, carefully putting in the numbers. Both wrists had pale rings of indigo about them. I kept one eye on Astrid and whenever it seemed that she might notice them I shifted my hands out of sight.

"Sixty dollars and forty-four cents," Astrid continued between bites of powdered-sugar donut. "Thirty-eight dollars and twelve cents." The fine white powder fell about her chin like a goatee. She didn't notice a thing. "Did you get that last one?" she asked. "Okay, let's see. Fifty dollars and eighty-three cents."

Slowly, I brought my left hand from my lap and rested it on the table.

Astrid continued reading, eating.

I took off the string bracelet, revealing the bruise.

But Astrid still didn't see. How could she not see,

never see?

"Only a few more, sweetie. Sixty-six dollars and no cents."

We were interrupted by three *pings* of the office bell.

Astrid rose and lumbered down the hallway.

I heard Frank Xavier's voice from the other side of the office wall.

"Unfortunately, Mrs. Clark, it's time for me to leave."

"I'm sorry to hear that."

"I've enjoyed my stay very much," he said. "As a matter of fact, I plan on returning."

"We'd love to have you," Astrid replied as she handed him his bill. "And be sure to tell all your friends about us."

"Oh, I will." Frank Xavier laughed as the screen door of the office swung shut behind him.

"I wish we had more like him," Astrid said when she returned. "Now where were we?"

I sat on my bed, rocking back and forth.

The tears, when they finally came, racked through me in torrents, wave crashing upon wave. I bit my lower lip until it was bloody to hold back the sounds but that only trapped them within where they shattered all they touched.

There was a trail of lava inside where he had been, where all of them had been. It burned through my groin, my gut, up through my throat.

I rocked, cried, clawed at myself for hours until I was finally spent, hollowed out, empty.

Sitting completely still, I slowly began to reclaim my body, my numb legs, my wasted lungs.

Eventually, I got up and scrubbed my face, patting it gently with a worn-out towel.

I wanted only to be good now, to be clean, to start again.

I still believed that was possible.

The following Monday, I went back to school.

I rose before dawn and put on opalescent Maybelline white eye shadow, black eyeliner, three coats of mascara, and a mocha frosted lipstick. I looked at myself in the mirror, and then I washed it all off. Clean-faced, I lay down on my bed to zip the jeans that were too tight to close any other way. I had showered in them earlier in the week to make them conform to my body, and then tapered the legs from crotch to knee in tiny hand-stitches to make them even snugger.

The newly built Flagerty High School sat in the morning sun unprotected by trees. The lawn that surrounded it was freshly mowed into a crisp green carpet with cement foot paths dissecting it like a web. It was completely empty when I arrived.

I was the first in my homeroom class, but nevertheless, I took a seat in the back row. When the other kids filed into the room twenty minutes later, bunched up, laughing, straightening books and skirts, they glanced over at me quizzically and then continued with their banter.

At lunchtime, I followed the crowd to the cafeteria. I did not sit with the other girls, avoiding anything that could be interpreted as an advance, as want or desire or need. Instead, I sat alone in the rear of the large gray room and ate my strawberry yogurt slowly, letting the pink-streaked goo drip from my spoon back into the container.

I felt someone watching me eat.

I glanced up quickly and then away. The boy eyeing me had stick-straight blond hair and sharp bones, and though he was seated in the center of a crowded table, he seemed separate from his friends. I looked back at him. His eyes, from the distance, were as blue-black as the sea at night.

When the bell rang, I hurried to my next class, English, and then to history and finally math.

The next morning, I saw him walking toward me with a group of his friends. We looked at each other as we passed.

I found myself looking for him in the cafeteria at lunchtime, in the hallway, outside the gym, but he was not there.

On the third day, Wednesday, I was walking down the front steps of the school and onto the cement path at three o'clock when he came up behind me.

"Hi."

"Hi." I took a pack of Winstons out of my back pocket and lit one, then offered him the pack. "You want one?"

"I don't smoke. Thanks, though."

As we walked, I stole a sideways glance. His face seemed to be pulled so tight I could see the shape of his skull through the skin.

"What's your name?" he asked.

"Marta."

"Marta what?"

"Marta Clark."

He nodded. "Jack Pierce," he said.

Eight

I NOTICED, AS WE CONTINUED WALKING, THAT PEOPLE were looking at us, girls, following our progress, querying it, their eyes squinted in puzzlement.

"Do they always watch you like that?" I asked.

"Who?"

"The girls. Your roving fan club."

Jack turned around, glanced at them, and shrugged. "I don't know."

I smiled. He was one of the boys who took it for granted, the attention, the ardor. It no longer even interested him. He could take it or leave it according to whim, his own damn whim. I knew that I would never be one of them, those girls eyeing him so proprietarily, never could be even if I wanted to. I would never be invited to their parties or their shopping expeditions, would never share giggling crushes on pop stars and movie actors and high school track stars like Jack. I only dimly suspected that was why he was walking with me, talking to me with a slight tremor in his voice.

"So rumor has it you're from Germany," he said. "How old were you when you came to America?"

"Nine."

"It must have been hard, leaving everything you knew."

"It was all right."

"Why did your parents come?"

I stared at him for a moment. "Do you always ask this many questions?"

"Only if I'm interested."

I shrugged. "Well, it's the land of opportunity, isn't it?"

I glanced up at him. He was half a foot taller than me, with broad shoulders and muscular arms. The narrow triangle of skin at the top of his white oxford shirt was deeply tanned. There was something overwhelmingly clean about him, despite the blond hair that fell rebelliously an inch longer than all the other boys', the loose shirttails, the buttons on his knapsack. "Pierce,

146

huh? Are you related to the Pierce store?" Pierce's took up a half-block downtown and was mentioned in every guidebook to the area, an unusual hybrid of expensive china and jewelry, gadgets both practical and rare, toiletries and silk scarves and homemade jams, that served tourists and locals alike.

"Yup."

"Oh."

He stopped short. "What does that mean?"

"Nothing."

"Right." He paused. "Sorry. It's just that people always figure they know something about me once they find out my family owns Pierce's. You know what I mean?"

"Yeah, I think I do."

We walked to the end of the school's property in silence and stopped when we reached the curb, hovering on its edges, uncertain of where to go next.

"Are you busy on Saturday night?" Jack asked.

"I'm always busy." The motel with its chores, its endless round of dirty laundry and soiled sinks, loomed just to the side of my days, my nights.

"Oh."

"No," I added quickly. "I mean, nothing I can't get out of."

"Will you then?"

"Will I what?"

"Get out of it?"

"Okay."

We smiled shyly at each other and then shifted our eyes nervously away.

Maybe it began with loving Jack.

I sat on the weathered wooden railing at the entrance

to the Breezeway, waiting for him. I could smell the grill being fired up by one of the weekend's party of fishermen, five fraternity brothers enjoying a twenty-year reunion. I could hear their raucous laughter, just beginning to be loosened up by beer; I knew the way it would hush and then ripple up behind me if I walked slowly past them. I kept my back to them.

When Jack drove up at exactly seven o'clock in a large green Oldsmobile convertible, I jumped off the railing and got into the car before he could get out to greet me.

"Am I late?" he asked.

"No."

He waited while I settled in beside him on the white vinyl seat and then he drove off.

"Where are we going?"

"I thought we could go to Mangrove Mary's for dinner. Have you ever been there?"

"No." The truth was I had never been on a date before, never sat in a car beside a boy, the entire evening ahead of us in all of its languid uncertainty. My left foot was jiggling up and down and I crossed my legs to still it.

"I want to hear all about your life in Germany," he said.

"Why?"

He laughed. "I've never been anyplace. I need firsthand reports. Come on, tell me one thing."

"I was just a kid."

"You must remember some things. What was your town like?"

"Dortmarr? Nothing, just an industrial town."

"Oh."

"I did go to Berlin once, though."

148

"You did?"

I swam in the excitement of his voice, in the reflection of myself I found there, cosmopolitan, sophisticated.

"Did you see the wall?"

"Sure." I offered up a brief description.

"God, you're lucky," Jack exclaimed.

"Why?"

"You've already done so much. I haven't done shit. Not yet, anyway."

I squinted and lit a cigarette, bending beneath the dashboard to keep the match from going out. The smoke blew back into our faces before streaming out into the wind.

"Didn't anyone ever tell you those things were bad for you?" Jack asked.

"I like a lot of things that are bad for me."

"Like what?"

"Like you," I replied with a bravado I did not feel. It was what I knew, that front, and I clutched at it now as if it were the sole familiar dialect in a foreign country. I tipped my head back and let the wind lick through my hair, opening my mouth to the soft night air scented with jasmine and insecticide.

"What makes you think I'll be bad for you?" he asked.

"Maybe you won't. Maybe I'll be bad for you."

He laughed. "Christ, I hope so."

We pulled up to a low wooden building nestled on a curve of the intracoastal, parked the car and walked up a planked deck lined with yellow hibiscus to the restaurant's entrance. Inside, potted palms stood in the corners and large ceiling fans whirred softly overhead. The dining room was filled with men and women freshly showered after a day of lounging on the beach. It was January, tourist season was in full swing. The hostess showed us to a table, but before we were seated, Jack asked, "Can't we eat outside?" The small round tables that lined the deck overlooking the water were completely empty, despite the crowd inside. "You sure?" the hostess asked doubtfully.

Jack glanced at me and I nodded in agreement. "Yes," he answered firmly.

We stepped out onto the deserted deck and took a corner table. The waitress brought us a small candle in a royal blue glass holder and the light shone up in our faces, a nimbus in the dark. We sat quietly for a moment, looking out at the motionless azure river.

In an instant, mosquitoes began to swarm around us, clustering on our legs, our arms, buzzing beneath our noses, tickling our cheeks, nibbling our calves.

"So this is why no one's sitting out here," Jack muttered as I swatted a mosquito on my thigh, leaving a tiny bulb of brown goo and blood. "I'm sorry. Do you want to go inside?"

"No. I like it here." The empty deck, quiet and distant from the busyness on the other side of the glass wall, seemed safer somehow, with no one to watch, to judge. Across the water, the state park was a singular wall of pines, black on black. And just beyond, the white lights of the highway curved brightly and then snaked off into the night.

When the waitress returned, clearly miffed at having to venture outside, we ordered grilled mahimahi steaks and Budweisers. No one asked for proof of age and we ordered a second round as soon as the waitress showed up with the first.

At first, there was only the cold beer, the darkness,

the mosquitoes. In the distance, I could see the docks of the Breezeway, the white boats moored for the night bobbing quietly in the water.

I moistened my lips with the tip of my tongue and tried to think of something to say. It was so much harder here, with Jack, than lying down with the men, where all I had to do was close my eyes, and no one expected anything except silence and malleability.

Jack looked down into his beer bottle as if searching for a topic of conversation there. "Do you have any brothers or sisters?" he asked.

"No. What about you?"

"No. It's just me. Maybe my parents wouldn't watch me so closely if there was someone else in the house. They have my whole life mapped out for me. You know what I mean?"

"No," I answered. "Actually, I don't. My mother doesn't know how to map out *her* life, much less my life. My mother does not know how to map out breakfast."

"You're lucky."

"You think so?"

"Sure. My parents have it all planned. I'm going to go to college at St. Delaville in the fall, where my father went. I'll study business. You know, how to increase efficiency, drive up profits, fascinating stuff like that. And then I'm going to come back and take over the store. I'm going to marry and have two kids and I'll probably never leave Florida."

"Do they have the girl all picked out?"

He laughed grimly. "Probably."

"Is that what you want?"

"I don't know. I guess I've never really thought about it." He leaned back in his chair, stretching his legs

151

beneath the table. I felt his calf brush mine. "They're older. You ever hear of the change-of-life baby? That's me. I'm their only hope. With the store and all. I guess I owe them that much."

"I don't see why you owe them anything."

Jack looked at me quizzically, as if the idea was so alien to him that he could think of no response.

"Have you ever been to New York City?" I asked.

"No."

"That's where I'm going to go. Someplace with more than three streets and five bars."

"When? "

"As soon as I can."

There was a long uncomfortable silence.

"You know the only time I ever feel really free?" Jack asked with a sudden intensity. "When I'm running. People think it's all about the meets and the trophies, but I don't give a shit about any of that. When I run, it's like I've discovered a way to suspend time. Everything else just disappears." He looked up sheepishly. "I guess that sounds crazy."

"No," I said. "It doesn't sound crazy at all."

He looked out at the water. In profile, I could see the deep planes of his cheekbones, the sharp line of his blond hair where it fell below his ears. I reached over and pressed my hand firmly to his neck. He turned, startled.

"Mosquito," I said. I smiled and took my hand slowly away.

"I lied a minute ago," Jack said quietly. "I have thought about it. You know what I want? To be a lawyer." He smiled, embarrassed. "Some big rebellion, huh? Right up there with Jack Kerouac. Right up there with goddamned Mick Jagger. Well, my mother

152

considers anything outside the famous Pierce's the same as running off to join the circus." He motioned for another beer and then leaned forward. "Did you watch the Watergate proceedings?"

I vaguely remembered the lineup of men on the television. "I didn't really pay too much attention," I replied, and saw a tint of disappointment wash across his face.

"See, this is the thing," he said. "The law works. It brought down the goddamned President, didn't it?"

"And that's what you want to do? Bring down presidents?"

"No. Well, I mean, if they're like Nixon, sure. But the law can change things, that's the point. Look at the Voting Rights Act. Look at the work the A.C.L.U. is doing." His blue-black eyes were an electric indigo now, backlit and excited.

I nodded silently. Beneath the table, I tapped my forefinger into the opposite palm, as if pressing the names into it. They were an orbit of details, of events, that I had only had the dimmest awareness. No one had ever told me that they mattered before.

Jack rested his beer on the table, looking wounded, mistaking my silence for boredom. "You probably think this is just a stage. That's what all of them think."

I didn't know if he meant his parents, or the other girls he had dated. "I don't think that," I said.

Our eyes met, assessing, approving.

"You shouldn't let them do it," I said.

"Do what?"

"Your parents. You shouldn't let them tell you what to do."

"It's not that simple. When my grandfather came here from up north, the town had gone bust. He built Pierce's

153

from nothing and turned it into the biggest store between Palm Beach and St. Augustine. He made it through the Depression, the 1935 hurricane, the war, all of it. That's the problem. I understand my parents wanting me to keep it going. There really is no one else. I don't know what to do. What about you? What do you want to be?" he asked.

I had never thought of *being* anything, just of getting out. "I don't care, as long as it's not here," I said.

"God, I know."

We both laughed and then it died out, this laughter which met above us, hovered, faded. We heard crickets in the distance, and the sound of dishes inside, and ceiling fans and couples having fun on a Saturday night. Inside, the band had begun to play covers of the Supremes.

"I lied about something, too," I said.

"What?"

"I never actually went to Berlin or saw the wall. The only big city I've ever been to besides my big ten minutes in New York is Hamburg. We had to go there to get the boat, but all we did was eat in a *Konditerei* and then go back to our hotel room. Not exactly what you'd call the grand tour."

"Why did you lie about something like that?" Jack asked.

"I thought you'd think I was more interesting."

He laughed. "You're pretty damn interesting as it is."

"It must be the beer."

After dinner, we drove to the public beach.

A cool breeze wafted off the sea and wrapped around us as we strolled on the hard wet sand. The ocean was a lapis-tinged black, the tips of its modest waves washing across our feet and then receding. The empty lifeguard

154

benches cast ominous shadows, and in the distance we saw other teenagers walking on the jetty, holding beers, holding hands. We headed in the opposite direction. He put his arm around me, finding a place in the curve between my waist and my hip. "I've never met anyone like you," he said.

"How do you know? You don't know me yet."

"I know that you're different from the other girls around here." He leaned over to kiss me.

I felt his lips, soft and salty, and then his tongue, tentative at first, and then bolder, drifting through my mouth, more intimate than all the harsh invasions of the past.

The next morning, I was carrying a stack of freshly laundered towels through the courtyard when I saw Jack drive up in his convertible. His arm, sinewy, perfectly proportioned, rested casually on the door. He was smiling as I walked over to him. "What are you doing here?"

"I thought you might want to go for a ride."

I ran my fingers through my hair, glancing back at the motel. I had fourteen rooms to clean, and the laundry to do. I turned back to him. There were pale purple rings, soft and puffy, beneath his eyes. I smiled. "Just give me a minute."

I hurriedly dumped the towels in the laundry room, keeping an eye out for Garner and Astrid. I didn't dare go back inside the apartment to get my swimsuit.

I sat a few inches closer to Jack than I had the night before as he drove. "Where are we going?" I asked.

"You'll see."

"I hate surprises," I said.

"You do?" He looked at me solemnly, gathering

155

information.

"Yes."

"I'm taking you to a place I know. A spoil island."

"What's a spoil island?"

"They were made when the Army Corps of Engineers dredged the intracoastal so boats could have easier access between the river and the ocean. They dumped these huge loads of sand and silt in piles just to get them out of the way and they became islands. Trees grew, shrubs. I don't know, somehow they just took. You can't keep things from growing here."

We pulled up onto an embankment and got out of the car. A rowboat was hidden beneath a large cluster of mangrove, and Jack pulled it out and threw the canvas bag he was carrying onto the seat. He launched the dinghy onto the water, held it while I climbed in, and then jumped in after me.

He began to row upriver. We were going against the tide and I watched the muscles in his arms bulging in a steady sinuous rhythm with his efforts.

"Is this your boat?" I asked.

"No. It belongs to this old black guy who lives in the trailer park out on Dohenny Drive. He doesn't use it much anymore because of his arthritis. He just fishes on the bridge over the intracoastal instead." He smiled shyly. "Sometimes I bring him coffee, or worms. That's how we met, buying worms one day. Anyway, he doesn't mind if I use his boat."

We passed a few tiny islands before we got to the one Jack had in mind. "This is it," he said.

He jumped out of the boat a few yards from the island's ragged shore, and began to pull it the rest of the way. I followed his lead and helped pull from the other side as the sludge of the riverbed seeped between my toes.

The air was suddenly still as we sat down on the white sand, heavy with the scent of heat and algae. Behind us, the center of the island was a compression of pines, dark and humming with mosquitoes. The only other sound was a far-off motorboat, cutting through the water and then waning. Jack reached into the striped canvas bag and pulled out a bottle of Mateus rosé, what we were all drinking that year. He nestled it into the sand at water's edge where the river would keep it cold.

"You knew I'd come?" I asked.

"I hoped."

We looked at each other.

"Do you want to swim?" he asked. "I'm pretty hot."

"I didn't bring a suit."

"Oh."

We stood facing each other awkwardly.

I shrugged, smiled. "What the hell." I quickly slid out of my shorts and shirt while Jack stared at a broken shell by his feet. I never wore a bra and I stood for a moment in my cotton panties, but that seemed silly, so I took them off too. Jack was wearing baggy green trunks, but he stepped out of them, smiling with a shy complicity at our daring.

We waded through the silt on the far side of the island and then we both dove in at once.

My hair streamed out behind me and my nipples hardened as I navigated through circles of warm and then icy water. I heard Jack break the surface, gasping, and still I stayed beneath.

After a half hour of swimming, we went onshore, running to our towels, both of us embarrassed to be naked in the open air. Jack held up his shirt to me. "Do you want this?"

"Thanks." I slipped into it, and the smell of him enwrapped me.

When we had both pulled on our shorts, our backs to each other, we sat down on the sand, hugging our knees to our chests while we passed the bottle of cold sweet wine back and forth.

"I've never brought anyone here before," he said. "I just want you to know that." He took a long gulp of wine. "Usually I just come here to get away from people. Do you ever want to do that? Just get completely away from everyone?"

"Yeah." I lay back, and felt the sand sink beneath my body. The sun and the wine were making everything warm and hazy. "There was a place I used to go in Germany," I said so softly that he had to lean closer to hear. "There was this building on our street that had burned down. It was just a shell, with rats and all. I used to climb inside the rubble and make a little fortress out of some of the loose bricks. Sometimes I'd stay there all afternoon, just reading or, you know, thinking. No one could find me there." I remembered the straggles of sun that would creep in through the cracks, carrying with it the distant voices of our street in Dortmarr, the women and the children hurrying about in the afternoon, and someplace out there Astrid, Astrid in her tight dresses and low necks, Astrid and her men. "I haven't found a place in Florida," I added quietly.

"You can come here," he said. "I mean, if you want to."

"Thanks." I took a swig of wine and wiped the dribble from my chin.

Jack propped himself up on his elbow, touching my neck with his fingertips. "Mosquito," he said.

He ran his fingertips down the side of my neck, my

158

shoulder, my arm.

My back arched and I bit my lip, suddenly terrified in a way I hadn't been with the others.

I rose quickly and, running, dove into the water, still wearing my shorts and his shirt.

It was late afternoon when we rowed back. Jack dropped me off a block from the Breezeway, as I requested. He reached over and when he kissed me, he tasted of wine and sand and sun. "Why can't I come in?" he asked.

"It's just better this way," I said.

He nodded and kissed me one last time.

Already, I knew I had to keep them separate, Jack and the motel, the others.

Garner was emptying the garbage by the pool when I walked by. "Where have you been all day?" he demanded.

"Out." I strode quickly to the office.

"Out," Garner muttered as he followed me. "Out. Well, we'd all like to go out, wouldn't we? But some of us actually have things to do. Some of us actually have duties."

In the kitchen, Astrid was humming along with Olivia Newton-John's "Have You Never Been Mellow" while she drenched a celery root salad with oil. She did not turn around.

I turned to Garner and found him looking at me straight in the eyes, and I looked back, emboldened by the day, by the very thought of Jack.

He left the kitchen without saying another word.

On Monday morning, Jack was waiting for me on the

school steps. His face broadened to a smile when he saw me. He did not kiss me hello, or reach to touch me amid the swirl of the other kids rushing past us. We only stood there for a moment, facing each other, flushed.

"Well," he said, "I guess we should go in."

"I guess."

"I have practice this afternoon but we could meet later," he said as we went through the door.

"Okay."

All day, I felt him moving through the hallways, densely fleshed, full-blooded, where everything and everyone else was suddenly reduced to shadows.

At three o'clock, I sat in the school library reading the *Flagerty Record* and the *Miami Herald* about the upcoming presidential election. The Florida primary was three weeks away and I studied the articles about the democratic field, crowded with names I had been hearing on the radio: Henry Jackson, George Wallace, Jimmy Carter. The words were suffused with an almost erotic vibrancy simply because I knew they were of interest to Jack.

I glanced out of the second-floor window at the track field below. A dozen boys in blue shorts and numbered tank tops were running, their legs suspended in midair as they flew over the hurdles. I got up and moved closer to the window, pressing my hands against it, looking for Jack.

When I spotted him, he was just finishing a heat. He turned around with his hand on his belly as he walked back to the coach. My heart quickened, certain that he would feel me watching him and look up, but he didn't. I gathered my books and hurried from the library.

I was standing by the bleachers, away from the few other spectators, when he noticed me and came jogging

160

over.

His breath was stilted when he reached my side. "Hi."

"Hi."

There was a film of sweat across his shoulders. "I'm almost done."

I nodded.

We stood six inches apart. Behind us, there was the steady sound of feet hitting the track. Jack reached over and slowly hooked his forefinger through mine.

We leaned in closer without speaking until our fingers were fully entwined, the heat gathering in our palms.

In the distance, the coach's whistle blew once, and then again, long and shrill. "You coming, Pierce, or are you too busy courting? "

Jack gradually pulled his fingers away. "I have to go." He took a few steps and then came back. "I'll meet you out front in half an hour."

I nodded and then watched him trot away from me across the near-empty field.

We did not go to the Hamburger Haven downtown or to the public beach where the other kids went, walking in couples or groups of three and four on the jetty, watching the late day surfers waiting in clumps for a wave, *the* wave. We didn't discuss it, discard it. We both understood the habit of solitude, I because I had been so much alone, Jack because he felt so much alone, so that now, together, we had a perfect excuse to indulge in what came naturally to us both.

We wanted only each other. Already.

Jack bought us Cokes, and we took them back to the track field and sat behind the empty bleachers.

The slats of the seats above us formed triangular shadows across the ground, where the scrupulously

161

groomed lawns petered out and sand poked through, even here, miles from the shore.

"I'll miss the beach," Jack remarked with the sad sweet air of one who is wavering on the brink of leaving but has gone no place yet, testing out the nostalgia before it has any real teeth.

"You mean when you go to college?"

"Afterwards. I think I'll have to live in cities. Washington, maybe." He smiled at me. "Or New York. If I do well in law school, who knows?" He took another sip of his soda.

"Oh, I'm sure you'll do well. You do well at everything, don't you?"

"Why do you say that?"

"You just seem the type."

"What type is that?"

"Your type," I said. "Anyway, cities are better. No one will know you're the Pierces' only son and heir. Isn't that what you want?"

"No," he answered. "That's not why I want to go away. I want to go away because I have to if I'm going to do anything that matters."

"Oh." Chastened, I felt my face flush.

"Were you serious when you said you didn't know what you wanted to be?" he asked.

I made rings in the dirt with the bottom of my Coke bottle. "Do you promise you won't laugh?"

"I promise."

"Well, I don't know exactly, but . . . See, I listen to the radio."

He waited for me to go on, to explain what I had only the haziest notion of myself.

"Not music," I said, "but the news. Maybe I'd like to do something like that."

"You mean journalism?"

"I don't know." I'd never actually defined it that way before. I only knew that the voices in the dark came from a different hemisphere, one that I longed to escape to. "It's nothing. It was just an idea."

He regarded me seriously and then smiled. "It's a good idea."

"You think so?"

"Sure."

That's how simply it became accepted between us, my future profession, his, secret dreams that we elaborated only with each other, turning them this way and that, expanding them, filling them in, until they began to feel like fact. How anxious we were to believe in each other, how young we were, how hungry.

I looked away, embarrassed, and noticed the Jimmy Carter button on Jack's knapsack. "He's got a lot of competition," I remarked.

"I know. But what are our choices, huh? Wallace, the fucking racist? At least Carter's talking about the right things. What does Ford care about, besides pardoning Nixon and getting in a good game of golf? The thing is, I think Carter is good," he said. "Maybe it's childish to divide people into good and bad, but I really think you can." He paused. "You must think I'm awfully naïve. "

"I don't think that."

"What do you think?"

"About what?" I asked.

"About me."

"You're all right, if you like the knight-in-shining-armor type."

"And do you?"

"It depends what's underneath the armor."

He smiled and leaned over to kiss me, and we fell to

163

the sandy ground, pressing, stroking, hurrying to learn each other's shape and taste.

There were none of the feints and parries of dating. We understood from the very beginning that the first and only thing that had ever really made sense was each other. Why should we pretend otherwise?

It was not easy to find time to be together, though. Jack worked most weekdays from three-thirty to six-thirty and all day on Saturdays at the store, helping customers, ordering stock, balancing the register at the end of the day. Afterwards, he was expected to drive home with his father for dinner. He had never done otherwise. And I had the motel.

We stole moments together before and after school.

We talked on the phone for hours.

Some evenings we met at the Carter campaign headquarters downtown, a tiny storefront behind the Five-and-Dime crammed with boxes of bumper stickers, buttons, and leaflets. We sat on the dusty linoleum floor beneath a tri-colored poster of the governor's toothy grinning face, stuffing leaflets into envelopes.

The windowless room was hot from lack of air-conditioning and our faces quickly grew a shiny film of sweat as we stole glances at each other when the other volunteers weren't looking, our knees touching, our arms brushing up against each other, all our righteousness and sense of mission mixing with our hormones so it was impossible to tell one from the other, and we had to sneak off to the hallway, kissing until our lips grew sore.

On the last Saturday night in February, I sat on the Breezeway's gate, swinging my legs impatiently back and forth as I had the first time Jack had come. It was almost nine when he drove up. The crescent moon was smudged with fog and I nestled close to him in the car.

"You've really never been to a fair?" he asked.

"Shocking but true. I'm not going to have to wrestle a hog, am I?"

"Absolutely. And rope a steer."

"That's okay, I've wrestled worse. And roped more."

Jack laughed and gave my hand a squeeze.

When we got to the site, we were directed by volunteers from the Jaycees wielding flashlights like batons to the makeshift parking lot across the road. We paid the two-dollar entrance fee and walked onto the muddy grounds. The fair swelled around us and we clasped hands tightly, adjusting to the crowds, the rides that made swooping arcs of light against the dark sky, the gongs of the nickel games, the cries of overexcited children, and the burnt sugary smell of cotton candy. I nudged Jack with the corner of my elbow. "Look."

A few yards away, we saw Mr. Dryer, Flagerty High's assistant principal, walking with a giant red balloon in one hand, and a half-eaten vanilla ice-cream cone dripping down the other. Jack pulled me quickly away before Mr. Dryer could spot us and we dodged behind a tent set up for prize pigs, enclosed in our game of hide-and-seek. We huddled behind a pole, assaulted by the smell of animal shit. "Did he see us?" Jack whispered.

"I don't think so."

We laughed, spies, thieves—momentarily safe.

"Let's go on the Ferris wheel," I suggested, and we wove through the crowd, ducking our heads so no one would recognize us.

We took our place in one of the seats and an old man

with a deeply pockmarked face buckled us in. "No standing up," he muttered apathetically.

The wheel lurched forward and we circled once and then stopped almost at the top, the fair below us an intricate network of bodies moving in and out of the green-and-white-striped tents, clustered about food stands and games, greedy for pleasure, for prizes. Jack put his arm around me and we kissed, our tongues lost in each other's mouths as we swung back and forth, suspended in the night.

It took a moment for our feet to adjust to the ground when we disembarked.

"Are you hungry?" Jack asked.

"Not really." I turned to him. "Aren't you going to win me something?"

"Like what?"

"I don't know. Anything."

He smiled and stepped up to a rifle range with three rows of moving tin ducks. Above, pastel teddy bears hung from a rope, waiting to be claimed. He handed over a quarter and took his position beside the other shooters. As soon as the gong sounded, the ducks started moving quickly by as Jack aimed and fired, aimed and fired, slower, more deliberately than his fellow players. When the gong sounded again and the ducks stopped moving, he had lost. He turned around to me. "Sorry."

"That's okay."

He looked at me for a second and then decided to try again. This time, he fired faster, and won a small teddy bear with coarse blue fur and a red bow tie. He handed it to me with a flourish.

I clutched the teddy bear as we wandered away from the booth. For a moment, I was a different girl, the kind of girl boys won teddy bears at state fairs for, and everything else just fell away. I gave his arm a squeeze.

We walked past a tent where the deeply guttural crooning of a country singer reverberated within, a Belgian waffle stand clustered with children wiping pink strawberry streaks from their sated chins, a picture booth with cutouts of a bride and groom. When we came to a fortune-teller's booth, Jack slowed. A gypsy with long skirts and large discs of gold earrings, a turban, and painted crimson lips called out to us in an indistinguishable accent, "Read your palms. See your future. Love, wealth, health, learn what's in store for you. Find out if your love is true."

"C'mon. Let's go in," Jack said.

I looked over at the woman with her heavily lined eyes beckoning us. There were pointy stars about her booth, and hearts, and dollar signs. The gypsy crooked her finger, Come in, come in. "The tarot can answer any question," she promised.

Jack began to reach into his pocket for the price of a reading.

"No," I said. "Why do you want to bother with that crap?" I took a few quick strides away.

He looked at me, puzzled, and then hurried to my side.

We wended through the crowds milling about, the tired parents searching for lost children, the groups of teenage girls and boys, the bored state troopers.

"Let's go," I said.

We drove with the top down, despite the cold, turning the heat on so that our feet grew hot while our faces remained chilled by the wind. It was close to eleven, but we weren't ready to go home. "Do you want to go to the island?" Jack asked.

"Now?"

He nodded.

"Okay. Sure."

We drove the rest of the way in silence, knowing where we were going, knowing why.

The boat was where we had left it hidden in the sea grape, and we pulled it out and launched it onto the river.

The sky, the water, were black, empty.

We heard the distant sounds of cars going over the intracoastal on their way home from the fair, and the ripple of the oars dipping into the water, pulling, withdrawing, dipping. We did not speak.

When we neared the island, we took off our sneakers, rolled up our jeans, and waded through the cold water to the shore, pulling the boat along.

"Are you okay?" he asked as we settled onto the beach.

I nodded.

He spread his jacket on the sand and we sat huddled on it, kissing. He slipped his hand beneath my sweater, touching my clammy skin, the knobs of my spine, the curve of my waist. I did not protest. I sank down into the soft sand. I felt his hair tickle the base of my throat.

He stopped, raised his eyes to me. "Are you a virgin?" he asked.

My elbow scraped against a shell as I dug it deep into the sand. "Yes," I whispered.

"Are you sure you want to do this?"

"Yes."

He nodded, smiling gently.

He kissed my breasts, tasting them, absorbing them, releasing them. We paused only long enough to slide out of our jeans, rushing now, rushing to it.

For a single fearsome moment, I wondered if he would feel something in me, an openness where he was expecting resistance, wondered if he would somehow feel the other men. I shut my eyes, willing the thought away. It was another girl in those dark afternoons, those rooms.

I wanted suddenly to feel Jack all the way up to my belly, my heart, my lungs, wanted him to wash out everything that had gone before. I was certain that he could.

When he came, he called out my name and his eyes rolled back into his head.

I felt the heat like circles in the water, spreading ever wider until that was all there was, and I let out one sharp cry.

We both lay completely still.

"Are you okay?" he asked.

"Yes."

He pulled me closer into his embrace, protective and warm.

We lay quietly in the dark, holding each other, staring up at the blurry slivered moon. "I love you," he said.

"I love you, too. " I did not fear saying it because it was so soon, I simply said it, repeated it, "I love you," my voice cracking with it, giddy with it, transformed by the revelation of it, because I knew that it was true.

He leaned up on his elbow and looked directly into my eyes. "I mean it."

"Me too."

Much later, he drove me home in the stillness, the absolute stillness of Flagerty at three A.M.

I sat up in bed watching the dawn rising from my narrow window. The grass of the Breezeway's courtyard was just beginning to glisten with dew. In another couple of hours, I would have to rise, wipe down the white metal tables, already mottled with rust, and open up the large blue-and-white-striped umbrellas. I watched the progress of a spider outside the pane, spinning its fragile sticky web. The smell of the bulging garbage bags behind the apartment crept in, foul with rotting fish carcasses, citrus rinds, beer cans, the weekend's remains. I lay back, running my hand slowly over my naked chest, my stomach, running it where he had been.

For the first time since we had moved here, the motel held my body but no longer contained my mind.

Jack drove by at three o'clock that afternoon. I stood with my hands on the convertible's door, looking down, both of us smiling shyly, testing the new ground we found ourselves on, testing each other—are you there?

And we each found the other waiting there, at the beginning, when the promise of love is an evanescent secret to be held aloft, full of promise not yet caught or scratched.

"Can we meet later?" he asked.

"Yes."

On the night that Carter won the Democratic primary by four percentage points, the first time George Wallace had ever lost in the South, I lay in bed listening to the radio.

It was ten o'clock when I heard a rapping on my window. Peering out, I saw Jack crouched in the path, grinning in the dark.

I opened the window carefully, but it squeaked loudly nevertheless.

"What are you doing here?" I asked.

"Come on, let's go celebrate."

I looked at him, with his disheveled hair and his grin, and I motioned for him to wait while I slid on a pair of jeans and a sweatshirt and slithered out the window.

We tiptoed down the path clutching hands, suppressing the laughter that erupted the moment we climbed into his waiting car.

"How did you know which room was mine?" I asked.

"I didn't. I think I gave an old lady two doors down a heart attack."

He had picked up a six-pack of beer and we shared one as we drove along Route 1. We did not go to the island that night, but parked by the new state park that was under construction across the street from the ocean. Jack cut off the ignition and we sat in the front seat staring out at the sea and the lights far up the shore.

I reached down and opened another can and we toasted Carter's success.

"I have something for us," Jack said. He opened the glove compartment and pulled out a box of kitchen matches. Inside, there was a single skinny joint wrapped in yellow paper. He lit it up, narrowing his eyes as he inhaled, and the musky sweet scent filled the front seat.

By the time the joint was finished, we were both so stoned that our laced fingers entranced us for a full five minutes. When he managed to disengage his hand, Jack turned on the radio, swimming through the dial until he found a station out of Palm Beach that was playing Donna Summer, K.C. and the Sunshine Band, Hot Chocolate, all the disco we usually despised. He got out of the car and went around to my door, opening it and offering me his hand. "Care to dance?"

The bass pounded from the tinny car stereo as we danced wildly about the tennis court, our arms and legs gyrating until, breathless, we came together, not quite dancing but swaying in a tight dizzying hug. I could feel Jack's erection grinding into me just above my pubic bone as we clutched each other, pressing in until neither of us could stand it and we ran to the edges of the woods, collapsing on a bed of fallen pine needles, diving burrowing carving into each other.

To this day, the dusky smell of pines still makes me weak and wet and sad.

We continued to avoid places where others went, and stole kisses in darkened stairwells, climbed out of bedroom windows to meet in the night, our desire lurking in corners and crevices, waiting only for the clandestine touch that claimed it. Sometimes, we just drove, the top down, the brilliant starry dome of the Florida sky above us as we talked about the thoughts and desires we kept hidden from all others—the future away from Flagerty, the law, journalism, each other, change. It all suddenly seemed so plausible now that there was someone else who believed it so.

We drove down Indian River Drive, with its newly built houses so large and imposing. We drove along Route 1 by the ocean. And we drove, most nights, to the boat hidden beneath the sea grape and rowed in the dark, the thin skein of white lights behind us, to the spoil island.

Neither of us spoke of it, of each other, to anyone else.

When Rosie called I almost mentioned Jack, wanting at least to say his name out loud, but I didn't. It was too important, too overwhelming, and too new to share, to be reduced to words, neatly contained in sentences and conventions. It had nothing to do, after all, with teenage dating, holding hands in the hallway, ice-cream sundaes, proms. It had nothing to do with anything but us.

Maybe it began with Jack loving me.

I kept waiting for him to change his mind.

As I went about my duties at the motel, changing beds, bleaching toilets, avoiding Garner, the specter of Jack was everywhere. I imagined him watching me as I went from room to room, guest to guest, as if he could somehow see my every movement, and I adjusted them accordingly. I was polite to the guests, and scrupulously distant from the men, lowering my eyes away from theirs.

I began to listen more closely to the announcers' voices on the radio, and carefully studied the reporters on television. I scoured the library for biographies of journalists, and worked hard to improve my grades.

Jack gave my best self back to me, that was his gift.

And it began to feel real, to feel right, even to me.

Lurking behind every well-planned sentence, though, every careful step, waiting for me when I climbed into bed at night, was the fear that Jack would see something, smell something—and turn away, repelled.

But he didn't.

How could I not do anything to hold on to that?

Nine

ALL THROUGH JUNE, THE ROTATING DIGITAL CLOCK and thermometer that towered over the front lawn of the Sun Coast Bank on Route 1 read 83°.

"Who do they think they're fooling?" Jack asked as we drove by. "The tourists?"

"There are no tourists," I replied. "Who'd be stupid

enough to come here in this weather?"

"Well, everyone else knows it hasn't gone below ninety-five in Flagerty since the middle of May."

I ran the cold can of Tab I was drinking across my forehead. Though it was only ten in the morning, the sun was everywhere, relentless and inescapable, drenching the open car in its scalding white glare. We drove the rest of the way downtown in silence. We had parted only a few hours ago, in the black pre-dawn, and exhaustion prickled beneath the surface of our skin, dulling the need for conversation.

Jack parked a block from the Pelican Diner and we got out of the car. The street sign on the corner was draped in plastic red, white, and blue ribbons. Flagerty had been gearing up for the Bicentennial for months. Store windows tried to outdo each other with the number and size of their flags, and the summer sales merchandise was bedecked in the trappings of patriotism.

Jack looked over at me as we walked. "Tired?" he asked.

"I'm all right."

When we reached the Pelican Diner, there was a handwritten sign taped to the front door: "Closed until September." The windows were dark behind blue-and-white gingham curtains.

"Shit," Jack muttered. "They always used to stay open in summer."

"It's too hot to eat anyway."

We headed back to the car, avoiding the corner that was dominated by Pierce's. Jack took my hand and our palms grew instantly moist. From a distance, we saw a young black boy in a suit and tie on the opposite side of the street. On both legs, he wore complicated metal braces that glistened in the sun as he walked alone in the direction of the Baptist church on Gladiola Street. He worked slowly, throwing his crutches a few feet ahead and then sliding his legs up to them. His hair was cut short and his oval face and large eyes were shiny. He was smiling beatifically. Jack turned and watched him, step, slide, step, slide, until he finally reached the front steps of the church.

"Why on earth would he believe in God?" I asked.

Jack didn't answer. He continued watching until the boy disappeared behind the heavy carved wooden doors. He turned slowly back to me. "What do you want to do? We can get some food and go to the island."

"All right."

We stopped by a 7-Eleven and then drove with our groceries to the boat.

"I've been thinking," he said as he rowed. "About September."

I flinched. In September Jack would be starting college in St. Delaville, three hours away. I had missed so much school that I had to make up a semester.

"Why don't you come to St. Delaville when you graduate?" he said.

"My parents would never pay for that."

"There are scholarships."

"I'd never get one."

"You make Chicken Little look like a goddamned optimist," he teased.

"And you make Pollyanna look like a fallen angel."

He laughed. "That's why we're so good together. We balance each other out."

"You really think I could get a scholarship?"

"Sure. Why not? Your grades are good now. And I could make some calls."

175

"Maybe."

When we got to the island, I watched Jack unpack our picnic lunch of cold chicken and beers. His back was smooth and browned, and I was filled with a pang of longing, forgetting for an instant that he was mine.

Almost mine.

We swam first, as we usually did, as if to wash off the external world, so that when we climbed out of the water, we were cleansed down to our truest selves, the selves that existed only when we were together.

"Did you mean it?" I asked as we dried off and climbed back into our clothes.

"About what?"

"About St. Delaville."

He wiped a single wet tendril from my eyes. "Yes."

We kissed once, wet on wet, and then sat down to eat.

"I've decided to tell my parents I'm going to go to law school," Jack said in between bites of his chicken leg.

"Why tell them now? Why don't you just wait and see what happens?"

"Because I've made up my mind. It's what I want to do. And I don't want to live under false pretenses for the next four years. If nothing else, I owe them honesty."

"What do you think they'll say?"

He smiled. "They'll probably blame it all on you."

I grimaced. He was joking, but his parents despised me and couldn't wait to see Jack safely out of my reach.

"And they'd be right," he said.

"What do you mean?"

He was serious now, resting his gnawed chicken leg back on the paper plate, reaching for my knee. "I want us to be together," he said.

"We are together."

"I mean for good." He leaned over and kissed me.

Everything inside pitched. "What does that have to do with law school?" I asked.

"I don't know. Nothing. Everything. I guess I just want us to be clear about things."

I took a sip of my beer.

"I was thinking," he said. "We could live together. In St. Delaville. We could get an apartment."

"Your parents would love that part."

"I wasn't actually planning on telling them."

"Honest Abe tells a lie?"

"I may be honest, but I'm not a fucking idiot."

I laughed.

"They have a journalism department," Jack said. "It's not great. But they have their own radio station. It's something, anyway " He looked out at the water and then back to me. "I can't imagine going without you."

He pulled me to him, and we kissed with greasy lips, falling back onto the scratchy wool blanket, melding into each other, here, just here.

He lay still inside of me for a long time after he had come, reluctant to leave. "Imagine this every day," he said.

"Imagine this every night."

We spent the rest of the afternoon talking about what it would be like to go to sleep and wake up every morning together, away from parents, away from Flagerty, away from everything but each other in a place where no one knew us.

"You're serious about all this?" I asked as we were packing up to leave.

"Yes."

"You really think we can?"

"Yes," he answered firmly. "Don't you?"

177

I smiled.

"Do I take that as a yes?" he asked.

"Yes."

We took a final swim at nightfall. As we tread water, he wrapped his legs around my hips and entered me, our bodies weightless but rooted to each other deep within. Everything other than where we were touching seemed to float away into the water, into the dark.

From that day on, we both considered our futures settled, entwined. The rest was just getting there.

Jack, elated, rushed headlong at it, our future.

He called the St. Delaville student union and found the name of a landlady in town who rented him an apartment by phone that would be big enough when I joined him. He called the financial aid office and got all the necessary applications. He continued on, tying up strings, knotting them twice, wary that I might change my mind.

Though I never gave him any reason to think that. A part of me was already there, in an apartment I imagined in a town I had never seen.

The present faded to a shadow, insubstantial, unreal, now that I was leaving.

I was in a light doze when I heard the door to room 203, which I was supposed to be cleaning, creak open. I opened my eyes and saw Garner standing in the doorway, looking down at me. He closed the door behind him. The air-conditioning had been off and the air was stifling, fetid. He didn't say anything, just continued to look down on me. Finally, he motioned to the cleaning supplies on the floor. "What's all this?" he demanded.

I didn't answer.

"You too tired from being out with your boyfriend all night to do your duty around here?"

"What business is that of yours?" I retorted, sitting up, hugging my knees to my chest.

"You little slut. You think your boyfriend is going to remember you when he goes off to college? Forget it. Not Mr. Pierce. He'll find some nice girl there and before you know it, he won't even remember your name. You can count on that."

"Did anyone ever tell you you're an asshole?" I hissed.

Garner tripped over the bucket filled with rags as he took a step closer to the bed, his face contorting into a sour laugh. "You know what you are to him? Practice, that's what you are. Just practice. You don't think you'll ever be anything more than that, do you? I don't care what he tells you now."

I lurched from the bed and slapped him across the face.

He grabbed my hand, still laughing. His other hand was reaching behind my back, pulling me to him.

Suddenly we heard the door swing open. Astrid stood in the doorway, the sun behind her, smiling nervously. "What's going on in here?"

Garner released me and stepped back. "Your daughter seems to think she's too good for the likes of us. Seems to think she's above doing a little cleaning."

Astrid, momentarily nonplussed, turned to Garner. "Someone's on the phone for you, hon," she said. "Something about a lawn mower, I don't know. You'd better go check."

Garner glared at me one last time and then stormed out of the room.

"Bastard," I muttered.

179

Astrid sighed as she bent down to pick up the bucket. "Come on, I'll help you."

I began to steal small amounts of money when I sat at the front desk checking people in and out. Ten dollars, maybe twenty. Astrid and Garner were too lax, too lost to realize. It would be money to live on in St. Delaville with Jack. And anyway, I had earned it. Garner and Astrid never paid me.

I did not tell Jack about the money that grew in my top drawer.

He, too, was working hard, saving what he could.

We told no one of our plans.

Only together during our stolen hours on the island did we let them out to prosper, the apartment we would share, the meals, the bed, the life.

The Bicentennial came and went, and the Democratic and Republican conventions, the Montreal Olympics; twenty-nine people died of a mysterious disease at the American Legion convention in Philadelphia. The summer gave every indication of passing.

What did we talk about then?

Labor Day Weekend, fast approaching.

Jack leaving.

Missing each other.

Writing, calling

January, when I would move to St. Delaville and we would be together all the time, forever. One of those words we used then, *forever*.

It is hard now to remember if I ever really believed we would get there.

Certainly Jack did.

180

But we were different. He had never been truly disappointed before, he had never been truly scared.

I clung desperately to the belief even as I waited for the blow that would destroy it.

Each day, I studied my calendar. Five weeks, three, now two weeks to go until Jack left.

The thermometer hit 98° by nine in the morning.

I was sitting at the front desk reading the back-to-school issue of *Glamour* magazine, filled with clear-skinned, clear-eyed girls, when one of our only guests, Mrs. Patrick, came in. Though she never went anywhere, she was dressed formally in a crisp white floral shirtwaist dress hanging on her skeletal frame, stockings and high-heeled white sandals. I left my forefinger on my page and looked up.

"I asked for more towels yesterday'" Mrs. Patrick said.

"No one told me."

She frowned. "Well, I'm telling you now, aren't I?"

I got off my stool, went to the supply closet and got down two towels. There was a cigarette burn in one but I folded it so that it couldn't be seen.

"Here," I said, going back out and handing them to Mrs. Patrick.

As soon as she was gone, I returned to my magazine.

When the office door swung open again fifteen minutes later, I hardly looked up, expecting it to be Mrs. Patrick complaining about the burn hole in the towel.

But it wasn't Mrs. Patrick's voice I heard.

"Hello, Marta. It's good to see you again."

I looked up.

Frank Xavier stood in front of the desk, smiling.

I felt everything sink, just sink.

The magazine slipped to the floor.

"Oh, Mr. Xavier, what a nice surprise," Astrid exclaimed as she came into the office, curious to see who the stranger's voice belonged to. "I was beginning to wonder if you forgot about us."

"Now how could I do that?"

"We're glad to have you back. Would you like a room overlooking the water this time?"

"You know, Mrs. Clark, I'm a creature of habit. Funny thing about being on the road so much, you take whatever familiarity you can get." He shrugged, smiling. "I think I'll take the same room as last time, if you don't mind."

"Whatever you want." Astrid handed him the keys to room 110. "Marta, show Mr. Xavier the way."

I frowned.

"Oh, there's no need for that," Xavier said. "I remember."

I knew right then that this was how the end began.

I left the office and went back to my bedroom, locked the door and lay down, afraid to make a sound, afraid to breathe.

I heard the television go on in the living room and the raucous gaiety of a game show. I heard Astrid and Garner in the kitchen as they ate lunch. Later I heard the lawn mower sputter and die, and a single splash in the swimming pool.

And still, I did not move.

I was supposed to meet Jack by the gate at seven o'clock.

At 6:55, I ventured out. Garner and Astrid were watching television in the living room. They hardly looked up as I passed.

There was no one about. The fronds of palms cast long shadows across the courtyard. The only noise came from the rattling of cicadas' wings rising and falling in waves. I walked quickly to the pool area where the gray metal switch box sat mounted on the rotting redwood fence. I needed to turn the lights on before I left. In my haste, I didn't see the pile of bricks that Garner had left there, the remains of one of his forgotten projects. My big toe rammed into them. Pain shot through my foot to the core of my spine. I bent down, cursing as I massaged my toe. As soon as I could, I straightened up, flipped the switch, and hurried back through the courtyard.

The ocher curtains of the few rented rooms were illuminated with the flickering of television screens. The path was a matte gray, leading out to black road. I paused just beyond the office door and took a deep breath. The air, though swollen with humidity, was a relief after the hours locked inside.

I was at the end of the path when the door to room 110 swung open.

Frank Xavier stepped into my way. "Taking a stroll?" he asked.

I looked up. His right eye had three dark freckles on the retina.

"I always like evening walks myself," he said. "Do you want some company?"

"No. I'm meeting someone."

"I bet you are."

I saw Jack driving up. He honked once and I ran to the car before Xavier could say another word.

"Who was that you were talking to?" Jack asked as we took off.

"No one, just a guest."

He nodded.

"Do you mind if we go to the Hamburger Haven before we go to the island?" he asked. "I'm starving."

"Sure."

The neon light of the diner shone on the table between us, illuminating archipelagos of ancient grease.

I watched Jack eat a cheeseburger and listened as he spoke of—what?

The new leather suitcase his parents had given him, course selections, the sheets he had bought for the apartment, our apartment.

Tonight, his optimism and his certainty seemed so alien.

"Are you all right?" he asked as he finished his dinner.

"Yes. Why?"

"You seem, I don't know, distracted."

"Just tired," I said.

He smiled, nodded, kissed me, and I shut my eyes, for a moment I just shut my eyes.

Xavier was waiting for me when Jack dropped me off just after midnight.

He met me on the pavement.

"So you have a boyfriend now," he said.

I quickly glanced back to the road. Jack was gone.

Xavier took a step closer and touched my hair. "Do you charge him, too?"

I began to walk away from him but he grabbed me and pulled me back.

"You're too good for me now? With your pretty boy? Pretty boys don't understand you," he said.

"He understands me just fine."

"Not the way I do. I know just who you are."

I glared at him. "I don't do that anymore."

He laughed, twisting my arm as he pulled me closer. "Girls like you don't change."

As I tried to wriggle away I saw the light go on in Mrs. Patrick's room. She was standing in the window, watching us.

"What would your boyfriend think if he knew what we'd been up to?" Xavier whispered in my ear. "You think he'd still take you to the prom?"

He tightened his grasp on my arm, yanking it behind my back until I felt a sharp tunnel of pain sear up to my shoulder.

"Let me go."

"Yeah, me and your boyfriend should have ourselves a little talk," Xavier said. "Maybe I'll invite him in for a beer next time he comes to pick you up."

"You wouldn't do that."

"Oh no? Then come in with me, Marta. Don't give me a hard time. "

"Leave me alone."

"Don't fuck with me," he said. "Come on, Marta," he said, "don't make this difficult. No one wants a scene."

The curtains of Mrs. Patrick's parted further.

"Yeah, your boyfriend and I could have a real interesting conversation," Xavier said as he pulled me to the door.

The room was brightly lit.

On the table, I saw that he had ropes again, already cut, waiting.

"You remember?" he asked, smiling.

I didn't move.

He came over and began to unbutton my shirt.

185

His hands were larger, more callused, than Jack's. His body heavier, less agile.

That was what I thought about, at least at first. How this feels different from Jack.

There are all different ways to lose yourself, and I tried this. Clinical, curious, a cataloging of parts and pressures.

I stayed completely still.

But I didn't lose myself this time, I didn't lose myself at all.

I was there, pinned beneath him, trapped.

This time, it was hell, only hell.

I felt the ropes tighten about my wrists, my ankles.

He rubbed the tip of his cock against my clitoris, back and forth, back and forth. His breath was hot in my ears. "You want it, don't you?" he said. "Tell me. Tell me you want it."

His fingers were inside me now.

He entered me just a hair's breadth, then withdrew. "Tell me," he said. His fingers moved round and round. "Tell me." Round and round.

But I didn't.

Angry, he rammed into me.

I thought about the way Jack's cock quivered within me, a single shudder, after he came.

When it was over, I walked silently, carrying my sandals, to the end of the docks.

The water lapped against the wooden poles as I dangled my feet above the black water. It was still hot, and swarms of mosquitoes and gnats clustered on my arms, my neck No one had barbecues anymore, no one sat outside, there were too many bugs.

A pelican was standing on the nearest pole, its beady

eyes staring out at the glassy surface below. Fred, we called him, the Breezeway's friendly pelican Fred, Astrid proclaimed to guests hungry for local color.

I closed my eyes, exhaled deeply.

Inside, it was all an open gash.

I pressed my fingernails into the edges of my scalp, digging them in further and further until that was all there was, that pure eradicating pain as I dragged them down my forehead. I thought of clawing my own face off, literally clawing at my skin until my flesh hung in ragged bloody clumps from my sharpened nails.

When Jack called the next morning to say he had to help with inventory at the store and wouldn't be able to see me until later that evening, I was relieved. It would give me longer to get clean. "I'll call you later," he said, "and let you know what time I'll be done. Okay? Okay?" he asked again.

"Yes."

I went into the bathroom and locked the door. The hot water of the shower pounded into me, hotter and hotter, scalding me, but it was still not hot enough to burn away what lay inside.

I spent the rest of the morning at the front desk while Astrid went food shopping. Looking out of the window, I saw Xavier go to the pool, swim laps, sun himself, leave. I saw Garner bent over the lawn mower, his face streaked with grease, his naked sagging stomach, brown as tobacco, flapping over the waistband of his Bermuda shorts. And Mrs. Patrick sitting at a table in the shade, staring out at the river.

Jack called back to say that he would pick me up at 8:15.

At 8:10, I looked in the mirror one last time, daubed makeup on my forehead to cover the scratch marks, and walked through the office. Astrid and Garner were in the kitchen, leaving their dirty dinner dishes on the counter while they rummaged for dessert. I closed the screen door quietly behind me and walked quickly to the pool to flip on the lights before going to meet Jack.

I didn't see Xavier, lying flat on one of the plastic lounge chairs, waiting for me.

"Where are you going?" he asked, rising.

"Out."

"Without me?" he teased.

I ignored him.

"I'd miss you," he said.

He grabbed my arm and pulled me to him. "Why don't you just stay in tonight?" His breath reeked of alcohol.

"You fucking asshole," I said. "Let me go."

He laughed and pulled me tighter.

Xavier's free hand slithered into my blouse and wrapped around my breast, pinching my nipple so painfully I had to bite my lip not to cry out.

I tried to wriggle free of him but he tightened his hold. His eyes were gleaming. He was enjoying himself, enjoying the game.

"Don't you think we'd have fun?" he asked. "More fun than you'd have with that rod-ass boyfriend of yours."

"Leave him out of this," I muttered.

"I will if you will," he said. His hand was going up my skirt now, pulling at my panties.

"Stop it." I tried desperately to pull his hand away. "Get away from me."

He gave me one great forceful lurch and I began to

fall, breaking it with my right hand on the pile of bricks by the fence.

But he followed me, grabbed me, would not let me go. I felt his rough forefinger working through my underwear, reaching my flesh. His other hand was wrapped around my throat. "Don't touch me, you bastard. I'll scream if you do."

"Go ahead, scream. But tell me, how are you going to explain the money? How are you going to explain my good friend Lewis Harmon? Huh, Marta?" He laughed. "Oh, I'm going to touch you all right."

My fingers wrapped around the brick.

"Nothing you can do about that," he said. His hand dug deeper into me, in and in.

I can still see it, still feel it, my arm rising in slow motion with the brick, and then coming down, swooping through the night air. The contact. Hard, and then soft.

I did not see Jack running through the courtyard.

I only saw Xavier's head, a rivulet of blood running down his forehead.

His body was flaccid, his eyes vacant.

And then there was Jack, standing beside me, looking from Xavier to me.

Slowly, I pulled my gaze away from Frank Xavier's body lying at my feet. "Oh God, what did I do?"

"I saw what happened," Jack said. "I saw what he was trying to do to you."

We both turned when we saw a light go on and Mrs. Patrick step out of her room.

"What's going on out here?" Mrs. Patrick called out.

Jack looked at me, and then he turned away. "There's been an accident," he said. "Call the police."

"That was no accident," Mrs. Patrick replied. "I saw those two. I know what they were up to."

"Help me, Jack. Please. Help me," I whispered.

"The man slipped," Jack yelled back to her. "We were having a fight and he slipped. Now, please, call an ambulance."

I looked down. Xavier's eyes were unfocused, completely still.

"Go in and get yourself cleaned up," Jack said.

I couldn't move.

"Go on." He gave me a push in the direction of the office.

I ran past Astrid and Garner and locked my bedroom door. My hand was shaking, but when I looked down, there was no blood on it, no evidence.

Outside, I heard sounds. Voices. A blur of voices.

His hand in the folds of my skin. "Oh, I'm going to touch you, all right."

The voices were gaining in momentum, rising.

Xavier's laugh. "Nothing you can do about that." His fingers tightening about my throat.

I had only wanted him to take his hand away, had only wanted him to stop, to finally stop.

Jack's face, his eyes, expecting an explanation I could never give him.

I turned frantically about. In an instant, I opened my top drawer, grabbed the money I had stashed there and thrust it into my pocket.

I unlocked my bedroom door. The apartment was silent, empty. Everything, everyone was outside, waiting for me.

I headed out the back door, and ran along the path behind the motel.

I cut through the neighbor's yard and kept on

running.

I stopped once, half a block away, and turned around.

In the white glare of the headlights, I saw Astrid and Garner standing in the road watching as Xavier was loaded into an ambulance.

I saw Jack being led to the police car.

I looked at them all a moment more, and then I ran.

Part Three

Ten

THERE HAD BEEN NO WORD FROM JACK, NO FACE IN the light, no signal, since my visit to his hotel room a week ago.

I found myself looking for him from the window of the town car as I drove to work, out of the corner of my eye in crowded restaurants at lunch, in the black air of the studio as I did the news.

I listened for him in every ringing telephone, leaning into the split-second before the other person's voice began.

I should have been relieved by his silence, his absence.

But I wasn't.

I blinked and returned to the papers on my desk. The debut of *In Step* was just two weeks away and I was still trying to grasp the minutiae of the ever-changing boundaries in the Balkans for my interview with the secretary of state.

It was almost noon when I sensed the air in the newsroom change.

I lifted my head up, looked through the glass walls that separated my office from the main newsroom, and saw others doing the same, raising their faces, sniffing. The crackling started in the far corner, where the voices over the police band radios had gone up an octave as they hurried over the ends of sentences. It radiated out through the room, a sputtering energy, wordless at first, shapeless, just nerves, senses—*something is happening*. I felt it creep beneath my door, those first tentacles of an event, a story, pulling me from my desk to the newsroom where it completely filled the air. It is, despite the denials, what every newsperson lives for.

I grabbed Susan Mahoney as she darted by. "What's going on?"

"I was just coming to get you." Her eyes skidded off of mine to the clocks, the maps, and then back.

"What is it?"

"An explosion," Susan said.

"Where?"

"Federal building in New Orleans."

"Terrorists?"

"Maybe."

"Casualties?"

"Three unconfirmed. We're breaking in on regular programming. Get ready to go on-air in four minutes. Perry will meet you in the studio. Where the fuck is Quinn?"

"Isn't he in his office?"

"No. And he's not answering his beeper. Oh God, I just remembered, he's supposed to be giving a speech to that 'Fairness in Media' group this morning. Just get going, okay?"

I rushed to the studio, where Al was directing the cameramen and scurrying about, checking lights, microphones, and TelePrompTers. "This is it," he said. "The main event."

I sat down at the desk and plugged in my earpiece, listening to the latest reports while I hurriedly scribbled notes. In a minute, Perry rushed in with her bag of tricks. She tucked a piece of paper toweling about the neck of my blouse and began to work on my face. I could feel her putting extra concealing cream on the black circles beneath my eyes. There was no talk of boyfriends this time, of sales at Bloomingdale's or the sexual proclivities of various ethnic groups. We were both silent.

We all knew that this was the test that all of the more mundane broadcasts led up to. This was the time to see if it had paid off, the relationship you built with viewers night after night, hoping to establish enough trust so that you'd be the one they turned to during emergencies for information, for assurance, for continuity.

This was the time, too, to see how you performed, without the carefully scripted copy, without the net. The newspapers always printed the ratings of each news department the day after any disaster, and gave much copy space to critiquing our performances. It is one of the most important things the network executives figure into their mysterious equations when it comes time to decide who will stay and who will go.

Perry combed my hair a little bit flatter, a little bit smaller than usual. It would be unseemly to appear too glamorous when reporting about dismemberment and death.

Over the loudspeaker we heard, "Sixty seconds to

193

cut-in."

The crew was positioning the cameras to hide the empty chair by my side.

Perry put down her brushes, quickly appraised her work, and yanked off the toweling that had been protecting my clothes. "Good luck."

"Thanks."

"And twenty seconds . . . and ten . . . and go."

The light went on and I read the hastily written copy slapped in front of me. "At eleven-thirty-two this morning, an explosion went off at the federal building in downtown New Orleans." I looked into the camera, through it. "There are unconfirmed reports that witnesses saw a jeep drive up right before the blast." I cut to Fred Jarred, our local affiliate's reporter in the street. "Fred, what can you tell us?"

There was a moment of silence while Jarred, his forefinger pressed to his ear, his eyes nervously roaming the screen, missed his cue. I held my breath and only exhaled, relieved, when he finally kicked in. "Laura, as you can see, rescue efforts are in full swing. There may be as many as seventy people still inside. We have no word yet on their condition." The screen filled with images of the tattered building facade and men and women with blood-splattered faces being pulled from the wreckage.

"Is there any word on the casualties, Fred?"

"All we know so far is that there are three unconfirmed dead. Two women and a man."

I heard Susan speaking into my ear, prompting me about what questions to ask, filling me in on information as it came to her that I could relay ten seconds later into the camera. "Fred, we're going to go to Belinda Kirk, who's standing with Orlando Samuels,

194

the New Orleans chief of police. Belinda, go ahead."

I was surprised and pleased when Susan whispered Belinda's name to me. We had worked together in Burlington, and had an easy camaraderie. We'd lost touch, but I was glad to find her again, working in a bigger market and looking well. While she grilled the chief for information, I studied the fresh wire reports that were being rushed in front of me.

"Thank you, Belinda," I said when she was done. "I wonder if I might have a word with the chief. Sir, what about reports of a jeep that was said to have driven up right before the blast?"

"We're looking into that, Laura."

"Can you tell us anything about the drivers?" In my ear, Susan was telling me to ask about their appearance, if they were dark-skinned, possibly Middle Easterners? "Did they appear to be foreign?" I asked.

"That would be highly speculative to state at this moment," Samuels answered testily. "Excuse me, but I must get back to the scene."

"Of course. Thank you, Chief Samuels. We'll go now to Hank Parson for some background on the federal building."

With the cameras on Parson for a minute, Belinda and I spoke. "Hey, girlfriend," she said.

"Good to see you."

"Likewise. You've been on my mind."

"Yeah, sure," I joked.

"Honey, you've been on a lot of people's minds lately. Congratulations."

"Thanks."

"Now I can tell everyone I knew you when."

"Give me a break."

"No really. This woman, what's her name, Harrison?

195

from *Vanity Fair* called last week asking about you."

"They're doing a profile."

"Well, aren't we hot shit?"

"What did she ask?"

"The usual," Kirk said. "Who you fucked, who you fucked over. I told her I'd fax her a ten-page list. Just kidding. Listen, I gotta run. The fire chief just got here." She ended our connection before I could say goodbye.

I stared down at the desk, wondering just how good a reporter Harrison would prove to be.

"Laura," Susan prodded. "Laura, pay attention."

As soon as the light indicated I was back on, I informed the viewers of the latest information. "We've just gotten word on the casualties. The two women are alive in critical condition. We have one confirmed casualty. A boy, ten or eleven years old. No name has been released yet. We're going to go to Gerald Nolan now at St. Barnabas Hospital. Gerald, what can you tell us?" I asked.

"Laura, as you can guess, the emergency rooms are packed. One minute. Here she comes now. We believe this is the mother of the boy who was just pronounced dead. Ma'am? Ma'am?"

The cameras panned over an enormous woman rushing past the cameras. Her face, beneath a frazzle of jet-black hair, was contorted by horror and disbelief, her eyes glazed with shock. It was far too early for grief. The cameras didn't leave her until she disappeared inside the hospital doors.

Nolan grabbed a doctor. "Sir, what can you tell us about the casualties you're seeing?"

For the next twenty minutes, I continued playing relay between the reporters on the street frantically nabbing whatever officials they could round up, and the

196

information that was coming over the wires. It was a treacherous and consuming juggling act, and the realization that a child was dead, someone's child, barely pierced my adrenaline. I knew that it would find me later. It always did.

Within an hour, all seventy people had been evacuated. After wild rumors, most of which I did not report but some of which I did—that it was the Iranians, the I.R.A., or our own right-wing terrorists—a fourth report surfaced that it was some sort of a gas explosion. No one's fault, except maybe the government's. It was their building, after all.

The decision was made to go back to regularly scheduled programming. Dreadful as the explosion was, it was not quite the cataclysmic event it had first seemed. The death count wasn't high enough, there was no sexy motive. "We'll keep you updated throughout the day on any further developments," I promised the viewers. "And of course, join us at six-thirty for all the latest information." I looked gravely into the camera for another three seconds and then we were off.

I unhooked my mike and took a deep breath.

"Good job," Susan said just before I unplugged my earpiece. I walked back through the newsroom, where people looked up briefly from their computers and nodded their approval.

Quinn was in my office waiting for me.

I sat down warily and waited.

"Nice job," he said.

"Thanks."

"So there was no jeep after all, huh?"

"No."

"No terrorists? No 'foreigners'?"

"No."

"Too bad. Anyone could have made the same mistake."

He stared at me for a long and silent moment. And then he rose and left without another word.

My blood was still pumping in a rapid sputtering rhythm, unable to slow, to steady.

It hits gradually, but completely, the power of witnessing the rawest moments of other people's lives, the randomness and ease with which they can be blown apart. I keep it at bay, all of us do, while we report. I'm not sure if this is a character flaw or a talent. But even for us, it is impossible to keep it at bay forever. There have been reporters who turn to drink, and others who quit suddenly to join the Peace Corps. There are those who become so brittle that nothing can penetrate the crust, and others who turn maudlin. No one ever really escapes the lesson taught again and again: how very fragile the strings are that tie our lives together, no matter how much we gild and knot them, trying to secure the connections.

I called Dora to check on Sophie.

I called David.

And then I called the Hotel Angelica. "Room six fifty-eight, please."

I heard the call being put through, then three rings.

"Hello?" Jack's voice was chafed but soft. Close. "Hello?"

I pressed the receiver tight to my ear.

"Hello?" he said again. I heard him swallow. "Marta?"

I placed the receiver carefully back on the hook.

An hour later, Carla buzzed to tell me Berkman wanted to see me. "What's this business about foreigners?" he asked before I had a chance to sit down.

Susan was standing by the window. She said nothing, certainly not that I had asked the question at her behest. I glanced at her and then back to Berkman.

"Do you have any idea how many letters we're going to get?" he continued. "Let me make this clear to you. We do not report unsubstantiated rumors on the air."

"I'm sorry."

"Yes, well." He looked down and shuffled some papers about. "You did okay otherwise."

"Thank you."

He looked back at me. "I want you to call the Townsends." The Townsends were the parents of the little boy who died. "See if they'll talk."

"Don't you think I should wait a day or two?"

"Do you think Diane will wait? Do you think Barbara or Dan are going to wait?"

I wasn't sure if the assignment was a reward for my reporting or a penance. Anyway, I had no choice. It is what we do.

I went back to my office and put in the first of what were to be twenty or thirty attempts to get through on the Townsends' constantly busy line.

The only call I took all afternoon was Jerry's.

"What's wrong, Laura?" he asked.

"What do you mean?"

"I've never minced words and I'm not about to start now. Something's wrong. I can feel it. It's creeping onto the air."

"Berkman was pleased with my performance."

"Did he say that?"

"Well not exactly. But . . ."

"I see. Well, I'm not only talking about this afternoon."

"What have you heard?" I asked.

"Nothing. Not in so many words. It's just a feeling, a sense. Call it a smell." Jerry's sense of smell was what made him one of the best agents in the business. I knew when it had gone my way, when I'd had the imperceptible sweet scent of a comer, and I knew too that once it turned there was little I would be able to do to bring it back. Hard work, even talent, rarely make a difference once there is an odor of disappointment about you.

"You just don't seem yourself lately," Jerry said.

"I'm trying my best," I said. "They're not making it easy for me."

He laughed. "Easy? Why the fuck did you think they'd make it easy for you? That's not their job. Get real, Laura. This isn't some goddamned college radio station. Do you want to keep this job?"

"Yes."

"Then show them." He paused. "I've got to go. Listen, if you need anything, anything at all, just tell me. Do you need anything?"

"No. Jerry?"

"Yes?"

"I can do this."

"I know you can."

I knew, too, that just the fact that I had to reassure him was not a good sign.

As I walked through the newsroom to the studio two hours later to do the evening news, pumping my fists, I repeated that famous mantra from the 1920s: Every day in every way I am getting better and better.

200

Silly, and yet.

I used to believe in the possibility of improvement, of perfectibility.

Perhaps I still do.

I don't know.

Maybe I sat up a little straighter that night.

Maybe I held on to the air, that great imperceptible of the broadcast, a little tighter.

Maybe I took up more of it.

Except for major gaffes, it is all intangibles, really, the shift of ions that makes one work on-air. Or not.

Whatever it was, Quinn held back, shrank into his own space and did not cross over into mine.

We smiled at each other as we said goodnight.

And then, the minute the cameras clicked off, we stopped smiling.

Before I left the studio, I had Carla send the Townsends a bouquet of flowers with a condolence note and I took their number with me.

"Their child just died," David said as I hung up the living room phone after another fruitless effort as soon as I got home that night. "Don't you think you should wait a day or two?"

"I wish I could wait ten years," I responded. "I wish I could wait forever."

"But?"

"Do you think Diane will wait? Do you think Barbara or Dan are going to wait?"

"That doesn't sound like you."

"I don't know what 'me' sounds like anymore. But you're right, it was Berkman's line."

David shook his head. "Oh, I forgot, someone called

for you earlier."

"Who?"

"I don't know. He wouldn't leave his name. Said he was a news source. Here." He handed me the phone number he had scrawled on the back of a magazine and then he went to shower and change his clothes before dinner.

I glanced down at the writing, chilled.

As soon as David was gone, I went into the den, closed the door and dialed.

"Hello?" Jack answered.

"How did you get my home phone number?" I asked.

"You can learn an awful lot in prison if you put your mind to it," he said. "That was you who called this afternoon, wasn't it?"

I looked nervously about the empty room. David was in the shower and I could hear him humming beneath the pounding water. He has a good voice, steady and melodic. Lately he had begun to write rhyming songs about mice and marionettes to play on his old guitar for Sophie.

"Yes," I admitted finally. I knew that I was admitting more than just the phone call, to myself, to Jack, though I wasn't precisely sure what. "It was me. But please. You can't call me here."

Jack took a deep breath. "Let me ask you something. How much does David know about what happened?"

"Nothing."

"You never told him?"

"No."

"Why not? Don't you trust him?"

"It's not a matter of trust."

"What is it a matter of?"

"Nothing. I don't know." But I did know, of course I did. David had fallen in love with a different woman entirely from the girl Jack remembered, and more than anything I simply wanted to be that woman. Sometimes I even thought I was.

"What kind of love is that?" Jack asked.

I flinched, suddenly defensive of David, of our marriage. I wanted to say he would love me anyway, he would love me despite anything, despite everything, but how could I be sure? I said nothing.

"What are you going to do?" I asked Jack at last. "Just tell me what you're going to do."

"About what?"

I heard the shower stop and the sliding glass doors of the stall open. "About us. About me," I whispered.

"I don't know." Jack paused. "I guess we're going to have to talk about that, aren't we?"

We both listened to each other's breath over the wires.

"I love you, Marta," he said.

I hung up as David walked in wrapped in a chocolate brown towel.

"Who was that? The parents of the dead boy?" he asked.

"No. I still haven't been able to get through to them."

"Why don't you take that as a message from God?"

"I thought I was supposed to be the superstitious one," I replied.

"Maybe it's contagious. Like head lice." He pulled the towel tighter. "Are you ready to eat?"

"In a minute. I just want to go in and check on Sophie."

I crept into her dark room on tiptoes and stood over her crib, listening to her heavy breath. Sophie sleeping, Sophie peaceful, Sophie safe.

I crossed myself three times before I left her.

Eleven

WHERE DOES BETRAYAL BEGIN? IN THE HEART, IN THE mind, in the past?

"What are you going to do today?" David asked the following morning as he sat on the edge of the bed tying his sneakers.

Lately, we had been dividing Saturdays in half. David spent the morning with Sophie, taking her to the playground in Washington Square Park, while I went off to do whatever I wanted. In the afternoon, we reversed it. It was the only way either of us had any time to shop or stroll or read, the only way either of us got to be alone.

"I thought I'd go in to work."

"On the weekend?"

"Yes." For years before we had Sophie, I'd used the compulsion to work to create a barrier of activity and achievement through which even I could not see in or out. Since her birth, I had shed the habit, resentful of any unnecessary time away from her.

David shrugged and wandered into the kitchen to get a cup of coffee.

I got up, showered, and dressed before Sophie rose. She likes to sleep late, ignoring the light that dances through the lace curtains in her room, often not rising until after nine o'clock.

I hovered in the foyer, making as much noise as possible, trying to wake Sophie without actually going in and shaking her. I hated leaving without seeing her, holding her first. As soon as I heard her first throaty cry, I went to get her. I bent down to kiss her on her damp brow. "Good morning, little pie."

She made a trilling sound as I picked her up and nuzzled the back of her neck where the dark hairs grow in a tender jagged border. Her breath had the sweet/sour smell of formula and sleep.

"Little angel," I whispered. She took my bottom lip in her fingers and yanked it strenuously.

Twenty minutes later, I left her having a bottle with David in the living room, batting at the paper while he tried to read it.

There was no studio car waiting for me and I walked up Fifth Avenue through the Village and past Fourteenth Street, festooned with racks of clothing leaking from the off-price stores, sweatshirts and wind-up toys in neon colors, perfumes and watches of dubious origin. When I hit Twenty-seventh Street, I turned right.

I pushed open the heavy glass door of the Hotel Angelica and breathed in the odor of dust, musty slipcovers, plastic potted palms. I walked quickly by the reception desk and went to wait for the single rickety elevator.

"Where you going, miss?" the desk clerk called out loudly.

I turned around. His eyes were boring into me.

"Room six fifty-eight," I muttered.

"Huh?"

"Jack Pierce."

"He expecting you?"

I nodded.

I waited another minute for the elevator. Every time I glanced up I met the desk clerk's eyes. Finally I ducked into the stairwell and began to climb. By the time I got to the sixth floor I was out of breath and a thin cold film

205

had formed across my forehead. The light of the hallway made me dizzy as I hurried down it.

I swallowed once and knocked on Jack's door.

Inside, a radio played softly and then stopped.

The door creaked as it opened.

"Marta." Jack smiled, "Come in." He was freshly showered and his cheeks, newly shaved, were pale. He had lost the last vestiges of the southern sun someplace in the city.

I entered without saying a word and, weak-kneed, sat down at the small Formica table by the window. For a long while Jack stood over me, watching as I ran my hand through my hair again and again, unable to look at him.

"You have every right to hate me," I said finally. "What I did was shameful."

"I wish I did." He walked to the window, looking out of the smudged pane, his long sloping back to me. He still had the slim tautness of a runner.

"Jack?"

He turned around to face me. "Yes?"

"There's something I've always wondered." I glanced up at him. "It would make it easier for me if you sat down."

He remained still another moment and then he settled on the edge of the bed.

I stared at his feet, sockless in scuffed Topsiders. The light shimmered off the sparse dark blond hairs. It took me a long time to speak.

"Why did you do it?" I asked at last.

"Do what?"

"Why did you say it was you who was fighting with Xavier?"

He looked away. "I don't know. It all happened so

fast. It seemed the right thing to do at the time."

"But you could have told them later. You could have told them at the trial."

He shrugged. "I didn't, that's all."

"Why?" I pressed.

"Because I loved you," he said simply. "I thought that mattered. I thought that was the *only* thing that mattered. Anyway," he added, "I'd already told the police that Xavier slipped accidentally and hit his head while we were fighting and they believed it. I was stupid enough to think that they'd just let me go. Forensics even backed me up. At least, they couldn't prove that wasn't what happened. The police were curious about you, of course, but they had no choice but to take me at my word. Everyone thought they'd just drop it, even my lawyers. Unfortunately, the D.A. decided to prosecute anyway. Do you think they would have believed me if I suddenly changed my story then?" He leaned forward. "Every day I sat in that courtroom I thought you'd walk in. Every time the door swung open, I turned, certain it was going to be you."

I stared down at the soiled carpet.

"I still see Xavier's eyes," I said after a long silence. "I still see them, Jack, every goddamned night. The way they were open and white and staring up at me."

"Why did you run?" he asked. "That's what I've never understood. It was clearly a case of self-defense. I saw the two of you struggling. I could have testified to that."

"I don't know. I panicked. Like you said, it all happened so fast. I was just so scared." I pressed my nails into the palms of my hands, harder and harder. "Not just about Xavier. Well yes, of course about Xavier. I mean, Christ." I released my fist, looked away.

"But there were other things, too."

"What other things?"

"Nothing. Never mind." I bit my lip. "Jack, I know you might not believe this, but I never thought you'd go to jail. When I called Astrid, she said . . ."

"You called Astrid?"

"Yes. I used to call to check on what was happening to you."

"She told me she never heard from you again," Jack said, bewildered.

"That's not true. I called her right away and she told me there weren't going to be any charges pressed. And then, when that changed, she told me she was certain you were going to get off."

"She was your mother. She loved you. Didn't you realize she was just trying ro protect you?"

"Jack, I got the Palm Beach papers and they said so, too. They said your parents had hired the most expensive lawyer in the state. It was clearly unintentional, you had no record, your family was well known in the community. No one thought you'd go to jail. I know that's no excuse, but Astrid told me you asked her to tell me to stay away. For both our sakes."

"And you believed her?" he asked.

"Yes."

"How convenient for you," he said. "But I never told her that."

We were both quiet for a long while.

"Well, my lawyers did believe I'd get a suspended sentence at most, probation, community service, whatever," Jack admitted. "But it didn't turn out that way. Maybe the jury wanted to make an example of me. The golden boy everything was handed to. I don't know. Astrid did a very good job of covering for you.

She said she'd seen me struggling with Xavier. There was some problem with your disappearance, but they still had an eyewitness and a confession. That's more than enough truth for most juries."

"What about the old lady, Mrs. Patrick?"

"Seventy-three years old and near-sighted as a bat? She didn't stand a chance. I don't think the judge agreed with the jury's decision, but there was nothing he could do. At least he had discretionary sentencing, so he let me off relatively easy. Ten months and five years' probation."

I rested my head in my hands and took a few shallow breaths. I felt his body near mine, coiled, waiting.

"I'm sorry," I said at last. "I'm so sorry for everything. I just could never find the way back."

"It's not that hard, really," he replied. "You just get on Interstate Ninety-five and keep going south until you hit Flagerty."

I flinched. "Yes."

He said nothing.

My fingers were knotted in my hair. "If you could do it over again, that night, I mean, would you? Would you do the same thing?"

"I don't know." His mouth curled down at the corners. I tried to remember if it always did or if this was new. "What about you? If you could do it over again, would you run?"

"I've asked myself that a million times and I'd like to believe I'd stay. I've been running ever since, I've never really stopped."

"You want me to feel sorry for you?"

"No."

He cocked his head. "You want me to forgive you? You want me to tell you it's okay what happened to me

209

while you got what you always wanted, you got out?"

I knew when he said it that it was what I wanted, what I had wanted ever since, though I had no right to it.

"I can't do that," he said.

"I know."

He took a deep breath and exhaled. "We each made our decisions," he said. "It's who we are, our decisions. It's all we have."

"Is it who you still are?" I asked.

"I don't know."

"Jack, I know it probably means nothing, but it was never you I was running from. It wasn't even jail. Not really. It was myself."

He came and kneeled before me. His hands were on my knees, their heat spreading up my thighs. His face was close, his breath brushing against me. "You want me to tell you why I did it?" he asked softly. "You want me to tell you why I never said a word to anyone? You want me to tell you why I'm here? It's because the only thing I've ever known with any certainty in my entire life is that you and I belong together. Everything else is just clutter."

Tears had begun to trickle down my cheeks and I wiped them with the back of my hand.

He moved closer and kissed my collarbone, his lips lingering on my neck. "Marta," he whispered, his mouth all over me. "The only time I was ever truly happy was with you. Tell me that isn't true for you, too."

I pushed him away, trying to resist. "No."

But he held on, wiping the tears that were still falling, licking them from my face as he pulled me onto the bed. "Don't you remember what it was like for us?" he asked. "Don't you remember?"

I heard my own breath catching in my lungs.

I wanted to say, No, I don't remember, I wanted to tell him to leave me alone, Please just leave me alone, I wanted to make him stop. But I didn't. Fear knotted through my chest, my brain, fear of turning away from him once again, fear of his proximity and his anger, fear of his knowledge and his reprisal.

He pulled me to him and his mouth found mine, his lips soft, open. Perhaps if I gave in just this once, it would sate him.

Our tongues met and gradually the fear began to meld with curiosity and the outlines of desire, as much for the past as for the man, for pieces of my lost self I had left behind. He cried out when he entered me, digging his nails into my skin, as if trying to pull me closer and closer in until that was all there was, all there could be.

He sank his teeth into my shoulder, trying to fill himself with me, buried his nose in my hair inhaling and inhaling and inhaling. I felt his hands clutching my upper arms, squeezing so hard it was as if he wanted to absorb my very flesh into his, a desire beyond time, beyond bruise.

Afterwards, we lay naked and entangled beneath the thin hotel blanket.

He ran his fingers up and down my forearm.

"What was it like?" I asked.

"What was what like?"

"Prison."

Jack was staring up at an amoeba-shaped water spot on the ceiling. "Ten months is a lot longer than it sounds," he said, "but in a way, it was far easier than what came after. At least there was no illusion of freedom there. Hell, I was the only guilty man in the whole place."

"What do you mean?"

"Everyone else was so busy protesting their innocence. I was the only one protesting my guilt. Funny, don't you think?"

I didn't laugh. I knew then that something had died in him there, something had been left behind, maimed.

"You just do it, that's all," Jack said. "You do the time, you do the fucking prison walk. I had a lot of time to think."

"About what?"

"You."

"What happened after you got out?"

"Like I said, I got five years' probation. I couldn't leave Flagerty, I couldn't even spit without the cops knowing about it. It was much, much worse than prison. So many open doors and I couldn't walk through a single one of them. I couldn't go looking for you. I couldn't go anyplace at all." He shifted his legs beneath the sheets. "All those months in jail I used to fantasize about running again. I craved that sensation of movement so much I used to dream about it. But you know what? I tried it once when I got out and for the first time it didn't bring me any sense of freedom. I realized there was no place I could go. I was trapped. I never ran again." He glanced over at me. "You want to know what I did the day I got out?"

"What?"

"I went to Astrid to find out if she knew where you were."

"She didn't. I never told her. I used to call her every few weeks for news of you, but after you got out I stopped calling except once a year at Christmas. That's how I found out Garner died twelve years ago. And then I called one year and some strange woman answered.

She told me she had bought the motel five months before. She told me Astrid had died. All of a sudden, I began to miss her so much. It took me a long time to realize she did the best she could." I looked back to Jack. "You were telling me about what happened after you got out."

"I went to work in the store."

"The one thing you never wanted."

"I didn't have much choice, really. I couldn't leave town, and people weren't exactly lining up to hire me. Anyway, my father died of a heart attack six months after I got out. He was never really the same after what happened to me. So my mother needed the help." He rubbed his chin with his forefinger. "In the end, I couldn't even save that for them. Most of their savings had gone to my defense, and then there were the taxes, and the malls were moving in. I just couldn't hold on to it." He rolled over, got a drink of water from the nightstand, and rolled back.

"After my mother died three years later, I sold the store for back taxes, pocketed the rest, and went to the community college."

"What about law school?"

His mouth turned down at the corners. "You can't go to law school if you have a criminal record."

"Jack, I . . ."

"It didn't matter to me anymore," he interrupted. "The law was bullshit to me then. I saw how easily it could be perverted. So I got a job drawing for the *Record*, I got married, I tried to build a life. I did what people do. But you know what it was like? It was like playing house."

"You mean with you and Carol?"

"Yes. It never felt, I don't know, real. It never felt like

it mattered. Not really, not the way it did with you."

"You're going to divorce her?" I asked.

"I'm working on it. We've been separated for eight months, but I'm having a hard time getting Carol to accept that it's really over. She's being treated for depression and her shrink thought it would be helpful if I attended some sessions with her, so I'm spending ninety dollars a week sitting in some stranger's office trying to get Carol to face the truth as painlessly as possible."

"Is it working?"

"I thought we were making some progress, but lately she's gotten it into her head that if we adopted a baby it would make everything okay."

"Would it?"

"No. It's too late for that now." He pulled on a loose thread at the end of the blanket. "She claims she's loved me since high school. Ironic in a way, wouldn't you say?"

"Did you tell her you were coming here?"

"No. I was supposed to meet her for a session the morning I left. I called to tell her I would have to miss it, but I didn't tell her where I was going."

We both lay completely motionless.

"I'll tell you what my life is like," Jack said. "After Carol and I split up, she kept the house on Hibiscus Drive. Do you remember the weird little pink stucco house we used to laugh at?"

"You lived there?"

He smiled. "Yes. Anyway, she stayed there and I moved into a two-bedroom Mediterranean at the end of Kinney Drive that used to be the servants' quarters to a large estate that slipped into the ocean long ago. I spend half my waking hours fighting the sand that's creeping

214

through the yard. And the rest of the time, I go around recording the events of the town for the paper, the political campaigns, the church bazaars, the swim meets. I'm quite good at it, actually. The *Miami Herald* asked me to come work for them. There would have been a shot at national syndication."

"Why didn't you go?"

He shrugged. "There have been other offers that would have meant more money, higher circulation. All the things I'm supposed to want. And Carol wanted to move. God, did she want to move." He licked his dry lips, went on. "But I just never could. I thought after the probation was up and I could finally leave, I'd go as far away as possible. But something happened, I don't know. I'd get so nervous whenever I left town, it was almost like a case of vertigo. I couldn't quite seem to feel my feet outside of Flagerty. That must seem ridiculous to you."

"No."

"It's funny about the work. People can't wait for me to draw them, but then they're always disappointed with the results. I guess I don't make things look pretty enough. They tend to think my depictions are so accurate about other people but never about themselves. I suppose no one ever really sees themselves clearly. Anyway, that's over now."

"What do you mean?"

"I lost my job two months ago."

"You didn't tell me that."

"Didn't I?" he responded flatly.

"No. What happened?"

"They decided to go with a syndicated guy out of Chicago with a 'broader view.' That's what they said, a 'broader view.' In the end, I was just too microscopic even for them."

"Now what?"

"Now what?" He laughed, but it was only half a laugh, really, the other half was lost in an abyss. "I'll tell you. Now, I only buy one day's food at a time just to make sure I get up and dressed every day. Which, for some reason, I actually think is important. As you know, I've always had a ridiculously heightened sense of discipline and duty."

"Do you wish you didn't?"

He snorted. "Of course I wish I didn't. What good has it done me?" And then, softly: "I've tried not to. I've actually tried to shut off the valve that controls that particular blood flow. But I can't. It seems I'm stuck with it. I'm not sure it's something you can change."

We lay in silence for a few minutes.

"You think I don't understand about fame?" Jack continued. "I'll tell you what it's like. When I went back to work in the store, people used to come in just to take a look at me. All our old classmates, their parents, they all found some excuse to come in that first week I was back to see if I had tattoos on my forehead or numbers on my arm. They still whisper about me. Even the ones who don't quite remember why whisper about me all these years later. Of course, I never quite hear it. All I hear is the silence when they stop at my approach, the silence just before they speak in these conscientiously regular voices. I'm a goddamned expert on silence."

"I'm sorry."

"You seem to be saying that an awful lot."

"Maybe I'm hoping for some kind of cumulative effect."

He propped up on his elbow, looking down at me. "All those early years stuck in Flagerty when I couldn't

216

leave, I used to remember how obsessed you were with moving to New York. I knew if I could only come here I would find you. I used to study every picture of the city in magazines looking for you. Even in movies set in Manhattan I used to scour the extras looking for you. So many times I'd spot girls with your long wild hair but I could always tell they weren't you even before they turned around. None of them had your walk."

"What walk?"

"You used to bend forward at the waist as if you were leaning in to get wherever you were going even faster. You don't have it anymore. You even managed to change your walk." He shrugged. "Anyway, they were just movies. I used to try calling information to get a phone number for you. I used every name I could think of. I tried Marta Deuss, because I remembered that was your mother's maiden name, I tried Marta Clark." He stopped abruptly. "I don't want to talk about all that. It doesn't matter anymore. None of it does. All that matters is that we're finally together again. Where we belong. I always knew we would be. That's all I care about now." He swept his finger round my skin in circles. "We can start all over again," he said softly. "It can be just the way we thought it would be. The way it should have been."

I didn't say anything. I didn't move.

"Close your eyes," he said. "Close your eyes and we can be back on the island. Just close your eyes, Marta," he whispered.

I shut my eyes.

In a little while, I heard his breathing grow regular.

When I glanced at my watch, it was close to 1 P.M.

Gently, I lifted his arm and placed it back on the mattress.

I dressed quietly, watching him sleep.

And then I walked down the six flights of stairs and back out into the afternoon.

I do know this about betrayal: Once committed, it is not something you can erase.

I smelled Jack on me when I took Sophie to the park that afternoon, smelled him on me when I kissed David goodnight and then good morning, smelled him on me the next day, no matter how much I showered, no matter how much I scrubbed.

Remorse, when you come right down to it, is meaningless.

It changes nothing.

Unless the one who has been betrayed is so deeply in love that he will find a way to excuse anything. It is usually the provenance of women, that kind of love that refuses to recognize action—*I understand you.*

It was Jack's kind of love. At least he said it was.

I did not think that it was David's.

But love is a difficult thing to calibrate or predict. Especially someone else's. It is, rather, an easy thing to be mistaken about, to underestimate or overestimate. It's rare that we ever truly discover the precise nature of another's love. I'm not sure we would want to if we could.

Why didn't I tell David about what happened that night twenty-one years ago?

The truth is, I tried, or at least I think I tried.

We lay in bed one early night in that sweet twilight period of an affair when no decision has been made yet but you are deep enough to know one will be. It was summer and we were drinking a carton of orange juice, passing it back and forth, still amused by the sloppiness of it, the wet sheets, the dribbling chins. It felt so much like intimacy.

"There's something I need to tell you," I began uncertainly, though I had been carefully rehearsing the words for hours, days, weeks.

David leaned forward with such a tender expectancy, waiting to hear of—what? Past lovers? Eccentric relatives? The most benign of confessions that he would magnanimously forgive. The flaw that becomes incorporated into the love itself, at least in the beginning.

I looked at him, so trusting and so earnest.

I paused.

And I froze. "Never mind."

I felt the moment, the opportunity slip out of reach, gone forever.

I never told him about Astrid and her low-cut dresses and her loose breasts and her money.

I never told him about Garner.

I never told him about the motel rooms or the ropes or those blue nights when I went diving into the very worst in myself, fearing it, loathing it, courting it. The nights that I finally ran so desperately from, the nights I am running from still.

I never told him that Laura Barrett was a name I made up my first day in New York twenty-one years ago, when I walked the unknown streets on a sultry late summer afternoon, a shell, hollowed out by guilt and terror and exhaustion.

It was dusk when I found a grimy hotel on Eighth Street that rented by the day or week, walking by its entrance three times before I finally went in and asked for their cheapest room, giving them a made-up name.

219

Laura, after a soap opera character. Barrett, from Elizabeth Barrett Browning. An embarrassing cliché, yes. But I was seventeen, remember. An age when we are ripe for mythology, particularly our own.

I huddled on the lumpy mattress of the single bed in the dimly lit narrow room, wrapped in blankets despite the heat, unable to stop shaking. Radios and sirens blared from the streets and I jumped at every piercing sound as the night deepened and the city swelled threateningly about me. Eventually, I must have shut my eyes, for it came to me then, the dream that has haunted me ever since. . .

Trapped in the heat, the wet Florida twilight heat, the gnats so thick they form an impenetrable sheath swarming angrily about my face, my arms. I am swallowing them, choking on them, gasping from them. Someone is coming toward me, a shadow man, and I wave the gnats from my eyes trying to make him out but they are everywhere, blinding, suffocating. He's on top of me now, his arms multiplied, omnipresent, a noose of octopus arms, tightening and tightening about my throat. I open my mouth to scream but the gnats swarm inside my lips, my tongue, my nostrils. My lungs heart stomach collapse in and in. There is no air, no escape. Xavier's eyes bore into me like neon, like fucking lasers through the gnats as I gasp. And then, somehow the brick is in my hands and in one final effort to break free I slam it down, slam and slam and slam, feeling it crash, sink, melt into his skull. But when I finally stop and look down it is Jack on the ground, Jack bloodied, Jack open-eyed and still, Jack staring up at me, and it comes then, the scream, ratcheting out, ripping my throat, out and out and out. . .

I woke on the other side of the hotel room in a

crouch, gasping frantically for air, sweat pouring down my face, my heart banging so hard and fast against my chest that I thought I was dying.

I spent the next four days and nights in the room, shivering, sleepless, living on Cokes and candy bars from the vending machine down the hall, counting and recounting my diminishing money, washing my hands until the skin was cracked and bleeding, terrified to leave, to move, to shut my eyes.

The only time I went out was to go to the pay phone in the lobby, carrying pocketfuls of change, to call Astrid. I believed her when she said Jack would be let go. "Everyone knows it was just an accident," she said. "You stay right where you are until this blows over, sweetie. That's what everyone wants." She was cheery, as if I was on vacation.

"Jack?" I asked.

"Jack is going to be fine. He's with his family. They're taking care of everything."

"Tell him I . . . Tell him . . ."

"I know." She brightened. "You be good now."

Astrid, holding both hands against the world, keeping it out, almost winning.

I did not tell her where I was. She never even asked.

Her voice, vague, dreamy, unattached, hovered in my ears long after I had hung up.

And everywhere, too, was Jack. Jack the way he looked when he ran track, untethered, omnipotent, free. Jack, his eyes fluttering when he came. Jack, calling out to Mrs. Patrick, "There's been an accident." Jack, alone, a universe away.

I called the bus station for the schedule back to Flagerty, writing down the times on the back of a magazine. Upstairs, I hurriedly packed my suitcase, zipped it, and headed for the door. But I turned back, paralyzed by the thought of Flagerty waiting open-armed and curious for me. I sat for hours holding the bus schedule, staring at the numbers until they became a senseless geometry.

The next morning I packed again, turned back again.

In truth, I didn't even have the money for the return ticket.

Slowly, inexorably, the days piled up.

On my fifth day, I was downstairs waiting for the phone when I heard the hotel's only maid quit. I talked the owner into hiring me in exchange for free rent and pocket money, all of it off the books. I started that afternoon. It was something I knew, anyway, and easier than the Breezeway. The rooms were only cleaned once a week each, and the hotel's numerous junkies often didn't even want to be interrupted for that.

I had been in New York nearly a week before I left the hotel for the first time, my eyes squinting into the light, my legs weak and wobbly.

There were days when I went no farther than a block, certain that people were staring at me, pointing to me, purposefully knocking into me. I rushed with my arms tight about my torso back to the room, the blankets, the bus schedule, overwhelmed by a new and encompassing fear of being touched.

It was only after dark that the city streets comforted me with their opaqueness, their lack of curiosity, and I wandered aimlessly for miles filled sometimes with dread, and sometimes with elation.

For there was this, along with the horror at what I had done and the shame and the fear, there was this, too: freedom.

A dreadful guilt-drenched freedom, but freedom

nonetheless.

The freedom of being in a place where no one knew me, no one knew anything at all. Freedom from Astrid, Garner, the Breezeway, the rooms and what I had done in them. Freedom from the past. There was suddenly so much air, so much space. I ventured out into it apprehensively at first, tasting it, testing it, then swallowing it whole, greedily, desperately.

There are no excuses.

I believe in right and wrong.

I did not go back. It was wrong. That is what I live with. Every day, every night.

I have looked up the word *guilt* in the dictionary. It is defined as "the state of having done a wrong."

Not just a single act, but a state of being.

Endless.

Always.

I never told David about the tiny roach-infested room I eventually moved into, or of the Upper East Side restaurant where I worked six shifts a week as I put myself through City College. I used to watch the women who came into the restaurant, rich women, women with elegant wardrobes and handsome men, women with country homes and confident gaits, women I studied as scrupulously as my books, analyzing them, envying them, copying them.

I starved myself until my rounded cheeks grew planes and angles, I cut my hair and bleached all the color out of it with drugstore peroxide before putting in the honey blond the restaurant women had. I changed the intonations of my voice by listening to myself night after night reading the dictionary into a Woolworth's tape recorder. There were mistakes made along the way, times when my hair turned orange, and when in an attempt to copy the clothes in magazines, I ended up looking cheap or matronly or clumsy. Years later, when I could afford it, I had my nose fixed. Afterwards, I stared into the mirror at my swollen skin, my black eyes, and wondered what I had done. I looked nothing like Astrid, nothing like myself.

I grew into the new contours slowly but completely until my own image in the mirror no longer surprised me but fit so thoroughly with what I had intended that I almost began to forget there had ever been anything else.

By the time I met David I was thirty-four years old. I had accumulated enough other stories to tell him. In fact, I was Laura Barrett. Am Laura Barrett. Why would he question that? Why would anyone?

Only at night the dream still comes to me, as vivid as the first time. The gnats swarming in my nostrils, my mouth, Xavier's arms tightening and tightening about my throat, the brick, the blood, Jack.

There were years when I tried drinking myself into a stupor at night to squelch it, and years when I tried sleeping pills. There were brief attempts at therapy, but I could never bring myself to confess the source of the nightmares, so there could be no help. I tried endless middle-of-the-night letters of apology and confession that I ripped up in the morning, and I tried working until I was so exhausted I could barely speak by the time I got home.

Still, it came to me, comes to me, the arms, the blood, and I wake across the room, breathless and shivering.

Early Sunday morning, I heard David in his study, tapping lightly on his keyboard. He had decided to write a new book and he spent every free moment there now, rising early, going to bed late. I listened to the steady sound of his fingers and then I knocked softly.

"Come in."

I entered and he swiveled partially around. The room is so completely his, with its pristine model of the city on pedestals, its carefully arranged books, its scent of erasers and Elmer's glue and old wood. What David craved, what he hoarded most was time. Time alone in this windowless room where he could sit and brood amid the carefully ordered spaces of the maquettes he created. "Hi."

"Hi." He had gotten his hair cut on Saturday afternoon and there was a shorn vulnerability about his ears, his neck. I bent down to kiss the pink uncovered skin below his newly crisp hairline.

He was waiting for me to get to the point of the intrusion, but there was none, not one that I could explain anyway.

"Is everything okay?" he asked.

I touched his cheek.

"What is it, Laura?"

I looked away. "I'm sorry."

"For what?"

"Disturbing you."

He looked at me curiously.

"I'll leave."

He bent his head back to his work, nodding. "I just want to get this thought down before I forget it."

I kissed him one more time and left.

All day as I played with Sophie, I saw David, the new skin, the concentration, the fingers tap tap tapping.

And I saw Jack too, Jack waking in the wintry midafternoon in that crummy hotel room.

I could not see after that, could not see what he did

next, felt next.

I only saw him opening his eyes in that empty gray light, and finding himself deserted again.

Twelve

I TRIED TO WILL MYSELF NOT TO THINK, TO WILL ALL the jagged pieces that cut, that mangled, away.

I threw myself into my work.

On Monday morning, I sat at my desk, doodling across the top of a memo from Berkman while I listened to the Townsends' phone ring for the fourth time.

I was just about to give up when a woman answered. "Yes?"

"Hello." I was so surprised that I had actually gotten through after so many days that I stumbled at first. "Yes. Um. This is Laura Barrett, from . . ."

"I know where you're from."

We were both silent for a minute.

"Are you Mrs. Townsend?" I asked.

"Yes."

I glanced down at the notes I had prepared, as if reading the words would somehow disassociate them from me, making them easier to speak. "I was wondering," I began, "if you would consider—"

"I think you're doing a fine job," she interrupted. "'Bout time woman was up there."

"Thank you." I swallowed once. "I'm so sorry about you boy."

Mrs. Townsend said nothing. I listened to her breath, heavy and labored.

"I have a little girl myself. She's five months old," I continued.

226

Still, her breathing, just her breathing. And my own.

"I won't pretend to be able to imagine what you must be going through," I said, though I could not help but imagine it, adding it to all the other permutations of loss I had imagined since the moment Sophie was born.

"What's her name?"

"Sophie."

"My boy was Kyle. Kyle Jason Townsend." She invoked his name softly, as if he was sleeping in the next room and she did not want to wake him. "You should be calling the government, not me," she added in a far firmer tone. "You call them and ask them what happened. I got me a lawyer now and we're going to make them answer for what happened to Kyle."

"I will call the government. Mrs. Townsend, I think it would help if you would talk. On television, I mean."

"Help who?"

"Help make sure this doesn't happen again."

"My husband thinks you're all a bunch of vultures, circling around here after Kyle died, pretending you care about our little boy."

"He's right."

"I'll tell him you said so."

"But that doesn't mean there might not be some value in you coming forward to talk about your experience. Maybe it will put pressure on the government to improve the standards of safety in their buildings. You know the expression 'a picture is worth a thousand words'? Well, I honestly believe your image on television will have more effect than a hundred investigative reports alone."

"I'll think about it."

"Fair enough. Why don't I call around and see what I can find out about the building?" I suggested. "In the meantime, will you at least consider doing an interview?"

"All right."

"Thank you."

We hung up without saying goodbye.

What would I have done in her position? Bolt the doors, curl up tightly with my mourning and my rage? Probably. But anger, grief are unpredictable. And the seduction of an audience of millions on which to play them out can be powerful, as if the image itself, magnified, refracted, will somehow deflect the pain.

That is the promise, anyway.

I began phoning everyone I knew who might have information, and many I didn't know. I was surprised at how much faster people came to the phone now that I was on a national show, and how obsequious they could be, even when they were lying. I found an engineer who had quit the G.S.A. eight months ago, disgusted with the shoddiness of their work. I discovered an internal review detailing the dangers in a number of federal buildings throughout the country. The more I learned of the government's negligence, the more outraged I became. I do not believe that all death is senseless but I believe that Kyle Townsend's was.

I kept digging. It is an aspect of reporting that I have always loved, unearthing the pieces, putting them together. It leaves no time, no space for the puzzles of your own.

I did not go to lunch.

I made lists of names, of numbers, of possibilities.

I juggled all the pieces once, and then again.

But it did not work this time.

In between the phone calls and the notes, I felt him,

heard him, Jack.

Close your eyes, Marta. Just close your eyes.

I shook my head and returned to the phones, the legal pad.

At three o'clock, I hurried from the studio to the pediatrician's office on Thirty-fourth Street for Sophie's monthly checkup. Dora was already there with Sophie, sitting in the waiting room crowded with push toys, pop-up books that no longer popped, and children in various states of distress. Sophie reached for me as soon as I came near and I took her from Dora's arms. "Thanks," I said.

Dora, still wearing her long navy down coat, nodded as she reluctantly handed her over. "She's been a good little girlie. She finished all her bottles and she had two bowel movements today. Nice and firm."

I smiled at Sophie, then turned back to Dora. "You can go if you want. David's meeting me here to take Sophie home."

Ten minutes later, I took Sophie into the examining room.

She cried as I stripped her and lay her naked on the paper-covered scale, her skin a mottled white beneath the brilliant lights, her veins a delicate blue network. I held her tightly while the doctor looked in her eyes, her ears, pressed her stomach and curled her feet, looking for defects.

"Everything's fine," Dr. Tetrasoni said at last.

I put Sophie's diaper back on and held her on my lap while she got a shot in her thigh. I watched the sharp tip of the needle press against her plump skin and then break through with a tiny popping sound while Sophie let out a howl of shock.

Dr. Tetrasoni wrote down Sophie's measurements

while I finished dressing her. "I don't need to see you for another two months," she said as she held the door for us.

I nodded thankfully. I'm always terrified that she will find something wrong with Sophie that will be my fault, and I am always surprised when she lets me leave with her.

David was in the waiting room, sitting beneath a giant blue Crayola crayon stuck to the wall. He kissed us both while I told him Sophie's frighteningly high percentages in height and weight, the superiority of her reflexes. "She has good genes," he said, smiling.

He paid the receptionist while I slipped Sophie into her one-piece snowsuit and then handed her to him.

We rode down in the crowded elevator together, Sophie's eyes beginning to close as she lay nestled froglike against David's chest.

Out on the street, I kissed her cheek, and then his.

"Our little glue pot," he said, smiling down at Sophie snug between us.

I watched as he stepped out into the bustle of Thirty-fourth Street to hail a cab. When he got one, he looked back once, smiled and waved as he ducked into a taxi, his large broad hand on Sophie's head to protect it as he maneuvered through the door.

I don't know which is the truer reflection, the person you were born as or the person you will yourself to become.

I only know that this, too, is real.

This child, this man. The woman I am to them, with them.

The life we have constructed.

I waited until they were completely out of sight and then I hailed a cab back to the studio.

Carla stopped me on my way into the office and handed me a stack of phone messages on yellow slips of paper. The top one was from Mrs. Townsend.

And the next was from Jack Pierce.

"He called twice," Carla said, her eyebrows raised, waiting for an explanation.

"Hold all my calls," I told her. "I've got to get an answer from the Townsends."

I closed the door and sat down at my desk.

I smoothed the papers out and stared at Jack's phone number at the Hotel Angelica.

Close your eyes, Marta. Just close your eyes.

I felt him pulling me in, pulling me back, felt the lure.

Like death might be, I thought, when you are very sick and weary to the bone.

Come, come. Just close your eyes and come.

Let go.

It is time now.

This is where you belong.

I did as he said, closed my eyes. I saw the island, just as we had left it, a compression of sand and pines I saw Jack. Jack young, Jack now.

But I could not see myself there, not any self I recognized.

I could feel Jack waiting for me, waiting for an answer I could not give him, for words I could not say, alone and waiting, waiting once again.

For the debt to be paid.

I folded up the yellow phone slip and put it deep inside my purse.

I called Mrs. Townsend and told her that I'd found an engineer from the G.S.A. who was willing to go on the record as a whistle blower.

"What's the G.S.A.?" she asked.

"Government Services Administration."

"Oh." She paused, and then she asked, "Your little girl, does she sleep through the night yet?"

"She just started to. The first time it happened, I was so scared something was wrong, I went in and woke her up just to make sure she was okay. I'm still not used to it."

She sighed. "He was the spelling bee champion in our school district, did you know that? Kyle was. He was going to the citywide meet next month. That boy just loved to spell. He was funny that way. The first thing he ever did with crayons was draw an 'H.' He was only two. Well, it's an easy letter I guess. I wish I had saved those papers. But I didn't. Save everything," she told me. "Take it from me. You never know. You just never know."

"I'm so sorry."

There was a long silence.

"All right," she said. "I'll do the interview."

"Are you sure?"

"I thought you said it would be helpful," she remarked, suddenly taken aback. "I thought you said my image on television would mean something. Now what are you telling me?"

"Nothing," I replied hastily. "You're right. That's just what I said. I think you've made the right decision."

"All right then."

I thanked her and told her I'd get back in touch with the details.

What I did not tell her is that the image, once sent out, is beyond your control. And, yes, maybe it will serve a purpose. Maybe it will even help free you from your pain.

But maybe, too, it will find a home in other people's hearts, and fester. Once gone, there is nothing you can do about it, nothing you can fucking do about it.

It no longer belongs to you.

As soon as I hung up, Carla knocked and came into my office.

"I know you said no phone calls, Laura, but there's a man on the line, and I can't get rid of him."

"Who is it?"

"He wouldn't give a name. But I think you'd better take it. He says it's urgent."

"All right." I picked up the receiver and waited until Carla left. "Hello?"

"Miss Barrett?"

"Yes?"

"Miss Barrett, you're familiar with a Shana Joseph?"

"Yes," I answered warily. "Who is this?"

"Mike Compton. I'm her parole officer." His voice was weary, put-upon.

"I see. How did you get my private number here?"

"Shana gave it to me."

"How can I help you?"

"When was the last time you saw Shana?"

"Two weeks ago."

"Did she make any mention to you of leaving town?"

"No. Is she all right?"

"That's what we're trying to ascertain, Miss Barrett." I could tell by the way he used my name that he despised me. There are some people who automatically hate me because they think that I would never understand what it's like for them, the unfamous, the people who actually work for a living. The flip side of all the unearned adoration we receive is a distorted

233

envy. Neither seems to have much to do with me. "She didn't show up for her meeting on Monday, and she hasn't gone to school," Compton said.

"Did you call her brother?"

"Her brother says he doesn't know where she is. I don't know if he's lying or he's just too doped up to notice, but he's no help either way."

"What about Jay?"

"Jay?"

"Her boyfriend."

"Jay who?"

I thought for a minute. "Actually, I don't know his last name."

"Oh." His tone made it clear that he considered this a personal failing of mine. "Anyway, if you hear from her, you'll let us know?"

"Yes."

Compton gave me his number at the Department of Corrections and got off the phone.

The next morning, I left the house early. I took a taxi to the Lower East Side and got off on Stanton Street. I headed south along the block dotted with broken pay phones and overflowing garbage cans, looking for number 104. The metal gates of the shops were just going up for the day and the loud clanging made me jump. I walked past a bodega with three men already drinking beers out front, and a mother helping her little boy pee onto a mound of black plastic garbage bags. Finally, I found "104" spray-painted in dripping white across a red door. It was surrounded by so much graffiti, hearts and lovers' names, indecipherable scrawls and a skull, that I had to look three times to be sure. There was no intercom and I knocked loudly in hopes that someone would hear me. I didn't notice until then that there was a hole where the lock used to be. The door swung open easily.

Inside, the stairwell was dimly lit and smelled of wet newspapers, cat piss, and years of cooking grease. The stairs were worn out and uneven, the railing swayed beneath my hand as I climbed to the third floor.

Televisions were blaring out of many doors, a disharmony of early morning talk shows and cartoons in Spanish, but there was no sound from apartment 3C. I knocked softly, then again.

No one stirred until the fifth knock.

"Yeah?"

"Can I come in?"

"Who is it?"

I didn't want to yell my name out into the hallway. "A friend of your sister's," I said.

"She ain't here."

"I know that."

"Then what are you doing here?"

"Please. Can I come in and talk to you? It will only take a minute."

"Shit." I heard the chain lock being slid from its holder and then two other locks being turned.

An emaciated man stood before me in low-slung blue jeans and a T-shirt. He had a tattoo of an inky blue mermaid across the slim rise of his bicep that seemed to swim when he moved. "You're that lady on TV," he said.

"Yes. And you're Cort?"

"Right." He stepped back and let me enter.

There was only one light on, a dim bulb in a pink-frosted gooseneck lamp over a wooden table cluttered with dirty dishes, loose papers, and overflowing

235

ashtrays. The walls were streaked with grease marks.

"Is Shana here?" I asked.

"I already told you that she wasn't." His eyes, beneath prominent brows, were a clear hazel, without layers, without depth, strangely childlike in his otherwise beaten-up face.

I nodded. "How long has she been gone?"

"What's it to you?"

"We're friends."

"Yeah, well, we don't exactly give each other our travel itineraries, if you know what I mean."

"When was the last time you saw her?"

"You sound like her fucking parole officer."

"I want to help her."

"Why?"

"I told you, we're friends."

"You don't look much like the rest of her friends."

"When was the last time you saw her?" I asked again.

"I don't know, last week, the week before. If I knew so many people would be interested, I'd have made a note of it in my fucking date book."

"What about her boyfriend, Jay? Has he been around?"

Cort laughed. "Now why would he be around if she's not? You think he's gonna come 'round here to have tea and crumpets with me?"

"You don't like Jay?"

"I don't got an opinion about him one way or the other."

"What's his last name?"

"Christ, how should I know?"

We stood in silence for a minute.

"Is Shana in some kind of trouble?" he asked. "I mean, besides the parole shit."

"I don't know. That's what I'm trying to figure out."

He sniffed loudly and wiped his nose with the back of his hand.

"Will you tell her to call me if you hear from her?"

"Sure, whatever."

I was just about to leave when I had a second thought. "Can I see her room?" I asked.

"Why do you want to see her room?"

"Just curious."

I followed him down a narrow hallway to a tiny bedroom with a window that looked directly into the window of the next tenement. There was a single bed covered in a shiny lavender spread, white frilly curtains, and one dead cactus plant, its needles dried and brown. On the walls, there were posters of boys in leather and studs I did not recognize.

And next to them there was a vast collage of faces that I did.

They were all mine.

There were the tabloid photos from three years ago when I first came to New York to do the news and a grainy newspaper photo of my last day at the local show. There was an eight-by-ten glossy with my signature in black across the bottom that the studio sent to those who asked for it. There were the pictures of me and Quinn that had run in ads announcing my addition to the *National Evening News,* along with reviews from all the local papers and some out-of-town ones. I stepped closer. There were Xeroxes of ten-year-old photos from Burlington and Pittsburgh, and reviews of the shows there. There was a copy of an interview I had given to a high school newspaper in Maryland thirteen years ago. There was a clip from a neighborhood weekly in Pennsylvania about the very first time I had appeared on-air at twenty-two. There were the tabloid wedding shots of David and me.

I stood stunned by all the disparate images of my own face for a long while before I turned back to Cort, who was standing in the doorway watching me impassively.

"How long have these been here?"

"What do I look like, a fucking interior decorator? How should I know?"

I took a deep breath.

"You done?" he asked. "Not to rush you or anything. But I got, like, things to do. Places to go."

"I'm done."

I followed him to the door. "Let me give you my home phone number in case you hear from Shana," I said, and scribbled it down on a loose sheet of paper I pulled from my purse.

He jammed it into the back pocket of his blue jeans as I turned to leave.

I heard him slide the chain lock into place as I headed down the crooked stairs.

Thirteen

JACK LEFT ONE MORE MESSAGE BUT I DID NOT CALL him back.

I knew that I had to and I started to, more than once.

Each time, though, I hung up.

I did not know what I could give him.

I did not know what I could ask him to do, or not do. How could I ask anything of him?

I jumped whenever the phone rang, fearful that it might be him. I listened from the doorway whenever David picked up and spoke.

238

I looked over my shoulder as I ducked into the studio car each night.

But Jack did not appear.

Did I really think he would just go away?

Berkman decided to let me do the interview with the Townsends live on the debut of *In Step*. Olivia Redding would get to do the secretary after all.

Jerry called every day to check on my progress, relieved that I once more had what he called "a fighting spirit." To say nothing of a good story.

During breaks in the nightly broadcast, Quinn checked on my progress, hopeful that it was good—we both needed *In Step* to be a success—but not too good. I told him just enough to make him curious, and nervous.

I called Mike Compton twice, but there was no word on Shana, and his hurried manner told me that unless I had information to add, not to call again. He was a busy man with other cases, other problems.

I met with Stacy Boyle, the field producer for the Townsend piece, for the first time. At thirty, she'd already won an Emmy for a story on a hospital in St. Louis that had used eyedrops that caused the blindness of fifteen babies at birth. She sat down in my office with a purposeful slouch, balancing a notebook across her legs and looking up at me with a skeptical expression. We had five days to pull the piece together.

It was only when I began to tell her all the people I'd already contacted and the information I had gathered that the look gradually wore off, replaced by one of concentration.

As she wrote down the last name and number, she said, "You've done a lot of legwork. It will make my life easier. Thanks."

"I assumed it was my job," I replied.

For the first time, she relaxed. I would not be just another diva then, reading the words and taking the credit for the hard work she had done.

Nevertheless, we both knew that she would be the one putting in the long hours in New Orleans, gathering the information and the initial film footage for the background introduction.

"I've talked to Berkman," Stacy said as she rose to leave, "and he agrees that you will only have to miss two nights' broadcasts of the evening news. I can send the footage back every night and we can do a lot of the work over the phone. It's just a two-hour flight, so I can go back and forth as much as I need to."

"Great."

She smiled. "Why give Quinn the extra leg room, right?"

It was not Quinn I was thinking of. I had never spent a night away from Sophie before and the separation already cleaved through my ribs. "Right," I said.

The day I was to fly to New Orleans, I did not go into the studio. I wasn't going to do the news that night anyway, and for once I did not care about appearing to be the most hardworking person in the office.

I left Dora sitting in the living room, drinking coffee with four sugars and watching Regis and Kathie Lee, and I took Sophie to the park alone.

The dried leaves crunched beneath the wheels of the stroller as I maneuvered it into the playground and closed the gate behind us. It was still early, and the air was chilled enough to keep the other children away. Sophie squealed with delight as I squeezed her puffy snow-suited legs into one of the black plastic bucket swings and began pushing her, singing a song that I had heard another mother sing, "Up, up, up in the air, baby goes up, up in the air."

I wonder where they learn these things, the mothers. Are they remnants of their own childhoods, does everyone but me come armed with heirlooms of charming ditties? All I can do is spy on them, listen and imitate, a maternal impostor. Sophie pumped her arms and legs, reaching for me each time she swung in my direction, her eyes and nose crinkling with expectation. This is what happiness looks like, I thought, as I sang the song once more.

I had just given the soles of her feet a playful tap when a shadow passed slowly over us.

I swiveled around and saw someone just outside the playground dip behind a barren tree.

But as I continued to watch, I saw no further movement.

The swing slowed down and Sophie banged her fist impatiently.

I started again, "Up, up, up in the air," while I kept on eye on the playground gate.

A few minutes later, when Sophie's nose had turned red and runny and my own fingers were numb, I lifted her out of the swing and we began walking home.

We had just gotten to the great arch at the entrance to the park when I heard footsteps behind us.

I turned around quickly, but I could not make out who it was among the people hurrying away from us.

I ran the rest of the way home, pushing the stroller in front of me.

Six hours later, I glanced out of the smudged airplane

241

window and saw Lake Pontchartrain, black as an oil slick in the approaching dusk, as we began to make our descent. I gripped the armrest, digging my nails into the itchy tweed covering as I listened to every whir and sputter of the engine.

I have always been a nervous flyer, but it got worse two years ago when David and I were flying back from a weekend in Chicago where he had gone to give a lecture. The takeoff went smoothly, but within twenty minutes we realized something was wrong. We heard the clanking of the wheels as they attempted to withdraw into the belly of the plane again and again. No one ever came to offer us coffee or a cocktail—not a good sign. We were clearly flying in circles.

I looked over at David, but he would not look me in the eyes, would not hold my hand. "I just want you to know that if anything happens, I love you," I said.

"Oh, please." He rolled his eyes.

Finally, the captain came on the loudspeaker. "We seem to be having some trouble with our hydraulic system," he announced. "We will have to make an emergency landing in Cleveland."

David continued reading his *Newsweek* magazine. "It's survivable," he said as he stonily turned another page. "It may be rocky, but it's survivable."

Which, of course, it was.

It's become a joke between us, "it's survivable," repeated on bad days, rocky or blue days.

There is something that I was too embarrassed to tell David then. For years, every time I flew I said a prayer before takeoff and landing. Just let me live and I will have a baby.

I finally told him of it last night as I packed for New Orleans.

"Did you really think having a baby would appease an angry God?" David asked.

"Maybe," I replied. "But the point is, I haven't flown since we had Sophie."

"So? Now He can kill you because you've fulfilled your part of the bargain?"

I didn't answer.

"Well, you'll just have to come up with a new prayer," he said.

"I don't even care about me anymore," I said as I put another pair of pantyhose in my suitcase. "But I can't stand the thought of Sophie growing up motherless. Promise me if anything happens you'll make sure she knows how much I loved her."

David groaned. "Nothing's going to happen. Laura, you have premonitions every time you fly. You have premonitions when you go to the bathroom, for God's sake."

And I had to admit that he was right. Still. "Promise me," I insisted.

"I promise."

The lights of the runway rose before me. As the front wheels hit the ground and we began taxiing, the overhead luggage rack rattled with a speed that felt uncontrollable, unstoppable. My foot jammed into the floor, as if to hit the brake, until at last we came to a complete stop.

When I stepped out of the airport, the air was thick and humid, like Florida air but without the bleaching clarity. Nevertheless, I recognized its presence. In the North, you can almost forget about air.

I found the car the network had ordered for me, and as I rode to my hotel in the business district of New Orleans, I thanked God.

I'm not one of those people who just prays for safety and salvation in especially worrisome moments.

I thank God every single day for what I have.

But of course that, too, is part of the bargain, part of the plea.

Stacy was waiting for me in the lobby, sprawled out in a floral wing chair beneath a crystal chandelier with her notes, newspapers, and a cellular phone arrayed across her lap. We had spoken four or five times a day for the last week, and when we greeted each other now we were both genuinely pleased. "How was your flight?" she asked.

"Fine."

"You sound surprised."

"Let's just say I still think flying defies logic. How's it going?"

"Good. I've checked you in. Come on, I'll take you to your room and then we can talk about dinner."

"All right. But how about if I show you the tape of the intro I wrote first?"

She laughed "You're worse than me."

Upstairs in my suite, I threw the video into the VCR and we watched the three-and-a-half-minute tape. All week, Stacy had been sending back shots of the federal building, the courthouse, and exteriors of the Townsend house. I'd spent hours helping to edit them and crafting the words to fit the images.

"Still no comment from the government?" she asked.

"No. It looks like we'll have to go with your footage of them shutting the doors on the camera. Then I'll read their official statement."

"With suitable irony in your voice, I presume?"

I smiled. "With the utmost objectivity."

"Good. We can finish editing at the local studio tomorrow. Are you ready for some Cajun food? I can fill you in on the Townsends while we walk."

"Great." Though I had spoken with Mrs. Townsend by phone a number of times, I had little sense of them as people and I was anxious for any insight Stacy could give me that would help with the interview.

We left the hotel and headed for Canal Street, lined with gaudy souvenir shops and liquor stores, glitzy hotels and men hustling chess for money. Crossing it, we entered the French Quarter. I followed Stacy along the cobblestone streets crowded with tourists pointing to the low pastel candy-colored houses, the ornate balustrades with plants dripping down like useless wigs. Everywhere there were seven-foot-high shutters painted bright blue or green or pink, once meant to protect against the southern sun, now locked against intruders.

"So tell me about the Townsends," I said as we skirted Jackson Square, crammed with clowns and mimes, jugglers and high-hatted horsemen offering buggy rides along the Mississippi.

"Well, you know she's a nurse's aide at the local hospital," Stacy said. "She's been on leave since the accident."

"What's she like?"

"Weepy. But hard as nails. She's definitely the tough one in the family. I don't think he's crazy about the lawsuit. Or about going on television, for that matter."

"What else?"

"She's fat and she collects dolls."

"Dolls?"

"You'll see."

"What about him?"

"He's more of a cipher. Getting him to talk will be a

245

piece of work. But that's why they pay you the big bucks." She smiled. "Look, I need to stop and get some aspirin and then I'll take you to the restaurant. It's only this sawdust-on-the-floor kind of dive, but the food is great. Is that okay?"

"That's fine. Are you all right?"

"Yeah, it's just all those hours staring at the monitor this afternoon."

We found a tiny grocery store on Royal Street and I waited outside, burying my head in a magazine guide to the city I had taken from my hotel room. The putrid stench of shellfish remains from a nearby restaurant's garbage filled the air and every time I looked up I saw people holding their noses as they jumped over the plastic bags, laughing as their drinks sloshed in their paper cups and their cameras swung about their chests.

From half a block away, I saw a solitary man headed directly toward me. I turned a page, pretending to be absorbed. There are tricks to avoid recognition—sitting with your back to a restaurant, never making eye contact. Sometimes they work, sometimes they don't. The man was wearing a purple mask with feathers that covered his entire face despite the fact that Mardi Gras was months away. He careened right to me as if I was a magnet. My hands trembled as I clutched the magazine.

He stopped when he was within four inches of my face. I could smell the whiskey on his breath as he leaned into me.

"I read a magazine once," he said. "It didn't help me." He came even closer, and one of the long dyed feathers tickled my forehead. "Don't you know you're going to die anyway?"

Suddenly, he broke into a maniacal laugh and wheeled around, rocketing back down the street.

I was shaking when Stacy came back out a minute later.

"Got it," she said, smiling. She looked at me. "Are you okay?"

"Fine. Let's go." I began walking quickly, my head down, my eyes lowered.

I should have laughed, I should have shrugged it off, turned it into anecdote.

But I no longer knew what was harmless and what was not.

I no longer knew how to divulge anything at all.

All through dinner at the Acme Bar and Grill, I tried to keep up my part of the conversation as we drank Dixie beer and waded through baskets of crawfish, snapping their heads off and sucking out the juice, but it was a struggle, and in the end, Stacy was obviously disappointed.

"I guess you would have liked something fancier," she said.

"No, this was great," I tried to reassure her across a distance I could not traverse.

I locked the door of my suite and flipped all the lights on, illuminating the pale grays and pinks of the rug, the couch and chairs, a sea of pastel swirls. I kicked off my shoes and sat down next to the telephone. The message light was dark. Outside the thickly paned windows, I could see the lights of the convention center along the Mississippi shining their endless promise of camaraderie and sales, but inside everything was silent.

I was filled suddenly with longing for Sophie. I missed the dead weight of her head when she fell asleep rocking on my lap, my forearm tingling because I was reticent to disturb her, I missed the twitching of her translucent pink eyelids when I finally carried her to bed and laid her carefully on her side. I missed the sound of her breathing. I thought of Mrs. Townsend and imagined Sophie being ripped from me. Surely she would take pieces of my flesh with her, that's how much she was a part of me now.

It was just ten-thirty but I was hesitant to call David in New York, where it was an hour later. The phone would startle him and wake Sophie. I pictured him sitting up in bed, papers by his side, a pen behind his ear, stretching out in the freedom my absence brought.

For years when I was younger, I used to try to picture my father, my real father, precisely picture what he was doing at any given moment. There were so few facts to build a fantasy on, though, that in the end he remained static, an immobile man with an immobile face.

I flipped through the guide to the numbers for various hotel services and closed the vinyl book. There were other times in other cities when I was so lonely I would call my horoscope late at night just to hear another voice.

I unbuttoned the side of my skirt and leaned forward, resting my elbows on my knees.

The room grew about me, expanding until there were no walls at all, only empty and unanchored space.

I reached over and rummaged through my purse until I found the crumpled yellow sheets of paper with Jack's phone number at the Hotel Angelica. I had put it off long enough, too long.

I smoothed them out across my lap and stared at them.

Finally, I dialed and listened while the phone in room 658 rang.

"Hello?" A woman picked up, her voice heavily

accented in Spanish. "Hello? Yes?"

"Excuse me. Is, um, Jack Pierce there?"

"Who?"

"Never mind."

I hung up and called the Hotel Angelica's front desk. "Jack Pierce, please."

"One minute. Pierce, Pierce. He checked out four days ago."

"Did he leave a forwarding address?"

"No. He didn't leave nothing at all."

I sat still for a long while and then I got up, rewound the video of the Townsend piece, and pushed the "Play" button, grabbing a notepad and a pen before I settled down again to work.

The Townsends' home was on a flat suburban street of one-story houses and neatly manicured lawns twenty minutes out of town. The camera crew was already there when we arrived the next day, busily transforming the Townsends' living room into an intricate web of wires and lights.

I stepped over the cables and looked about the narrow room. The couch and chairs were of a matching brown and gold nubby wool, so new looking I doubted if they had been fully paid for yet. There was an aqua ceramic vase filled with pastel silk flowers and drapes of a diaphanous white nylon. The walls were lined from floor to ceiling with glass cases. A thousand dolls stared out of them.

There were Madame Alexander dolls with rouged cheeks and enormous eyes, dressed in tutus and taffeta gowns, kewpie dolls with blond mohawks and nun dolls in old-fashioned habits, their painted eyebrows thin and arched on their pale innocent faces. There were Marine

Corps Barbies in navy dress uniforms with medals on the chests, blond hair cascading down, and Hawaiian Kens in floral shirts. There were little boxes of baby dolls, swathed in pink and white, with names like "Hope," "Faith," and "Love" written across them in gold script. There were dolls in high chairs and dolls in ornate wicker carriages, their chubby plastic arms outstretched, forever waiting to be picked up.

"Good Lord," I whispered.

Stacy, who had been there all afternoon, just looked at me and smiled.

Mrs. Townsend was in the bedroom getting her hair done by a local aficionado who had been called in for the occasion. It was another half hour before she emerged. She was, as Stacy had said, a large woman with beefy arms and legs, and a large rotund face that swelled about her eyes and mouth. Her hair, shiny with a fresh coat of lacquer, was a uniformly stiff flip. It was hard to believe she was only twenty-eight. She patted her hair nervously. "Do I look all right?" she asked.

"You look fine, Mrs. Townsend." I couldn't really blame her for worrying about her hair. Once I had to interview the mother of a college student killed in a plane crash by a terrorist bomb and all she could talk about when I went to meet her in makeup was whether she should get a perm. It's nerves. Television-shock.

"Call me Jane Ann."

"Laura." I offered her my hand and we shook. "Thank you for doing this. I realize how hard this must be for you."

She nodded.

Barry Townsend came in a minute later. He was half the size of his wife, a knotty man wearing a baseball cap and a denim jacket that reeked of cigarette smoke. He

250

had a sunken sun-hardened face that made him look sixty-five, though he was probably in his early thirties. He hardly mumbled hello when I introduced myself.

We spent the next hour making small talk and doing light and sound checks for the crew.

Finally, it was fifteen minutes before airtime.

"Tell me again what you're going to ask me?" Jane Ann insisted.

"About your son. About what happened that day. About your lawsuit," I said. I didn't want to be too specific. I wanted her answers to be fresh, the more emotional the better. The makeup man powdered our faces and we settled into chairs in the living room while the thousand glassy-eyed dolls looked on.

The pre-taped intro played over our monitor, ending with the exterior shot of the Townsends' house and then Stacy motioned to me with her forefinger. We were on.

"Good evening. Thank you for letting us into your home, Jane Ann, Barry. I realize how painful this must be for you. You are living every parent's nightmare."

Jane Ann's lower lip trembled. "It is a nightmare."

"Why don't you tell us about your son?"

Jane Ann's eyes filled suddenly with the tears I had not seen all day. From the corner of my eye, I noticed Barry's Adam's apple lurching up and down as he rested his hand on the spread of his wife's thigh.

"He was a good boy," she began. "He placed second in the citywide spelling bee last year. That boy just loved to spell. He knew the alphabet before he was two, if you can believe that. There's no telling what he could have done."

I paused, waiting as the camera closed in on her crumbling face. For a moment I, too, was lost in it. But even then I realized how well this would play on-air.

Sometimes I wonder if I'll ever feel anything firsthand again.

"Can you tell me what happened that morning? Why were you in the federal building?"

"We were going to the passport office. Kyle was hoping to go to England with his church group for Christmas. We'd saved for it for years. They go every winter, you know, They call it a Medieval Christmas."

Barry tapped impatiently on his wife's leg, as if to tell her to move on.

"Let's talk about the lawsuit," I said. "You're convinced that it was negligence on the government's part that killed your son?"

Suddenly, Barry leaned forward and began to speak, his voice gravelly from cigarettes, from exhaustion, from pain. "Did you know that the G.S.A. was supposed to replace the entire heating system last year?" he asked. "Did you know that the inspector never even went downstairs to the basement, that he lied on his report? They spend two goddamned years repatinating the statues on the courthouse roof from the goddamned 1898 World's Fair and they can't secure the safety of their own citizens." His eyes bulged from his shriveled face and it was hard to know how it would appear on screen, righteous anger or nuttiness. The camera magnifies certain parts of your personality—a tic, a desire for attention, sadness, vitriol—and negates others. Everyone becomes a caricature of themselves on television.

We spoke of the upcoming court case and then once more of Kyle.

"He was my only one," Jane Ann said at the end, "my only one." A flicker of a smile appeared on her teary face. "He's in heaven now. And I know God is taking care of him. He's eating strawberry ice cream in heaven. That's what he liked best, strawberry. He used to slice the strawberries with his spoon until they were nothing but little red specks before he'd eat them." She wiped her wet eyes with a soggy tissue.

When the camera clicked off, all three of us remained seated, unable to quite emerge from the tunnel we had been in for the last nine minutes. Finally, I rose and shook the Townsends' hands one last time. "You're very brave. Let's hope you did some good."

"Can you stay for coffee?" Jane Ann asked.

"Thank you, but I really think we'd better leave."

"Maybe they want something harder," Barry said.

"No, really. Thank you anyway."

They hovered about us, watching our every movement, making it difficult for us to leave, as if they knew that as soon as the door was closed we'd be moving on to other stories, newer ones, fresher ones, while this one was theirs to keep, to keep forever.

At last, the cameramen finished packing up their bags and carried them out to the van parked on the front lawn.

I was still standing in the center of the living room when Jane Ann bent down and picked a large doll dressed in a lace christening gown out of a wicker carriage. She cradled it in her arms and then she handed it to me. "Doesn't it feel just like a real baby?" she asked.

It was still dark out when the taxi took me to the airport at 4:30 the next morning. Inside, the stands that sold red plastic crawfish and popcorn, postcards, and paperbacks were still closed. I managed to find an early edition of the *Times-Picayune* just as I boarded the plane.

As I settled into my seat I tried to practice square breathing—inhale for four counts, hold for four counts, exhale for four counts, hold for four counts. It was something I had once heard a radio call-in psychologist say helped with anxiety attacks.

The flight attendant brought me a glass of orange juice and I took a sip before I buckled my seat belt. There was no one else in first class.

By the time the plane began its descent into Newark Airport, the sun had risen sharp and incessant. I shut my eyes behind my dark sunglasses and repeated my new prayer: Please let me live so I can raise my daughter.

It was just eight-thirty when I opened the front door to the apartment. The foyer was quiet, the marble table empty except for a neat stack of yesterday's mail.

I walked to the edges of the living room and looked in. It was untouched, unmarred. Everything was precisely as I had left it.

I heard sounds in the kitchen and walked back. Inside, David was fixing himself his first mug of milky coffee. He looked up sleepily and smiled. "Welcome back."

"Hi, honey." I went over and embraced him. His body was warm and slouchy, still redolent of pillows, sheets, slumber.

"You were great last night," he said.

"You say that to all the girls."

He laughed, kissed me.

"How's Sophie?" I asked. "Is everything okay?"

"Of course everything is okay. She's sleeping. Just like she always is at this hour."

I smiled, shrugged. It is one of the oddly disconcerting things about travel that life goes on while

254

you are gone with so easy an adjustment.

"Let me just rinse my face with some cold water," David said, "and then you can tell me all about your trip."

"All right."

While David went back to the bathroom at the far end of the apartment, I returned to the foyer, hung up my coat, and began to flip through the mail. On the bottom of the stack of bills and business correspondence there was a large manila envelope, thick with bubble lining. I pulled it out. It was marked "Photo—do not bend."

I put down the rest of the mail and opened the package, certain that it must be the pictures that the photographer from *Vanity Fair* had promised to send of Sophie with me.

But it wasn't.

It didn't register at first what it was.

And then it did.

It wasn't Sophie at all.

It was a different girl, a different place.

Me at the Breezeway's gates.

Caught unaware, squinting into the Florida sun.

I looked at it closely.

The high cork platform sandals.

The cutoffs.

The eyes lined in black.

I turned it over.

On the back, written in script in a silver Magic Marker, it said, *Everyone has to pay. Even you.*

Part Four

Fourteen

LATER, YOU REMEMBER EVERYTHING.

Every detail of the day, that day, that at any other time would pass effortlessly into the effluvia of the past. Inconsequential. Meaningless.

Later, you scour every moment, every movement.

Looking for clues.

Looking, too, for those last shreds of time, time before the single slice that literally cuts through life itself.

Innocent time.

Ignorant time.

Time that you wish only to stop.

But of course, you can't.

I rose at 6:45 the next morning. As I always did. Just as I always did. I kissed David, looked in on Sophie, and then I did my exercises. I remember that my left wrist hurt as I did push-ups. At the time it was little more than an annoyance, but now it is one of the things most vivid to me, that sharp stab of pain in my wrist.

By the time I was done, David was dressed for an early meeting with a student. I remember wondering if it was a girl, one of those fresh-faced eager long-haired girls that clustered in his office.

Sophie was still sleeping.

I remember the smell of her room when I looked in on her, a blend of Desitin and diapers and talc and something else, something milky and sweet, Sophie-dom itself.

I showered and dressed in a fitted black-and-white tweed suit. Later, I incinerated it. How could I ever wear it again without thinking of that day?

Sophie woke at eight-thirty. I listened to her cooing happily as she rattled a teddy bear with bells in its belly before I went in to get her.

This is what I remember: lying her on the changing table, the swell of her white belly rising up, the impossible smoothness of her flesh as I bent down and kissed it, moving up her body with my mouth, over the transparent skin of her chest that barely covered the pale blue veins, the rolls of her neck, her fat red pudding cheeks. She pursed her lips in pleasure and began to razz, bubbles spilling down her chin, and I razzed back, our lips touching, our tongues, our saliva mixing.

I dressed her in navy flowered leggings and a navy turtleneck, snapping the padded elastic of the pants against the hollow of her back as she laughed at the sound it made. She wore white socks on her still flat and puffy feet, and white sneakers. It was hard to tie her shoelaces with her feet waving madly in the air, and I grew frustrated and impatient with her play, grabbing her meaty calves firmly to stop it. I wish it had been otherwise, I wish I had laughed, tickled her toes, held her tight and never let her go, but I didn't.

And then, when Dora came, I kissed Sophie three times on the forehead, and I went to work.

I spent the first two hours in my office reading the early news over the wires and taking notes for possible future projects for *In Step.*

The debut had been a success. We had come in second in our ratings period with an 11.6 share, which meant that just over eleven million people had watched, not bad considering we were up against a Schwarzenegger movie. The reviews were reasonably good and my interview with the Townsends was generally considered the highlight of the show. Jerry's nose was twitching as he sniffed the wind, pleased with what he found. Even he returned my calls faster than he had before, when the odor was less certain.

Buoyed, I suddenly found myself percolating with ideas for the Nightly Notes as well as for future segments of *In Step*. As I read, I underlined potentially incriminating evidence about the auto industry's illegal levels of emissions in an article in the *Detroit Free Press*.

It was 11:46. I don't know how I know that. I must have looked at the digital clock on my desk or at my watch. Newsrooms are rife with clocks, with the strictures of time. Anyway, it was exactly 11:46 when Carla knocked on my door and came in with an alarmed look on her face. Two men I didn't recognize followed closely behind.

"These men say they are detectives," Carla said. "They want to talk to you."

"Yes?"

One of the men, his overcoat still buttoned, his yellow hair greased straight from his forehead, turned to Carla. "If you'll excuse us?"

She looked at me and I nodded. She left the door ajar on her way out.

The detective reached over and closed it. He was so blond, pasty and soft, he looked as if he only had to shave once or twice a week. He turned back to me. "Miss Barrett?"

"Yes?"

"I'm Detective Flanders." He opened up a battered black leather fold and showed me his badge. "And this is Detective Dougherty. We're from the Sixth Precinct."

My heart stopped. It was my home precinct.

I did not want them to speak again. I didn't want it to start, whatever *it* was.

My blood began pumping in a rapid staccato rhythm.

Flanders shifted his weight nervously. He glanced once at his partner before he began in a faltering voice. "Miss Barrett, um, there's been an incident."

I rose, panic jutting up through my throat. "What kind of incident?"

He paused. "It's your daughter," he said quietly, unable to look me in the eye.

"Oh God, oh my God." My skull turned to ice. "Is she all right?"

"We don't know yet," he said in a strained voice.

"What do you mean, you don't know?" I screamed. "Is she hurt? Is she in the hospital? Where is she? Where's Sophie? Where's my baby?" I leaned across the desk, my arms grasping for something, anything. I grabbed Dougherty's coat and shook it. "Where's Sophie?" I cried again.

"Miss Barrett, maybe you should sit down," he suggested helplessly.

"Just tell me where is she," I repeated. And then, for just an instant, a still calm came over me. "This is ridiculous. I know where she is. She's with Dora. I just have to call Dora and she will straighten this all out. She's fine. Sophie is fine. Of course she is."

Dougherty and Flanders exchanged a brief look before Dougherty spoke. "Ma'am. I'm sorry. But . . ." He inhaled, steeling himself.

"But what?" I demanded frantically.

He exhaled, paused. "Someone has taken her."

The words bounced off of me, at once meaningless and horrific. "What are you talking about?" It was a foreign language they were speaking, an underwater language. I could make no sense of it.

Flanders's mouth moved in a nervous mime before the words began to come out. "Your baby-sitter, Dora Rickley, was walking your baby in Washington Square Park when someone," he said quietly, "someone took her. Sophie," he added haltingly.

"Dora would never let anyone have Sophie," I protested. I had to make them understand that they were wrong, they had to be wrong.

Flanders's eyes blinked nervously. "She had no choice. I'm sorry, Miss Barrett. The man had a gun."

My legs buckled and Dougherty slid his hands beneath me as I fell back into my chair.

When I looked back up at him, my peripheral vision had blackened. The detective's face was blurred and then sharp, too sharp. "Where is Sophie? Is she all right?" I pleaded. "Just tell me where she is."

"We're looking for her, ma'am. We have men everyplace, covering the park, the streets, going door to door to see if anyone got a license plate number. We've put out a felony alarm over the radio with a description of the car," Flanders said.

I stared over at his doughy face and then I bolted up and rushed to the door. "I have to find her. I have to find my baby." I clawed desperately at the knob while Dougherty gently tried to calm me. "Where is she? You must know where she is. Please. Just tell me where she is." I was shaking Dougherty now, shaking and shaking him.

"Miss Barrett, maybe you'd better come with us," he

suggested.

"Where's Sophie?"

Flanders put his hand on my shoulder to steady me. "We'll take you downtown."

"I have to call my husband."

"Two detectives went to his office to notify him. He'll meet us at your apartment. Ma'am, really, why don't you let us take you home?"

I followed them numbly out through the newsroom, where people stopped picking up the wires and typing into their computers to stare at us.

An unmarked car was waiting downstairs and I followed the two detectives into it.

I stared blankly at the backs of their heads from my seat in the rear and mumbled a litany of prayers, Sophie, Sophie, Sophie.

I dug my fingernails into my skin, deeper and deeper, as a chill fear pooled in every cell.

Sophie, Sophie, Sophie.

The smell of cheap aftershave filled the car, making me nauseous. No one spoke. We seemed to be moving through the city streets in slow motion. I banged my hand once against the glass window and cried out. Flanders turned around but my hand was in my mouth now and I was gone, just gone.

Sophie, Sophie, Sophie, I pleaded, aloud or silent, I don't know.

In the background, the police band radio pattered on and on about other crimes, other concerns. My stomach and bowels convulsed.

I crammed my fingernails into my scalp, in and in and in, repeating her name with each stab, Sophie, Sophie, Sophie.

261

When we got to the apartment, David was already there, standing ashen and lost in the center of the living room. "Laura." He reached for me with outstretched arms, but I broke away and ran to Sophie's room.

I pushed open the door, smelling her, sensing her, ready for her.

But inside it was dark.

The crib was empty.

I turned the lights on, my hands gripping the door frame.

Nothing.

I leaned against the wall and slid down to the floor, beating my fists into the thick carpet over and over. "No, no, no."

"Laura, stop." I felt a hand on my back. David was kneeling beside me.

I looked up and saw the tears in his eyes. "David."

He wrapped me in his arms.

"I can't believe this is happening," I cried. "How can this be happening?" I felt his heart pounding in his chest as he held me, or maybe it was mine. "Who would do this to us?"

"I don't know." His voice was filled with cracks and splinters.

We clutched each other and did not speak for a long time.

Finally, he said, "We have to go back to the living room. The detectives need our help."

He waited while I struggled to catch my breath, and then we helped each other up.

The four detectives, talking softly to each other, quieted as we approached, watching us nervously.

We stopped in front of them. David touched my arm

and I buried my face in the hollow of his neck, my sobs half-hidden in his flesh. The detectives averted their eyes, embarrassed.

Suddenly, a single thought pierced through my pain. "Where's Dora?" I demanded.

"She's at the precinct, ma'am," Flanders said. "Our detectives are questioning her there."

"Is she a suspect?" David asked.

"Everyone's a suspect in a case like this. But aside from that, we're hoping she can remember something that might help us."

One of the detectives who had accompanied David stepped up and introduced himself to me. "I'm Detective Johns," he said. "And this is Detective McElvey."

I stared at him. I didn't care about their names, I didn't care about anything at all. I only wanted Sophie.

"Do you have any idea who might do something like this?" he asked.

"Christ, no," David said.

"Miss Barrett?"

Before I could speak, the doorbell rang. I ran to open it, certain that it would be Dora, walking in with Sophie—that this was all just some horrible mistake. I hurried to undo the lock, smiling, open-armed, here I am, Sophie, waiting here.

A tall ruddy man with brilliant auburn hair strode purposefully in, followed by another man with deeply lined skin and coal black eyes.

I fell back.

The first man took a quick glance around the room before introducing himself. "Miss Barrett, Mr. Novak. I'm Detective Mike Harraday. Major Case Squad." Flanders stiffened but said nothing as he stepped aside.

Harraday held out his hand and I looked down at it, unsure of what to do with it. It had nothing to do with anything.

He withdrew it. "And this is my partner, Detective Carelli."

Carelli nodded. The worried expression in his eyes terrified me.

"Where's my baby?" I demanded. "Where's Sophie?"

"We're doing everything we can to find her. I promise you," Harraday said.

"Where is she?" I insisted.

"Maybe it would help if you sat down," he suggested.

But I could not seem to move.

"Please," he said, as if he were the host of an awkward party.

David helped me to the couch and then perched beside me, our fingers intertwined. Harraday sat down opposite us while the other detectives stood a few feet away, watching.

I leaned forward. "Where's my baby?" I pleaded again. I knew that if I asked enough, someone would tell me, someone would have to tell me, please just tell me.

Harraday took a deep breath. "This is what we know so far," he began, his voice gentle, concerned, calm. "Your baby-sitter, Dora Rickley, was walking your daughter in the park this morning when a man in a ski mask ambushed her . . ."

My throat constricted, David moaned.

". . . held a gun to your daughter's head . . ."

I shut my eyes.

". . . and took her from the stroller."

"He didn't use the gun?" David asked, his words nearly smothered by fear and pain.

"No."

264

"Where did he take her?"

"We don't know yet. They got in a car. Unfortunately, no one got the license number. When Dora screamed, the foot patrolman on duty in the park, Officer Pike, came to her assistance and radioed in for help."

"How could this have happened?" I cried angrily. "How could you have let this happen? Why didn't anyone stop him?"

Harraday shook his head sympathetically but didn't answer.

"Do you have a description?" David asked.

"Not much to go on. As I said, he was wearing a mask, and a heavy jacket. Dora seems to think he was about five-nine or ten, slight. And we can't be sure, but from her description, we think it was probably a .38 handgun."

The words, the faces were unreal to me, distorted and grotesque. I rose suddenly and ran for the door. David caught up with me as I fumbled with the lock. "Where are you going?"

"I have to find her."

He put his hand on mine. "Laura."

I struggled against him, pounding his chest with my open palms. "Let me go. I have to find her. She needs me. Don't you understand? She's going to wonder where I am. She's going to think I forgot her."

"I know, I know." He clutched me so hard and tight I could not fight back and finally my arms were still. I collapsed against him.

"She needs me," I repeated.

"We'll find her," David whispered. "We'll find her," he said again. His litany, his prayer. "We have to."

He led me back to the couch.

Harraday waited patiently while we tried to figure out how to breathe, how to be.

Finally he leaned forward, his hands hovering midair as if they would touch us, console us, if they could. Both hands fell to his knees. "Please believe me, we are doing everything in our power to find your daughter. Everything," he said.

David nodded.

I did not move, did not speak. I was numb. Beyond numb. There are no words.

"It would help if you could answer some questions. All right?" Harraday asked.

"Of course," David answered. "Anything."

"I have people scouring the neighborhood," Harraday assured us as he got out a tiny spiral notepad. "As I said, we don't have much of a physical description, but I have men circling the park looking for other witnesses, and going door to door. You never know what someone might have seen. I have my men handing out 'Get Out of Jail Free' cards to the drug dealers if they'll talk. Someone must have seen something." He paused and looked directly at me. "But we've got a special situation here," he said carefully.

"What do you mean, special?" David asked.

"Your wife is a celebrity," Carelli said. He uttered the word delicately, as if it was not quite proper for mixed company.

Harraday glanced at Carelli and then turned back to me. "That always makes it more, well, complicated," he said. He was in his midforties with the beginnings of jowls and chapped lips caked with tiny white flaps of skin. "Do you have any idea who might do this?"

"No," I answered.

He looked at David.

"No."

"Have you gotten any threatening phone calls or messages recently?" he asked.

I blanched. "Oh God. There have been . . ." I looked at David and then away. All six of the detectives were watching me, waiting. "There has been someone .

"Sean McGuirre," David interrupted.

"Who's he?" Carelli asked.

"A nutcase. He was following Laura last year. He broke into our house. Left notes. He was sent away. They were supposed to let us know when he got out, but . . ." David stood up. "I'm calling Hank Baldwin."

"Who's Baldwin?"

"Head of security at the network."

We listened while David called Baldwin and explained the situation.

"He's coming right down," David said as he hung up.

"Good. Did you save any of McGuirre's notes?"

"No. The police took them to use as evidence. I don't know what happened to them after that."

"We'll look into it. Is there anyone else you can think of?" Harraday asked. "Anything out of the ordinary? Anything you can tell us?"

"What about Shana and Jay?" David asked me.

"Who are they?" Carelli asked.

"She's someone my wife sees. A teenager. Didn't her parole officer call last week?"

"Yes, but . . ."

Harraday's eyes lit just a fraction as he turned to me for an explanation. "Who's Shana?"

"Shana Joseph. She's my little sister. Well, not really my little sister. You know, part of a program."

"What was she in jail for?" Carelli asked.

"Breaking and entering. But it was over a year ago

and she was just an accomplice. She's not like that."

"And Jay?" Harraday asked as he scribbled notes.

"Her boyfriend. I don't know his last name."

"What's this about her parole officer calling?" Carelli asked.

"She disappeared," David said.

"She'd never do anything to hurt Sophie," I interjected.

"Do you have the parole officer's name?"

"Yes, someplace." I dug in my purse, my eyes blinded by tears. "Where did I put it?" My fingers worked maniacally, but they were clumsy, unattached to my body or my brain. "Here." I finally found where I had written Mike Compton's number down.

Harraday glanced at the slip and then handed it to McElvey.

"Anything else you can tell us about them?" Carelli asked. "Do you have an address for her?"

"One-o-four Stanton Street. I went there last week." I tried to swallow but there was no saliva in my mouth. "There were all these, I don't know, pictures of me."

"What kind of pictures?"

"From newspapers, the studio. They went back years. It was weird."

"Did she ever threaten you in any way?"

"No. She's had some trouble but she's basically a good kid."

Harraday and Carelli were both writing away in their little pads while everyone looked on. "All right, McElvey," Harraday said. "Get on it. Call her parole officer. He'll have her social security number, a list of her friends. Get men out to the neighborhood. And check out her apartment. I want a report on this personal photo department she seems to be running. Now."

McElvey grabbed his coat and left.

"Before we go any further," Harraday said as the front door closed, "I'd like your permission to call TARU—"

"TARU?" David interrupted.

"Technical Assistance Response Unit. If you agree, they'll set up a wiretap on your phone. If this is a blackmail case, the schmuck could call anytime."

"Of course," David said.

Harraday motioned to Flanders. "Get them here as soon as possible."

Flanders phoned it in. "They're on their way," he said.

"Good."

I turned to Harraday. A single strand of hair had fallen across his forehead and he brushed it away self-consciously. "What did the man look like?" I asked.

"I told you, Dora couldn't see him. He had a mask. Unfortunately, there's no point in even sending her to Central Photo to look at mug shots."

Everything was falling.

Someone brought me a glass of cold water, though I don't remember asking for it and when I took it in my hand, I didn't know what to do with it. I no longer knew what it was for, what anything was for.

"He'd never do it," I muttered.

"Who?" Carelli asked.

"There's someone. It's crazy. He'd never do anything to hurt her." I was talking to myself really, only to myself.

"What the hell are you talking about?" David asked.

I paused.

"Miss Barrett," Harraday said, "if you know anything that you think could help us, anything at all . . ." He spoke so softly I had to lean closer to hear him.

"Jack."

"Jack who?" Carelli asked.

I looked up at his face, impassive, illegible, and then I turned back to Harraday. "There's someone. Someone I used to know. Jack Pierce. I hadn't seen him in many years." My voice was flat, dead. It felt like betrayal, another betrayal. And it didn't feel like anything at all. All I cared about was Sophie.

"But you have recently?"

"Yes."

He waited for me to go on, they all waited.

"What the hell is all this about, Laura?" David demanded.

I looked at him, and then away.

"Can you tell me the circumstances?" Harraday asked more gently.

"He came to New York."

"To see you?"

"Yes."

"How do you know him?"

"I knew him in Florida, when I was young," I said quietly.

"When, exactly?"

"Twenty-one years ago."

"Have you been in touch with him since then?"

"No."

"I see. And he just reappeared?"

"Yes."

"What did he want?" Harraday asked.

"I don't know. To see me. Just to see me."

"And you did? See him?"

"Yes," I whispered.

"I don't believe this," David muttered. He stood and

began pacing, his teeth clenched.

"Where is he now?" Harraday asked me.

"I don't know. He was staying at the Hotel Angelica on Twenty-seventh Street, but he's gone now."

"Was there any reason for him to be angry with you?"

I didn't look at David. "Maybe."

Harraday leaned forward and took a breath before speaking again. "Why might he be angry with you?"

I looked into his eyes for a moment, they were a soft brown, helpful, composed. And then I shook my head. "We were . . . friends. And then we weren't."

"And he would have preferred it otherwise?"

"Yes."

David stopped pacing. "Why didn't you tell me about this?"

"I thought I could handle it."

"That's great, that's fucking great." He started pacing again. I looked back at Harraday.

"Did he ask for money?"

"No."

"Did he ask about your daughter?"

"Not really. Just the way you do, I mean. Talk about your life."

"Do you have a picture of him?" Carelli asked.

I bit my lip, nodded. "Yes, but it's very old."

"I'd like to see it anyway," Harraday said.

"All right." I felt David's eyes on me as I disappeared into the den, where I opened the bottom drawer of my antique desk and pulled out a lacquered paisley box from the rear. I dug out a small black-and-white photo from beneath a stack of papers inside it. It had been with me, in the papers in the box, locked up through years of cheap apartments and hurried moves, through marriage and now this.

I came back out and handed it to Harraday.

It was Jack, Jack on the spoil island the summer I left. Jack laughing into the camera, his chest out with adolescent sexual pride, his bones sharp but not yet brittle, his eyes teasing and trusting and gay.

Harraday rested it on his lap. "We'll also need a current photo of Sophie."

David reached into his back pocket and pulled out his wallet. He opened it up and slid out a picture of Sophie I had taken last weekend, standing above her as she lay on the rug between my legs. She was wearing just an undershirt and diaper, her tongue curled out as she raised her face to the camera, smiling up at me as I snapped away. Afterward, she had turned over and begun to suck on my big toe. A sob escaped from somewhere deep within as I watched him hand it over.

Harraday was saying something to David but I could not make out the words.

"Laura? Laura?"

I forced myself to focus on David.

"They need to know how much Sophie weighs," he said.

"Nineteen and a half pounds," I replied automatically, remembering our visit to the doctor. "And she's twenty-six and a half inches long."

I sank back inside the thick blanket that was covering me now. David and Harraday were talking again, something about birthmarks, anything that could distinguish her, anything they should know?

"She sneezes in the sun," I interrupted.

"Excuse me?"

"Whenever her face gets in the sun, she sneezes. She always has. I took her out when she was just two days old and she sneezed as soon as those first rays got on

272

her face."

Harraday nodded.

"She sneezes in the sun," I repeated.

I did not bother to wipe the tears away. One fell on my thigh.

We all just sat there.

The doorbell rang again and Dougherty got it.

Hank Baldwin hurried in. "McGuirre's out," he announced grimly.

"What do you mean, he's out?" David demanded. "We had an agreement. They were going to give us advance warning."

"Well, they didn't," Baldwin said.

"Where is he?"

"We don't know yet. But we'll find him, don't you worry."

"Jesus fucking Christ," David said. "What's wrong with you people? My daughter is missing. Do you hear me? My daughter is missing."

"Calm down," Baldwin said.

"Don't tell me to calm down," David replied harshly.

He continued to glare at Baldwin while he gave the detectives the background information on McGuirre.

When Baldwin was done, Harraday turned to Johns. "All right, this one's yours. Get to his relatives. Get to his goddamned cell mate. Get to his lawyer. You know the drill. There'll be men waiting for you back at the precinct." He turned back to me. "Where were we? Oh yes, you were telling us about Jack Pierce. Go on."

When two officers from TARU arrived fifteen minutes later with their cases of electronic equipment, David showed them where the main phone lines were and they got to work. As soon as they were done, one of them

273

turned to us and explained how the tap worked. "This is a voice-activated recorder," he said. "It will go off whenever someone calls. We'll be here to listen in, but in case someone's not, don't worry. It will all be on tape. Now legally, as soon as you realize it's a friend on the line, or anyone who has nothing to do with the case, you have to turn off the recorder. Do you understand?"

We both nodded.

When they had gone, Carelli, who had been pumping his olive hands impatiently, stepped forward. "This Pierce guy. You got any idea where he went?"

"No."

"Where's he from?"

"I told you already. Florida. Flagerty, Florida."

"Do you have any idea where he might go? Any idea what his habits are?"

"No." I realized suddenly how very little I knew about Jack's time away from me. "I wish I did. But, no."

The doorbell rang again.

"Christ," David muttered. "What is this, Grand Central Station?"

Flanders opened the door.

Both Harraday and Carelli stood up, exchanging looks, as a man in an expensive pin-striped suit entered and held out his hand to us. His hair was lacquered to a high shine and even his skin seemed buffed. "I'm Frank Browning," he said.

His taut face fell a little when we didn't recognize the name.

"Chief of detectives."

"Of course."

We shook his hand.

"I just want you to know that we're doing everything we can," Browning said. "We are, of course, highly

274

concerned. Every resource will be at your disposal. We'll have all the backup we need from the FBI, though it will remain within our jurisdiction."

"Thank you."

Harraday and Carelli filled him in for a couple of minutes, and then Browning returned his attention to us. Or, more accurately, to me. "The chief of police is on his way. The mayor has asked me to relay the message that he will personally be monitoring this case. He'd like to stop by later this afternoon to speak with you himself."

I looked over at Harraday, whose already florid complexion was growing more flushed by the moment. He had not made eye contact with Browning once.

"Would you like a glass of water?" I asked him.

"Yes, thank you." Harraday followed me out of the room while Browning continued to reassure David about the high-level interest in finding Sophie.

As soon as we got to the hallway, I grabbed the lapels of his jacket and pulled him to me. "Detective Harraday, do you have any children?" Desperation made my voice high-pitched, shrill.

I leaned into his weathered face. He had a single scrawl of a purple scar above his right eye and a long broad nose.

"Yes." His eyebrows knit in apprehension. Maybe he was thinking of them, seeing them. I hoped so. "Two. A boy and girl."

"Then help me. Please. You have to help me," I implored him. "Find Sophie. Find my baby."

"I'll do everything I can."

"As if she was your own?" I asked.

He nodded and I reluctantly let go of his jacket.

"Miss Barrett?"

"Yes?"

"Is there anything you'd like to tell me? Confidentially?"

"Look for Jack, okay? Jack Pierce."

"I'm sorry, but I have to ask you this," he said. "How's your marriage?"

"Fine. Why?"

"Most kidnappings of children turn out to be family matters."

"No. I'm sure it's nothing like that."

"Here's my home phone number," Harraday said, pulling out a card. "If you want to talk. Anytime. About anything."

I slipped the card into my pocket while he began to head back to the living room.

"Wait," I said.

"Yes?"

"Tell me honestly, will it help to have them all here?" I asked, motioning to the living room.

Harraday looked at me closely. We were both trying to figure out how much to trust each other. "Yes and no," he answered carefully. "There are benefits, sure. And I plan to use them. The FBI will let me into their computers right away. And they'll let loose every piece of equipment and manpower they can muster. No one wants bad publicity, least of all the mayor or the police chief. But as far as them standing around out there, no."

"Why not?"

"Let's just say a case like this . . ." he continued.

"Like this?"

"High profile," he explained. "Everyone wants a piece of it. But it can get in the way of the investigation. Too many chefs."

"The only thing I care about is finding Sophie."

276

"I know."

"You have to find her," I cried, touching Harraday one last time, as if marking him.

As soon as I returned to the living room I went up to David and whispered in his ear. "Can I talk to you for a minute?"

He glared at me and stood his ground.

"Please," I said.

He followed me into the foyer.

"David." I tried to reach for him but he moved instinctively away.

"What the hell is going on, Laura? Why didn't you tell me about this Pierce guy?"

"I'm sorry—"

"Sorry? What do you mean, sorry? Sorry is not an explanation."

"Can we talk about this later?"

"No, we cannot talk about this later. I want an answer now."

"It's complicated."

"Obviously."

"Look, I promise you, we'll talk about it later."

"You're damn right we will."

"I'll tell you everything you want to know. But right now, we've got to figure out what to do."

"What do you mean?"

I told him what Harraday had said about all the political hot shots. "They're worried about how it's going to play," I said. "He's worried about Sophie. He needs room to work."

David listened closely, then turned around without saying another word to me.

Back in the living room, he went up to the chief of detectives. "I appreciate your concern. More than appreciate it. I'm going to count on it. But right now, I think it would be better if the mayor didn't come. You understand. We could use some privacy."

Browning relented, though he was clearly not pleased. "Of course. Well, I'll be in close touch. Rest assured that I will be supervising the entire team of detectives at all times." He glanced back at Carelli and Harraday, and then he left.

Harraday exhaled, and cocked his head almost imperceptibly in my direction.

Half an hour later, Dora walked in the front door, escorted by a burly policeman in a green suede baseball jacket.

"She said she had to come," the cop explained. "It's her choice, really. I mean, she's a free woman."

"It's all right," Harraday said.

Dora rushed over to me and grasped my forearms. "I'd never do anything to hurt her, I'd never do anything to our little girlie." Her voice was so frenzied, the island accent so thick, that it was hard to fully understand the jumble of words. Her eyes, beneath her wire-framed glasses, were red and swollen.

The detectives watched her closely.

"The man, he had a gun," she cried. "He had a gun to her head. I tried to stop him but I couldn't. He had a gun to her head." She was shaking me ferociously now.

I pushed her away.

Later, I wished I hadn't. Later, I realized she had no choice but to give him the baby, my baby, Sophie. Still, in my heart of hearts, I cannot help but believe I would have found a way not to if I had been there.

But I wasn't.

That is what it came down to, then and forever, in my

mind: I wasn't there.

"The gun was pressed against her head. Here." Dora put her finger to her temple.

I stared at her finger pressed to her skin, my Sophie's skin, where it was most soft and vulnerable. Sometimes I rest my mouth there in an open kiss, feeling her pulse thrum against my lips.

"It all happened so fast," Dora cried. "I'd never let anyone hurt her. Lord, oh Lord."

"I know," I murmured. "I know." And then, quietly, I asked, "What did he look like?"

"I told them, I didn't see his face."

Harraday and Carelli listened cautiously.

"Who would do something like this to a baby?" Dora sobbed. "Evil, there's evil people in this world." She reached to embrace me once again but I slithered away from her touch.

David stepped forward. "Dora, I think it would be best if you left now."

"Miss Barrett . . . . ." she pleaded.

I turned away.

I heard her let out one last cry before she was led to the door.

"I've got to get going myself," Harraday said. "We're going to set up a command post back at the Sixth Precinct and work out of there. I'll be there putting the team together if you need me. Of course, we'll call the second we know anything. In the meantime, Flanders will stay here to work the phones with you."

I grabbed Harraday's sleeve as he began to slip into his coat. "What happens now?" I asked frantically.

"I wish I could tell you, but I don't know." He tried to disengage my hand, but I wouldn't let him go.

"What usually happens?" I beseeched him.

Harraday paused and in the split second of silence that followed I saw all the children never found, the ones that disappeared on the way to a school bus, a play date, the ones that simply vanished from the earth. I pulled Harraday to me. "Tell me. Tell me what happens now."

"We'll do everything humanly possible," he said softly.

"Tell me she's going to be okay."

"We'll do everything we can."

"When? When are you going to bring her back to me?" I shook him. "They won't know what to feed her. She must be hungry by now. I'm sure she's hungry, I have to give her lunch. She still gets formula. Not milk. Formula. The kind with extra iron. What if they don't know that?"

David pulled me off of Harraday. "Laura. We have to let them go do their job."

Harraday looked painfully at me. "We'll check all these people out," he said. "But, unfortunately, in a case like this, there's always the X factor to consider, too."

"The X factor?" David asked.

"Fame. We'll look into everyone you've told us about, believe me. And there are some strong leads. But there are an awful lot of people who know you, or think they know you, who we have no idea of. It could be someone who just wants your attention, Miss Barrett. It could be someone who wants money. It could be someone who fantasizes about you. It could be anything. Christ, it could even be some nut off the street who has no idea who you are, totally random. Just a case of being in the wrong place at the wrong time. You know, bad luck."

"Bad luck?" I repeated, aghast.

"I'm sorry, Miss Barrett."

Baldwin turned to me as he prepared to follow the detectives out. "Laura, what do you want to do about the press?"

"The what?"

"The press. We can try to keep a lid on this for a little while, but I don't think I can keep it out forever. There are always leaks." He looked accusingly at the detectives.

"This is my baby you're talking about. My baby."

"I know."

"Keep it quiet," Harraday ordered sternly. "I've never seen it help a case yet."

Baldwin nodded and in a moment they were gone.

We were left in the room, our room, no longer ours. David, Detective Flanders, and me.

I sank onto the chair, burying my head in my hands.

I saw Sophie, the gun pressed to the delicate skin of her temple, saw her arms flailing out to me, heard her crying for me.

I called out to her, reached for her. . .

But there was only emptiness.

I heard David in the bathroom being sick. The toilet flushed, and then he was sick again.

Flanders looked at me and then away.

When he came out of the bathroom, David pulled me into our bedroom, away from Flanders's earshot.

"I can't believe you didn't tell me about this Jack Pierce," he exclaimed.

"I told you, I thought I could handle it."

"Good fucking thinking, Laura. Our daughter is missing and you thought you could handle it."

"David, Jack didn't have anything to do with this. I

281

know he didn't."

"If you're so certain, why did you tell the police about him?"

"I don't know. I . . ."

"You don't know?"

I shook my head. "I can't take any chances, that's all. Nor now. Not with Sophie."

"You should have thought about that before."

"I would never do anything to jeopardize her," I cried. "You know that."

"I don't know anything anymore," he replied. "You kept some guy's picture for twenty-one fucking years and you never even bothered to mention his name to me. Then he comes to New York and you see him and you tell me—what? What, Laura? What did you tell me? Were you shopping that day? Were you working? What the fuck did you tell me?"

I didn't answer.

"Is there anything else I should know about?" David continued. "Or, should I say, anyone else? Please, if you don't mind, I'd rather hear about it before the police," he said sarcastically.

"David."

"When did you see Pierce?"

"Last month."

"Is he in love with you?"

"I don't know."

"Are you in love with him?"

"No. Of course not. It has nothing to do with that. It was all so long ago."

"What was all so long ago, Laura? What exactly is going on?"

"David, I'm sorry." I began to sob. "He was just someone I knew a long time ago. In a different life. I didn't know how to explain it to you. I thought it was over. It *is* over."

"Do you think you could get any more cryptic?"

"David, stop. Please stop." I looked up at him. "All I can think about right now is Sophie."

He watched me cry. "We're not done with this, Laura," he said and left the room.

We spent the rest of the afternoon pacing the apartment in our separate corridors of pain.

Somehow, time passed, seconds, minutes.

I called the precinct every fifteen minutes but there was no news.

No one found the blue car.

No one contacted us for money.

I crossed myself three times on the forehead. And then in three sets of three, again and again.

I stared out the window, looking for Sophie, my forehead pressed against the pane.

It was three o'clock, four o'clock.

At four-thirty, Harraday called. My heart leapt. They had found her.

Flanders, David, and I grabbed various extensions.

"No sightings," Harraday said.

The receiver loosened in my hand.

"But the FBI let us use their computers," Harraday continued. "Case like this, they always agree. Anyway, we ran a check on Pierce. Seems this guy has a record," he told us. "He served time in Florida for involuntary manslaughter for the death of a man named Frank Xavier."

"Did you know about this?" David asked when we had all hung up.

He and Flanders both looked at me.

"Yes."

They stared incredulously.

"You're going to have to talk to Harraday," Flanders said, "and tell him what you know."

David ignored him and took a step to me. "You knew this guy killed a man and you never thought that maybe seeing him was not such a great idea? That never fucking occurred to you?"

"David, please."

"What's wrong with you? Our daughter could be dead because of you."

"Don't say that." I reached over and slapped him hard across the face. "Don't say that! Don't even think that! They're going to find her. They have to find her. You said so yourself."

David turned his back to me while Flanders called Harraday back.

"Don't you think you'd better call the studio?" David asked me when Flanders was done.

"About what?"

"To tell them you won't be doing the news tonight."

There are no rules of conduct for a time like this. No rituals to observe that would distract us from our grief.

Not grief. I was not going to feel grief. I was not even going to imagine it.

No rituals, anyway, for this.

There was nothing.

The light changed, evening fell.

At some point in the night, I heard David bang his fist into the wall and cry out.

And at some point in the night, I went into Sophie's room and shut the door.

She was everywhere in the smell, the dust, the very

284

air.

I opened the bureau drawers and touched her neatly folded clothes, the fuzzy one-piece sleeping sacks, the leggings, the tiny flowered socks.

I reached over and took the white netted bag we used for her laundry from its hook. Inside were the clothes she had worn for the past three days, the soft cotton side-snapped undershirts, the terry cloth stretchies. I held them close, breathing in her scent. I pulled out a white velour shirt with two purple stains from the jelly I had let her lick off my finger, her velvet gummy toothless mouth clamping around my forefinger.

I picked the teddy hear with the bells in its belly out of the crib and hugged it to my chest, rocking back and forth, back and forth.

She was out there someplace, someplace without it, someplace alone.

I touched the towel we rolled up and leaned her against to sleep so she could not roll onto her stomach and suffocate.

Were they doing that for her? Did they know?

I crawled over to the almond-hued metal diaper pail by the side of her dresser and opened it up. Inside there was a single Pampers from the morning that no one had thrown out.

I opened up the plastic strips covered with bunnies holding pastel balloons and buried my face in it, the loose shit, cold now, smearing across my face.

I don't know how long I lay there.

Later, I got up, washed my face.

I could hear David still pacing.

I could hear Flanders in the living room, slurping coffee he must have made himself.

I crept into the den and shut the door.

I didn't turn on the lights.

I sat down on the floor, hugging my knees tight to my chest.

And then I picked up Harraday's card from the top of my desk and slowly dialed his home number.

Fifteen

HE PICKED UP ON THE THIRD RING, HIS VOICE HEAVY with sleep. "Yeah?"

"It's Laura Barrett."

"Miss Barrett." I could hear his voice kick into alert. It was five in the morning, but neither of us mentioned it. There was a long silence. David was in the bedroom, finally asleep.

"There's something I need to tell you," I said quietly.

"Yes?"

"The other day, a photo came in the mail."

"What kind of photo?"

I paused. "Can we keep this confidential?" I asked.

"If it has nothing to do with the case, I'll keep it to myself. I won't even tell my partner. That's all I can promise."

"And if it turns out that it does have something to do with the case?"

"I can't give you any guarantees."

"All right." I rearranged my legs on the cold wooden floor. And then I told him about the picture of the Breezeway and the scrawl on the back, *Everyone has to pay. Even you.*

"Pay for what?" Harraday asked.

I took a deep breath.

All the years spent avoiding questions, running and ducking from them, now came down to this, sitting in an expensively furnished den in the dark, talking to a stranger I prayed could help me.

I no longer feared the questions.

The worst had already happened. Sophie was gone.

My voice was a hoarse whisper as I began to tell Harraday about the August night twenty-one years ago when I had struggled with Frank Xavier, told him how Jack had come up the path, seen us battling, seen the brick.

"Miss Barrett," he interrupted

"Laura."

"Laura, I have to warn you before you say anything else. You should know, if you say what I think you're about to, legally, I'll be obligated to inform the D.A."

"Even though it was twenty-one years ago?"

"It doesn't matter. Homicide cases never get closed out. As long as I have probable cause to believe a felony was committed, I've got to act. I want you to know that." His voice softened. "Look, my only concern right now is finding your daughter. But, like I said, I can't make any guarantees."

The glass panes rattled in the brisk night wind. "All I care about is getting Sophie back."

No sound came in from the streets below as I continued without interruption, summoning that long gone night from the subterranean cave where it had lurked for so many years. Gradually, it entered and filled the room, the soupy humid air, the smell of chlorine from the pool, the fear, the blood.

And something Harraday would never see, never smell: Garner, the men.

"So Pierce went to jail?" he asked, his voice

287

objective, uninflected.

"Yes. He got ten months and five years' probation."

There was a long pause.

"It would certainly give him a motive," he said finally.

"I know it looks that way, but if he wanted to hurt me, why would he have waited all this time? It doesn't make sense."

"He didn't know where you were before. He didn't know *who* you were."

"Maybe. But I don't really believe that. He's a good man," I said softly. "I don't know how to explain it to you, but he's a good man."

"Good can turn bad," Harraday replied simply.

"Now what?" I asked.

"I'll make some calls as soon as I get in this morning."

"Is one of them going to be to the D.A.?" I asked.

"I don't know. Give me a little time to work on this." He began thinking out loud. "It is a different jurisdiction, after all I can keep it quiet for a little while. I'm not really sure what purpose it would serve at this point. You did instruct us to look for Pierce. We'll have the photo to go on. And we already know his record. You deserted him, he resents you for it, that's motive enough for now. Laura?"

"Yes?"

"Who else knows about this?"

"No one."

"All right. I'll come by this morning and pick up the photo. We'll check for fingerprints, handwriting. That much will have to become common knowledge. What did the postmark say, by the way?"

"There was none."

"Then whoever sent it not only knew where you lived, they knew how to get in. I'll send some men to talk to the doormen, the postman, whoever else might have seen something."

I was just about to tell Harraday about the postcard of the Breezeway that had come to my office last month when I heard a rustling and I looked up, startled.

David was standing in the doorway, his face shining in the darkened room.

When I met his eyes, he turned and disappeared.

"I've got to go," I said to Harraday, and hung up the telephone.

I followed David into the bedroom and sat on the edge of the bed, looking down at him, his eyes weary and distrustful' his body limp, bruised, near defeat.

"I don't know who you are," he said.

I took a deep breath, searching for an answer to give him, but I found none.

"You killed a man," he uttered in disbelief.

I stared at a wrinkle in the quilt. "Yes."

He clutched the sheet in his fist tighter and tighter until his knuckles turned white. "Who was Xavier?"

"He was staying at my parents' motel.'"

"And?"

I looked at the back of David's head, mossy and soft. "He was . . ." I stopped.

"What?"

"We were struggling. I only wanted him to stop touching me. I never meant to kill him. Oh God, I never meant that."

"But he died," David said harshly.

"Yes."

"If it was self-defense, why did you run?"

"I panicked. It was a mistake, David. An awful mistake. I know that. I was just so scared." I looked at the window, then back to him. "I know it's no excuse, but I never thought Jack would go to jail. I called my mother and she told me he was going to get off. The way the brick hit Xavier, forensics couldn't prove he hadn't just fallen on his head the way Jack said."

"You're right. That's no excuse. You knew about the trial. I just don't understand. How could you not have gone back?"

I longed suddenly to tell him all of it, to be bleached, emptied out.

"David, I know nothing I say will ever change what I did. Nothing can make it right. But I need you to at least try to understand. There are things I never told you, things I never told anyone."

He lay completely still, waiting. The room was silent except for our breathing.

"I don't know where to begin." I paused.

"Try," he said bitterly.

"I told you I only met my real father once."

"Yes."

"David, my mother, Astrid. She wasn't just the brokenhearted teenager I made her out to be. Maybe she started out that way, I don't know. But it's more complicated than that." I stopped, shifted my legs, began again. "We were very poor in Germany. She was just a teenager when she had me. Her mother had died and her father was so mad at her he kicked her out. She never finished school, so it was hard for her to find work. She took in people's clothes to sew, she tried to get work in the factories. Astrid always had some plan, some idea that would magically make things better, but they never worked out. The only way she ever really made any money was men."

"What are you talking about?"

"She was . . . she went with . . ."

He turned to look at me. "Are you telling me your mother was a prostitute?"

"In Dortmarr. Before we came here."

"Good Lord."

"Then she latched onto Garner, or he latched onto her, I don't know. And that was almost as bad. Maybe it was worse. Oh God, David, I don't know how to make you understand what it was like then. I've kept it all buried for so long. I know I lied to you. But it was only because I was trying so hard to forget it all. Astrid, Garner, all of it. None of it was what you think."

"They ran the motel?" he asked, no longer certain of what was firmament and what was illusion.

"Yes. They ran the Breezeway."

"And were there . . . did your mother . . . were there men there, too?"

"No. Yes. There was Garner, first of all there was Garner." I stared up at the ceiling. "It's funny, but I thought I'd feel some relief when I found out he died, but I didn't. I didn't feel anything at all."

"What did he do to her that was so awful?"

"Everything. Nothing. To me, too," I added faintly.

David raised his head, the tendons in his neck bulging and tense. "What did he do to you?"

"Not as much as he wanted. He tried, but it never got that far. But it was like living in a warped world, David. I was frightened of Garner, I was ashamed to have friends, ashamed that they might learn about Astrid, about what my family was really like. About what I was really like."

"What do you mean, what you were really like?"

291

"All my life, I was terrified that I'd turn out to be like Astrid."

I stopped.

"Why would you think that?"

I buried my face in the pillow. I didn't want him to see me. "Because I did. I was."

"What are you talking about?"

"Frank Xavier. I had slept with him before."

"For money?"

"Yes."

"How old were you?"

"Sixteen."

"I don't believe this. How does that happen? How do you start sleeping around for money at sixteen? Tell me. I really want to know. Tell me how that happens."

Before I could attempt to answer, David's voice softened. "Did your mother know? Did she put you up to it? Is that it?"

"No."

He fell back, deflated. "I suppose Pierce knows all about this?"

"No. You're the only person I've ever told."

He took a deep breath. "Why didn't you tell me any of this before?"

"I loved you. You were the best thing that ever happened to me. Would you have still wanted me if I had told you?"

"I don't know." He looked directly at me. "You didn't give me the chance to decide. You took my choice away from me."

"Don't you see, David, I wasn't hiding it from you. Not just from you, anyway. I was trying to hide it from myself. For years, I thought I was like Astrid, that I had to be like her. And then I escaped. And all I wanted to do was wipe her away. I even made sure I didn't look like her anymore. It wasn't her, of course. I know that. It was myself I was trying to erase. But I would have gone mad if I didn't pretend they never existed. That Marta never existed. It didn't work anyway, how could it? I could never wipe away what happened that night. I can never change what I did." I stopped and looked at him. "I never meant to hurt you. That's the last thing in the world I ever wanted." Even to my own ears, the words sounded hollow, inane. Nevertheless, they were true, if that mattered.

"Tell me about Pierce," he said quietly. "When did You meet him?"

"We were young. Teenagers."

"You're going to tell me all this was just a case of puppy love?"

"No. No, it was nothing like that. At the time it felt like . . ."

"Felt like what?"

"I don't know. Everything. It felt like everything. Didn't you ever have anyone like that, when you were young? Someone who meant the world, literally meant the world to you?"

David didn't answer. I knew that he had never had that first love that burns everything in its wake, burns youth itself. Not everyone does. I'm not sure who are the unlucky ones, the people who have known it and spend the rest of their lives comparing every love to that, or the ones who never knew it to begin with.

"He was the first person who made me feel I could get out," I said. "That was an incredible gift."

"Have you been in touch with him all this time?"

"No."

"You never heard from him until now?

"No."

"Why should I believe you?"

There was no reason, really. Even I knew that. I didn't answer.

"What does Pierce want?" David asked angrily.

"I don't know."

"You let the man go to jail for you. He must despise you."

"I know. If I could change what I did, I would. You have to believe that, David."

"You can't, though. You can't change what you did. Even if I come to understand what led you there, that doesn't mean I'll ever think there's an excuse for it. I don't care what happened or who your parents were, nothing could make it right."

"No."

"Pierce must want revenge."

"I don't think so. No matter what, I honestly don't think Jack has Sophie." At her name, my voice caught. "It's just not the kind of man he is."

"How can you tell what kind of man he is? I thought I knew what kind of woman you are and I wasn't even in the ballpark. I wasn't even in the fucking universe."

Outside, a car honked loudly and then sped off. Dust motes caught the morning's first rays and did a slow waltz through the air.

"David?"

He ignored the question in my voice.

I moved to touch him but I felt his thigh flinch from my fingers in revulsion. "I love you," I said quietly. "I've always loved you."

David looked over at me, his face contorted by pain and confusion. "I just want Sophie back," he said. "That's all."

"I know."

We sat for a long time in the quiet room as the dawn began to break and a sunless gray light filtered in.

There was nothing left to say, not now, not yet.

There was only Sophie, wanting Sophie.

Was she crying?

Was she being fed, changed?

Touched?

I thought of the coffee stain in the shape of Africa on her left calf. The slash of white on her ribs. Her wayward patch of curls.

These are the things that break your heart.

We heard the papers slap against the door just after six o'clock that morning.

I left David lying there, his back to me, his eyes open, glazed, and went to get them.

The first time I saw my picture in a newspaper fifteen years ago in an article about my initial foray into television in Pittsburgh, I stared at it without comprehension for long minutes before it began to register who it was. An inexplicable nausea filled the gap between the picture and the person I knew myself to be. It was Sophie I recognized on the covers of the *New York Post* and the *Daily News,* Sophie's sweet and rounded face laid out in the black and white dots of the tabloid pages, at once familiar and unknown. And then my own face in the background, our foreheads touching as I held her. "Jesus Christ."

I went back to the bedroom and dropped the papers on the bed next to David. "So much for keeping it out of the press," I said.

He picked them up and I watched him study them.

"How the hell did they get these pictures?" he demanded.

"That shit from *Vanity Fair* must have sold them."

"What shit from *Vanity Fair?*"

"I told you. When they came to do the interview they took pictures."

"I thought we had an agreement that no one in the press gets Sophie's picture?"

"He said they were just for us."

"And you believed him?"

"Yes."

David glared.

He scanned the stories in the tabloids and read bits and pieces out loud to me.

" 'The only child of network news anchor Laura Barrett and her husband, David Novak, was taken at gunpoint yesterday morning. . .Baby-sitter Dora Rickley was held for questioning and later released. . . No blackmail message has been received. Anyone with information on a blue sedan seen in the vicinity of Washington Square Park between nine-thirty and eleven-thirty yesterday morning should contact . . .' "
He continued to scan the article. "There's no mention of your friend Jack Pierce."

"At least the cops managed to keep some things confidential."

"Only if it helps their investigation to keep it out of the papers. If not, I wouldn't count on their munificence." He flung the papers down and they landed with a thud on my lap.

"I had no control over this," I said.

"Of course not."

"David, that's not fair."

He turned around, looked at me once, and went into

the bathroom, slamming the door behind him. I knew that he blamed me. Blamed me for everything. I understood. So did I.

I picked up the phone by the bed and dialed Harraday's number at the precinct, figuring he'd be in early. He was.

"Have you heard anything?" I asked.

"I'm sorry, Laura. Nothing yet. You know we would have called you if we had."

My chest filled once more with dead weight, I could hardly breathe. "How could she just disappear?" I cried.

"I don't know."

"Someone must have seen something. It was broad daylight."

"We're looking into every lead we get, Laura."

"You're not looking hard enough," I accused him.

Harraday didn't answer.

"You told me you'd keep this out of the press," I said.

"I'm sorry. There was a leak."

"Obviously."

"I don't know how it happened. Maybe when Pike radioed it in from the park someone overheard. The press monitors the police bands all the time, you know. Well, of course you know. Or it could have been someone from your own studio. Baldwin must have told more than his confessor."

"Will there be other leaks?" I asked carefully.

"Not now. Not yet," he answered just as carefully.

I pressed the receiver closer to my mouth. "Do you think she's okay?"

"I hope so."

"You're going to find her, aren't you?"

"We're going to do everything we can."

I hung up without saying goodbye and curled up in

fetal position.

When Sophie was first born, I didn't know the words to any lullabies so I used to sing her "Silent Night, Holy Night" over and over again as we swayed gently in the rocking chair, her warm body pressed tight to my chest until, finally, she slept.

I pulled the covers over my head and began to sing it now, *Silent night, Holy night, all is well, all is bright. . .*

I sang it again and again, in whispers and in tears, hoping that somehow, somewhere she would hear me.

The day spread itself out before us, empty, unknown.

By eight o'clock when David went to the windows to open the curtains, our building was surrounded by the press, leather-jacketed men and women with a mass of indistinguishable faces, jumping up and down to keep their feet warm as they clutched paper cups of coffee, laughing with each other, trying to get a better angle, avid, eager, bored, their long-lens cameras and their eyes all trained steadily on us as they waited for something to happen, the next line of the story.

He quickly pulled the curtains closed. "Your fellow travelers," he remarked.

I stayed in bed, unable to move.

Still when David glanced down at me, I caught his eyes just once and saw a glimmer of shared pain despite his anger.

We were hostages together, inexorably connected by our yearning and our fear. By our love for Sophie.

I only rose when I heard Flanders talking on the telephone. I ran through the apartment until I found him in the kitchen.

He was hanging up when I entered.

"Did you hear anything? Did they find her?"

He shook his head. "Nothing so far." His face was bleary from lack of sleep.

My shoulders sank.

What we all knew but did not mention was that the longer we went without hearing anything from the kidnapper the worse Sophie's chances were. A simple blackmailer wants the money quickly. It is a business deal, after all, an exchange of goods, the cleaner the better.

It is the more perverse of the criminals who drag their wretched escapades through time to their horrible conclusion.

Or worse, to no conclusion at all.

I walked barefoot back to Sophie's room and settled down in the corner away from the window, hugging her teddy bear close to my face.

"Laura?"

I looked up.

"Harraday's here," David said.

He stepped gingerly into Sophie's room, his eyes haunted as he took in the crib, the changing table. He offered his hand to help me up. "Come on," he said quietly. "He needs to talk to you."

I started to follow him out. We were almost to the door when he took the teddy bear from my arms and laid it gently on the changing table.

"Do you want to get dressed first?" he asked as we started down the hallway.

I shook my head.

"How about at least rinsing your face or brushing your hair?"

"It's all right." The simplest rituals, washing, eating,

were abstractions to me now.

Harraday was standing in the living room with Carelli, waiting to pick up the photograph. His hair was freshly slicked back and his ruddy cheeks newly shaved. His breath smelled vaguely of menthol cigarettes and coffee.

"Good morning," he said.

"Morning," David replied.

"Quite the crowd out there," Harraday said as he unbuttoned his coat.

"Crowd is a polite word for it," David muttered.

"Actually, it can help us if it makes more people who might have seen something come forward. Of course, it can also bring out every lunatic between here and the Mississippi." Harraday told us that a phone line had been set up for tips and the "800" number had been given to the media.

"What have you found out about Pierce?" David asked.

"The police in Florida went to his house but there's no sign of him. As far as we know he hasn't been back in weeks. We're running credit card checks, but nothing's turned up since he left the Hotel Angelica. We talked to his wife, Carol, this morning, but she says she doesn't know where he is and we have no reason not to believe her. As you told us, they're separated, so it's not so surprising. I gather they're not on very good terms, so I doubt he'll contact her."

"What about Shana Joseph?"

"We haven't found her yet, but we did learn that her friend Jay's last name is Lopez."

"Did they find him?"

"No. We talked to some of his friends. They think he left town about a week ago. No one knows where he went, but wherever it is, it's probably with Shana."

Carelli turned to me. "It seems your friends are running a regular missing persons bureau all their own." He glared in my direction. He'd had to clean up after more than one errant celebrity before, no doubt. Manhattan was cluttered with them. When he did his job right, the public never even heard about it, so untarnished did the image remain.

I said nothing as I gave the photo of the Breezeway to Harraday. He picked it up with tissues and turned it over, examining the message while Carelli peered over his shoulder.

"We'll dust for fingerprints and have our handwriting experts check the scrawl on the back," Harraday said as he slipped it into a plastic evidence bag. "I want a list of everyone who has your home address as well as everyone who could have had this photo to begin with. Besides Pierce, of course."

"My parents ran a motel. Hundreds of people went through there."

"I would assume hundreds of people wouldn't have a motive, though. Think. Think of who you knew then." He waited, his pen and pad at the ready.

I ran my fingers through my knotted hair. "I just don't know."

"Well, you work on it."

"What about Sean McGuirre?" David asked. "Any more news about him?"

Harraday let an uncomfortable pause ensue before he spoke. "His aunt in Poughkeepsie says he came by to collect some things on the night of his release three weeks ago. No one's seen him since."

"This wasn't supposed to happen," David said. "We were supposed to be warned. How could he just be let

301

go with no word?"

"There appears to have been a breakdown in the system," Harraday responded flatly.

"That's great. That's just fucking great."

"Unfortunately, it happens."

Harraday put the photo in his briefcase and began to tuck his charcoal gray wool scarf about his neck. When no one was looking, he reached over and touched my arm lightly. "Hang in there."

I knew then that he hadn't called the D.A., not yet anyway. I walked him to the door. "Thank you," I said softly.

He looked closely at me, and he nodded without saying a word.

Ken Draper, the vice president of the news division, showed up with another man in tow as Harraday and Carelli were leaving. "This is Thomas Borstein, from the network's public relations office," Draper informed us as David reluctantly took their coats.

Borstein looked at me curiously and I tightened the sash of my bathrobe.

I realized suddenly that I was a problem. As much as the network might sympathize with my situation, they were terrified of any whiff of scandal when it came to the news division. The kidnapping was terrible, it was heartbreaking, yes, but what exactly should the spin be?

"Do you mind if we sit down?" Draper asked.

"Of course," I said dully as I led them into the living room.

"What are we, running a cocktail party here?" David mumbled.

Draper and Borstein looked at him condescendingly. "It's important that we talk to Laura," Borstein said.

"I don't think this is exactly the time for career counseling, fellas."

"It's all right, David," I reassured him. They were nothing but meaningless chess pieces to me now, these men in their suits, part of a senseless game I used to play.

Draper and Borstein stared down at their shoes and then back up. "Of course," Borstein began, "we can't begin to express our sympathy and concern. Whatever we can do to help, you just let us know. The network's entire resources are at your disposal."

"Thank you," I answered numbly.

"People in the public eye can pay a very high price," Draper said. "It's one of the things we report on all the time, but until it happens to you, well . . ."

"It's not happening to you, is it?" David said. "It's happening to us."

"Yes, of course."

We all sat down at once as if through some silent agreement.

It was Draper's turn. "As you know, we made no announcement on the news last night about your absence."

I nodded. I hadn't watched the news, hadn't thought of it.

"Now that it's in all the papers though, we have to discuss how to handle this. What would you like us to do, Laura?"

"Do?"

"Would you like Quinn to make some sort of statement on-air?"

"What kind of statement?"

"Well, that's why Thomas is here. We thought he could help you draft something appropriate."

"Just what do you consider appropriate?" David demanded.

"I'd rather there not be a statement for now," I said.

"I'll try to keep any mention off the air for another day," Draper answered. "But after that, we're going to have to reassess. Is there anything we should know about? Not for public consumption, necessarily, but anything that might be, well . . ."

"No."

He smiled. "Of course, whenever you are ready to, I mean, whenever this thing resolves itself, your position is waiting. The calls of support are pouring in from the public."

David stood up. " 'This thing,' as you put it, is my daughter. Our daughter. My wife's Q ratings are not exactly our gravest concern at the moment. If that's all, gentlemen?"

Draper rose. "Of course. If we can do anything to help, anything at all, you'll let us know. In the meantime, we'll get out of your way."

"They were only trying to help," I said to David as he shut the door behind them.

"Help what?"

When Jerry called later, offering his assistance, I asked him not to come.

I knew that his job was image, perception, play, damage control.

I even knew that I would need him again.

But I could not face him now.

The phone rang all morning. Dougherty had come back to take up Flanders's post on the telephone, and each time it rang, we picked up simultaneously. "Hello?" I asked hopefully.

But it was never anyone we wanted, never anyone who could help us, never anyone with Sophie.

Dougherty flicked off the recorder and hung up his extension while I tried to get rid of whoever it was as quickly as possible, my heart sinking.

Frank Berkman called to offer sympathy, support. "Anything, anything at all you might need," he said, "you just let us know." That great corporate "us." The "us" that could do nothing for me now.

Susan Mahoney called, sighing and tsking as she commiserated, and subtly pumping me for details, for inside information.

Perry called.

Olivia Redding called.

Carla called to relay messages that had come into the office from numerous people, rich people, powerful people, people I had met at cocktail parties for a minute or two, who had called to offer help. "I'm praying for you," she said. "We all are."

"Thank you."

Dora called so frequently to find out if we knew anything that we had to tell her we were trying to keep the line free and not to phone again.

I didn't want to speak to any of them.

They were on another shore now, across an infinite divide that no amount of their sympathy could conquer.

The phone rang once more. "I'll do it," David said.

I watched while he and Dougherty picked up at the same moment.

"Hello?" David said.

He listened for a moment and then put his hand over the receiver. "It's Hartley," he said to me while Dougherty hung up. "Do you want me to get rid of him?"

I started to nod and then I changed my mind. "No, I'll take it."

David shrugged and waited while I went to pick up another extension.

"Laura," Quinn said. "I know there's nothing I can say. What you're going through is unimaginable." There was something in his voice, worn out, flat, far beyond the clumsiness of commiseration that even the best-intentioned could not avoid, that held me.

"Yes."

We were quiet for a moment.

"All those times you come back from an assignment, from some horror," I said, "and you feel so sorry for the people, but all the time you're thinking, Thank God it's not me."

"And now it is you."

"Yes."

"They'll find her," he said.

"Do you think so?"

"Yes. We report on miracles, too. Don't forget that."

I was so desperate that I believed him and felt, for the briefest moment, better.

The door to Sophie's room was ajar.

I took a step in and turned on the lights. A soft white came to the frosted-glass shades, illuminating the eerie neatness.

I was eight months pregnant when we furnished Sophie's room, and the day we chose her furniture she lay still in my stomach. For weeks she had been kicking and swiveling against the walls of my body, restless and vehement. But that day, she did not move. When we got home from the furniture store I lay in bed reading a

306

pregnancy handbook that spelled out all of the inherent dangers, all of the ways to lose the unborn. I tried everything they suggested to budge her, drinking sugary liquids, changing positions, tapping on my hard belly, until finally at one A.M. just as I was about to call the hospital, she awoke. I remember the sudden joy of that first kick—ah, here you are. Here you are again. I felt the outline of her foot through my skin and I clutched it while she moved.

Hope is a surprisingly sturdy affair. It withstands extraordinary assaults—absence, neglect, violence. It even withstands the imagination, the most subversive and effective weapon of all.

I pictured Sophie bruised.

I pictured her hungry, cold, wet, scared.

I pictured her alone, abandoned.

I pictured her until my bones ached from the inside out.

But I always believed that we would find her. The alternative was, as Quinn said, unimaginable.

I do not know what David believed. I never asked him, he never asked me.

It was easier to hope believing that he too thought we would find her. It was what bound us during those hours, bound us despite everything.

I stood by Sophie's window, peeking through the lace curtains, watching the streets turn dark on the press corps, the curiosity seekers, the neighbors walking home from work irritated by the invasion.

I recognized someone doing a remote from *Hard Copy,* and someone from the *New York Times,* which, we would soon find out, had decided to cover the people covering the event, as if that was somehow a more dignified approach.

I let the curtains fall and turned back inside.

Dougherty sat in the living room eating take-out Chinese food and watching us from downcast eyes. The first few times I passed him I smiled wanly, and then I didn't bother. I was anecdote to him, something to tell the boys back at the precinct about, something to tell the wife.

Maybe that wasn't fair.

Maybe he had kids, too. Maybe he thought about missing them, losing them. I don't know. I didn't ask.

He sat tentatively on the edges of the velvet couch, as if he was afraid to spoil it, and glanced about the well-appointed room. It looked suddenly alien to me as well, the Aubusson rug, the precious traveling clock, the Mies van der Rohe table, the decorator touches, someone else's idea of a life I no longer had. I don't think I ever had it to begin with, not really.

The smell of grease from Dougherty's General Chao's chicken made me ill and I rushed to the bathroom and threw up.

At six-thirty I flipped on the television in the bedroom and watched Quinn begin to speak. "Good evening," he said. "As you may have heard, my esteemed colleague, Laura Barrett, is in the midst of some personal difficulties which we have every hope will be quickly and happily resolved." He looked directly into the camera and his solemn face filled the screen. "On behalf of all the people here at the *National Evening News,* let me say that our prayers are with you and your family, and we look forward to your speedy return." He waited a beat, glanced down and began again. "And now, the news. Earlier today, the President met with the Speaker of the House to iron out . . ."

308

I turned off the television and sat down, picking at my cuticles until they bled.

And then, at 8:04, it came, what we were waiting for, hoping for, dreading.

I picked up the phone on the second ring. "Hello?"

Dougherty was listening in on an extension, his hand over the receiver.

There was a deep breath.

"Hello?" I asked again.

Another breath, a pause.

"Who is this?" I demanded impatiently.

"I have your baby."

I let out a single sharp cry. "Oh my God. Where is she? Where's Sophie?"

"I want five hundred thousand dollars by two A.M. Wait for me on the third row of benches at the departure gate of the Staten Island Ferry. If I see cops, I'm gone And so is your baby" The man's voice was muffled, unrecognizable.

"Is she all right? Is Sophie all right? Please, let me hear her," I pleaded.

"She's safe," he said.

"Please just let me hear her."

"Two A.M." He hung up.

"Wait, please . . ." I shook the dead receiver in my hands. "Wait . . ."

Dougherty looked up, grinning. "Got it." He had the phone number scrawled on a pad.

I clasped David's trembling hands in mine. "She's okay," I cried. "She's okay. We're going to get her back."

"I don't believe it," he said, kissing my cheek, my neck.

We hugged tightly for the first time.

Dougherty was already on the phone to the precinct. As soon as he got off, he said, "It's a pay phone. They'll find where it was located. The place will be crawling before this guy knows what hit him. Harraday's on his way here to go over procedure."

"You heard him, no cops," David said.

"Look, we don't know who this guy is. We don't even know if he really has your daughter."

"What do you mean?" I asked, horrified.

"It could be real," Dougherty replied, "or it could be anyone who reads the papers. Either way, the best chance you have of getting your baby back is cooperating with us. We know what to do."

David and I looked at each other, terrified of making the wrong decision.

"All right," David said at last.

When Harraday arrived he told us that the phone the blackmailer had called from was inside the ferry terminal. "I've already sent plainclothesmen out there. They'll be in the park, in subway stations, they'll be in the streets. They'll be everywhere," he said. "And the money's on its way."

"From where?" David asked.

"We have a fund for things like this."

"You'll give him all of it?"

Harraday glanced away. "Sometimes we put in phony money, sometimes we mix up the two." He looked back up to me. "But it's real this time, all real. Marked, of course, but real."

"Good."

"TARU's sending over a special suitcase, too."

"What kind of suitcase?"

"It'll have trace-and-tracking capabilities. We'll have a car positioned nearby that can follow wherever it goes."

310

"You mean in case you lose him?"

"Sometimes we have to let them go a little if we think they'll lead us to the baby."

"But I thought he was going to bring her to the terminal." My panic rose.

"Did he say that?"

"No," I admitted.

"Precisely. He didn't say anything about Sophie's location at all. Even if he did, it wouldn't mean anything. Whoever made that phone call is not exactly a paragon of virtue. We're not about to take his word for anything. It's strange that he didn't tell you to drop the money."

"Drop it?"

"In a garbage can, under a bench. There were no directions about that."

"What do you think that means?"

"I don't know. For some reason, he might want a face-to-face encounter with you. Or he might have other plans. We'll have to be ready for a number of contingencies."

"Oh God, please just let him have her. It's a good sign, isn't it?" I asked. "Isn't it a good sign that he called?"

"It's a good sign," Harraday said. "Now, let's get to work. We've got five hours to get this right."

Sixteen

IT WAS EXACTLY ONE-THIRTY WHEN WE LEFT THE building in a taxi for the trip downtown to the tip of Manhattan. The driver, a plainclothes cop, said nothing as we sped through city streets that were nearly empty in the nowhere hour between midnight and dawn. David and I held hands in the backseat, the suitcase beside us, as the car wove through the narrow winding streets of the financial district.

When we reached the terminal, we got out alone and walked up the curved ramp to the new building, rebuilt after a devastating fire a few years earlier.

Inside, the vast space was nearly barren, filled only with the ghosts of commuters who in just a few hours would jam through, clutching papers and coffee, jostling each other, glancing at their watches as they hurried to work. The lights hanging from the aqua pipes overhead shone on the few homeless people asleep on the benches, a bag lady in tattered stockings hugging armfuls of day-old newspapers as she chanted an indecipherable mantra, a young man in a navy warm-up suit waiting for the boat. Though I was not supposed to, I searched their faces, trying to discern who might be plainclothes cops.

And I looked for Sophie, looked for her in the corners and the crevices near the shuttered newsstand, behind the change machine, looked for her knowing that she wouldn't be out in the open but hoping nonetheless that I would see her on a bench, in a stranger's arms, waiting for me, for us.

David walked beside me, carrying the suitcase. When we got to the departure gate, we stopped. Overhead, a clock told us that the next ferry would leave in twenty-three minutes. Outside the wall of windows, we saw the East River, black and still, and in the distance, the Statue of Liberty. A few yards away, a man was sweeping and the rhythmic swiping of the broom melded with our hearts beating out of time, the precise sound of our waiting.

I looked at my watch. It was one-fifty-six.

No one appeared to be watching us. No one approached.

I heard David's stomach grumble.

One-fifty-seven.

At exactly one-fifty-nine, a thin wiry man in a black knit ski mask, the kind they sell on the street as soon as the weather turns cold, darted out of the men's room.

My pulse quickened as I clutched David's hand.

The man looked quickly to his left and right and then hurried toward us.

He was empty-handed. There was no sign of Sophie.

His eyes were focused only on the suitcase, the prize.

In a second, he was beside us, grabbing the leather handle.

But David grasped it tightly, pulling the man to him. "David," I whispered.

He let go and the man swiveled around. We watched as he ran toward the side door and down the ramp, clutching the suitcase to his chest.

I looked hurriedly about the terminal, expecting Sophie to suddenly appear, but all I saw were three plainclothes cops tear out and another two run to check the bathrooms. They came out shaking their heads. The benches were empty. She was not on the floor. She was nowhere. I sobbed as we began to run after him.

By the time the man had gotten to the bottom of the ramp he was surrounded by nine policemen, their guns drawn. "All right, freeze! Now!" one of them yelled.

The man swiveled around, looking both ways. There was no place to go. There were more cops behind him, and beneath the ramp, only the black and icy river.

When David and I reached the cluster, two cops were holding the man's arms to cuff him. Harraday stepped

313

forward and squeezed through the cops still kneeling, their guns aimed steadily at the man's chest. Harraday grabbed the wool mask from the bottom and yanked it off roughly.

"Christ," I exclaimed.

Cort Joseph stared at the ground with his rheumy eyes and runny nose.

"Where's our baby?" David demanded.

Cort looked up, panicky and shell-shocked. "I don't got her," he cried.

"Where is she?"

"I don't know."

"What do you mean, you don't know?"

"I didn't take her." He was shaking now, shaking all over.

"Who did?"

A policeman began to read Cort his Miranda rights.

"I don't know," he repeated, ignoring the familiar words. "I swear to you. I don't know anything about her."

"Where is she? Where's Sophie?" I felt hysteria rising up my throat, escaping.

Cort looked away. "Fuck."

"Please. Please just tell us where she is," I implored him.

"How many times I gotta say it? I didn't take her, man. I just read about it in the papers," Cort said. "I just, you know, wanted some money. You got to believe me." Mucus ran down from his nostrils.

David lurched forward and grabbed Cort's neck, his large hands tightening about it as he shook him until the cords began to pop out. "You fucking turd."

The cops watched impassively for a few long seconds before they pulled David off.

314

"He's ours," Harraday said.

Without another word, they hurried Cort into an unmarked police car waiting at the bottom of the ramp.

By the time David and I arrived at the precinct house on West Tenth Street, Cort was already booked and being questioned upstairs. Flanders was waiting for us. "Come on, I'll take you to the interrogation room. Excuse me, the interview room." He shook his head. "I'm surprised we're even allowed to call them cells anymore." We followed him up a dark dusty staircase to the second floor and then down a long corridor lined with gray steel lockers past the Bomb Squad room with a red blow-up of a torpedo hanging over its door. "This way," he said as he led us through the detectives' main area filled with cluttered desks and typewriters into a small cubicle stuffed with case files and a computer. Flanders turned off the lights and we peered through the rectangular two-way mirror to the adjoining room where Harraday and Carelli were questioning Cort.

"We're just interested in the truth here," Harraday said calmly. "Everyone makes mistakes. I understand. Why don't you just tell us how it got started?"

Carelli was standing in front of the door, as if to show Cort that the only way out was to deal with him.

"Cort, we want to help you," Harraday continued. "But it's a two-way street. You're going to have to talk to us." He smiled amiably. "They say confession is good for the soul."

"I want a lawyer. Get me a fucking lawyer."

"You're gonna need more than a goddamned lawyer to get out of this one, boy," Carelli said harshly. "You're gonna need divine intervention. Now why don't you just start giving us some answers? What the fuck were you thinking?"

Even before Harraday came out to talk to us we knew that Cort was telling the truth, that he had read the papers in the morning and gotten the idea to cash in. I had given him my private number when I went looking for Shana two weeks ago. It must have looked easy to him with his junk-addled brain. Detectives had been dispatched to search his apartment on Stanton Street, but I knew that they would find nothing.

"What happens to him now?" I asked.

"We charge him with extortion. That's grand larceny, second degree."

"How long will he get?"

"Well, it's a felony. Minimum, a year and a day."

"I'd like to kill that little fuck," David said as we made our way back downstairs, past the large American flag and out of the precinct house.

It was still dark when we returned home.

Upstairs, I went into the bathroom and washed my face. When I looked into the mirror, my cheeks, my eyes, seemed to be sinking beneath the bones, all shadows and caves. I saw in the reflection intimations of the old woman I would be, gaunt, hollow as a death mask.

I dried my face and went back out to David.

There is a separate language for nightmare. Terse, objective. As if any adornment, any use of adjective would open a floodgate that could never be closed.

"Are you okay?" David asked.

I nodded. "You?"

"Yes."

We sat down on the edge of the bed, our palms resting open on our knees.

316

I moved my hand slowly over to his, tentatively, desperately, and he took it, his fingers closing around mine.

And then our other hands, our arms.

I felt his pulse, his heat, his exhaustion as I collapsed against him. He turned and grasped me fiercely and we fell back onto the bed, grappling, pulling and pushing at each other, tearing clothes off, our mouths open as we gasped for air, for flesh, for release. It had nothing to do with desire or love or pleasure. We were beyond that, caught in our private hell, trapped in it, united in it. He slammed into me, deeper and deeper, our bodies crashing into each other with each thrust.

But when we came to, nothing had changed.

We lay without touching, unable to look each other in the eyes.

"Try to get some sleep," David said, and pulled the quilt about us.

I closed my eyes, finally drifting into that bottomless gray air between consciousness and sleep, suspended, unrelieved, falling deeper, when it wriggled into my marrow, piercing my dreams, the stabbing sobs of breath Sophie cried when she awoke.

I bolted out of bed, still tangled in sleep, running down the hallway to get her.

I slammed open her door and bent down to the crib open-armed, ready to scoop her up, comfort her—*I'm here.*

It was only when I saw the empty mattress that I fully awoke and remembered.

Sophie was gone.

Outside, I heard the neighbor's cat wailing.

I shut my eyes and listened for a long time before I

317

went back to bed.

I lay watching the sky gradually lighten.

This is one of the things that haunts me: I don't truly remember what Sophie looked like when she was born. I replay those first hours over and over again, but I cannot quite find her in them.

And something else, something I am deeply ashamed of: When the nurse's aide wheeled Sophie in, snug in her bassinet, the first morning, I didn't recognize her. "I don't think that's my baby," I said. The aide, her face impatient and censorious, checked the plastic bracelet and assured me that it was.

It was only later that I felt it, her flesh as mine.

I would give anything to have those first moments back, knowing her, loving her as I do now.

David slept lightly beside me, grinding his teeth in slow angry circles. There was a time when he used to laugh in his sleep, his mouth curling into a delighted smile, his closed eyes crinkling.

It was just past six when I heard the elevator door open, the thump of the neighbors' papers being delivered, and then ours.

I walked past Flanders, dozing on the couch, undid the chain lock, and opened the door. The tabloids were on top. The *Post* and the *Daily News* both had pictures of me on their covers.

I turned to the *Post* first.

On page three, I began to read. . .

New Information in Case of Anchorwoman's Missing Baby
New information has come to light in the case of network anchor Laura Barrett, whose six-month-old

318

daughter was abducted three days ago. Our sources have learned that the day before the infant disappeared, Miss Barrett received a threatening package that included a photograph of the Breezeway Inn in Flagerty, Florida. On the back, there was an inscription, "Everyone has to pay. Even you." The girl in the photograph was Laura Barrett, or as she was known then, Marta Deuss Clark.

It was at the Breezeway Inn, owned by Miss Barrett's mother, Astrid Deuss Clark, and her stepfather, Garner Clark, on the night of August 26, 1976, that Frank Xavier died in an altercation. Jack Pierce, a friend of Miss Barrett's at the time, was arrested and stood trial for. . .

I fell back against the kitchen wall, breathless.

I had dreamt of this, of course. My name, *names,* laid bare.

I had dreamt of being split apart, opened. Revealed.

For years, I had dreaded it so fiercely that the very thought made me sick with night sweats and sores that I picked into my arms in my sleep.

I had thought it was the worst thing that could happen.

Now it was just another cog of a nightmare far more horrific.

I threw the paper into the trash atop the banana peels and coffee grounds.

By the time David woke up an hour later, the size of the press corps outside our building had tripled.

"David," I said carefully, "the papers got hold of the story about Xavier."

"How did that happen?" he asked as he sat up in bed.

319

"Someone from the police department must have leaked it. I'm going to kill Harraday."

"How bad is it?"

"There are no specific allegations about my role in Xavier's death. I'm sure even the *Post's* lawyers had to veto that, but it's still pretty bad. Do you want to see them?" I asked.

"Why the fuck would I want to see them? I'm living with it. Isn't that enough?"

Something crashed against the bedroom window.

"What the hell was that?" David exclaimed.

"I'll go look." I walked over to the window. When I peeled the curtains back to investigate, a million cameras clicked.

I let the curtains fall and buried my face in my hands.

David got out of bed, showered.

When I went to the kitchen to get us both coffee, I found Flanders, standing at the counter in his sleep-wrinkled suit, reading the wet and soiled copy of the *Post.* He looked up, flushed. He did not say good morning, but I caught him glancing back curiously at me, searching for—what? Pieces of a past he thought he could suddenly lay claim to? A truth, some inexorable truth that he could seize and hold against me? Or was he looking for the lie in my face, my voice, my name?

I flinched and turned away from him.

This is what exposure feels like, I thought. True exposure, when the air itself can kill you and there is no cover to be found.

Distracted, I spilled hot coffee on my hand and cursed, bringing the flesh to my mouth to blow on. For a long while, I simply stared at the reddened skin, raw and angry.

I went to David's study to bring him his coffee, waiting quietly while he spoke on the phone to his department chairman at the university. His voice was strained as he went over some intricacies of student grading, his face contorted with the overwhelming struggle of keeping up the facade.

"God only knows what he was thinking," David said as he hung up the phone. "He's too polite to come right out and say anything, of course. Christ, in a way I almost wish he would. I'm just beginning to understand what it's going to be like out there. If I ever leave this apartment again, that is." He turned angrily to me. "I didn't bargain for this," he said.

"No."

"It's not fair, Laura. It's not fucking fair."

"I don't exactly love this either, you know."

"But you wanted to be famous," he spit out. "You courted it."

"And you courted me," I retorted. "Besides, I certainly didn't want this."

"No, you thought you could have it all free of entanglements."

"I don't consider Sophie an entanglement."

"That's not what I meant. Never mind, Laura. Just leave, okay? Just leave me alone."

"Please, David."

"Go," he said wearily. "Just go."

I stood holding the doorknob, looking back at him. David's hands were pressed to his glistening maquette of the city's piers, squeezing the papier-mâché walls between his fingers, harder and harder, until they cracked.

I went around the apartment, making sure that all the

blinds and curtains were tightly drawn.

Still, I could feel the press, with their telephoto lenses and their microphones, feel them moving in, climbing up, no longer worried about manners or professional courtesy. I wasn't the Madonna anymore, cruelly robbed of her child. That angle was over now.

There was a new avidity to their clamoring, hungry and menacing. I had betrayed them and they would make me pay. Who did I think I was? All boundaries were gone.

Besides, they knew a good story when they came across it, its scent, its heat.

The missing baby had been all right for a few days, but with no new word, it had begun to fade.

Until this.

It would seep onto the airwaves, creep into news broadcasts and talk-jock monologues, it would smear itself onto supermarket tabloid covers and into editorials.

They owned me now.

I went into the bedroom, locked the door, and called Harraday.

"How did the papers get hold of the story?" I demanded. "Was it you?"

"No," he answered calmly, "it wasn't."

"Who was it then? Carelli?"

"I don't know who leaked the info on the Breezeway photo. But Laura, once they had that, it probably wasn't all that hard to get the rest. We all leave paper trails. Your immigration papers. Your official request for a name change from Social Security. It's just a matter of knowing where to look."

"I'll bet it was Carelli. He's hated me from the very

beginning."

"It's not our job to hate you or love you, Laura. It's our job to find your daughter."

"Well, you're not doing that very well either."

Harraday took a deep breath. "We're doing the best we can under the circumstances. Look, given a choice, I would not have had the papers print the story. But then again, it will be all over the country within hours. Who knows? If the kidnapping did have anything to do with the past, maybe this will flush someone out."

"It could also flush out every lunatic from here to Kingdom Come. It's open season now."

"Yes, I realize that. We've already had to add six operators to our '800' tips line. Unfortunately, people seem to be dialing up just to express their opinion of you."

I exhaled loudly. "Where's Cort?"

"They took him down to Central Booking."

"Haven't there been any new leads?"

"Only one that we give any credence to. A woman called twenty minutes ago saying she thought she'd seen Sean McGuirre coming out of a crack house in the East Village. We sent some men down there but I haven't heard back yet."

"You'll call me when you do?"

"Of course. "

"Anything else?" I asked.

"Nothing worth reporting."

"It's been three days. Three days."

"I know, Laura."

"You don't know," I spit out. "No one knows," I said, dissolving into sobs.

Despite the melee outside, it was strangely quiet within

the apartment's confines.

David stayed in his study and Flanders sat molelike in the living room while I paced the hallway between my bedroom and Sophie's, touching her door, sometimes caressing it, but not entering.

No one from the network called. Not Carla, not Draper, not Berkman. Not Quinn. I could imagine them huddled in their offices, coming up with a plan, with a statement, with deniability. With distance.

Of course, they could not come right out and disown me just yet.

There was no evidence of clear misconduct, after all. There was no proof.

And there was still the matter of the missing baby.

It didn't make sense strategically to be too condemning when there was an infant involved. No reason to risk turning public opinion against the corporation.

They turned it this way and that and in the end, the network did nothing at all. Nothing I could see, anyway, nothing I could hear. Not yet. It would come later, I knew, the midday press release that would say I had decided to resign from the evening news broadcast to pursue other interests.

No one from the mayor's office called, as they had been doing every day before.

No friends called to offer support, too embarrassed or too shocked.

There was suddenly no one but us.

At least those in mourning have a fact to grasp, no matter how horrific. At least they know.

But we knew nothing at all.

All we had was the snail-paced agony of seconds, minutes, hours, passing with no word.

I continued to call the precinct every half hour even though Harraday assured me he'd let me know the minute he heard something. I couldn't stop myself. It was hard not to call more than that, not to call every minute. I crossed myself again and again. I waited.

"This isn't happening," David muttered. "This can't be happening."

Harraday called back in the early afternoon to say that the lead about McGuirre hadn't panned out. "We'll find him, Laura," he tried to assure me. "No one can disappear forever."

But we both knew that wasn't true.

"By the way," he added, "I just got back the fingerprint checks on the photo you gave us."

"And?"

"There were three sets. Yours, Flanders's, and another pair."

"Whose are they?"

"We don't know yet." He paused. "But we got Pierce's up from Florida. And they're definitely not his."

"I told you."

He didn't answer.

We were getting no closer, we both knew that, only dancing along the perimeters bumping into no one but each other.

The only other person I spoke with that afternoon was Jerry. "My phones have been ringing off the hook," he said. "You could have at least warned me about this."

"I didn't know about it."

He sighed. "Is it true?"

"Is what true?"

"All of it."

"Yes."

"I gotta hand it to you. You've got balls. Marta, huh?" He said the name curiously, rolling it about his mouth.

"Changing your name isn't a crime," I replied.

"Of course not. If it was, half of Hollywood would be under arrest. To say nothing of Park Avenue." He swallowed loudly. "I just wanted to let you know, I've already gotten three book offers for your life story when this is all over."

"Are you serious?"

"Completely. And so is the money. Seven figures. What do you say?"

"Jerry, my daughter is still missing."

"I realize that. I said when this is over, didn't I? Didn't I say that, Laura? Didn't I say when this is over?"

"I've got to go, Jerry."

"All right. I'll keep them dangling for now. It will only make them hungrier."

"Goodbye, Jerry."

Dusk finally crept in through the lowered blinds.

Outside, the press jumped up and down to keep warm.

When Johns came to take Flanders's place, the two detectives whispered in the foyer, no longer trying to disguise their gossip and their disdain.

David remained in his study and didn't come out until nine o'clock.

We didn't turn on the radio, or the television.

We hardly spoke.

We lay behind the carefully secured curtains of our

326

bedroom, avoiding each other's eyes.

We were cut off now, alone inside the thousand-watt spotlight.

The only thing we could not see was Sophie.

Seventeen

THE NEXT MORNING, WE SPOKE LITTLE, ATE NOTHING, and resumed waiting, picking up our hope where we had left it. But it was not the same hope we'd had before, it had been badly bruised by Cort.

Flanders returned to take up his post, listening in on the phone whenever it rang, avoiding my eyes.

In the morning's tabloids, there were continued updates about our crisis, part fact, part rumor, part absurdity. Dora had gone into hiding, and though the media had staked out her apartment in Brooklyn, no one had found her yet. There were reports that she had gone back to St. Lucia, but they were unconfirmed. Her previous employers were interviewed, as well as her sister in the Bronx. Her record as a nanny was, much to the press's chagrin, spotless. There were photos of our shuttered windows. Our wedding pictures were resurrected. They used my old name, Marta Clark, as much as possible, a weapon, a joke, a lie. We warned everyone we knew not to talk to the press, and David kept a running list of those who did and those who didn't.

Outside, life proceeded and we watched it as if from another continent. It was far away, minuscule, remote, absurd.

We did what we could. We offered a reward for information that led to the capture of the kidnapper and set up another hot line. We gave more photos of Sophie to the police.

My ritual of crossing myself three times, knocking three times, tapping my foot three times, grew ever more complicated.

When David wasn't making lists, he baked bread, pounding the dough with his fists so hard that the china in the frosted-glass cabinets shook. While it was rising in the oven, its sweet yeasty scent filling the apartment in a not entirely pleasant way, he rolled out pasta, putting the dough through his shining hand-cranked machine and then draping the kitchen with the long and fragile strands.

Harraday called at ten that morning. The police were checking into the hundreds of tips that were pouring into the hot line from people who wanted the reward money, people who got off on simply attaching themselves to a news event, and people who genuinely wanted to help.

Sightings of Sophie came from lower Manhattan, New Jersey, Idaho, and even Israel.

"We're doing our best," Harraday said, but even he was beginning to sound less certain, less strong. Time was the most invidious enemy of all.

David went back to the kitchen, coming out only when the chairman of his department at the university stopped by to go over substitute lecturers with him. Flanders let him in while I hid in my coffee-stained robe in the back. I did not want to see anyone. I did not want anyone to see me. Since yesterday's papers, every pair of eyes that fell on me scoured for Marta in my face, my stance, my words. Had they suspected it all along? Had they distrusted the mask? I could see them going back, back, convincing themselves that they had.

When the doorman rang that afternoon to tell us a couple was downstairs, I assumed they were network emissaries sent to fire me. I didn't ask their names before telling him to send them up.

But when I opened the door, Shana and Jay were standing in the hallway, bundled in matching leather jackets, their faces reddened by the cold.

"Good Lord, where have you two been?"

Shana had tears in her blue-shadowed eyes. "We just read about it this morning."

"Where have you been?" I asked again. "Don't you know that everyone's been looking for you?"

"Why have they been looking for us?" Jay asked warily.

"Well, first of all, Shana broke parole," I said, irritated now. They were standing so close that their arms were touching even as they walked in. "Do you know anything about Sophie?"

Flanders stepped out of the living room and was standing beside me.

Shana and Jay stared at him nervously. "We read that she was missing," Shana said.

"What else do you know?" Flanders asked.

"What do you mean?" Shana asked.

"Do you know where she is?" David demanded as he came forward.

"Oh man," Jay said, turning to leave. "You think we got anything to do with that? You're fucking crazy."

"Just one minute," Flanders warned. "I don't think you're going anywhere just yet. What about your brother, Cort? Did you know about that?"

"What about Cort?" Shana asked.

"He tried to get a ransom from us," David said, still

329

not trusting them. "Thought he could make some quick money out of this. What do you know about that?"

"Fucking hell," Shana said. "You're shitting me?"

"No," I replied. "We are not shitting you."

"That asshole. That fucking junkie bastard." She looked up at me. "I'm sorry. I got nothing to do with him, but I'm sorry. I'll kill him when I see him."

"The only place you'll see him is in Rikers," Flanders muttered.

"You still haven't told us where you two have been," David said.

"Virginia."

"What on earth were you doing there?" I asked.

"We eloped," Shana said, her eyes shining with the pride of new love, with conquest. She held up her hand for me to admire the hammered gold wedding band. Her nails, bitten and ragged, were painted an iridescent white.

I nodded numbly.

I realized that we were all still standing in the foyer. "Come in," I said, ignoring David's scowl.

"These two are coming with me downtown to answer some questions," Flanders said.

"I'd like to talk to Shana first," I told him. "Shana?"

She nodded and I led her back to the kitchen, closing the door behind us.

Shana leaned against the counter, her head bent, her eyes lowered.

I studied her before I spoke. "I went to your house," I said.

She looked up defiantly. "Why?"

"What do you mean, why? I was looking for you. I was worried."

"I'm sorry."

"Shana, where did you get all those clippings of me?"

She glanced away sheepishly. "I photocopied some of them from microfilm in the library. I got some from the stations. I called out-of-town newspapers. It's easy, really."

"But why?"

"You'll laugh at me."

"No I won't."

"I used to want to be you."

I rested against the butcher-block counter, waiting for her to go on.

"Not be you. But you know, be like you." She was playing with a saucer filled with toast crumbs that someone had left behind and she brought her forefinger to her mouth and licked it. "I thought maybe it was something I could learn if I studied closely," she said, "like arithmetic or something."

"But why?"

"What do you mean, why? Man, look at your life. I thought you had everything." She shrugged. "I didn't know about all this other shit. Jesus."

There was an uncomfortable silence.

"I'm pregnant," Shana said, brightening.

I didn't answer.

"Aren't you going to congratulate me?" she asked petulantly.

"Of course," I responded dutifully.

"It's not a crime, you know. I love Jay, and he loves me."

"You're very young."

"Not too young to know what we want."

"What you want can change."

"But it doesn't always," Shana said. "Does it?"

"I don't know."

Shana rubbed her stomach unconsciously. "I'm sorry about your little girl," she said.

When we got back to the living room, Jay and David were sitting in opposite chairs, avoiding each other's eyes while Flanders stood above them both, scowling. It was clear that no one had said a word. Jay stood up immediately and put his arm protectively about Shana's shoulder. She leaned against him and kissed him on the cheek, her eyes half-closed.

"Okay," Flanders said. "Why don't you two just come with me and we'll talk things over at the precinct house."

Shana looked at me with real alarm.

"I think you two had better go," David said.

The press stood ready to snap everyone entering our building, but few came. I could feel them, all of them, my friends, my bosses, in their offices and their dining rooms, distancing themselves from me.

"What do you care?" David asked. "I'd think you'd be relieved not to have to keep up the pretense anymore."

"It wasn't a pretense," I replied.

He looked at me, not understanding, and walked away.

When Quinn arrived unexpectedly at three, the press swarmed greedily around him, and he smiled his practiced smile. A funeral smile, used for reporting bad news. It would be in all the papers the next day. Which, of course, he knew.

David let him in.

After a polite exchange, David excused himself. Quinn and I were left alone in the living room. "Thanks for coming," I said quietly. It had, if nothing else, been brave of him. We both knew that.

He nodded.

"Do you want any coffee?"

"No. I can't stay long." In fact, he wouldn't even let me hang up his coat. We sat uncomfortably across from each other, with out a script for this specific type of meeting.

"So you have the show back by yourself," I said. There was an acidity in my voice that surprised even me. I was striking out blindly, striking anywhere. What, after all, can you do with an anger so overwhelming?

"It's not what I wanted," he said calmly.

"Oh, you suddenly want me back? I don't think so."

"I wanted a fair fight, Laura. Not this."

I nodded. "I'm sorry."

"You'll be back," Quinn said.

I smiled. "I don't think so. I'm damaged goods. No matter what happens, I'll always have the stink of unwanted headlines. Scandal may be all right for Hollywood starlets, but I've never seen it help a news anchor. No, the best I can hope for is a shot on *Oprah.* Or maybe if I play my cards right, a talk show of my own."

He laughed and I did too. It was the first time I'd heard that particular sound for as long as I could remember.

"Don't knock it," Quinn said. "There's a lot of money to be made in that racket."

"Where defrocked celebrities go to die."

We smiled and then it faded. I knew that he wanted to ask me more, ask me about Xavier and Pierce, about who, precisely, had been sitting at the news desk beside him, but he didn't. We both shifted in our chairs.

"How are your girls?" I asked.

He shrugged. "Miserable, but okay. All that stuff about staying together for the sake of the children is beginning to make sense to me." He looked away. "Unfortunately my wife and her new boyfriend don't see it quite the same way." He laughed briefly. "My daughters are now seeing therapists three times a week. Individual therapists, family therapists, group counseling. All these experts and all three girls are still pissed off as hell. Who can blame them? Kids don't understand shit like this. All they really want is continuity. That shouldn't be so hard to give them, should it?"

"Things happen," I said.

"Things happen," he repeated.

"You're doing the best you can, Quinn."

"Maybe." He straightened his legs. "Anyway, I have to get going. I have an interview with an automobile executive who's willing to talk anonymously about systemic lying in Detroit about pollution levels. Do you know they actually installed a device without telling anyone that lets cars emit completely illegal levels of carbon monoxide?"

"That was my idea."

"Was it?"

"You know it was. What did you do, find my notes on my desk after I ran out the other day?"

"A good story is a good story, right?" Quinn said. "Jungle rules."

"Jungle rules," I muttered. I saw him to the door.

"Laura?"

"Yes?"

"Is there anything I can do?"

"No."

"I didn't think so." He finished buttoning up his coat.

He looked up once, embarrassed, and then he left.

I locked the door behind him and went to find David in the kitchen. The bread he had baked earlier sat neglected in the corner. The pasta was hardening on the cabinet doors. No one was hungry. He was standing with his back to me, his open palms pressed against the wooden counter as he stared out the window at the approaching dusk. "Quinn's gone," I said. "It's safe to come out."

David didn't move, didn't speak.

I walked up quietly behind him and ran my hand down his back.

I felt his muscles tense, and then relent just a little.

He turned slowly around and I saw the tears in his eyes.

I reached over to wipe them away but he wouldn't let me.

"David."

He swallowed once and blotted his eyes. "I was just thinking," he said. "Do you remember when we went to Cape May? Do you remember how scared Sophie was when I dipped her toes into the ocean the first time?"

"But she loved it by the third time."

He smiled. "She loved it then." He bit his lip. "All these things I wanted to do with her. All these plans." He shook his head. "You know what I was really looking forward to? It sounds silly, but what I was really looking forward to most of all was just walking down a street holding her hand. The way fathers do."

I fingered a lock of hair from his forehead. "I know." I wrapped my arms around him and he held me against his chest.

"I love you," I said quietly.

He looked at me and then away. "Not now, Laura."

If there had been anger in his voice, perhaps it would have been easier. But there was only an endless well of sadness.

He turned back to the waning light.

I watched him for a moment, and then I left.

When the telephone rang an hour later, I picked it up dully, expecting nothing. "Hello?"

"Laura?"

"Yes?"

"Alexandra Harrison. *Vanity Fair.*"

"Oh yes, of course. I'm sorry, Alexandra, but I have no comment for the press right now." I turned the tape off.

"I think you might want to reconsider when you hear what I have to say," Harrison insisted.

I remained still, waiting.

"I'm in Florida," she continued. "Flagerty, Florida, to be precise."

I sank into a chair. "I see. What are you doing there?" I asked warily.

"The dailies may have scooped me on your identity, but I thought it might be worthwhile to come down here and read Pierce's trial transcripts myself. Laura, what exactly happened on the night of Frank Xavier's death?"

"You just said yourself, you read the transcripts."

"There seem to be certain gaps. It's clear you were there. But it's just as clear you disappeared. Now this is what I don't understand: If you had nothing to do with his death, why didn't you testify?"

"I don't have to answer your questions."

"Of course not. But I'm going to print the story anyway, so you might as well give me your side of it."

336

"I don't have a side, as you put it."

"According to that woman's testimony, what was her name, Alma Patrick?, yes, according to Mrs. Patrick's testimony, you were struggling with Xavier when Pierce ran up the courtyard path. Then you suddenly disappeared. She also said that Pierce was your boyfriend. I don't know, it just makes me kind of, well, suspicious."

"The jury had another opinion."

"So it seems. But as we all know, juries are far from infallible."

"The tabloids already went over most of this," I said impatiently. "By the time your publication comes out, it will be old news."

"I have things the dailies don't have." She paused. "I've just come from talking with Carol Pierce."

"Jack's wife?"

"Yes."

I shifted my legs nervously back and forth. "The police already talked to her."

"Yes, I know. But they didn't ask the right questions."

"What do you mean?"

"She's a nice woman, Laura. A little lonely, maybe, but as you well know, lonely women can make for very good stories. They want to talk. They *need* to talk."

"What did she have to say?" I asked despite myself.

"She remembered you very well from high school. She said you had something of a reputation with the boys. Of course, I get the feeling there was a certain amount of tension between you and her over Jack. Was there, Laura?"

"I never even knew her."

"Is that your on-the-record response?"

"It's my on-the-record and off-the-record response. It happens to be the truth."

I was about to hang up when Harrison began to speak again.

"Be that as it may, she had some rather interesting ideas about what happened the night Xavier was killed."

"I'm not going to talk about this right now. Look, Alexandra, my daughter is missing. Do you understand that? Do you have any idea what that means?"

"I'm sorry. I truly am," Harrison replied.

I took a deep breath. "Did she know where Jack is?"

"I realize you may think that I put the story above all else. And maybe I do. But believe me, I would have told the police if she knew where Jack was. All she said was that he was on a business trip but she was certain that he'd be returning soon."

"They're separated," I replied dully.

"Yes, so I understand. But Carol seems pretty sure that they'll work things out as soon as this is over. She's convinced that despite their rough times, he cares too much about their baby to leave for good. To tell you the truth, I have a feeling they've been in touch all this time. Maybe she's protecting him for some reason. What do you think, Laura? Is she?"

I hardly heard her last words. "What baby?" I asked as I clutched the phone in my shaking hand.

"Their little boy."

"But . . ." My lungs sputtered to a stop.

"What's the matter?"

"Nothing," I stammered. "I just didn't know they had a baby. Did you see him?"

"Who, the baby? No. He was napping in the next room. Carol stopped the interview when he began to cry. Why?"

I was standing now, my palms sweating as my mind jagged about in concentric circles. "No reason. Look, Alexandra, I've got to go. Someone's at the door."

"Wait. Aren't you going to comment on—"

"Not now."

"But—"

I hung up in the middle of her protestations.

It was Sophie.

It had to be.

Sophie.

What other baby could it be?

Mine. Ours.

Sophie.

I had been wrong. Dead wrong.

It was just as David had said. Jack hated me after all.

Eighteen

I WALKED AS CALMLY AS I COULD PAST DOUGHERTY and found David in the kitchen where he was soaking white beans to make a soup.

"Hurry," I said as I began to pull him by the arm.

"What are you doing?"

"Sshh. I need to talk to you."

"Give me a minute," he protested as he tried to dry his wet hands.

"Now," I insisted.

I dragged him into his study and locked the door.

"She's okay, David," I whispered. My eyes were blinded by tears as I reached for him. "Sophie's safe." I was laughing and crying at once.

"What are you talking about?" he asked

incredulously.

"That was Alexandra Harrison on the telephone."

"Who?"

"The reporter from *Vanity Fair*."

"So?"

"She's in Flagerty. She just interviewed Carol Pierce. Jack's wife."

"That's nice," David retorted wryly. "Another full-length feature. That's just what we need."

"David, she has Sophie."

"What are you talking about? Who has Sophie?"

"Carol."

David's eyes widened. "Did Harrison tell you that?"

"No," I admitted.

I saw him sink with disappointment, another disappointment.

"But Harrison said that when she went to interview Carol, she had a baby. David, don't you see? Carol and Jack couldn't have any children. It's Sophie. It's got to be." The words were tumbling out, tripping over each other.

"Hold on. Maybe Carol was just watching a neighbor's kid."

"No. Carol specifically said it was hers and Jack's. And Harrison thinks Carol's been in touch with Jack all this time."

David slammed his fist onto his desk. "I knew he was behind this."

My eyes fell. "You were right." It was a moment before I could look back up at him. "But Sophie's alive, David. She's safe. That's all that matters."

"What proof do you have it's her?"

"I just know it."

"Did Harrison actually see her?" David persisted.

"No, but . . ." I didn't tell David that Harrison had said the baby was a boy. I knew Carol was lying.

"Laura, the police already talked to Carol. Don't you think they would have known if something was wrong?"

"She obviously lied to them," I replied impatiently. "All she had to do was keep Sophie out of sight. Why would they have suspected her? David, listen. Jack told me that Carol has had emotional problems. Serious ones. I wouldn't put this past her."

"I wouldn't put it past him," David muttered bitterly. He began to reach for the phone on his desk. "Okay. Let's call Harraday and have him get some men down there to check it out."

I grabbed David's arm. "No."

"What do you mean, 'no'?"

"Sophie's safe. I know she is. No matter what, I'm sure Jack would never hurt her. But I think it would be better if we went to get her ourselves."

"What the hell are you talking about? The Florida police can be there in ten minutes."

"David, I can't send Jack to jail again. Not after everything I've done to him."

"Are you fucking serious? If he is behind this, you won't have to send him to jail. I'm going to kill him." His face was suddenly red, contorted. "Look, aside from everything else, it could be extremely dangerous to take this into our own hands. For Sophie. And for us. Let's at least arrange some backup. They can do it undercover. Nothing to jeopardize Sophie's safety."

"No."

"Laura, this is a national case. Even if it is Sophie, do you really think we can simply reappear with our baby, no questions asked? Get serious."

"I'm completely serious. We can tell the police the

truth after we have her safely back.?" I took a step closer and grasped David's arms. "Don't you understand?" I asked hoarsely. "I'm scared. I don't know what Jack would do if he saw the police coming for him again. It's the one thing that might make him hurt her."

David took a deep breath, pausing, not so certain now, not so strong.

"We're not even sure if it is Sophie," he said quietly.

"I'm sure."

We both stood completely still.

"Please, David. All I care about is getting Sophie back unharmed. Let's do it my way."

"What if you're wrong?"

"What if I'm right?"

Our eyes met, held. I saw David's chest moving in and out with each breath.

"Laura, this is crazy. Assuming Pierce took Sophie, what makes you think he'll just give her to us?"

"He will if I talk to him."

"What makes you so sure? You were wrong about him already. You thought he had nothing to do with this."

"I know," I said softly. "I'm sorry. But I still believe if he sees me, if we speak . . ."

"We can't just go down there and get her even if we wanted to," David interrupted. "What about Dougherty?"

"I turned the tape off when Harrison introduced herself. I didn't think it would be anything we needed. Dougherty didn't hear the conversation and there's no record of it."

"We still can't waltz out of here with no one noticing."

I stopped and, for the first time, began to panic. "What do you mean?"

"Don't you think they're going to be suspicious if we suddenly march out of here together for the first time in days with a suitcase in hand?"

"We won't take a suitcase."

"Laura."

"We won't go together," I added quickly, grabbing at anything.

"What do you mean?"

"I'll tell Dougherty I need to get some air. What can he do? He can't keep me from taking a walk, after all." The words were coming out only partially formed as I began frantically to think up a plan, any plan.

"This is crazy," David interrupted.

I didn't hear, didn't stop. "Just listen. There's a phone booth around the corner from the Wayfare Diner on the corner of Sixth Avenue and Waverly Place. Do you remember? We've had breakfast there."

"I remember."

"Okay. I'll go there," I continued, "and call the house."

"So?"

"You can pretend to be in the bathroom so Dougherty has to get it," I said impatiently. "Then while I have him on the phone, you sneak out."

"Excuse me?"

"Just do it, David. Please."

"What are you going to tell Dougherty on the phone?"

"I'll pretend to be Harraday's secretary, I don't know."

"Harraday doesn't have a secretary."

"Jesus, David. I'll think of something."

"And just what happens when they realize we're gone?"

"I don't know. I don't care." I was crying now, pulling on his shirt, pleading. "Please."

David ran his hand through his hair. "Do you really think it might be her?" he asked, his voice cracking.

"Yes."

I saw the first pale hues of hope wash across his face. "Oh God, I hope so," he whispered to himself. Tears began to cluster in his eyes. "I hope so."

"Give me fifteen minutes," I said. "Then as soon as I call, hurry out. I'll be waiting for you at the phone booth."

"You realize this is nuts?" he remarked.

"If you're not there, I'll go without you," I replied harshly. "I mean it."

David leaned back against his desk. He stood with his face down, completely still. I could not see his eyes. "All right," he said at last. "All right. But Laura, don't get your hopes up. It might not be Sophie."

I wasn't listening. I was moving, moving already. "Call the airport and get us on the next flight to West Palm Beach."

I left David in his study and, trying not to run, went to get Sophie's favorite white blanket from her room, cramming it into my large black leather pocketbook. I stood with my hand on her crib, inhaling the fading remnants of her smell. Soon, soon. I took a deep breath and then I walked carefully into the living room, where Dougherty was flipping disinterestedly through a two-week-old *Time* magazine.

"I'm going out to get some air," I said casually, fearful that he would hear my heart, thrashing so loudly against the confines of my chest wall.

He put the magazine down immediately and rose. "Wait a minute and I'll arrange an escort." He began to reach for the telephone.

"I don't want an escort," I snapped. I relaxed my shoulders and tried to smile reassuringly. "I'm just going to the corner drugstore. I need some . . . things. Female things."

Dougherty looked uncomfortably at me. "I'm sure the drugstore delivers. Or we can send someone. Just tell us what you need."

I took a step closer to him. "I'm going crazy in here," I said softly.

"Miss Barrett, you can't go out alone. If nothing else, the press is gonna jump down your throat."

"I'll go out the service entrance. I'll cover my head and keep my face down. You'll see. They'll never even know." I spoke quietly, conspiratorially.

"It'll take more than that. Miss Barrett, let me just get one of the guys to come down. It will only take five minutes." Once more, he made a move for the phone.

"No. Please." I laid my hand on his arm. "You have no idea what it's been like," I said as tears began to well up in my eyes. "I think I'll lose my mind if I don't get out."

He stared down at my fingers on his shirtsleeve.

"I'll be okay. Really," I assured him. "But please. I need a little time alone. This is just so hard." I let go of his arm, giving it a final squeeze. "It can be our secret. I promise I'll be back in twenty minutes. A half hour, tops. Please. Try to understand."

Dougherty averted his eyes.

"You're sure?"

"Yes. I'll take full responsibility."

345

Finally, he shrugged his shoulders in defeat.

Before he could change his mind I hurried to the front hall closet and yanked on my long coat. I wrapped a scarf high about my neck and pulled my cloche low on my forehead. I did not turn around.

The back elevator was filled with old newspapers corded for recycling. Three bags of bottles and cans were balanced precariously against the far wall, and a discarded dust rag hung from the railing. I pressed the bottom button and prayed no one else would get on as the elevator lurched down eleven floors. Finally, the door opened onto the poorly lit lime green hallway that snaked through the bowels of the otherwise elegant building. The serviceman who usually sat at the tiny booth near the door had left at five o'clock. His perch was empty. I pushed open the heavy metal door and walked out onto the street.

The cold early evening air slapped into my face. I took a deep breath, relieved to be out, to be alone, to be moving. A light flurry was falling and tiny white specks of snow landed on my coat. I walked quickly, my legs cutting across the pavement with nervous energy as I passed Seventh Avenue and continued east. I was going at last, going to her. I glanced at my watch. I had left the apartment exactly six minutes ago. No one looked my way.

When I reached Sixth Avenue, I saw the first Christmas decorations beginning to go up in some of the record and book stores. Tinsel and garlands in brilliantly colored foil were strung across the windows, glistening shyly in the growing dark. It was something David and I had been talking about recently, Sophie's first Christmas. David, who had grown up Jewish but not

346

observant, suddenly wanted Sophie to observe Hanukkah and I, who remembered haphazard holidays, Christmas celebrated days after the fact or whenever Astrid found it convenient, craved elaborate Christmas Eve dinners, Christmas mornings with presents and punch. We had agreed to give her both. I pictured it quickly, tasting it, believing it now.

I continued north, thinking of Sophie.

And thinking, too, of Jack. Jack, his head bent as he ducked into the police car on that suddenly lit black-top street all those years ago, Jack, handing me the crumbling picture he had drawn of me in prison, Jack the way I had last left him, sleeping in the Hotel Angelica, alone.

Finally, I reached the side street behind the Wayfare Diner. A shuttered entrance to the subway lay black and forbidding on the corner. Piles of the diner's garbage lay against the wall, and a river of stinking sour milk ran to the gutter. I stepped around a sleeping wino, his hands lost down the waist of his filthy jeans, and reached the graffitied pay phone.

My fingers twitched as I fumbled for a quarter in my pocket. It took two attempts to get it in the slot. But when I brought the receiver to my ear, it was dead. I pressed the coin return and banged the receiver before I tried again.

Nothing.

I grabbed my quarter and, panicking, looked at my watch. Thirteen minutes had gone by since I had left David in his study. I looked up the narrow side street, but there was not another phone in sight.

I had no choice but to run around the corner into the bustle of Sixth Avenue. A block and a half away, I spotted another pay phone in front of a large discount

347

drugstore. Brilliant white neon poured from its large windows and I paused, looking in both directions, before running to it just as another woman stepped up to use it. "Bitch," she muttered as I angled past her.

I pressed my forehead to the cold metal box as I slid in my quarter. After a few seconds of static I heard the dial tone. I quickly dialed my home number and listened to it ring as I put a Kleenex over the receiver. Silence. At the second ring, I looked down at my watch. Seventeen minutes. More silence.

After three rings, Dougherty picked up. "Hello?"

"This is Officer Kyler," I said in a rapid high-pitched voice. "Detective Harraday asked me to call and go over scheduling for the next few days with you."

"Who?"

"Kyler. I'm new."

"All right. What do you have for me?"

I held Dougherty on the phone as long as possible, purposefully confusing days and dates and shifts. As soon as we hung up, I hurried back down Sixth Avenue to Waverly Place and rounded the corner. The same bum was still sleeping two feet from the phone where I had told David to meet me. I leaned sideways against the brick wall behind the diner and, with my face lowered, I began to wait. I figured it would take him about eight minutes to get here.

The snow thinned and then thickened, the fat white flakes clustering in my eyelashes as I watched people hurry home, groceries in hand, to their warm apartments. Across the street, a couple stood pondering the offerings of an expensive wine store. Beside me lay the deserted subway station, its blackened stairs leading nowhere. My hands were growing numb. Four minutes had gone by since the phone call.

The bum began to stir, his eyes flickering open. He pulled his jacket tighter about his neck and sat up, his glance roaming from my feet to my face.

I tried to ignore him, peering up the dark street. There was no sign of David.

The bum pulled a brown paper bag from his pocket, brought it to his mouth, cursed, and then flung it into the street, where it crashed with a thud.

I shifted my weight anxiously.

A car went by with a loud boom box playing rap.

Around the corner, I could see a line begin to form in front of a movie theater.

A taxi let out an elderly woman in a plaid coat a few doors away.

I pretended not to notice that the bum was still looking intently at me.

Seven minutes had gone by, and still no sight of David.

I stamped my feet to warm my toes.

I could feel the man at my feet, waiting to speak, to acknowledge, to attend to me.

"This is my corner," he said at last.

I nodded.

"Mine. Go on," he admonished me. "Go on someplace else."

"I'm waiting for someone," I told him in a whisper, fearful of a scene.

"Aren't we all?" He pulled his socks up and continued to stare at me. "You look like someone," he said.

I turned my face away from him.

Ten minutes.

If David wasn't here in five more minutes, I would

leave without him.

"Hey, I'm talking to you. Are you someone?" he demanded.

"No."

A man with a briefcase hurried by, glancing curiously at us

"What you looking at?" the bum called after him. "Haven't you ever seen a man talk to a lady before? Jeez."

I pulled my hat lower.

Thirteen minutes. I wondered if David had changed his mind, or been caught by Dougherty. I bit my lip angrily. He should have been here, should have come.

"You got any money?" the bum asked.

I dug in my pocket to get out the extra change I had brought for the phone.

The man took it, laid the coins out in his soiled palms and then glared back up at me. "Ninety-three cents? You serious, lady? You expect me to believe all you can come up with is ninety-three fucking cents? Haven't you heard of inflation?"

"Sshhh," I implored him.

"What do you expect me to do with ninety-three fucking cents?" he continued to rant, louder and louder. "That doesn't buy me a paper cup to drink out of. Go back into that big black bag you got and see what you can come up with. Go on."

"All right, all right. Just keep your voice down. Please." I'd had enough. Enough waiting. Enough of this. It was time for me to go.

"What's the matter with my voice? You got a problem with it?"

"No, it's just that—"

"What?"

"Here." I reached into my bag for more money, threw a couple of dollars into the man's hand, and began to hurry back to Sixth Avenue.

I would go alone then. I would go to Sophie.

"Hey, lady, come back," the bum called out. "I thought we were friends."

I ignored his rising voice and continued, my head down, my feet slipping dangerously on the wet pavement as I walked.

I was almost to the corner when I felt a hand on my left arm. Startled, I turned around, ready to free myself from the wino.

But it was David, breathless and flushed.

"Wait here." He darted out into the oncoming traffic on Sixth Avenue to hail a cab while I hid my face.

"La Guardia," David told the driver as we clambered in.

We were the last people to board the plane.

While David tried to read a magazine, I paid close attention to the stewardess standing in the front giving safety instructions, pointing out the emergency doors, talking about the flotation devices. "If the oxygen masks drop, those traveling with small children should be sure to put their own masks on first before securing their child's," she said. I reached over and put my hand over David's.

We flew into the starless night.

All through the flight, I kept my face turned away from the other passengers, but I could hear one or two of them whispering, the murmur gaining in momentum. Strangers began to take repeated trips to the bathroom, walking slowly by our seats, staring over, glancing back.

351

It didn't matter. We were going to get Sophie. I was sure of it. David turned the pages of *Business Week* two at a time.

As we began to descend and the wheels locked into place, I saw the lights of West Palm Beach glittering in the distance, globules of pure white in the black sky. I pressed my hands to the cold glass of the tiny window and prayed.

We angled out of the airport and drove in our rented car ten miles above the speed limit up Interstate 95. The headlights of the oncoming cars formed beacons of light, momentarily blinding and then receding. A child's car seat was buckled into the back, its safety belt lying open. I opened my window a crack and breathed in the familiar thick humid night air, an echo of an echo in my lungs.

When we saw the sign for Flagerty, my leg began to rattle up and down, and even when David put his hand on it to still it, more out of annoyance than affection, I could not stop.

We drove past the sporadic cavities of half-empty strip malls, gas stations, and the public tennis courts nestled in the triangular park along the road. The Intracoastal Waterway, as we made our way across the overpass, was green and still. A solitary pelican floated lazily in the dark. Jack had told me that Carol lived on Hibiscus Drive, three blocks south of where the Breezeway Inn used to be, and I directed David to turn right. The palm trees that lined the road cast long graceful shadows, their fronds motionless in the still night.

We saw the house from half a block away, a small pink stucco daub nestled between a Circle K

352

convenience store and a motel with turquoise balconies overhanging the yard. We pulled into the driveway and David cut off the ignition. A light was on behind the sheer gold curtains. "All right. Let's go," David said. He touched my hand just once and we got out of the car.

We walked up the red stucco steps of the minuscule front porch lined with pots of dead herbs balanced on the ledge and David banged the wrought-iron knocker.

On the third knock, a woman came to the door. She was tall and thin, her blond hair straggly and limp, her pale blue eyes encircled by deep black rings. Everything about her was a little out of focus, her eyes, her clothes, as if she were struggling to keep them from sliding away and not entirely winning the battle.

"Carol?" I asked.

Looking at me, she gasped once and then stared into my face, trancelike, expressionless, mute.

I tried to peer around her into the house. "Can we come in?" I asked carefully.

She didn't move.

"Who is that?" a man called out.

"No one," she replied and tried to slam the door. David reached over and stopped it with his foot.

"What's going on?" the man asked.

"Nothing," Carol called back urgently.

"Who's in there?" David demanded.

"No one. A friend."

We were just about to push our way in when Jack came to the door.

At the sight of us, he stopped short. His face, exhausted, shadowy, and sunken, crumbled even further. "Laura." I hardly recognized his voice. It was beyond surprise, beyond pain.

"Jack." I leaned forward, my face inches from his.

"Do you have Sophie?"

There was a gulch of silence. For a moment, all four of us were lost in it.

"Yes. She's sleeping inside," Jack admitted.

I shut my eyes. "Thank God."

David lunged at Jack. "You fucking bastard."

"David, stop." I grabbed his arms and pulled him away. "Not now."

Jack's eyes were hollow, bleary. "Come in," he said dully.

He reached around Carol and opened the door.

We entered the house and Jack shut the door behind us. I could feel David, coiled up with fury, beside me, but I did not look at him. The living room had a grease-stained gray carpet and eroded furniture, but it was otherwise neat, barren of the clutter of other people's lives. There was no evidence of a baby.

As soon as we were inside David lurched once more for Jack. "Where is she?"

Jack stepped back, eluding David's grasp. "I'll go get her."

"No," Carol protested.

"Carol, it's over," Jack hissed.

"No," she cried again.

"Shut up," Jack told her.

She watched, glazed, as he began to walk slowly, carefully from the room.

"Let me come." I began to follow him.

"No," he answered firmly. "Wait here. I'll be right back."

He disappeared down the hallway.

David took my hand and we listened to Jack's footsteps as the headlights of the cars driving up to the Circle K flashed against the walls. Carol fell back against a desk on the far wall, her back to us, her fingers nervously playing with a drawer.

"I'm going to kill him," David muttered. "What kind of man does something like this?"

I hardly heard.

Sophie was here.

Sleeping just a few feet away.

Here.

Jack would come out with her.

Give her to us.

We would have her, hold her, once again.

David's hand pulsed in mine.

In a minute, Jack returned with Sophie over his shoulder. She was rubbing her still drowsy eyes with her fleshy boneless fists, her inky hair standing up on end, revealing the rolls in the back of her neck.

"Sophie." I took a step closer and a thin skein of drool snaked down her chin as she smiled, I'm sure she smiled. "Sophie."

I reached for her warm sleepy marshmallow body.

"Thank God," David whispered, as he too reached for her.

My hands were inches from her body, my eyes locked on hers, only on hers.

I was so close that I could smell her sleep-scent.

"No!" Carol hissed as she slammed the drawer one final time and swiveled around to us.

I turned, startled, my arms hovering in midair.

Carol had a .38 handgun pointed at my chest. "Get away from her."

"Oh God," I cried as I took one last step to Sophie, my hands outstretched, open. My fingertips grazed her terry cloth pajamas.

"Move back," Carol warned. She aimed the gun

355

directly at Sophie's face.

"Now."

I froze.

"Do it."

I shuddered and stepped back, away from Sophie, her warmth, her scent receding. "Please don't hurt her," I pleaded.

Carol glared at me, the gun wavering slightly in her hands.

I turned desperately to Jack. "How could you do this?"

His eyes were grievous, pained. He parted his lips to speak but nothing came out.

"He can't help you this time." Carol took a step closer, the gun steady now, unmoving. "I was the one who took your baby, not him."

I looked at her, stunned. "You?"

"I followed Jack to New York," she said, staring defiantly at me. "He followed you and I followed him. I guess that's the way it's always been. Funny, isn't it?" Her bleached eyebrows raised. "You're not laughing." She waited, then finally continued. "That morning when he called to tell me he wasn't going to meet me, I went to his house. I told the landlord Jack had asked me to pick something up for him and he let me in. When I saw that magazine picture of you that he had colored in next to the old photograph, I knew exactly where he had gone."

"But Dora said it was a man."

"She made a mistake. It was easy, really. Jack and I still had the same credit cards so I was able to find out what hotel he was staying at, and he led me right to you. After that, all I had to do was figure out your baby-sitter's schedule. Do you realize she takes the baby to the park at almost precisely the same time every day?

356

Ten-fifteen. I even talked to her there a few times and admired what a pretty little girl she was taking care of." She was proud now, shameless, as if she had to prove to us, to Jack, that she was not a fool after all. "No one was looking for a woman, so it was easy to ditch the car and get on a plane. When the police came the next morning, all I had to do was keep the baby in the back. They never even looked."

Jack took a step in Carol's direction while Sophie burbled her protest.

I stared at her soft red mouth, her moist dark eyelashes, so close.

"Carol, this has gone far enough. Now give me the gun," he said.

Carol looked at him icily, and waved him away. "Step back. I mean it."

No one made a sound, no one made a move. Sophie's eyes were on the light gleaming off the gun, entranced as if it were a toy. The curls on the side of her head were damp. I wanted only to smooth them, to dry them.

"He saved that picture of you at the Breezeway all these years," Carol continued. "And the postcard I drew the coffin on. He thought I didn't know about the box where he kept all his pieces of you, but I did. I never said anything. I thought I could wait it out. I actually thought he would change." Her breath caught in her mouth. The gun shook dangerously.

I shifted my weight from one foot to the other. "Just let me have Sophie. Please," I beseeched her. "We'll leave. You'll never see us again. Just let us have our daughter."

"No."

David turned to Jack. "Do you expect us to believe you had nothing to do with this?" he asked furiously.

Jack glanced at David and then at me, only at me. "Did you really think I'd do anything to hurt your baby?"

"I didn't know what to think," I stammered.

He looked at me sadly. "I've been on the road since I left New York ten days ago. Just driving. Funny, in all these years, I've never just driven. I needed time, that's all. Just time." He shook his head, debilitated, confused. "I heard about what happened with Sophie while I was traveling. But it wasn't until I saw the papers today that I learned about the Breezeway photo. Then I pieced two and two together. I knew the photo was mine. The only person who could have gotten it was Carol."

"Why didn't you call us?"

"I had to be sure first. I knew if it was Carol she wouldn't do anything to hurt the baby. I was in Georgia, ten hours north of here. I got here as fast as I could. I tried calling you when I got here about three hours ago, but the police answered the phone."

"Did it ever occur to you to tell them?" David said bitterly.

"I thought it would be better if I could get Carol to turn herself in," Jack replied. "I've been trying to talk to her. Trying to get her to agree . . ." He stopped. "She needs help. I thought I owed her that much at least."

"Owed her?" David said, incredulous. "What about us? Sophie is our baby, for God's sake. Our baby."

"I'm sorry, Laura," Jack said in a low and broken voice. He turned and took one more step to Carol. "Put down the gun," he told her. "Please."

Suddenly the windows flooded with brilliant blinding lights as cars screeched loudly to a halt outside the front door.

Carol turned to the window, panicked and confused.

358

I felt David give me a tap on my hip. "Now," he whispered.

David lunged suddenly for Carol, his hand reaching for the arm that was holding the gun.

And I leapt to Jack and Sophie.

I never reached them.

I fell to the floor as the explosion tore through the room, a single black sulfuric rip cord shattering the air, shattering time itself.

When it was over I looked up, across my own blood-splattered legs, to where Jack and Sophie lay.

There were rivulets of blood dripping down Sophie's face.

I crawled over to her and took her in my arms.

Sophie.

Her flesh, her weight, her heat, met mine, filling me, completely filling me.

Tears ran down my face as I kissed her scalp, her fragile white neck, her cheeks, burying my lips in her, losing myself in her.

She began to cry.

"Police."

The door broke down and three policemen with their guns drawn burst into the room.

I looked over Sophie's head to David, kneeling three feet away.

"Police. Drop the gun."

Carol, glazed, shaking, slowly dropped it.

It was only then she saw what had happened.

Her eyes filled with horror as she began to scream. "Jack."

She ran to where he was lying, his chest ripped open,

pooled with blood.

I clutched Sophie tighter as she wailed, wiping Jack's blood from where it had splashed onto her face.

Carol stroked Jack's cheeks, cupping his head in her arms.

I did not reach for him, did not touch him. He was hers now.

When I looked up again, a fourth policeman stepped into the room. He came and knelt by Jack's side, feeling for a pulse.

I glanced over at David.

"I called Harraday before we left," he explained as he wrapped his arms around me and Sophie, kissing the top of her head. "Sshhh, sshhh? little peanut," he whispered. "It's okay, we're here now. We're here."

The policeman shook his head. "Call an ambulance," he instructed one of the men. "And the medical examiner." He reached down and gently closed Jack's eyes. "I'm Detective Florio," he introduced himself.

Outside the gauzy curtains we saw two more police cars drive up, and behind them, three vans, the logos of the networks' local affiliates emblazoned on their sides, satellite dishes on their roofs.

Detective Florio wiped a drop of blood off his forefinger with a tissue. He touched the side of Sophie's cheek once lightly and then he turned to me. "Is she all right?"

"Yes." It was only then I truly realized that she was safe. Safe. My chest heaved forward as I began to cry.

Florio nodded slowly. "What happened?"

As we rose and began to answer his questions, the enormous klieg lights the news crews were setting up flooded the lawn.

I turned back to the living room. One of the policemen was picking up the gun with a handkerchief and putting it into a plastic evidence bag. David finished describing what had happened while two policemen coaxed Carol up and began to recite her rights, but their words were a distant cacophony to me. I stared down at Jack, his body sprawled two inches from my feet. My chin rested heavily on Sophie's head, rubbing into the dank heat of her cherry wood scalp.

Florio put away his notebook. "You're going to have to go to the local station and give a formal statement," he told us. "The FBI will need to talk to you, too."

"All right," David agreed.

"One minute," I murmured. With Sophie tight in my arms I bent down to Jack. I shut my eyes and touched his soft cotton shirt just once with my fingertips. Slowly, I rose.

"Ready?" Florio asked softly.

I took a deep breath. "Yes." I kissed Sophie's forehead, the iron salt taste of Jack's blood brushing across my mouth.

And then I buried her face in my chest and stepped out into the glare of the television lights.

Dear Reader:

I hope you enjoyed reading this Large Print book. If you are interested in reading other Beeler Large Print titles, ask your librarian or write to me at

Thomas T. Beeler, *Publisher*
Post Office Box 659
Hampton Falls, New Hampshire 03844

You can also call me at 1-800-251-8726 and I will send you my latest catalogue.

Audrey Lesko and I choose the titles I publish in Large Print. Our aim is to provide good books by outstanding authors—books we both enjoyed reading and liked well enough to want to share. We warmly welcome any suggestions for new titles and authors.

Sincerely,